THE TRAIL TO CHURNYG

THE TOKEN BEARERS — BOOK THREE

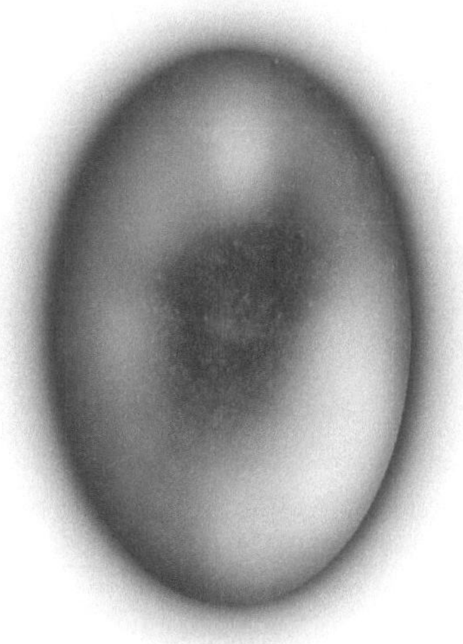

THE TRAIL TO CHURNYG

DERIN ATTWOOD

The Trail to Churnyg

A Wordly Press Publication
Ashhurst, New Zealand
Phone 64 6 326 8066

First published by Wordly Press in 2014

Set in 12/18/24 Adobe Garamond Pro
This text uses English (UK) spelling.

ISBN 978-0-9941108-2-4

A catalogue record for this book is available from
the National Library of New Zealand.

Wordly Press
www.wordlypress.com

Dedication

For Ron — Always

Acknowledgements

Special thanks go to Elaine Hand of Brightchick Photography, for gifting me the divine photographs to use on the book cover. A wonderful gift, doubly appreciated because she had to trek for over an hour to re-shoot them to the excessively high standards demanded by the cover artist.

Llyvonne Barber for again creating the cover I wanted. She has always seen my vision, and then made it better. Thank you also for formatting the book interior.

My writing friends around the world who support me and help me solve problems when I have them, and celebrate with me when I don't. Those dear writers close to home who pop in for tea, coffee, occasionally wine, and always lots of laughter. They allow me human contact in what is effectively, a very solitary occupation.

Last but not least, my family, particularly my son Garreth and my dearest, wonderfully supportive husband, Ron.

Characters on this Adventure

Name		Relationship
From the Green Valley		
Amethyst	F	Found in the desert, adopted by Kirym
Arbreu	M	Token brother to Kirym, Teema and Bokum
Kirym	F	Veld and Loul's daughter, aligned to Teema, Arbreu and Bokum
Loul	F	Headwoman, Kirym's mama
Mekrar	F	Kirym's sister, twin to Mekroe
Mekroe	M	Kirym's brother, twin to Mekrar
Tarl	M	kirym's older brother
Teema	M	Aligned to Kirym, Arbreu and Bokum
Veld	M	Headman, Kirym, Mekrar and Mekroe's papa
From Faltryns Tower		
Elm	M	Boatman
Granite	M	Guard
Oak	M	Guard, Wind Runner's great grandson
Starshine	F	Wind Runner's great granddaughter
Storm	M	Wind Runner's grandson

Name		**Relationship**
Willow	F	Healer (deceased)
Wind Runner	F	Headwoman at Faltryn's Tower
Bryn's Family		
Bryn	M	Family head
Dashlan	M	Eldest son
Enliah	F	Eldest daughter
Jeresaya	F	Bryn's wife
Larqeba	M	Youngest son
Quinita	F	Youngest daughter
Rargo	M	Orphan, adopted by the family
From The Rock		
Ashistar	M	Guard
Baketer	M	Guard
Borboncha	M	Guard
Churnyg	M	Tree dwarf — Oak Family
Gynbere	M	Leader — Yew Family
Jetara	F	Shormel's maman, Oak Family
Mrilan	M	Old man
Rookham	M	Guard
Rosisha	F	Varitza's maman
Shormel	m	Child
Shurlyn	F	Old woman
Slaslow	M	Head guard

Name		**Relationship**
Thipin	M	One of triplets
Vellysh	M	One of triplets, sent to pick up ibith
Zeffyn	M	One of triplets

From the Winterisle

Name	Sex
Faltryn	M
Iryndal	F
Ubree	M
Othyn	F
Egrym	M
Arymda	F
Borasyn	M

Prologue

Solid horns and a short snout dripped water as the huge black head rose above the surface of the sea. The wet skin shone although no sunlight showed in the thick fog. Dark blue eyes stared broodingly at the flimsy boat and its three occupants, the colour a reflection of the tokens worn on the foreheads of two of them.

The beast paused, moved closer, and the water heaved as it slowly, majestically rose into the fog. Its thick body touched the side of the boat, the rasping sound drowned out the lap of water against the hull.

Massive wings flexed and wrapped around the craft, closing and squeezing until the hull creaked. Suddenly it released its hold and spread its wings. They seemed to ripple and the beast's head disappeared into the fog. The tail gently rubbed against the side of the boat as it rose. Amethyst reached out and touched the tail. The beast paused, its skin pulsing to the wee girl's pressure. Kirym grabbed her hand, and in doing so, brushed against the monster's skin. She could feel the tail flexing beneath her fingers. It knew she and Amethyst were touching it.

Kirym gently pulled Amethyst's hand away, and the creature shot skyward. Drops of water showered the boat as the beast flew overhead, an indistinct shadow in the sky.

It seemed like a dream.

1

Kirym Speaks

"What — what was that creature we saw?" Teema glanced up at the night sky, as if he expected to see it descending on us again.

I shrugged. "As to what it was, well, I have as much idea as you do."

"You haven't told anyone about it," he said.

"Nor did you."

"Well, I feel like I dreamed it."

"If you dreamed it, so did I. The reason I didn't say anything was because I just couldn't imagine the conversation," I said.

"What do you mean?"

I laughed. "Well what could I say that wouldn't make everyone think I'd lost my mind? The fog thickened and a huge sea monster took our boat away from land, and then it flew away?"

He nodded. "Yes well, doesn't sound believable, does it?

That's not even adding the bits about how it tried to hug us or kill us. I'm not sure what it was doing there, and I have no idea how you and Amethyst found the courage to touch it. Even in my head, I can't find words to explain what we saw." He leaned forward, his voice low. "What was it? We did see it, didn't we?"

"Yes, we did. It was so big and gone so soon, I can't put it into any perspective. The pictures we saw in Faltryn of the dragon came to mind, but that thing was huge. I never imagined any beast so big. Was it a dragon? I don't know. Initially, I thought it was a sea monster, but then it flew. Do sea monsters fly?"

"I thought you were joking when you said we'd look for the dragons. But — you found it straight away, if that's what it was."

"It might not have been a dragon, but I'm deadly serious about looking. It's important, Teema. Finding one, if that's what it was, isn't enough. There's a mystery here, and we have to know more."

"What sort of mystery?"

"Why there's nothing in our written history about them. They were so important we acknowledged them when we named the boat. It's more than that even. What did we see on the prow? What had walked across the sand?"

"It may not have been a dragon. I mean," he paused, frowning. "What if it was just a run-of-the-mill sea monster?"

"It doesn't matter. We still have a mystery to solve, but we'll do that after we find Papa, and settle Wind Runner's people in their new homes."

Quest had seemed reluctant to leave its winter home that

morning. It drifted slowly in the dawn breeze, its sail occasionally attempting to billow. Teema and Mekroe tightened and loosened the ropes, although the light tendrils of wind tended to disappear before they could be of much use.

We had chosen Quest because she was twice the size of Venture, the first small boat Armos built, and could comfortably hold all ten of us. Far to the north a rainbow had appeared over the crown of a large flat-topped hill. It was there we had found the token-cave, inaccessible now because the ancient dry river bed on the ridge above it had suddenly begun to flow last spring.

The rainbow had been small when we climbed aboard the boat and cast off. Our friends from Faltryn's Fortress couldn't completely understand the phenomenon, no matter how I explained it. But as in past days, the rainbows would grow and multiply as the sun rose higher.

It was hard to believe only six days had passed since we had walked eagerly along Tarjin's Path to find the dwellings in The Green Valley deserted.

I remembered my moment of panic. I'd never seen the settlement look this empty. Then as I grasped the significance of the empty settlement, I realised my expectations of a welcoming homecoming would not be realised.

Everyone else had been shocked. "What's happened?" asked Mekroe. "Where is everyone?"

"Papa received our messages. He's taken the family to welcome the people from Faltryn. Everyone must be really excited, they've all gone to meet them."

Initially exhausted from the long journey from Faltryn's Fortress, we revelled in hot water, good food, comfortable beds and clean clothes. However the lack of people and something meaningful to do soon began to pall. While it had been wonderful arriving home, to find no one there left us initially deflated. It soon became disturbing, and ultimately too quiet.

I mentioned the idea of my doing a short excursion on the evening of our fourth day at home.

"It should only take me a couple of days," I said casually. "I'll climb the hill and see if Papa's in sight."

Mekroe snorted. "Alone? Do a rethink, sis. When do we leave?"

"Someone should stay, Mek." I said. "Our guests have had a long trip. I can't ask them to do another one."

Storm laughed. "Oh I think we'll demand to join you …"

"And," interrupted Teema, "we're not letting you leave without us. Now I'm sure you've checked the path to Bildon's Rest. Is it still flooded?"

I nodded. "Yes, but the low ridge is above water and the land east of that is clear. I was going to follow the ridge north, but if you're all coming why don't we take one of Armos' small boats. It'd be easier and quicker."

"And do you really think it'll only take a few days?" asked Teema.

I'd shrugged. "Had I been going by myself, I'd have made sure I took no longer than six days. But if we're all going, we'll be together and it won't matter how long we take. It really depends what we see and decide to do."

Storm, Starshine, Granite and Elm, our friends from Faltryn, were intrigued by the new way of travel. They used paddles to propel their small boats, and the thought of sitting about as the wind did all of the work, delighted them.

Elm prowled around the deck asking questions and helping as he learned.

"An inspired decision to travel this way," said Storm quietly. "Boats have always been Elm's passion and I can't think of anything that would haul him out of his melancholy. I haven't seen him so animated since we were boys."

"It's not the final answer, but seems to be doing some good. Losing Willow was ghastly, but realising he could never tell her how he really felt, well I thought he might try something so stupid, he'd follow her. Learning new skills is always a good thing, but we still need to watch him carefully in case he withdraws again," I said.

Bobbing along in Quest's wake was one of the boats from Faltryn. It would be handy if two or three wanted to make a short journey to check on something. Teema, Mekroe and Granite had returned to the inlet to collect it, when Mekrar suggested we might not get close enough to the ridge to safely wade ashore. Quest had mainly been used for fishing trips on the lake, and the frequently discussed jetties to be built elsewhere, had not yet come to fruition.

Soon after midday we passed over Bildon's Rest, now covered with water. It was sobering to realise the amount of water that had come out of the canyon. It lay deep on land we had walked across, hunted and camped on.

When evening approached we dropped the anchor, ate and enjoyed the serenity of the lake, celebrating Amethyst's second moon with us. As the moon rose, everyone found space below deck to sleep.

Morning came early — the nearby ducks objected noisily to our presence, and once we were all awake and had eaten, it seemed sensible to continue our journey. We soon covered the distance to the base of the hill and sailed east, passing the entrance to the ravine before the sun was high enough to shine over the trees that shaded it. Even knowing where it was, the shaded entrance was virtually invisible even with the water pouring out of it.

The water on the eastern side of the entrance was more turbulent, but we utilised a strong eddy to sit Quest alongside the ridge. We ran the boarding ladder to the top of the ridge and it was just a few steps to get ashore.

Unpacking Quest was easy. It was simple to pass our equipment along the ladder. Teema and Mekroe then sailed Quest into deep water and anchored it securely, returning to shore in the small boat.

The travel-stained remains of the clothes we had worn from Faltryn had been washed and mended where possible, but we had raided the stores from home to replace most of them. The late summer weather was settled and warm through the day, although cool at night. We carried cloaks and rugs on a triangle frame.

The vicious storm that hit us while we were in the bay was long gone, and the autumn weather continued to be mild.

I now carried Amethyst in a proper baby sling. It was a lot easier and everyone helped with her, freeing me to do the things needed to lead the group.

Now we travelled on the eastern side of the small ridge, land I knew less well. The low ridge had successfully held the water in the lake area, and the eastern side was unaffected by the flood. There was no path here, and occasionally we pushed our way through quite dense undergrowth.

We were north of the ravine, the roar of the water was a mere whisper in the distance. Our search for somewhere to set up a camp was halted when Storm tripped in a kellich hole, turning his ankle.

I eased his boot off, knowing we'd go no further today, and probably not for the next two or three days. His ankle was already blackening with the bruise, although I was sure there were no bones broken. It seemed to rotate well, but painfully and he needed to rest it.

Dosed with harkii, a hot sweet tisane and with his foot wrapped in cool damp moss to reduce the swelling, Storm declared himself to be 'extremely comfortable'. Then, with instructions for him to stay still with his foot raised, we set up camp around him.

Over the evening, I dosed him with a tea of basil, mint and passionflower to help him relax, a mixture of a pulped lemech root mixed with the juice of trandor berries, that I dried in front of the fire, to stop the pain, and a little harkii to help him heal.

As night fell, we talked of how to occupy ourselves for a few days. Days spent sitting around camp tend to get boring. I'd packed some of the stories of our trip from the Land Between the Gorges into my pack, along with more parchment, quills and ink, so Storm would have plenty to do. I also had material from Mama's store, brought with the idea of replacing the festival clothes we had worn out on our trip to Faltryn.

We spent two days relaxing, taking turns at reading, stitching, talking and playing with Amethyst, but before the evening meal was cooked on the second day, the men had organised a hunting trip for the morning. By the time their plans were finalised, it was obviously a men only thing.

Before the dew was off the grass, Storm was the only man in camp, wondering whether to be pleased or annoyed.

I had suggested to Mekrar and Starshine that they plan their own excursion, but Mekrar declined, so as soon as the men had disappeared, I placed a few items in a pack.

Mekrar watched, amused. "Aha, you have plans. I wondered

why you would allow such a chauvinistic men only thing to happen in such a small group. It's not at all like you."

I shrugged. "Sometimes they need time away, and it's nice, because it gives us time to do other things they'd be less interested in. Are you sure you want to stay here?

"Oh, definitely. The monster I was born with will be back soon. On these hunting things, after they swim and brag, they always make the youngest person gut any animal they shoot. They call it practice. Mek bypasses that by coming home early. He'll claim I need him because I'm not over the upset of thinking he was dead. We'll have a nice day together and we'll look after Amethyst and Storm. Do you want to be by yourself? You could take Starshine with you."

"I planned to, unless you want her to stay. I thought I'd climb the hill. Once I'm above the tree line, I get a good look at the surrounding area and maybe see if Papa is in sight.

"That's a good idea, but why didn't you ask Teema? He would have gone with you. All of them would have."

"I know, in fact he'd have insisted and then everyone else would've joined us. But they're noisy and intrusive and it would have turned into a hunting trip. With me there, they wouldn't have had as much fun. Truth to tell, I'm happy with a day away from them too. Anyway, I won't be alone. I'll show Starshine the result of Faltryn's tears. You're safe here and there isn't anything more I can do for Storm. Keep his foot elevated and bandaged like I showed you. Don't let him walk on it too much."

"Do I tell Teema where you've gone?"

"If he specifically asks, but I should be back before he returns. If I'm not, I won't be far away."

2

Kirym Speaks

Starshine was good company. She hadn't been at all keen on exploring alone. She was unsure of the strange terrain — finding the masses of trees overwhelming — but she was happy to join me.

The lower part of the hill was covered with trees and dense bush, but large areas were clear and easy to walk through. By mid-morning, we were above the thickest of the tree growth. We sat in a clearing and nibbled at nuts and dried fruit, looking out over the surrounding countryside.

There was a lot of animal movement and plenty of fresh water in the form of small lakes and streams.

"There's no sign of Papa," I said, "although I didn't expect to see him. I wonder if he planned a hunting trip along with meeting Wind Runner, although he might not have realised how long her trip would take."

"It took you less than a season to get to us," said Starshine. "I thought they would have arrived by now. Could something be wrong?"

"I'm sure everything will be fine. It's only been three moons since they began. They can't travel as fast as we did, nor as far each day," I said as I thought about the trip. "When they get to the stream, Bokum may let no more than ten travel through to the stone circles at a time, and maybe fewer at the start. More later, but it needs to be carefully planned. The first men through will need to widen the place they'll stop at overnight, and that may take a day or longer. Also Bokum will need to rest for a day after each two days in the water. He'll need that, so groups would go through only every six or seven days at best."

"That will take so long. How did you do it so quickly?"

"We journeyed every day, but you can't do that when travelling with a large group of all ages. But really, there'll be ways they can cut that down. They were already discussing how before they left Faltryn."

"Why did Veld leave so early then? He'll have to wait for ages until they arrive."

"I suspect he's taken the family to explore the land to the north and east. He will want to know the land he offers you for a home." I gathered our things together. "It's nice to sit in the sun and talk," I said to Starshine, "but we'll never make it to the top at this rate."

It was just before midday when we finally looked into the canyon. The air was full of rainbows and the water still thundered over the edge. In the canyon though, the water was lower than when I had last seen it, less than a quarter of the way up the cliff. The tops of the caves were now showing above the water.

It still amazed me, and it took a lot of explanation for Starshine to understand what she was looking at.

"All of that water came from Faltryn?" she asked.

"Water can move incredible distances, and there may

be a link with the flow through the cave of tears and the waterfall, but there's no way of being sure. It's a long way between here and there." I paused. "I wonder if the cave will be different when we return."

"You'll go back in there? I mean, it's beautiful, but it seems such a dangerous place."

"This is where we get our tokens. When a child is named or when two people join, we come here."

"What if the water doesn't go away? There will be more people joining. When two families meet, there's generally an increase in relationships. Intrigue in new customs is often the basis of attraction."

"There'll be an answer — Amethyst's token found her. Tokens always find a way to do what they need to do."

As the day progressed, clouds had scudded across the sky. When they covered the sun, the air was chilly, and I was pleased for the protection my cloak gave me. There were few trees up here, but a stand just below us caught my attention. These were old, although not really big, the cold and wind up here had stunted them.

As the sun was again covered by cloud, we slipped into the grove. The trees grew in a circle and were much older than they looked from above. The trunks were gnarled and twisted, giving them an almost human appearance. We sheltered here and shared a meal.

The ground beneath the trees was thick with leaf mulch and mushrooms. Between two of the furthest trees were some tall bushes covered with tiny black berries. New to me, I decided to pick some to experiment with. The blackest and ripest were at the back, and I pushed my way through to get them. I pulled a branch towards me for easier access and stared into a dark hole in the hill.

The entrance was narrow, but once we were inside there was plenty of room. The floor was sandy and the walls were of stone. It was dry and didn't smell at all musty. I loosened my knife in its sheath, pulled a lamp from my pack, lit it and handed it to Starshine.

The passage angled down quite steeply from the entrance, and then levelled out. It was wide enough for us to walk abreast, and it widened more the further we went in. It was quite dark inside. Initially the trees kept out a lot of the light, but further in, we were below the level of the entrance. I was pleased for my cloak and the lamp.

Starshine, holding the lamp, was a little ahead of me as we rounded a corner in the tunnel.

"Oh, it's a dead end," she said.

The tunnel had been blocked by two large stones. Dark grey and white with long streaks of shiny black, they were very different to the light grey walls of the tunnel.

I took the lamp and lifted it high to study them. They didn't reach the roof. "They're standing stones," I said in amazement. "They've been lodged across the tunnel. I wonder why?"

Just above my eye-level and against the edge of the stone, someone had etched three lines of three chevrons. I followed the point of the chevron to the right, and found it was echoed in the dark shadows on the second stone and beyond that I found a third stone and a fourth. Now I was in a narrow passage between the stones and the wall of the cave.

The stones had been set in a curved line around the edge of a large cave. The cave got lighter as we followed the stones around, and when the circle of standing stones started to curve back towards the entrance, daylight streamed in from another tunnel.

We sat on the ledge and looked over the canyon. I stared up to where, at the beginning of spring, I had first spied this cave.

I understood now why it wasn't visible from the canyon

floor. It sat at a sharp angle looking northwest and from below would appear simply to be a crease in the rock.

Back from the entrance, water bubbled out of the wall filling a small depression in the rock. From there it boiled over into a stone bowl below. Someone had carved into the wall around it, so it was depicted as a waterfall falling into a pool. Around the pool they had created strange creatures that looked like rocks and the trees, but with faces. To one side was a massive stylised tree with a hole in the trunk. There were more strange creatures in the tree, obvious only because of their eyes, although there seemed to be a mixture of bird beaks and noses. On the tunnel side of the waterfall, the carving depicted a wall with a large arch in the centre, the paved road curving out of sight. Another narrow path followed the wall. Away from the arch, the wall seemed rougher as if the carver was in a hurry. And yet there was still a lot of detail, fallen bricks, trees and bushes, with insects, two mice, a hairy creature with a long tail, and a number of small birds. The wall ended against a rough shallow cave, and beyond that the carving stopped.

"I must take a rubbing of this. It'd make a great wall hanging," I said.

Eventually Starshine and I continued following the path around the standing stones. There were twenty stones, not in a circle as I had first thought, but a spiral that led into the centre of the cave.

At the heart of the spiral was a massive flat topped boulder. Pictures were engraved around the edge, each different. The first was made up of suns and moons, the next a tree with flowers. Another was of fire, the ocean with fish swimming through.

Water oozed out of the standing stone that backed the flat rock, and ran across one of the carvings. In the centre of the boulder was a double circle.

My tokens lit up as I studied the pictures and the large tokens began to vibrate. I opened the pocket holding them, taking them out one at a time and sitting them on the rock.

Starshine stood to one side watching, as fascinated as I was. When each token was placed on an engraving, the pictures seemed to come to life. I placed the yellow token on the top picture. The token glowed, and as I moved, the sun and moon appeared to rise and set. The facets of the blue token made the water seem alive, the fish swam, appearing and disappearing in the waves. The tree appeared to grow, and the flowers bloomed under the green token.

One image was left uncovered. This was where the water ran. I sat the rainbow token there, but it didn't glow and the engraving remained hidden. This space belonged to a different token. Everything seemed almost perfect.

Light from my lamp flickered. As I picked it up to trim the wick, I knocked my flask over, spilling the water. The water soaked into the floor — the empty flask rolled out of sight.

I went after it and because I was near the ledge and wanted time to think about what I had seen, I took the flask to the small waterfall to refill it. I lodged the flask under the rock lip, studying the picture while I waited.

With the water diverted, the wall behind it now showed a series of engraved chevrons. Because they were out of balance, they channelled the water towards the bowl. Without the chevrons there, the water would have missed it completely. I checked lower on the wall. Lines where water had eaten away at the softer rock, evidence that water had once flowed straight down the wall and run off the ledge into the canyon.

Why was it diverted? I wondered. *If the water ran straight, it would miss the bowl.*

I plunged my hand into the water bowl. It was deep, almost to my shoulder before I felt the bottom. It was surprisingly clear of debris and smooth for the most part. On one side was a lump which moved as I felt around it. I grabbed hold and pulled it up.

I held a purple token, and already the other tokens were singing. I took it to the centre of the spiral and sat it on the last engraving.

They all lit up. Rays of light joined, leaving the centre circle in darkness. I slipped the rainbow token onto the double circle. It fitted the smaller circle leaving the larger visible around it. The six tokens seemed to grow in size, dwarfing the rainbow token. Then each connected to it and appeared to feed it so it also rose up and eventually towered over them, losing colour as it did. Now white, the lines engraved beneath it suddenly came to life. An image appeared, what looked like a large clearing with a tree in the centre. The tree grew until it was massive, ancient. Then a mist surrounded the lower trunk, the branches bent and thrashed. It looked as if it were in battle. Slowly it toppled over.

When the mist cleared, the tree lay on its side. A new mist covered it, twisting and thickening. Again, it appeared to be fighting, although the details were hidden. The mist seemed to settle, sitting heavily on the stump. It looked like great coils of the thickest rope were leaning against it.

Deep within the stone, the rainbow colours again glowed. The shape of the original stone was clear. It appeared to be trying to push its colours up through the stone above. Suddenly a rainbow erupted from the top and arched up towards the northern wall of the cave. The colour was so intense — it looked as if it had cut right through the wall. Slowly the rainbow drew back into the token and the light died.

I glanced at Starshine. She was backed against a standing stone, her eyes wide.

"Did you understand any of that?" I asked.

She slowly shook her head. "I didn't realise the tokens did things like that," she whispered. "That showed something. What? Why?"

"I don't know, but we'll find out eventually."

I thought about it as I packed the tokens away. "The tokens needed to be together. Now they are. I wonder where the rest of the peace stone is."

"The myths, the stories aren't always correct, are they?" asked Starshine. "Faltryn had the red token, not the peace stone. But maybe he had both of them. If that's so, then he'll have it back in his cave and we'll never get it." She sighed. "Maybe we just need to get the families together."

"Possibly. We won't know until we do. Each token means a family. Wind Runner's prophesy said, 'when they return, who wear the token, the land will begin to be whole again'. I think it needs everyone to be whole. We have members of six families, but can one person actually be called a family?" I shrugged. "I may have it all wrong anyway. The myth said the peace token broke in two. Half became the rainbow token. Here it grew into a massive white stone, so perhaps it really is complete now and we just have to understand what we saw."

As I wrapped each of the tokens, I realised that water no longer oozed out of the standing stone.

Everything seemed different, as if what I had seen had changed me. I felt hollow, as if something was roaring inside me. Then I realised it wasn't something I could feel or hear, but rather something I couldn't. An absence of noise. And I knew! The waterfall no longer flowed.

I ran to the ledge overlooking the canyon. Water still swirled around the bowl below me, struggling to get out through the ravine. The large gash in the rim was again visible. I thought it was deeper than it had been, although I wouldn't know for sure until I could see it from the floor of the canyon.

A rainbow still arched over the hill. There was only one now, but bigger and deeper in colour than when there had been many.

The flask was still lodged under the rim of the rock lip, water spouting out of it and spilling down onto the ledge.

I lifted it off and again studied the engraving while pushing the stopper into the spout. Nothing in it gave me a hint about the picture I had seen in the cave.

It was quite cold now, Starshine was shivering, so we made our way out into the sunlight and found a sheltered place to sit and eat.

I looked over the land to the massive rock in the northeast and the huge hills in the distance beyond it. It amazed me that the expansive flat area between here and the hills could exist. From my time down there I knew the land had small hills and gullies, but from here, it looked like a wide plain. In my mind I heard the description from Wind Runner's prophecy. The leader of The Green Valley in his anger, pushed the hills apart creating a wide plain ... I had a sudden thought.

I opened my token pocket, chose and unwrapped one, clicked it to my blue token and sent a message to Papa.

Tell Wind Runner — The tribes were called to meet for a great celebration in the middle of the vast plain to the east of the canyon. She will understand and explain.

I felt his bewilderment, but he acknowledged my message.

With our meal over, we packed and started back. The trip home was quiet, we both had a lot to think about.

Before we got to the camp, Starshine stopped me. "Kirym, when you found the red token you didn't show us straight away. Was there a reason for that?"

"Why do you ask?"

"Well, I don't want to have to tell everyone about the purple immediately. Such a lot happened here, and I need to think about it first. I feel mean, but well ..." She looked troubled.

I was surprised she was so attuned to the token and that her feelings had mirrored my own so completely.

"Tokens reveal themselves. I leave it up to them. You have the ability to read them. You're a worthy holder of the bronze token."

"You said there were six families. I can only think of four. Yours and mine, Findlow's and Amethyst's."

"Bildon's family came from The Hills north of The Land Between the Gorges, and Sundas was born way to the south east of those lands. That may be wrong though, because although Arbreu has been adopted by us, his family was unknown. It's possible we all have an ancestor in common. There aren't that many differences between people."

Starshine brightened and smiled. "Will Amethyst carry the purple token in the ceremonies?"

"Perhaps at some time in the future, but she is far too young at the moment. Her name doesn't imply a connection to the tokens or any one token except the one she wears. Her token aligned with Teema's, Arbreu's and mine. We are her family, but things in the future will align her to others. Her history is important — her birth family. I'd like to find her people."

She looked appalled. "You'd give her to people who dumped her?"

"I'd do nothing to jeopardise her. She's mine and I'll protect her with my life. I don't know why she was left and we may be surprised when and if we find out. She will know where she came from. When she is old enough, she'll make her own decisions."

3

Kirym Speaks

I watched the hunt from my vantage point at the top of the ridge. The deer raced past the rocks fanning out across the hill. The direction they were taking meant they would be beyond Teema's arrow range.

Just below me, a path ran along the side of the hill. Familiar blond curls bobbed along it, sticking above the line of bushes that edged the path. Arbreu was much closer to the deer. Possibly he could turn them. As he came close I called out.

"Arbreu! Arbreu, help ..."

The bushes thinned. He turned towards me, eyes widening, surprised. Then his eyebrows climbed up his forehead.

He looks different, so young.

A dry branch cracked behind me. Something smelled ghastly. I turned.

A massive hairy animal towered over me, arms outstretched. It reared up, roaring. Its arms flailing, it knocked me to the ground.

Arbreu's lost his token, I thought, and everything went black.

4

Teema Speaks

The deer didn't follow the line in the land I had expected. Instead they fanned out across the rough ground. Maybe they realised it was a trap. I didn't want to return to camp empty-handed. One animal was all I needed, but now they were moving towards the bottom of the hill away from me. Something had spooked them.

Then I saw Arbreu.

He raced out of the trees at the bottom of the hill, panicking them, turning them back up the slope.

I could hear him crowing and yahooing. My arrow settled on a fat young stag. The beast raced towards me, not realising the danger.

I took a deep breath, steadied and loosed the arrow.

I felt the loss just as the arrow left the bow. A deep void. A sudden blackness similar to when as a child, I missed my first kill with everyone watching.

This was different though, I knew this arrow had flown

true. The stag faltered and fell in front of me. I struggled momentarily, trying to sort out my feelings.

Arbreu stopped, stricken.

I raced towards him.

"What happened?" I screamed. "Kirym! Where is she?"

Arbreu looked stunned. "She was ... then ..." He shook his head. "She's gone. How?"

I leaned over, panicking, trying not to vomit. I couldn't think. I struggled to make a decision. "We have to get back, find out what's going on. It can't be like that. When my Papa died, it wasn't like that. It ... well ..." I was lost for words. "Maybe she lost her tokens." I clung to the thought but deep down I felt — I knew. She was dead!

The sun travelled almost two hand-spans before Arbreu and I raced into camp.

The normality of the area seemed shocking, no panic anywhere.

I was so out of breath, even talking was impossible. I leaned over, trying to cope with the pains in my side and chest. I had really pushed myself getting here.

Now Mekrar was beside me, concerned, but seemingly calm.

"Kirym," I gasped.

"Breathe deeply," she said. "Now what happened?"

"Where is she? Where's Kirym?"

She looked surprised. "She followed you. Didn't you see her?"

"I think she's dead. She must be. Her tokens are gone. I can't read them."

"She's not dead!" Mekrar was adamant. She went to the baby basket. Amethyst was playing with her feet — her token glimmered slightly — unchanged. Mekrar clicked her token. "It's different, but ... well ... I don't know." She rounded on me. "But she isn't dead!"

"Then where is she?"

"If her tokens are gone, could you connect with the large ones? Kirym's used them before when she needed to. So …" Starshine paused, "couldn't you?"

I stood up, happy at having a new avenue of search. I frowned as I concentrated, thinking of one colour after another. I got no response, just cooing and gurgling from Amethyst. The sound distracted me, and I kept losing my concentration.

"Keep her quiet?" I snapped.

Mekrar frowned at me and went to Amethyst's basket. She picked her up and gasped.

"Oh! The tokens are here. Kirym left them in the basket."

My heart sank. "Why would she do that?"

Mekrar pulled me back from the edge of panic. All I could see and feel was the loss, but she was unwavering. "She is alive!"

She organised everyone to pack the camp ready to move by the time I got my breath back and had eaten the meal she placed in front of me.

"You need energy," she said. "You're of no use to anyone if you collapse. We need to do this together."

Storm backed her and even Arbreu seemed to think it was a good idea. I just wanted to race out and search.

"She'd have followed the path you took," said Mekrar. "So we will too."

We had little time to travel before the sun set, but I felt better for having started. I still found it difficult to think about Kirym without a feeling of terror. I was amazed at how calmly Mekrar coped. She was so practical and efficient.

Just before the sun set, I felt my token glimmer. 'I'm imagining things,' I told myself, 'wishful thinking — clinging to hope beyond hope.' Already, I grieved.

As night fell I tried to sleep. At midnight I gave up the pretence and joined Mekrar in guarding the camp. I was restless, on edge, eager to start searching although I knew that all I'd do at night was destroy any signs Kirym may have left.

"If you don't rest, you'll have no energy in the morning."

I felt so wretched.

Mekrar rubbed my shoulder. "You can't protect her from everything, Teema."

I shook my head miserably. "It's not about protecting her. I think I threaten her life every time I turn around these days."

She waited quietly for me to carry on.

"When we first found Arbreu, Loul asked me to care for Kirym, protect her. And yet I haven't. The boat sank in the rift because I didn't wait for Storm to call the direction. I just went blithely ahead. She could have drowned. I should have made her go with you at the arch. I could have picked Mek up. Kirym almost died there too. We get here and I thought a day away hunting would be great, her safe in camp looking after Storm and Amethyst. I was so frightened when I found she'd gone. She returned with the food I should have collected. I'd said I would hunt, and I didn't. I spent days sulking around camp ignoring her. When I did decide to go hunting it was unnecessary. The goat Kirym killed would have lasted, but suddenly I decided to prove myself. Be the big hunter. I don't blame her for needing to check up on me, and now she's dead."

I was shocked when Mekrar giggled.

"Oh dear, do you have it bad. This isn't a forced march you know. Kirym would ask you to do something if it was required. She understands that everyone needs time off. As a leader, she does what leaders do. It's automatic for her."

"But it shouldn't be. She's just a little girl. She should be playing and, well stuff like that."

"Oh Teema. She is grown up. Are you the only one who hasn't noticed? Don't let her size deceive you. On the river — well I wish you'd talked to Storm. He blames himself because he didn't know what route to call. He feels guilty too. He was pleased you made the decision. He said later that either way, you were going to hit a rock there. At the arch, Kirym made the right decision. You were the only one who could handle Elm. No one could have anticipated the boat breaking up."

She left me to think about that while she checked around the camp, collecting Amethyst and bringing her back to be fed. "Back in the settlement, Kirym said she wanted to climb the hill, and she told me she was going to look in the canyon. If you'd asked, I'd have told you, but you didn't seem interested. We all need time off. You wanted to show the men the land, and she wanted to check the canyon. It wasn't a difficult trip and Starshine was with her. Since then, you've avoided everyone. She foraged because that's what she does. She killed the goat yesterday because it had broken its leg and needed to be put out of its misery, not because we needed food. She didn't follow you to check on you. She wanted things to be right between you. And now? Well, she is alive even if you don't believe it."

At dawn we were ready to travel.

Initially Kirym's trail was straightforward as she had clearly followed the path I had taken. Then we lost her on a large rocky outcrop.

"Let's set up camp here," said Mekrar. "There's access to water and the site is easily defendable. Storm shouldn't walk any further, he'll damage his ankle. We can split up and search from here. Two small search groups will be far more efficient than if we stay together."

Storm, Starshine, Amethyst and Elm stayed in camp while Granite and Mekroe went north. Mekrar, Arbreu and I followed the path I had taken while hunting the day before.

The stag I had shot was now just a few chewed bones. Predators had dragged the carcass over a large area. There was no sign of Kirym.

Arbreu pointed to a line of trees to the north. "If she was in there when we were stalking, she may not have seen us. She could have gone further east and been over the next ridge before we sighted the deer."

With no more suggestions, we crossed the valley and climbed the low ridge searching for signs.

Below us was a shallow overgrown valley. We followed the ridgeline north until we found a deer trail through the tall grass.

I wasn't sure if Kirym had used it, but as Mekrar pointed out, she was more likely to follow a path than create a new one and this was the only one there.

"Hoo looooo!"

I felt an instant surge of hope. And then I realised. It wasn't Kirym. But then it wasn't any other voice I recognised either. The sound came from behind me, from the north.

I felt relieved. If this was the first of Wind Runner's outriders, there would be more people to help search for Kirym.

A tall slim figure pushed through the tall grass. His clothes were the same pale brown colour those from Faltryn used for travelling, although the style was different.

"Hello, I'm Rargo."

I had never seen him before.

5

Arbreu

Rargo approached Arbreu, his hand extended, a half smile lurking under a dark fringe and heavy eyebrows.

Arbreu grasped his arm. "Arbreu," he said. "Teema and Mekrar." He pointed to each as they joined him. "Are you one of Wind Runner's people?"

Rargo, ignoring the question, discounted Teema and turned to Mekrar, his eyes widening. He looked slowly from her head to her feet, staring intently at her long trouser-encased legs.

He smiled brightly and took her hand. "I never expected to find such a jewel in this wilderness."

Arbreu hated him instantly.

"We're looking for my sister," said Mekrar woodenly. "Have you seen her?"

Rargo shook his head. "I've not seen anyone for many winters. I've travelled alone and lonely for countless seasons. I'll help you search though. Where have you looked so far?"

He seemed eager to assist. "I've come from the north," he said. "I think you should look further south. Something's worried me over the last few days. Lots of animals were travelling towards me. It was as if something had unsettled them. Perhaps whatever it is has stopped the child from getting back to you."

They picked up their weapons and packs. "We'll look," Arbreu said.

He wanted to send Mekrar back to camp, but thought if he suggested it, Rargo would volunteer to accompany her. He didn't trust him. Anyway he doubted Mekrar would allow him to send her off. Besides, if Rargo knew the land and helped find Kirym, Arbreu felt he could overlook almost anything.

They travelled until sunset and made camp.

Mekrar lit a fire and started to prepare a meal. She chatted quietly to Rargo, asking him questions about his life.

Arbreu listened with half an ear, wondering where to go and what to do next. He was jolted out of his reverie when Rargo landed on the ground at his feet.

"Touch my bum again and you're dead!" Mekrar screamed.

Rargo, the imprint of Mekrar's hand on his face, scrambled backwards away from her. "She's crazy! It was an accident!" he yelled.

"He pinched me!" She turned back to the fire, her face bright red, her lips tight with anger.

"I didn't," screamed Rargo. "I just bumped her."

Teema leaned down, his face in front of Rargo's, his voice steely. "You don't do that. It's unacceptable. Show respect."

He offered his hand, but Rargo ignored it, scrambling to his feet.

"Crazy," he muttered. "I was trying to help." He rubbed his face. "She hit me. She had no right."

"You're lucky this time," said Teema. "She carries a knife and has been known to use it. Step carefully."

Rargo's pale face highlighted the anger in his eyes.

Arbreu smiled to himself. "Are you all right?" he asked Mekrar softly.

She glowered at him. "Don't use him for guard duty," she said, "and watch him carefully!"

Arbreu stayed beside Mekrar, helping her prepare the meal.

Everyone was unusually quiet as the sun disappeared.

As they started to eat, Arbreu tried to fill in the awkward silence, talking about the search in the morning. "We've seen no sign of anything. Are we going in the right direction? Maybe we should have followed the treeline east."

"I've just come from there," interrupted Rargo. "I would have seen something."

6

Teema Speaks

By the following evening I was even more deeply depressed.

I was setting up the shelter when my token glimmered. I looked up.

Mekrar stared at me, and in two quick steps was beside me. She clicked my token.

"Has this happened before?"

I nodded. "Just after I got to camp yesterday. I thought I imagined it. I can't feel her. Maybe her tokens just want us to find them."

Rargo came towards them. "Is something wrong?"

Mekrar waved her hand dismissively. "Talk later," she said quietly.

It was past midnight when Mekrar joined me as I guarded the camp. Arbreu handed us a drink, and settled his cloak around his shoulders. "I won't be sorry to sleep. Searching like this is exhausting."

"Don't go just yet," said Mekrar quietly. "There are things we need to discuss." She checked that Rargo was asleep and beckoned us away from him.

"Arb, just on sunset Teema's token glowed."

"Mine didn't," said Arbreu.

"Your connection to Kirym is different," she said. "The blue token glowed, not the green. I clicked it within moments, but felt nothing. She wasn't wearing it then, but it would only glow for her. This proves she's alive."

"But that doesn't tell us where she is, does it," I countered.

"Are we looking in the right place?" she asked.

I shrugged. "With the information we have, it's the logical place."

"And who gave us that information?" Her lip curled derisively. "That lying worm."

Arbreu and I both objected, but she was adamant.

"Look at him. He says he's been by himself for a long time. But in the two days we've known him, he has gone from being clean and neat to a grubby, untidy mess. He hasn't the equipment he'd need for travelling alone and his hunting skills are appalling. He can't forage. He just doesn't know the plants. Earlier today he was collecting nightshade berries for dessert. I was tempted to let him eat them, except we'd have to nurse him and explain his death. Someone has been looking after him and quite recently, they must be close by. Why didn't he tell us?"

"Hold on, Mekrar. Why would he leave people who cared for him? Anyway, that doesn't mean we're going in the wrong direction."

"It does if you think about it, Teema. Why would Kirym come this far? You know her. What's your gut feeling?"

I was quiet for a long time as I thought about all I knew of Kirym and her abilities. "She wouldn't come south knowing where we were. She'd get to us as quickly as she could or she'd return to the camp."

Mekrar nodded. "The sun had moved about a hand-span when she followed you. She must have almost caught up when she disappeared. Three days back! We have to get back there and change our search pattern. We're chasing will-o'-the-wisps down here. Rargo took us away from there. Why?"

"I thought she might have been attacked. Met up with a wild animal of some sort," said Arbreu. "They were around."

"We only thought predator, because Rargo suggested it," said Mekrar. "When he first turned up, he said something about a predator stopping the child. Kirym's not a child, but she is small, so if you didn't know her, you may think she's much younger than she is. He knows something. Why hasn't he told us? Also have you seen any animals going north? I haven't. It doesn't make sense anyway. When animals stampede it's only for a short distance. Predators tend to be territorial and at this time of the year they don't move far. He's hiding something and I'd like to know what it is." She frowned. "He's been careful with his pack. I wonder what's in it."

"Kirym had a fair idea where we were headed, so she'd have kept to the tops of the ridges to get an overview of each valley. That's the best place to start." I turned to Arbreu. "We need to let Starshine know where we are and what we're doing. Do you think you could find the camp from here?"

Arbreu nodded. "There's a stream a little way back that goes in the right direction. I can follow it. It's about three ridges to the west. Once I've told Storm, I can track Kirym towards you. I'll make sure she didn't go elsewhere." He nodded at Rargo, "What about him? I could take him with me."

"We'll take him," said Mekrar quickly. "You're going against the grain of the land, so it'll be a harder trip. We at least just follow the valleys north. Anyway, I don't trust him not to kill you when your back's turned."

"Shall I wake him up?" Arbreu started to rise.

"No," I said. "Wait until morning and see what his reaction is when we tell him we're going back. He may drop something vital and if he annoys us enough we'll have an excuse to search his pack."

7

Larqeba

It was early evening when Larqeba finally approached the lodge. After racing noisily across hills and through the bush, he was now very wary and quiet, cautiously checking for sentries. He knew they'd be out watching for him.

There were three paths to choose from and all of them probably guarded. Dashlan's foot hung from the big rowan tree ahead. Dashlan dreamed in trees and if disturbed was likely to fall out.

Rargo's haunt was further west so Larqeba chose the northern path to the lodge.

Ahead was the rock, and he knew Enliah would be sitting in the shade there. In all probability she would be asleep, or so near sleep she wouldn't react until he was well past her. It was the only choice he had, short of — no, there was no other choice. He had to get help fast.

Nothing else for it, he put his head down and ran.

"Hey!" Not Enliah, but Rargo.

Then Enliah's voice. "Rargo! Wait for me. We're just watching for him."

Damn, they'd been together.

Larqeba could hear Rargo getting closer.

Larqeba leapt over a small log, sidestepped some bushes and sprinted across the open area towards the lodge. Ma was there. She would be the one to talk to.

"Ma!" he called. "Ma!"

She looked up, first a smile — relief, and then — well of course she would be annoyed, but anger? Not at him fortunately, although it may have been so under different circumstances.

Larqeba felt Rargo's fingers grab at his hair, a sharp pain as he took a flying leap and landed in the dirt at his Ma's feet. He knew a large chunk of his hair would be in Rargo's fist.

"Stop that! Rargo! You were asked to find which path he took, not to attack him." Ma stepped forward protectively.

Rargo turned away scowling and kicked at one of the washing frames. It collapsed in the dirt, the damp washing again streaked with dust.

"Rargo! Pick that up and wash it all. Jeresaya has enough work to do."

Larqeba was picked up by his tunic. "You lad, can go to bed, now! And I don't want to see you until morning."

"But, Pa!"

"Nothing from you!" he thundered. "Two days away. We were worried sick. How many times must you put us through this? Count yourself fortunate I'm not thrashing you."

Rargo slipped to the edge of the trees, smirking as Enliah picked up the grimy laundry.

"Rargo! I told you to do the washing! Enliah, leave those to Rargo and help with dinner. Rargo! Now! And don't lose any."

Larqeba slipped into the lodge and opened one of the

large storage containers, searching through the contents. He hauled out a long lidded box.

Qwinita sat on her sleeping platform. "Pa will beat you if he catches you touching that. Pretend to sleep. Ma will bring you some food later, and you can sort out the rest in the morning."

He looked up, frowning grimly. "I don't have time. She'll die if I wait." He noted Qwinita's shocked expression, then grabbed the carved speaking stick from its padded case. He slipped back through the door, Qwinita breathing down his neck.

Larqeba hit the bottom of the stick on the old drum by the door. Everyone looked up.

Pa was furious. He stood up and took a step towards him, but Ma put her hand on his chest.

"Listen first, Bryn."

"She might be d…" Larqeba faltered, not really knowing where to start. He took a big breath. "There was a girl and an animal and she fell and it grabbed her and she might be dead and I don't know and we have to go an' see." Tears filled his eyes. "We have to help her."

"We don't make contact with others, lad. It's too dangerous. You know the rules, forget about her. Animals kill. It's nature's way." Pa shook his head. "We'd be too late, anyway." He hunkered down beside Larqeba and stroked his hair. "It's hard, but we'd be far too late."

"She called for help, Pa. She looked at me and asked for help. But she called me by your name."

"She called Bryn?" Jeresaya looked stunned. "Why? How? You must have misheard."

Larqeba shook his head. "And she had this," he said holding out his hand. "I found it on the ground where she fell."

Jeresaya took the green stone he held out. It glowed slightly.

"Oh my goodness," she gasped. "It's a token. Bryn, it's a token."

"It can't be. They're myths, stories for winter nights." He looked at the stone and shook his head. "We can't get involved. It's too dangerous. We've already lost too much. I'll not jeopardise what little we have left. People are treacherous." He stood and turned away, but Jeresaya caught his arm.

"What right have we to expect that our family remains safely together, and as we'd wish them at birth. We may have lost, but we've gained too. She asked for you by name, Bryn. If we ignore her call, we'll be cursed. Then we will lose everything. When you think about it, we've not lost that much."

He turned back to her, his eyes flinty blue with anger. "Not much? A son? A community? All of our friends? If that's not much, then ..." He stopped and sat heavily on a log, rubbing his hand across his face.

Jeresaya knelt beside him. "We have two strapping sons, two beautiful daughters and Rargo. We have each other. The community, our friends, they made a choice. It was their decision to make. Our son, well I would wish that had he needed help, someone out there would do as much. This is somebody's daughter, and she's asked for your help. To refuse her ... and she wears a token."

"Not any longer, she doesn't. Does the power leave them when the token leaves?"

"It still glows, Bryn. She might still be alive. We must do something to help her." Jeresaya slipped the token into the pocket tied around her waist.

Bryn looked around the clearing. "We were happy here. I wondered if it was too good to be true." He sighed deeply. "Very well, we'll leave at dawn. Do we pack up, or leave this here and hope to come back?"

"Pa," Larqeba handed Bryn a handful of long coarse red-brown hair. "This was caught on a bush near where it was. Can you tell what it is?"

Bryn teased the fibres out. "Looks like a bear. I didn't think they lived this far north. They prefer colder weather." He pulled the boy to him. "Lad, if it's a bear, she will be dead. But I'll check it out, and kill the beast! Will you be satisfied with that?"

Larqeba nodded.

Bryn picked up his spears and started checking the points.

8

Larqeba

"Ma!" Qwinita shook Jeresaya's shoulder.

Jeresaya sat up, noting the darkness of the lodge. Just before dawn, she thought, automatically reaching for Qwinita's forehead.

"Are you all right? What hurts?" she asked quietly.

Qwinita put her finger to her lips and moved away from the sleeping platform. Jeresaya followed, tying on her overdress as she did.

In the dim recess of the lodge, Qwinita turned to her. "I'm fine, but something's wrong. The air vents are closed and the windows are covered. Rargo's bed hasn't been slept in. He didn't waken Dashlan for guard duty. I can't find Larqeba and other things have disappeared, my neck and ear jewels. We need to tell Pa, but ..."

"Get some air in here." Jeresaya went back to her sleeping platform and shook Bryn's shoulder as Qwinita opened the ceiling vents and then the windows.

Sunlight streamed in and by then, Bryn was through the door. He looked around the camp. The fire was out, containers were open and scattered.

"I'll thrash them both for this. Larqeba knew I wanted to leave early."

Jeresaya sifted through the ashes trying unsuccessfully to find a glowing coal. "It hasn't been fed since dusk. We'll have to start from scratch." She picked up a flint.

"Leave it," said Bryn. "We need to get after them."

"We won't get far with empty bellies, Bryn. A little longer will make no difference at all. Anyway, why would Larqeba run off? He knew we were leaving at dawn. It doesn't make sense. Ask Dashlan, he may have heard something."

Qwinita handed Jeresaya a container of water. "They went into the stream, but I don't know what direction they took. Common sense says they went downstream, but we need to look upstream first. If they went that way, they won't have stayed in the water long, it gets too deep."

Bryn ushered Dashlan and Enliah out of the dwelling as Jeresaya set fruit and bread on the table for them to share. She bustled around filling packs to take with them.

"Bryn, I can't find my pocket. I was sure I left it beside your knife, but I can't find that either."

Bryn's hand went to the empty sheath on his belt. He entered the lodge and returned again a few moments later, his face black with anger.

Sharp questions from Bryn soon showed that Dashlan knew nothing. "Not that I'd expect him to," Bryn sighed. "That boy lives in another world."

Jeresaya smiled. "He's a dreamer, an artist. Not like Larqeba and Qwinita, and that makes Larqeba's disappearance so wrong. We planned to leave early to search for the girl, so why would he hold us up like this?"

With weapons in hand and packs on shoulders, they began

the search. Bryn crossed to the far bank of the stream while Qwinita kept pace on the near-side.

They soon returned, and with the rest of the family in tow, continued the search downstream.

Qwinita found a well-used animal track going west and while there was no proof Rargo and Larqeba had left the stream there, it was an obvious path, and the grass was damp, showing that something had used it overnight.

Just before midday, Bryn found a mound of grass piled on one side of the track. "Who left it and was it done on purpose?"

He sifted through the pile, holding up some grasses, plaited together, and tied in a circle with a tail of seed heads.

"Larqeba did that," said Qwinita. "I taught him how to make them last spring. What's he trying to tell us? Why is it hidden, and why now and not sooner?"

Jeresaya took it from Bryn. "It lets us know we're on the right path. Maybe Larqeba isn't here by choice."

It was frustrating. The trail, though well used was covered with resilient springy grass. It bounced back quickly after they passed, and effectively hid previous users from discovery. A number of tracks ran off it. Bryn couldn't tell if the boys had left the path or continued on.

Late in the afternoon, Bryn found footprints on a patch of sand. "Rargo's," he said studying them. He's running, but there's no sign of Larqeba."

Telling everyone to wait, he quickly followed the footprints up the hill ahead, surveying the land around.

"It looks like he went into the long grass there," he said when he returned. "I wonder why he changed direction."

"Well whatever it was, we can do nothing more until

morning," said Jeresaya.

"Pa, there are animal trails in the field. Is this where Larqeba saw the girl? Could that animal have its cave nearby?"

"I'd not expect to find a cave in this sort of land, Qwinita. Caves form in rock. It's predominately soil here and a cave in these hills would collapse. I don't know what direction Larqeba took yesterday, but probably nowhere near here."

"If Larqeba was here and had run into the field, he'd be hidden by the tall grass," she said. "Maybe Rargo went to high ground to find him."

Bryn nodded. "Well the trail is easy enough to track and if there's a chance Larqeba went that way, we need to follow it. It's our only option. I have to assume that both of them went into the field."

9

Teema Speaks

I had expected an argument from Rargo, but with sidelong glances at Mekrar, he mumbled excuses and agreed he may have got it wrong. He gave us no excuse to look in his pack, but clung to it possessively.

I felt better once we were on our way, although possibly only because I believed we may finally be making progress in the right direction.

The trip back was slow. Soon after we started north, Rargo tripped over a log. Although there was no sign of swelling he declared his ankle to be twisted and too sore to walk on.

"It's no good. It won't carry my weight. It should only take a day or two and then we can go on, but …" He shook his head.

"You're right. It's best you stay here then," declared Mekrar. "We'll leave you some food and enough wood to keep a small fire going. We can come back for you after we've found Kirym."

Rargo panicked. He realised Mekrar was pleased to have a reason to leave him.

After some heated words, Arbreu bandaged Rargo's ankle firmly and I gave him the choice of joining us or staying put.

Rargo moaned and complained as we walked away, but followed us, limping heavily. We had to adjust our speed to his. I placed him in front of Mekrar, knowing she would take less nonsense from him than Arbreu would.

It was harder after Arbreu left. Together we'd shared the lead checking the path ahead and keeping an eye behind. Now every time I went to check the land ahead, Rargo would slow down further. Mekrar was coming to a slow boil that I knew would come to a head very soon.

I knew Mekrar's assessment of Rargo was right. He was totally untrustworthy. I seriously considered walking away from him, but I was sure he would get himself into danger and we'd have to waste time rescuing him or feel guilty. The sooner we could hand him back to his people, the better, although I privately wondered if they would refuse to take him back.

Just before midday, while checking one of the few steep gullies in our path, I saw movement in the distance. Something appeared to be following the track we had made yesterday and it was big enough to be a threat. The grass was tall, well over our heads and we would be easy prey for something large and predatory.

I sped back to Mekrar.

Rargo sat down as soon as I approached. His resentment at being pushed by Mekrar had grown through the day, just as hers had for him holding us back.

Mekrar and I hunkered down in the long grass discussing possibilities.

Rargo yawned. "Well, be careful. It could be the animal

that attacked ya little sister."

Mekrar's eyes widened. In one swift movement, her knife was in her hand and at his throat. "Where?"

Rargo tried to sink into the ground and skitter away from her. "No, no, no. Joking! Honestly, just joking." He looked at me. "Get 'er off! I didn't mean it!"

I grabbed him by his tunic, lifting him off the ground, my face close to his. "You are a lying scumbag." I saw the fear in Rargo's eyes, and was sickened. Dropping him heavily, I turned to Mekrar. "If he moves, kill 'im."

Rargo grunted as he hit the ground. "Kill me and you'll never know where his lair is."

Mekrar took a step back, whipped out her bow and shot, her arrow pinning his sleeve to the ground. A smear of blood stained his tunic where the arrow nicked his arm.

"He can wear a lot of arrows before he dies."

I nodded shortly, picked up my bow and sprinted away.

I crawled into the gully. Once below the skyline with bushes behind me, I raised my head, to check the creature's path. There was too much movement in the grass for there to be only one of them. This was a family group. These were large animals, and anything that big giving birth in spring would still be overprotective of their young. We'd have to be careful.

They followed the track we'd made coming south, but was that accidental? This was not its territory. Animals are creatures of habit, and they tend to keep to the same tracks. We had created the path through this field, and that implied we were being followed. I remembered the height of the growth here, well above my head. I would not see these animals until they were pretty much on top of me. I needed somewhere safer where I could control the encounter and make the decisions about attack or retreat.

Close to the base of the hill near a stand of trees, the grass reduced in height. I sprinted towards the shelter, hoping the shadow would give me a momentary advantage. If there was a suggestion of danger, I could dodge through the trees and retreat over the hill to warn Mekrar.

I loosened my knife in its sheath. My bow was already fitted with an arrow. I made it with moments to spare.

The nearer grasses rustled as the animal approached. I automatically adjusted my bow.

A head appeared, but not what I expected. It was human.

A man pushed through the thinning stalks and stepped clear of them.

He was quick. His spear was pointed at me before he was clear of the grass.

I looked him over, dropped my bow and stepped forward, my hand outstretched.

As he hesitated a woman appeared beside him. She murmured something and he lowered his spear, brushed seed from his hair and stepped forward smiling.

"I'm Bryn," he said. "Jeresaya, my wife. Are you looking for a girl?"

I smiled and relaxed. "Teema. Yes, we are. Is she with you?"

Two girls and a boy stepped out of the grass.

"Not with us, but my son knows where she is. Unfortunately he's missing. I thought we were following his track."

I nodded and gestured over the hill. "He's safe, but he hasn't told us about Kirym. He's been mucking us around a bit."

Jeresaya looked surprised. "That's not like Larqeba. He's normally ..."

"Who?" I felt nauseous again. "He gave his name as Rargo. He's led us on a bit of a wild goose chase."

Jeresaya sank to the ground, obviously upset.

"Our son Larqeba saw the girl," Bryn explained. "He'd

been away for two days, but I assumed he came for help as soon as he saw her. It was evening and I said we'd find her in the morning. I expected him to lead us to her."

I nodded. "Rargo isn't yours?"

"We care for him. He's an orphan." said Bryn. "I thought they'd left together, but it didn't make sense. We'd agreed to help the girl, so I can't understand why Larqeba would jeopardise the search."

"Hold on," I said. "Rargo knows more than he's let on, so let's stop for a meal and talk." I indicated the clearing. "This is as good as any place. Let's get everyone together."

I sketched out a quick plan and went to get Rargo and Mekrar.

10

Teema Speaks

Rargo still lay on the ground where I had dropped him. His sleeve was stained with blood where the first arrow scratched his arm. Three more arrows pierced his clothes. Mekrar held another in her bow. As I approached, she plucked the arrows from the ground releasing him.

"Next time I won't miss," she hissed. She raised an eyebrow in my direction.

I shook my head. "A couple of deer," I said. "There's a place over the hill where we can make a meal."

Mekrar glanced at the sun, only just at its peak. "We could go on for a while."

"I'm tired," I said taking a deep breath. "It was easier when Arbreu was here. Anyway, it's a good spot, plenty of wood and water. We'll move faster after a good meal." I turned away from Rargo and winked at her.

She frowned, shrugged and picked up her pack.

Rargo sat up. "I'm not walking anymore. My arm hurts.

And my foot."

I grabbed him by the front of his tunic and hauled him to his feet. "You have been pushing it since we met you. If I let Mekrar loose, you may survive, but I doubt it'll be long when I tell her papa what you've done," I paused. "Actually, stay put. I don't care. But if you're not with us, you don't eat."

I gathered dry grass and piled it up with twigs to set a fire. Mekrar collected water and pulled some grains and dried fruit from her pack, adding the remains of the meat from this morning.

"Where's Kirym? Rargo, where is she?"

"I dunno. I only said that 'cause you were mean to me. If I knew, I'd tell you, honest."

"You wouldn't know honesty if it bit you on the bum."

Rargo jumped up and spun around. "Bryn! You found me. Thank goodness. These people, they kept me prisoner. Look they shot at me. I don't know what they've done with the kid."

He seemed shocked to find himself lying on the ground. Mekrar's punch took everyone by surprise.

She shook her hand. "Ouch! What kid?" She backed away from the strangers, her knife pointed at them.

My hand closed over hers pushing the blade down. She relaxed, jamming her weapon back into its sheath.

Bryn lifted Rargo off the ground by his tunic. "Where is Larqeba?"

"I sent the little runt packing. He'll be back at the lodge with Jeresaya. He'll be in his element," he sneered. "Fussed over like a baby."

"And Kirym?" I interrupted. "You care to tell me what you

know about her?"

Rargo took a quick breath, glanced at Bryn and looked away. "So I knew the kid had seen her. But I didn't know where she was," he blustered. "Anyway, Bryn said she'd be dead. I didn't do anything wrong …" He stopped.

Jeresaya, Qwinita, Dashlan and Enliah stepped into view.

"Where are my ear jewels?" Qwinita demanded.

"Looked in your brother's pack?" sneered Rargo, pulling himself free of Bryn's hold.

Qwinita launched herself at him and was hauled back by Bryn. In the commotion, Mekrar sliced through the strings of Rargo's pack, snatching it away.

"You can't do that," he screamed. "It's mine." He lunged for it as she upended it on the ground. A number of pockets and pouches, two knives and other tools lay on the ground.

Mekrar picked up one of the knives, its distinctive engraving of three boats shone in the midday sun. "You thieving scumbag! And don't say he gave it to you," she yelled as he opened his mouth. "He wouldn't have given it away, and especially not to you."

Bryn sheathed the other knife, handed a small soft skin pouch to Qwinita and a pocket to Jeresaya.

Jeresaya opened hers and pulled out a token, handing it to Teema. "This belonged to the girl Larqeba saw. He thought she had another."

"We'll help you find the animal, and retrieve the stone. I doubt there's much hope though," said Bryn. "Laqeba brought some of its fur, and I'd say it's a bear."

Mekrar relaxed, flexing her hand. "She's alive," she said. "Tokens are different when the owner is dead. Now we know why we got no response from this one. She's not wearing her others although she's close to them. What about Lar…?" She shook her head. "Well, where's he, Rargo?"

"I don't know!" he shouted, backing away from her. "He

followed me and I sent him packing. He said he was going back to the lodge. It's not my fault he wanders."

11

Kirym Speaks

The pain in my hand woke me. My head ached. I had hit it when I was knocked over.

The animal! I remembered! The appalling stench! The scream! Arbreu looking so young and different without his token.

My tokens! They were gone!

Had I lost them when I fell? The holder was gone too, and it was unlikely to have fallen off. My forehead felt bare without them. Worse, it cut off my ability to contact Teema and Arbreu. I didn't have the large tokens either. Because I'd wanted to travel quickly, I'd left them in Amethyst's basket.

I was thirsty. My throat burned. My damaged hand was wedged under my hip, throbbing with my weight on it. I needed to move.

Something grunted in the distance, the sound diminishing. Then silence. I knew I had to look. I opened my eyes, just a little and quickly.

Dirt.

I lay against a wall, my nose almost touching it. I looked again as I carefully lifted my hip and slid my hand forward. I tried desperately not to moan as the blood rushed back into it. I hugged it to my chest, analysing what I could see.

Just above me something pale stuck out of the wall. From this angle I couldn't tell what it was. There were more of them higher up and in more light. It was dim where I lay, but daylight. The same day? I thought so.

The animal had carried me here, and most beasts didn't stray too far from their den.

I sat up and looked around. Not much to see. I was in a tunnel, the opening at one end looked onto another dirt wall. But there was a light source further around to the left. All was quiet.

The pale thing I had noticed in the wall was a bone, a skull. It was partially buried, the jaw jutting out, the eye sockets still filled with dirt. Further on more bones stuck out of the wall at different heights. They looked old. They had been buried for a long time and had absorbed the tannins of the soil.

My knife and sheath were gone. I had tied them to my shoulder for easy access. It couldn't have fallen off and it didn't feel like it had been wrenched off.

I'd lost my herb pouch. That had been tucked securely into my waistband. There was a rope around my waist, tied at the back and looped up towards the roof and around the corner of the passage. At least it offered room to move.

I still knew nothing about where I was or what was around me. I crept close to the entrance of the passage and peeped around the corner.

It was cave-like, the walls, dirt not rock. There was an open central area with a number of passages like the one I'd been in, four in all like fingers branching off. The ceiling and most of the passages were wreathed with cobwebs. The passage I'd been in showed signs of cobwebs which had been recently removed. Thick walls between the passages supported the roof. In the open area, tree trunks were used as extra support. Roots hung through the roof. Some had been cut off but the thickest grew down through the floor of the cave. Spider webs crossed some areas thickly. Tunnels in them showed the paths most often used.

It was rather dreamlike.

A platform sat against a wall, a pile of smelly skins heaped on it. At one end sat a skull, the eyes staring blackly at me. More skulls were stacked against two walls and had been placed like sentinels around the platform.

One wall had arm and leg bones stacked to the ceiling. Further around, rib cages and finger bones were heaped, seemingly higgledy-piggledy, in a large hollow in the wall. Some of the skulls showed damage, but the skull on the platform was intact. It was decidedly strange.

The fireplace in the middle of the floor held the smouldering remains of a fire. There was an acrid smell, not one I was familiar with. I picked up a stick and poked through the ashes. Burned bones sat amid charred logs. These bones were different, not aged as the others had been and not human.

Nearby was a woodpile. I grabbed some thick twigs and a small log and placed them on the embers, watching until the twigs caught. In with the wood were piles of dried dung. The animal obviously used them for fuel too.

Near the door was a strange contraption built into the wall. It looked almost like a fireplace, but I had not seen anything like it before. The opening was too small for it to be efficient as a hearth or oven, but the inner walls were black with soot. I only thought of it as a fireplace because of the ash remains. It didn't seem to be made to heat the cave.

I wanted to study it, but this wasn't the time.

The rope around my waist was cleverly fastened to another tied between two tree trunks. The knot tying the ends of the rope was well above my head. If yanked very hard, it may come down, but it might also pull the trunk and possibly the roof with it. I would be lucky to escape.

Against the wall was a large flask similar to those we used for water storage in the settlement. I checked, yes water and seemingly fresh. On the shelf beside a number of gourds and platters was my herb pouch. It had been opened. Three of the inner packets had been unfastened and roughly tied again.

Using a gourd from a shelf nearby, I drank deeply. I swallowed a pinch of an herb, three small seeds and sucked on a square of trandor berry juice mixed with the pulp of lemech root and dried. With another drink, I felt a lot better.

I'd had time to think now, and there was a lot that worried me here. This wasn't the den of an animal. Animals don't build platforms. They don't have fire and they don't consistently steal. The flask came from our settlement, as had the two pots sitting near the fire. At least one of the baskets had been woven by Jorlenta. She had been experimenting with new designs and it had her distinctive touch. A hanging on the wall was one I'd last seen in the large chest found on our boat, Dragon Quest.

I eyed the leg bones. I needed a weapon and they were my only option. I placed three of them around the walls where I'd have the opportunity to grab them if needed.

I was surprised to be alive. The creature I had seen towering above me had looked and sounded ferocious. This cave was full of death although the bones appeared to be treated with respect.

The rope allowed me to get to the entrance. The cave

entrance faced northeast. It was late afternoon, the sun was approaching the western horizon.

A stream meandered to the east. The area in front of the cave was clear of plants although pieces of wood, bone, decaying skins and broken frames were scattered around. The hill above me was covered with grass, bushes and trees.

I was aware of something approaching through the bush. The thing — the animal — was returning. It didn't travel quietly. It groaned, muttered and occasionally bellowed. It crashed through the undergrowth, seemingly blind.

I fled into the cave, slipping into the shadows of the walled area. Not right in however, but able to see most of the cave. Just behind me, partially hidden beneath my skirt, was a femur, a long solid thigh bone. It was my only protection.

12

Kirym Speaks

He was big and smelly. Human, not an animal, the costume he wore implied that. A large brown fur robe was topped with a wolf's head. The wolf skin hung over his shoulders like a cape. There were stones set in the eye sockets of the head, giving it the strange appearance of being blind. I could see a human eye quite clearly through the wolf's partly opened mouth. The rest of his face was obscured by a matted beard that fell to his chest.

He sat on the platform and opened the skin bag he carried, dumping the contents into a nearby woven basket. A gutted kellich wrapped roughly in its skin fell to the floor. He kicked it towards the fire. He roared as he did so, pulling his foot close to his body, rocking and moaning in pain. That foot, his right, was wrapped in a skin and tied with rope. It was bulky and obviously padded. The other foot was in a rough boot. Under the robe, his legs were wrapped in badly tanned skins. He smelled dreadful.

I looked at the items he had placed in the basket. My knife and sheath, a few root vegetables, some fruit, kindling and other things I couldn't see properly.

Seemingly unaware of me, he sorted through the basket, pulling out my token holder. He picked up the skull, crooning to it, holding up the tokens as if showing them off. His voice was muffled by the wolf head, but I didn't think anything he said was intelligible. He placed the skull back on the platform and burrowed under the skins, pulling out another skull attached to some skin. These were good kellich skins, well-tanned. Two had been sewn together, stuffed and another piece of skin attached as a hood ensuring the skull remained in place at the neck. He placed my token holder across its forehead and laid it carefully on the platform. This human skull was tiny and he treated it with care. It looked like a baby, a doll.

He pulled at the ties holding the wolf mask and yanked it off his head. He was hairy. His matted beard and hair hung past his shoulders and had seen neither water nor a comb or teasel in many moons. He hauled the robe over his head, throwing it on the end of the platform. His body was wrapped with skins and they looked as if once on, he had never removed them, just adding more as necessary. He smelled like a dead animal. There was something about him, he looked familiar.

I wracked my brain. The truth when I realised it, was unpleasant. "Salcan!"

Salcan had disappeared on the day we first stepped on these shores after we escaped from our former home, The Land between the Gorges.

He must have heard, but he ignored me. He put some wood on the fire and went back to the doll.

With the sun's angle lower, I could make out more details in the walls. There was evidence of many more bones. Salcan had made his home in an old burial mound. A lot of people had been buried here.

"Food!" He was talking to me.

He kicked at the kellich that lay near the fire, cursing as he hurt his foot again. Tears ran down his face, disappearing into his matted beard. He was in a lot of pain. He took a deep breath, holding his knee to his chest. With his hands gripping his leg halfway between his ankle and knee, he rocked to and fro until the pain dissipated. Then he took another deep breath.

"You make food." He actually smiled, although only just discernable through the matted beard.

I picked up the kellich and pulled the smaller pot towards me. Using the gourd, I added water and hung the pot over the embers. There were a number of large wooden stumps littering the room. I pulled two close to each other, one to sit on and one to use as a cutting block.

Salcan didn't seem inclined to hurt me. I decided to act normally and hopefully he would relax enough for me to escape. I went to the basket where he had dumped everything and sorted through it, picking up the root vegetables, my knife and sheath.

He ignored me.

I cut up the meat, and put it in the smaller pot, then put water in the bigger pot and scrubbed the vegetables, chopping them and adding them to the meat.

Salcan's attention was on the small skull, rocking it and crooning to it. He had placed my tokens around its neck as they kept slipping off its forehead.

I cleaned my knife, picked up the sheath and tied it around my waist. I put the knife into it, but pushed it back onto my hip out of his sight.

The food was heating nicely, the smells just beginning to permeate the cave. I realised how hungry I was. I stirred the mixture and opened my herb pouch to get some dried onion and garlic and a few other herbs to flavour the meal.

He was suddenly beside me. He grabbed the pouch and pawed through the contents, pulling out three packets.

"What?" he demanded. These were the packets he had opened earlier.

I wondered why they were important to him. I opened the first, some seeds.

"I grind them and put them in bread. It sweetens and adds a lovely flavour. They taste nice." I ate one and offered one to him.

He bit into it. He really needed fresh breath, although his breath smelled sick as well as uncared for. He smiled at the taste, showing brown and yellow teeth and a few gaps.

The second was a mixture of dried berries. I explained that I used them when treating children with fever and cough.

He nodded his acceptance of my explanation.

I opened the next packet. This was bulky — broken soap-nut pieces.

"I'll show you," I said and added a small handful to the big pot with some clean water and put it on the embers to boil and reduce. He watched as I finished preparing the meal.

When the soap-nut mixture was ready I poured most into a small flask, leaving a small amount to cool. I used some to wash my hands and face.

Salcan reached over to the platform and handed me the doll and a scrap of absorbent kellich-skin. "Wash."

Now I got a good look at it. The stuffed skins looked and felt like a well-wrapped baby. I was sure now that this was what he had created, his own baby.

I wet the kellich-skin and wiped over the skull and down in around the neck. As I did so, I pressed the blue token, feeling it glow. I kept my hand over it until the glow was gone. The message would be relayed back to Teema — that

I was alive.

While washing the skull, I thought about the packets Salcan had opened. He obviously knew the knots I tied most of the packets with. There were five basic knots showing varying levels of danger, along with extras for further identification. They were fairly universal. Salcan's mama, Jalkam had been a revered healer and I suspected he had picked up an amount of knowledge from her. The packets he'd questioned were all things she wouldn't have known about. They were produce of this land and fairly common here although unknown in the hills where she had lived. Salcan hadn't experimented with the new things around him, I wondered if he knew how to.

I pushed the bowl towards him. He ignored it and reached for the doll.

"No," I said, pulling it away. "You can't hold her when you're dirty."

He growled, but started to wash, first his face and then his hands. The water was black when he finished.

I handed him the doll and disposed of the water. The sun had set and it was almost dark. There were herbs growing on the banks of the stream. I wanted some for the meal, but the rope wasn't long enough for me to reach them, so I returned to the fire and asked Salcan to get some.

I was surprised when he handed me the doll and obeyed, especially as his foot was obviously bothering him. Grunting with pain he picked up a crutch-shaped branch to support him.

It was getting quite cool. After Salcan handed me the herbs he went back to the entrance and swung a screen from against the hill outside, covering part of the entrance. He filled the open space with skins he had tied and sewn together, tying them into place. The cave became quite cosy.

The meal was now ready and I looked around for some

platters. Salcan saw me searching and lifted down two white circles.

At first I thought he had found a way of curving a pelvic bone, but once I held them I realised that these were made of something new. They were bleached, smooth, strong, and unlike anything I'd used before.

I handed him a filled platter. He hardly touched the food. At first I thought he didn't like it, but then realised that whatever was affecting his foot would also affect his desire for food. His eyes were bright with fever and infection. I took some of the meat and vegetable juices and mashed a few of the root vegetables in it, encouraging him to eat that instead. I was pleased he took some, although he didn't consume as much as I wished.

13

Kirym Speaks

While I cleaned up after the meal, Salcan staggered down one of the cobweb infested passages. He returned with a ground mat, a stuffed sleeping-pad and two warm rugs. These were sweet smelling and of good quality, and yet he obviously hadn't thought of using them himself, sticking to his rancid vermin-infested skins.

I wondered at his kindness. Did he not recognise me? Did he think of me as a friend? He seemed to respect my knowledge of herbs and powders. That could be my protection. Maybe he was lonely.

I slept amazingly well. I didn't feel I was in danger and I had eaten an excellent meal. Early in the night, Salcan had roamed the cave, although restricted by his crippled foot. I wondered how he had injured it.

As morning light seeped past the door frames, I busied myself getting the fire going to heat water and a meal. It was cold. The wind, blowing from the north filtered around the edge of the frame making it uncomfortable. I shivered as I worked on the fire.

Salcan disappeared down the storage passage again, returning this time with a warm cloak. I settled it around my shoulders and poured him a hot drink.

I wondered what else was stored in the dim passage way. So far he hadn't objected to anything I'd done, and was only tense when I went to the entrance. Even then he only watched to ensure my return. I walked past him and under the cobwebs.

The passage opened up to a storage room, lined with rough shelves. It was a treasure trove. Good skins, clothes, rugs, platters — things he could have used.

Most of them had been taken from the settlement. Normally we had guards on duty, although not when we visited the token-cave. There was no specific routine to our visits, although we generally went two or three times each season cycle. He must have watched us.

His cave was five or six days from the settlement. I wondered how many times he had made the trip. He would have needed at least five trips, probably more, and yet most of the items were unused. Perhaps ownership was more important to him. Maybe he had a guilty conscience over the thefts, although as a member of the family he was entitled to a portion. He could have asked for all of this, and we'd have given it. I had a lot to reflect on.

I chose a tunic, jacket, trousers and soft boots. I added a teasel, a washing cloth, two towels, and after some thought, a sharp shell for a shaving blade. I returned to the main area where I added the small flask holding soap-nut liquid and placed them on the edge of the platform.

"Why don't you have a bath? You'd feel a lot better wearing clean clothing," I said. "You could bathe in the stream. Little ones like to be held by someone who's clean. She'll become infested if you are."

He looked at the small skull lying on the platform beside him and pushed away the skins near it. Standing abruptly, he picked up the pile of clothes and his crutch and staggered towards the entrance.

As soon as he was gone, I put the large skull and the doll aside and swept everything else onto the floor and outside, as far away from the living area as possible. I took two pieces of burning wood from the fire and threw them on the pile, satisfied when the flames caught. I didn't want these things burning in the cave, mainly because of the smell, but also because I didn't want anything living in them to stay in the cave, and possibly find a new home.

I returned to the platform and scrubbed it clean. I'd used three bowls of water before I felt it was hygienic enough for use. From the storage area, I brought out a sleeping-pad and some rugs for him.

He was gone a long time and looked like a different person when he returned.

Without his hair and beard, I could see the effects of the fever. His face was flushed and his eyes were bright, but he was shivering. I wrapped the rugs around him and brought some well-tanned skins and a cloak from his storage area. I'd mixed some herbs and powders to try to lower his temperature and encouraged him to drink.

He had left his injured foot uncovered and dropped the unused boot on the floor beside the platform. Now I could see the extent of the damage. The foot, ankle and lower part of his leg were mangled, a pulpy mess with part of his leg bone visible through the blackened wound. I split the trouser-leg to his knee to ensure it wasn't restricted. The poisons were obvious above the wound. It must have really hurt to put it in water.

"What happened?" I helped him lift the limb onto the

platform and placed a pad of absorbent moss under it.

"I cut down a tree. It fell wrong. I got caught. It'll be all right, won't it?"

I couldn't say yes, and I wouldn't say no, because I really didn't think I could do anything about this.

"Nah, you're right, it's a mess," he said quietly. "I knew that."

"It's beyond my experience, Salcan, but I'll do all I can."

In reality I was his only help. The skin around the wound was dead and poisoning his system. Without something drastic the wound would kill him.

"There's one possibility," I said. "Amputate it. Cut it off. If I took it off just below your knee. Otherwise ..." I shook my head.

He went white and turned away.

I knew he would need time to think about it. In the meantime I got together what things I could to relieve his pain and cleanse his system. I really didn't have anything strong enough. I felt mean now that I'd made him bathe. It must have been so painful. It said a lot about him, that he did as I'd asked. Again, it gave me food for thought.

He threw off the rugs, his temperature was rising. I wet a cloth and placed it on his forehead and another across his throat. His eyes were sinking, his skin tightening over his skull. He was beginning to look like the dead he lived with.

I ate my meal and tidied up. The water was getting low. He was unable to get more for me.

I told him I'd get some from the stream and promised I'd return. He looked at me and turned away, resigned. We both knew I could leave whenever I wanted. I cut the rope from my waist and picked up a waterproof container.

He was asleep when I returned. It took five trips to the stream to fill the flask. I could only carry one container at a time. My hand still ached, I'd damaged it when I returned to The Green Valley from Faltryn, the Fortress in the north.

While I was waiting for the container to fill, I got a look at the cave from the outside. It was obviously not a natural cavern, but it was cleverly done. A few of the trees above the cave had been cut down removing weight, but the stumps remained there, helping to hold the hill together. In the bank near the door was a similar opening to the strange fireplace within the cave. I got a good look at it, and remained mystified. It backed onto the inner construction. Although similar to the inside fireplace, it contained no ash, although there was evidence of great heat. The internal wall was made of clay, and there was evidence an outer clay wall had been built in at some time in the past, and then broken down again. I was intrigued.

I built up the fire and infused willow and poppy seed with other herbs.

I heard him move behind me. "You still here?"

I nodded. "I said I'd stay. I will until you don't need me." I fed him the infusion and spoke again of amputating his leg.

Even with the best odds, it would be hard work. I had seen toe and finger amputations — a number of healers had helped each time — but I'd never done anything like that before. While he was asleep, I checked what tools I could use. He had a good size axe and a heavy serrated blade.

"It needs to be done soon. The longer we leave it, the less chance there is of it being successful."

He looked at me, his eyes travelling from my head to my feet.

"You couldn't do it. You wouldn't have the strength."

He was right. I scarcely came up to his armpit, but I wasn't giving up.

"I can wield an axe, but there are others nearby who could

help. They're very close, I could get them."

He shook his head. "No. It won't help. It's too far gone."

He split the leg seam of his trousers further, showing me the signs of poison running towards his groin. He knew enough of wounds to know he had gangrene.

"It'll only be a short time," he said.

Throughout the day, he sweated and shivered. The pain relief did less than I'd hoped, but he was stoic. He took what fluid I offered him, but refused to eat.

I didn't feel like eating either, but I knew I'd need my energy. I hadn't attempted to get my tokens, they were safe and when it came down to it, I saw no reason to upset Salcan.

I was surprised Teema and Arbreu hadn't found me. I wondered if Salcan had killed Arbreu when he took me or if maybe something else had happened. Without my tokens, I couldn't contact them, but I was sure they would be searching for me, no matter what.

As night approached, Salcan slept. I ate the meal I'd prepared. I wasn't hungry, the smells of the wound weren't conducive to eating, but I needed energy. This ordeal could last some time.

14

Larqeba

A hand grabbed Larqeba's mouth. He struggled, recognising Rargo's smell.

"Shhhh! I won't hurt you."

Larqeba backed away on the sleeping platform.

Rargo turned to the door, beckoning him to follow. Once outside, Rargo quietly shut the door and walked over to the fire.

Larqeba followed, not getting too close.

"Did you really see a girl?" asked Rargo.

Larqeba nodded.

"Bryn don't believe you. I heard him talking. He's taking us all north tomorrow, away from here. He said if there are people, there'll be a war and we'll die. He said even if there is a girl, she'll be dead and we'll be blamed, so we're leaving."

Larqeba tried to think what he could say to convince his Pa to help the girl. "I'll talk to him again, make him change his mind." He started back towards the lodge, but Rargo grabbed his arm.

"Got a better idea. Why don't we go find her? You and me. He won't leave without you and it won't take long."

Larqeba wasn't sure, this didn't feel right. "I'll talk to Ma. She'll change his mind."

"Listen!" Rargo grabbed his arm, pulling him back. "She agreed with him. She's scared she'll lose more family. I've got a pack here, we can go now." He paused. "You don't have to come. If you're too scared, tell me where she is and I'll go get her. But if I can't find her and she dies, it'll be your fault." He picked up Larqeba's cloak and held it out.

Despite misgivings, Larqeba took the cloak and grabbed his boots. He was hesitant. He really didn't trust Rargo. He was still trying to decide what to do for the best when he stepped into the dark of the trees.

Rargo was right behind him though, pushing him on. At the path Rargo stopped him.

"I was thinking, if they wake and find us gone they'll follow and they might catch up with us before we get to the girl. If we use the stream, they'll have to wait until dawn. Then we'll have found her and Bryn'll be real proud of you. An' Jeresaya will be pleased 'cause she'll have a new daughter."

"All right, but we have to leave a sign when we leave the stream."

Going downstream was easy despite the darkness under the trees. When Larqeba found the animal track, he climbed onto the bank, dried his feet on his cloak and tied his boots on. While Rargo fiddled with his boots, Larqeba knotted two pieces of twig together. He wrapped the tip with russet thread from his cloak, laying it on the trail so the thread pointed in the direction they were going.

Then Rargo was beside him. He gestured Larqeba into the lead, slinging the pack and a rope on his shoulder. He kept urging Larqeba to go faster and faster.

Larqeba wasn't happy. The path was indistinct and it was difficult to see obstructions in the dim light. When the moon went behind a cloud, he stopped and refused to go on.

Rargo paced up and down ranting and raving about the need for speed.

Larqeba picked a handful of long grasses, measuring to find some the same length. He plaited them, and because the moon was still hidden, he pulled more grass and continued.

"I'm not moving on until the moon is free of clouds. It won't be long and we'll go faster when we have some light." When he had three plaits, he twisted them into a circle and tied them together so the seed heads were protected in the centre of the ring. The cloud was thinning, so he dropped them on the ground, and pushed them under the grasses he had discarded.

As the moon reappeared, he wrapped his cloak around his shoulders and continued along the path. Rargo was again right behind him, pushing him, stepping on his heels.

It was after midnight when Larqeba stopped for a short rest.

This time, Rargo didn't complain. He opened the pack and brought out a loaf of bread, some apples and kullith nuts.

Larqeba knew the bread was the loaf Ma had made for their breakfast, and these were the best of the nuts, he felt guilty about eating them. Rargo could just as easily have taken the older bread, and food that hadn't been put aside. He felt more and more uneasy about the trip, wondering now if he should have gone to talk to his parents before leaving the lodge.

It wasn't like Bryn to change his mind like that. He always

explained his reasons for doing something and listened to everyone's point of view.

"Gotta go, boy. We need to be there by light." Rargo prodded him with a stick.

Larqeba batted it away.

"Don't do that." His eyes widened as the stick landed in a patch of moonlight. The end of it was wrapped in russet thread. He picked it up and turned back to Rargo, but he had disappeared.

Larqeba felt the rope around his throat, tightening. He struggled to breathe, clawing at the rope. He got his fingers between it and his throat, fighting to take a breath. Then Rargo flipped him onto the ground and pushed his knee into his belly. His fingers tightened around Larqeba's throat.

Larqeba felt his blood congesting in his head. He tried to scream, but heard only a faint gurgle.

Then everything went black.

15

Teema Speaks

If I hadn't been so worried about Kirym and to a lesser extent Larqeba, it would have been one of the better evenings I'd had in a long time.

We shared a good meal, and Dashlan volunteered to share the first watch with me.

At first I thought he was a strange lad, but I began to understand that he saw things differently to other people. He talked of dreams, light and shadows. He spoke of rainbows he'd seen and I was reminded of Kirym's love of them. He was intrigued with the descriptions of the different places I'd seen, and was fascinated when told of the sea journeys I had taken. He wanted to visit The Green Valley to experience new things.

"I love being with people," he said. "We've been isolated for so many seasons, and I know that's what happens when you travel. When I talk to you, I learn so much. It's nice to dream, but finding out the dream could be true is even better. Just the thought of meeting a few more people is great."

I laughed. "Well there are a lot more than a few people coming this way. Hundreds! Other than those from The Green Valley, there are over four hundred coming from Faltryn."

His look of delighted amazement was wonderful.

"I remember a gathering we went to when I was little," he said. "I thought there were hundreds of people there, but the number may have grown in my head. It's what happens when you're little. My brother died soon after that, and it really affected the whole family. That's why we decided to travel. After that, I drew things I'd like to build, but Rargo said my ideas were stupid. He said you couldn't build a dwelling on more than one level, and that they had to have straight walls."

"Rargo seems to have many words and little real knowledge. I'll enjoy introducing you to Armos. He's a builder. Does well with our dwellings, but even better with boats, and he curves the side in two directions at the same time. He reckons he could build a round house."

"Out of wood?"

I nodded.

The evening went by so fast, and I was surprised when Mekrar woke and reminded me it was time to sleep. She was joined by Jeresaya and Enliah for the middle watch.

I woke well before dawn to find Bryn and Qwinita had taken over. I was restless and knew I wouldn't sleep again, so I sent Qwinita back to her rugs while I joined Bryn.

"We're searching for two people now. Do you want to split up? Go in two different directions?"

Bryn shook his head. "If Rargo is telling the truth, he sent Larqeba back to the lodge. Knowing my son he'd have gone on to find your Kirym."

"And if Rargo is lying?"

"Then it's still better to find Kirym first. You claim she's alive. We have to ensure she stays that way. Larqeba will go to her, or return to the lodge. My instinct tells me he'll be attempting a rescue."

He looked at me and raised an eyebrow.

The relief I felt must have shown on my face, because he laughed quietly.

"Well," he said. "My heart tells me to search for my son. Jeresaya may say the same thing. But it comes down to practicalities. Larqeba would tell me to find Kirym."

Bryn's guilty feelings for his children were similar to mine for Kirym, but he had a balance that came with maturity and age. He talked vaguely of a community he'd been happy in, but lost. He didn't enlarge on it and we moved on to other subjects. He had travelled huge distances and was very experienced. One point he made was that too many people complicated a search.

I felt he was right and in the morning when I talked to Mekrar, she agreed. We sent messages to Arbreu and Mekroe to stay in camp for now and ensure everyone else did also.

We were watched in this by a bemused Bryn and intrigued Jeresaya.

"I always wondered what tokens were for," said Jeresaya.

We shared a hot meal and were on the path as the sun left the horizon.

Rargo lagged behind and slowed us down. After he had been hauled into the centre of the group twice, Bryn lost patience.

"You've a choice, lad. You can keep up or we'll leave you behind, and this time we won't come back for you."

Rargo straightened his back, and curled his lip in disdain. "I don't need you, or them." He eyed the hills to the west.

"They won't welcome you, lad. Not after these two send

them a message to shoot you on sight." Bryn turned away, and motioned for the rest of us to join him.

Rargo hung back, but as we set off without him he casually followed. For the rest of the day, he made sure he didn't lose sight of us.

I questioned Bryn about Larqeba's last trip. He was surprised to discover how much he really knew, much more than he realised.

Together, we decided on a direction to search in when we arrived back at the field where we met Rargo.

We both felt better for having a plan.

16

Kirym Speaks

Salcan was a good patient. He suffered silently, thankful for what I gave him in the way of drinks and medications. I gave him the heaviest pain relief I could, but I knew it wouldn't work for long. As hard as I tried, I couldn't draw the poisons from his system.

He wanted to talk, but didn't seem to know how to begin. After a few false starts, I realised it was easier to ask questions. He was happy to answer and it took his mind off the pain.

"Where did you get the platters?"

"I made them using that." He pointed to the fireplace in the wall. "I add stuff to clay and make them. Then I put them in the outside part when it's warm, and close it off with thick clay and soil. The fire burns for a couple of days. Lots of them break, but those that don't are good."

"You collected all of those things in your storage area. Why didn't you use them?"

"They weren't mine. I couldn't use stuff that wasn't mine. I thought I'd find someone and they could use them. Then I realised there wasn't anybody. The land's empty. Except there." He pointed to the large wall hanging. "Creepy place. I got the wee skull there." He sighed. "I shouldn't have taken her. They were angry, tried to kill me, but I got out. The guards followed, but stopped." He frowned. "Black vultures! They didn't leave their tree, but they watched. I wanted to talk to them about her, explain what was going on, but they kept me away with a line of arrows whenever I approached. Then I realised telling them the truth there wouldn't make any difference. All they'd see was that I'd stolen it. I stopped letting them see me and they went away. I tried to think of who else could help, but before I could decide for the best, things started to go wrong. The tree fell, and well I couldn't figure out a plan anyway. Perhaps they cursed me."

It didn't really make sense, but I needed to know other things first.

"If you knew you were dying, why did you bring me here?"

"I knew you would do what I wanted."

"And that is?"

"Return her." He nodded at the little skull. "Tell them I looked after her. I didn't mean any harm. I tried to prove something, but when I thought about it, I realised it probably didn't matter."

"Won't they try to kill me too?"

"Nah, you'll be safe. You wear tokens. There was a carving of a girl holding stones. They looked like your two big tokens, but she had more. Churnyg treated it special. You'll be fine."

"Why didn't you ask to join them instead of taking her? Most people will take in someone who's alone."

"Some of them are strange, not like real people."

"Why didn't you come back to us? You knew where we were."

"I couldn't. You knew how Kamdra died."

Confirmation! He knew who I was.

"Anyway, I'm not good with people. Wary o' them. Voices in my head tell me things. Well Mama said they were in my head. I know sometimes they're wrong, especially when there are lots o' people around, but they yell at me. With one person, it's not so bad, but who'd give up their family for me?"

"Kamdra would have died from his wounds. Why didn't you just let it happen?"

"I was scared. He discovered things and he'd have had to tell. They'd send me away. I'd lose everything I loved."

"What did you love?"

"My family. Kamdra and his daughter, Laydra. She loved me. She was always happy to see me. Babies, children accept me. After I ..." he paused, stared at the wall, and took a deep breath. "Tindra never liked me. After we went through the waterfall, she said she didn't want me near them. I told her I wanted to care for her and Laydra, look after them. I'd make a dwelling for them, and hunt and grow stuff like Kamdra did. She said she'd make Veld and Raff send me away. I knew Kamdra wouldn't have told her, but ..." He paused. "They were all I had. I got angry and I thought about ..." His voice faded, his eyes were bright with tears. "I had to leave."

I brewed more willow bark and he slept fitfully for a while. When he woke, I changed his dressings and tidied the platform, making him comfortable. I hadn't bandaged the wound, just covered it to protect it, but the moss I'd piled under it absorbed leaking fluids and needed to be burned.

Maggots had hatched in the wound. They ate away at the

dead flesh, not hurting him, so I left them. I didn't tell him about them. They were doing a good job, but I wasn't sure what his reaction to them would be. I hoped they would be the help that tipped the odds in his favour.

I ate the meal I prepared and encouraged him to drink some broth. He took a little, but preferred plain water. I tied the skins into place at the entrance and built up the fire. I was looking at the wall hanging when he woke again. He drank more water, refusing more than a sip of the broth I offered. He was sweating less and his temperature was high. Not a good sign.

I was preparing to sleep when he called me over. He was holding the tokens.

"You had a green one, didn't you? I thought it must have fallen off when I knocked you over. I went back to find it, but it wasn't there. I don't remember the white one."

"Early this spring I travelled far to the north to a place called Faltryn, The Place of the Dragon's Tears. I was given the white token there."

Salcan stared at the tokens and handed them to me. "You're definitely the person to take her back," he whispered.

I placed them around the doll's neck, keeping them covered while they glowed. "She looks after them well," I said. I laid her beside him. He smiled and closed his eyes. I thought he was asleep, but he started to talk again.

"Wear them when you take her back to Churnyg."

"Where do I go?" I asked.

"Walk east until the water talks, then north. You can't miss it. There's only one way in."

It was drizzling when I woke, not heavily and it would clear by mid-morning. I built the fire up and made a hot fruit pottage, hoping to encourage Salcan to eat a little.

He wouldn't or couldn't, but he drank some of the liquid diluted with water. I didn't know if I was doing the right thing, he seemed determined to die.

I untied the skin door, letting in the fresh air, but left the large frame in place. It was too big and heavy for me to move.

I made the strongest willow bark infusion I could and added a poppy seed extraction.

Salcan dozed for most of the morning.

The water was getting low and with Salcan asleep, I had the time to fill the flask. While the container filled at the stream, I picked herbs and fruit for the next few meals. Although Salcan was eating less and less, he drank more when the cooking smells were nice.

I balanced the small basket on one hip with my sore hand, picked up the water container and turned to go back to the cave.

"Pssst!"

He stepped out from behind some bushes, so close I almost walked into him.

"Arb …" I hesitated and gasped. "Oh! Who are you?"

"Larqeba,"

I realised how different he was to Arbreu. His hair, a comparable curly mess, but had I caught more than a brief glimpse of him days earlier I'd have known he was a stranger.

He was ill at ease. Now I got a good look at him, he was looking decidedly battered, much more than when I saw him before.

Still wet from the rain, his tunic was good quality, but ripped at the neck. His throat was grazed, a rope burn, the rope still tied tightly and hanging down his back. His cheek was bruised, one eye black, even his hands were bruised and there was dried blood on his fingers. He carried a loosely coiled rope in each hand. He looked cold, tired and miserable.

"Where's that animal?" His voice was soft, his throat damaged internally as well.

"We're safe. Why are you here?"

"I wanted Pa to help you, but Rargo lied and now they'll be gone." He rubbed his nose with the back of his hand. Tears tracked through the dirt on his face.

"First things first. Are you hungry?"

He nodded.

"Good, a meal and we'll get you cleaned up. Then you can tell me what happened and we'll figure out how to find your Pa."

I cut the rope from his neck, and realising that the ropes he carried were tied around each wrist, I cut them off also. The ropes had bitten into his wrists and the hairy fibres were imbedded in the dried bloody wounds.

He looked around the cave, taking in everything as I dished a meal for him. He briefly glanced at Salcan, asleep and mostly hidden under a large rug.

I let him eat while I heated water for his wounds. Cleaning them would take some time.

I was looking through my herbs when Larqeba gasped. I glanced up. His eyes were wide with fear, his mouth half open.

The throaty growl from behind me raised the hair on my arms. I sprang to my feet and swung around.

Salcan struggled to get off the platform, his eyes wild. He growled like a feral animal.

"Stop it, Salcan!"

He looked from Larqeba to me and calmed slightly, although his fists were still tightly clenched. "Who's that?"

"It's just a little boy, Salcan. He's hurt, like you are. He needs my help."

The colour drained from his face and he slumped back onto the platform. His attempt to stand had drained him.

I helped him to get comfortable.

"I don't want people here," he said belligerently.

"He's not people. He's here because I'm a healer."

Salcan settled, the wild light gone from his eyes.

"I always get it wrong," he mumbled. "The voices — they tell me things."

I brought over some more willow bark, but he closed his eyes, pretending to be asleep. I watched him for a short time, until the sleep took over and then I went back to help Larqeba.

He eyed Salcan suspiciously. "Is that?" he paused. "I thought you'd escaped from him. I can help you get away," he whispered.

"He won't hurt us, I promise. He just wasn't expecting you. He hasn't injured me and he won't. Knocking me over was an accident. Like you, he needs my help."

Larqeba shook his head. "He looks different, I almost didn't recognise him."

While Larqeba finished his meal, I poured warm water into two bowls. He washed the worst of the dirt off and then soaked his wrists. I cleaned the dried blood away. The fibres of the rope took quite a long time to worry free. To distract him, I asked him what happened.

17

Larqeba

It was dark when Larqeba woke. He lay on his side against a tree, one arm stretched out under his head, the other down his body. He felt stiff and sore.

He fell asleep.

When he next opened his eyes the sun had risen. His head ached, his eyes felt gritty and it hurt to swallow. The rope tied to each wrist went around the tree, tight enough to keep his arms outstretched, not allowing him to bring his wrists close enough to his mouth to worry the knots with his teeth. Another rope was tied tightly around his neck, although it didn't seem to be attached to anything.

He pulled his left wrist towards him. The rope moved slightly. He hauled it in the opposite direction.

All through the day he worked the rope. It bit into his wrists, and the bark on the tree rubbed them to a bloody mess. By evening he was worn out. He continued to work on the rope as night fell, until he was too exhausted to carry on.

He lay with his head against the tree, feeling very sorry for himself. He knew his family would be worried and searching for him. He regretted his decision to follow Rargo instead of talking to his Pa. He wondered now if Rargo had really heard something or had he made the story up? What did he think he'd get out of it?

Larqeba woke before dawn, cold, stiff and aching from being unable to move much. Dew had formed on the plants around and he sipped at every drop he could reach. It wasn't enough to assuage his thirst, but it helped his tongue feel less sticky.

As daylight strengthened, he continued to work the rope, first one way and then the other. He didn't know what was worse, the pain in his wrists or the ache in his arms.

By afternoon he seriously considered giving up. He lay with his head on his arm, tears streaming down his face.

A leaf from the tree above floated down and landed on his cheek. He flicked his head in frustration and rubbed his cheek on his shoulder. Then he realised his shoulder moved, that his arm could bend just a little more than before. The rope had stretched some. He could now grip it with one hand. He grabbed the rope and pulled. His other wrist stretched painfully, but he felt the rope give slightly. He screamed with pain, sure he had dislocated his wrist, but he kept pulling.

The rope snapped with such force, he fell back hitting his head against a fallen branch. He lay still as his vision wavered and cleared.

He hadn't considered what he'd do when he escaped. He honestly hadn't thought he could. Now he was so overwhelmed by his freedom, he couldn't decide what to do first. Then common sense set in and he stood slowly, allowing his head to clear. He looped the ropes so he could carry one in each hand. The one around his neck was short and hung down his back.

He followed the track Rargo had made, wondering why no one had found it. When he came to a stream he understood. He washed his mouth out and drank, bliss for his parched throat. After the first few sips, the pain set in and he could drink no more. He stripped his clothes off and rinsed them through, grimacing as he hauled wet trousers on, and opting to carry his tunic for now.

Decisions! Upstream or down?

He knew Rargo was lazy and apt to take the easiest path. Most likely Rargo would have come downstream especially as he had been carrying a heavy load.

Larqeba waded upstream.

Rargo had left no track on the stony bed, and that was good luck on his part.

Larqeba knew Rargo wouldn't have thought the strategy out and he wouldn't have realised it in the dark, but it was enough to lose anyone who followed.

Larqeba turned west when he got to the path. Something had used it recently, he hoped it was his Pa. A short distance on, and he found a green ribbon, one of Qwinita's, proof his family had passed. He followed, hoping they had found the girl, but when he reached the field where Rargo left the path, he knew they had tracked him instead.

It was evening, the decision of which path to follow could be made in the morning. It wasn't a decision really. Ma and Pa would find Rargo and they would return. The girl had asked for help. It had been days and Larqeba was now scared he was too late.

Decision made.

He settled into a bank, protection for his back. His belly grumbled from lack of food, but his throat was too sore for him to swallow the berries he'd found. Even water wasn't easy to take in more than small sips. He closed his eyes, sure he wouldn't sleep. Moments later it was dawn.

He climbed the hill to where he'd first seen the girl, and followed the vague track the animal had used.

18

Kirym Speaks

Larqeba was suffering from dehydration and was exhausted, more from fear than lack of sleep. I bandaged his wrists, put salve on his neck and gave him an infusion to sip. He wrapped up in a cloak and slept while I washed and mended his clothes.

With both of them asleep, I foraged for fruit for the meal, and found a kellich caught in one of Salcan's traps. When I returned, Larqeba was kneeling on the edge of the platform helping Salcan drink.

Salcan ruffled his hair. "He's a good lad." He seemed genuinely pleased to have him around and had perked up considerably. Maybe this was a good sign.

Larqeba was an excellent companion. Through the day they kept each other company while I foraged for the roots and herbs I needed to try to purge the poisons that had built up in Salcan's system.

I was relieved to know Salcan wasn't alone while I was

away searching. The maggots were feeding happily. More had hatched, doing the work nature made for them.

Larqeba knew enough of herb lore to know what he saw when he was out, and bring me useful things to experiment with.

I considered sending him to get Mekrar, but I was sure she would have moved the camp once everyone started to search for me.

Anyway, I felt Larqeba was more help here than away.

Salcan's temperature rose again, and although he drank more than over the previous days, I spent a large part of the night caring for him.

He settled just before dawn and I slept, waking late.

Larqeba had prepared drinks and was cooking grains and fruit for me. He had replaced the dried mosses under Salcan's leg and foot. They were both eager that I rest, and as they were coping well, I allowed myself to be spoiled a little.

Larqeba showed me some carved figures Salcan had given him to play with. They were likenesses of animals, bizarre tree stumps with faces, small thickset people, strange vultures and what I thought was a dragon. These were all made from the same material as the white platters.

"Salcan said they're for you," Larqeba said. "He made them."

I was stunned. Where had Salcan seen a dragon? Its head was very similar to a drawing I had seen in Faltryn, although the stance was different. He had put a lot of work into this piece. The scales were there in intricate tiny detail, along with two tiny twisted horns set close together on his forehead. It had what may have been a scar on its shoulder, although I wondered if it was a flaw in the process Salcan had used to make it. That was different from the monster I had seen in the inlet as we arrived back from Faltryn. That monster was so big, and I had seen it for such a short time,

I didn't know what to think.

After I had eaten, I set about producing the medicines I needed for Salcan. One in particular would take a long time to make. I had found the root late the previous evening and had soaked it overnight. Now it needed to be cooked, rinsed, mashed and strained.

Larqeba wandered in and out. As with most boys he healed well, and after a good sleep he was making up for the days of no food. He had much of his energy back. His throat was mending well, although I encouraged him to rest it on occasion. He was a chatterer, and would have filled every waking moment with noise given half a chance. I replaced his dressings sure the scars would fade with time.

He hadn't told me much about the boy who had attacked him. I wondered what would happen when we found him. And we would find him. I would make sure of that.

Salcan was brighter than ever. I'd not mentioned amputation again, but I'd given him a lot of different things to cleanse the poisons from his system. The wound was looking better too. He wasn't healed, but I thought I may now have time to get the help I needed.

It was late in the afternoon when Larqeba rushed in to me. "There're people near where we got apples," he whispered, with a glance at Salcan. "I saw two, and I think one is a girl, but she looks like a boy."

I smiled at his description. That had to be Mekrar. When she was young, she constantly borrowed Mekroe's clothes to go exploring. Eventually Mama gave in and made her a similar set. She wore them when she hunted or explored. Now she always dressed comfortably when she was travelling and with her hair up, she looked almost as boyish as her twin.

Salcan heard him and struggled to sit up.

"I'll keep them away, Salcan," I reassured him. "No one

will come in here unless you want them to. Larqeba will stay with you while I see who it is."

He looked desolate. "You'll leave," he said.

"No! I promised! I will stay until you don't need me anymore."

19

Teema Speaks

We reached the hill overlooking the field where I had killed the deer.

"My mistake was going to where I'd been, instead of to where Kirym would be," I said. I pointed to the top of the ridge. "Knowing her, she would have stayed high looking for us. Probably up there somewhere."

The springy grass obliterated all signs of passage, but there were areas that looked like paths. Bryn and I decided to do a cursory check before dark, hoping to eliminate some of them.

Mekrar and I followed one, Bryn and Qwinita another. Jeresaya, Dashlan and Enliah foraged for fuel and food. Rargo sat against a tree glowering at everyone.

The track we followed took us down the hill, across a stream and then northeast towards a humpy hill in the distance.

The route was covered with the springy grass of the area. It was difficult to tell if anything had used it at all except, as Mekrar pointed out, "It's obviously a path, so something must have used it, to differentiate it from the surrounding area."

However was the something, the animal who took Kirym or the herds of deer and other animals that abounded in the area?

We couldn't tell.

We disturbed a few animals as we travelled, but nothing that looked remotely like the monster Bryn described.

I checked the sun, considering how much further we could go before needing to turn back. As much as I wanted to continue, I knew we had to stop here.

"We'll carry on tomorrow," said Mekrar. She hoisted her pack on her shoulder and turned back.

And then Kirym was there, running through the trees towards us.

I blinked, sure I was dreaming. She seemed unchanged, but then it was only five days, although it felt much longer. Then I saw the difference. All of her tokens were missing.

She called, and Mekrar swung around, laughing delightedly when she saw her.

I raced towards her, with Mekrar close behind. I was so relieved, and then my arms were around her, my face buried in her hair.

Mekrar's hand was around her sister's shoulder, her face against Kirym's.

"Where's Arbreu?" Kirym asked softly.

"He's fine, back at camp getting them ready to join us." I stepped back and pulled a small bag from around my neck, opened it and handed Kirym her green token in the holder I'd made for it.

I clicked mine to hers, feeling Arbreu's acknowledgement as well, and then she turned to her sister.

There was so much to say, for a moment no one said

anything. Then everyone talked together, laughed and talked again.

"Kirym! Kirym!" A boy ran through the trees, changing direction when he saw us. He held out a small package.

"He told me to give you this."

My questioning look was echoed in Mekrar's face.

Kirym opened the soft skin package. Her other tokens lay in the centre. She stared at them, frowning.

"Oh, no! What has he done?"

20

Kirym Speaks

The cave looked surprisingly normal, for all of my fears. But there were changes.

A leather herb pouch sat open on the platform beside the large skull. The herb packages had been removed and placed in a semicircle in front of it. Two of them were open, one held a mound of dried plant fibre, the other ten flat hairy seeds.

The plant fibre was a strong anti-convulsant. I had never seen the seeds before, but I knew them instantly. An old healer had visited Mama when I was a child, and had drawn them for her. She called them poison nuts, described them as seeds of death and said there was no cure. Few healers carried them, they were so dangerous.

Now I understood why Salcan had checked the new things in my pouch. He was checking to see if I had an antidote.

The pouch was very old and had been handed down many times. Pouches owned by men and women were distinctively different and this was a woman's pouch. Each of six previous owners had put their mark on it after using it for twenty winters. A pouch this old would be revered. The owner would hand it on before death or it would be buried with her.

This pouch belonged to Jalkam, Salcan's Mama.

Healers often travel long distances, passed from one sick person to another. It was assumed that someone had come for Jalkam through the night, and that she had gone on to wherever she was needed. However, she'd never have left the pouch behind and because of that, she had to be dead.

"How many?" I asked, nodding at the seeds.

"Enough," said Salcan. "It'll be quick.

I indicated the large skull. "And that was …?

"Mama."

"Oh! Kamdra found her healing pouch. He realised?"

He nodded.

Now I understood the full extent of Salcan's sickness, his guilt.

"It was the night before the attack," he said. "He never even yelled at me. He said we would talk about it in the morning. After he died, I got scared. I knew you'd figured most of it out. Why didn't you tell Veld or Raff?"

"I did, and we talked about it for a long time. We knew you were close to Kamdra, so there had to be something else going on. Papa wanted to handle it quietly, so we could figure out a way to help. Raff asked for time to think about it, but you left before he made up his mind what to do. Papa regretted not insisting they talk to you straight away. No one in our community is condemned without the opportunity to explain and sort it out. We wanted to understand and help — I wanted to. After you returned, everything moved so fast. Everyone was busy and it was impossible to talk to you privately."

He looked surprised. "You invited me back, to go on the boat. I was sure you knew. I couldn't understand why everyone didn't start laughing and throw me out. The voices kept saying you'd wait and use it against me. I couldn't make sense of it. I stopped thinking about it while we were on different boats, but then we landed here and when I saw you again, I got scared. The fear just got bigger and bigger." Tears ran into his growing beard. "I can't live with lots of people and I hate living alone. I like having you and the lad here. I wish it could go on forever." He shook his head. "That's not fair on you two, and it doesn't matter now anyway. For all you have done for me, this I can do for you. You're a great leader, Kirym. You always were."

There was nothing I could do or say. I wished it hadn't ended like this, but I knew bringing him back to the family was fraught with problems. He was right, it wouldn't work.

I offered him food and a drink, but he refused.

"It's better not to," he said. "Drink causes all sorts of other problems."

Larqeba crept in and climbed onto the platform. "The man has gone to tell his friends. Mekrar is waiting outside. She wants to know if she can do anything."

"Tell her to set up camp by the trees at the end of the clearing. Say goodbye to Salcan before you go."

He looked up at me. "But he's getting better."

I put my arm around his shoulder. "He felt better, and that was due in a large part to you. Some wounds can be helped for a short time, but not cured."

Salcan rubbed his shoulder. "You're a good lad. Always be loyal to Kirym. Off you go now. There'll be things to do out there. Mekrar will need your help. She's all alone."

When he'd gone, Salcan handed me the small skull. "Take her back to Churnyg. When you take her, go through the tree. Follow the path and when you see the arch, look for a trail on the left. Use that. Don't under any circumstances go through the arch, 'twill be your death. Be wary! Trust no one."

"How do I go through a tree?"

There was no answer, Salcan stared straight ahead, his smile fixed and his body stiffened as the first convulsion started.

This seizure was short, but I knew they'd get longer as time passed. The anti-convulsive wasn't strong enough to overcome them.

I stayed with him to the end.

His final words were, "If only I'd known. If only things had been different ..."

I covered him with a rug and walked away.

21

Kirym Speaks

It was after midnight and Mekrar had a fire blazing. A man sat at the fire with her and Teema. There were others asleep under a skin shelter.

Teema had found Larqeba's family.

Arbreu, Mekroe, Storm and the rest had not yet arrived.

Mekrar fussed around with hot water and clean clothes, her actions so similar to Mama's, I could almost believe it was her with me. It was nice to be able to wash. She had a hot drink and food ready for me.

I accepted the drink, but refused the meal.

I felt numb. I knew everyone wanted to know what happened, but no one asked, and I couldn't have told them. Well not yet, anyway.

I wrapped a rug around me and slept.

22

Teema Speaks

I was concerned at how quiet and withdrawn Kirym was. She sat against a tree seemingly lost in thought. When we spoke to her, she appeared not to hear us.

"Give her time," said Mekrar. "She's a leader, and naturally enthusiastic about everything. Instinct will take over," she said.

It happened surprisingly quickly, much sooner than I thought it would. When it did I almost wished it hadn't.

Jeresaya dished the midday meal and handed an extra platter to Qwinita. "Take that down to Rargo, please. Bring back the platter he used ..."

"No!" Kirym was on her feet. "If he wants to eat our food, he can eat it here. I will not have him skulking out there, cared for as if nothing has happened. After all he's done ..."

"He's embarrassed!" interrupted Jeresaya, looking shocked.

"He should be more than embarrassed. He needs to take responsibility for his behaviour. Your way means he stays away cared for and cosseted until so much time has passed, it'd seem petty to bring anything up."

"It was my fault, Kirym," I said. I didn't want any argument between the two families. "I should have thought about what he was saying. Anyway, it took us away for a few days, but you were safe."

"What?" She looked mystified. "It's not about me, Teema. It's what Rargo did to Larqeba. He could have died."

Our faces showed a lack of comprehension and Kirym realised no one knew what she was talking about.

"Didn't you wonder what happened to him?" she asked. "Did no one ask about the bruises and scars?"

Jeresaya went red. "I assumed the animal that attacked you got him also. He told us how it hurt you."

The anger went out of Kirym's eyes. "That animal was a man and he didn't attack me. He accidently knocked me over. He was badly injured, and had banged his wound. That's what Larqeba saw. Salcan didn't hurt either of us."

Mekrar's eye's widened and I gasped.

"Yes. Salcan! He's been living here since he left us," Kirym explained.

Larqeba had stayed close to Jeresaya since he'd left the cave. Now, his face black with anger, he planted himself in front of Kirym.

"Why didn't you heal him? He said you were a healer, but you let him die."

"I didn't need to," she said gently. "You did it for me."

He looked shaken. "I didn't do anything. He died. You should have fixed him."

She shook her head. "It wasn't that simple, Larqeba. Salcan had a sickness in his head as well as the poisons in his leg. He had been very unhappy. You made him happy and you gave him peace. The days you were with him were the best he'd had in a long time."

"But why didn't you fix his leg?"

"The poisons in his system were very strong. He knew that, and he knew it would be hard to eliminate them. He didn't want to live, and sometimes a healer's job is to allow a comfortable death."

Larqeba's eyes filled with tears. "I didn't want him to die. I liked him."

Kirym hugged him. "I did too. He wanted a friend and he didn't want to be alone. In the end, we gave him what he wanted, and now we have to make sure he's remembered. That's the best thing you can do for a friend." She paused. "I think you need to tell your ma and pa what happened to you since you saw them last."

Everyone settled around the fire and the story was told, first by Larqeba and then Kirym.

At the end, Jeresaya was in tears and Bryn looked drawn.

"There's no need to deal with Rargo immediately," said Kirym, "but meals will be eaten together. For now there are other more important things to do. First I want to bury Salcan and I want my family here."

"All right," said Bryn. "Let's dig a grave."

Kirym shook her head. "I'd prefer to collapse Salcan's cave over him. It needs to be destroyed. You'll understand when you see inside. However, I want it emptied first."

Bryn frowned. "Shouldn't a man be buried with his possessions?"

"He will be. He asked me to give specific things to people he loved, and return some items he'd borrowed."

We removed the door panel to allow easier access to the

cave. I suggested we use it as part of a shelter to store the contents in. "When Veld returns, we can get a group together to carry them home. It'll be easier than hauling it all there ourselves."

The cave was cold and sad inside, and no one wanted to linger. Everyone was amazed at the display of bones, but agreed they must be re-buried. Many workers made short work of emptying the cave.

"Where did all the bones come from?" I asked. "It's a massive mound. There must be hundreds of people here. How did they die?" I paused. "Wind Runner told us about a battle between the tribes. Could this be their burial site?"

Kirym shrugged. "Anything's possible, Teema. However, don't assume the whole hillock is bodies. It's more likely that just a small part of the mound is the burial site and the rest is just soil. I'm not really prepared to dig into the hill to find out. There's no way of knowing if the bodies were buried all together or over a long period of time. I suspect the amount of soil between the bodies may imply it was an extended rather than mass burial, however I could be wrong."

Kirym sat Jalkam's skull beside her son. She had buried the remaining poison seeds deep in the cave so they would never be found nor have the opportunity to sprout.

Salcan had given his tools and weapons to Larqeba, and a few things including Jalcam's healing pouch to Laydra. The small skull, the wall hanging, the white platters and carved figures were safely stored with Kirym's possessions.

With the cave empty of all but the dead, Bryn and I attached ropes to the tree trunks Salcan had used to support the roof. Anticipating a lot of dust, we tied damp cloths around our faces. Everything in camp had been covered or moved some distance away.

Bryn dug a trench in front of and slightly under the

supporting trunks hoping they would tip and fall easily.

The rope Salcan had used to tie Kirym was attached to one trunk, and a firm heave immediately felled it along with the back half of the cave. The other trunk needed our combined muscle to bring it crashing down.

The cave was gone and the hill now had a dent on one side, with dark brown soil harshly obvious against the surrounding green grass. Three large trees on the hill fell as the cave collapsed and a few others looked unsteady. They would take a season or two to decide whether to strengthen their roots or fall. In the meantime, Kirym suggested the hill be avoided until it stabilised, and then be treated as the burial site it was.

Dashlan picked up a handful of soil. "It looks so raw and new."

"Nature will take care of that surprisingly quickly," said Kirym. "Within a moon, the grass will grow and by midwinter, it'll look untouched except for the fallen trees."

Kirym had said words for Salcan and the other dead, following Veld's style. She talked of Jalkam and her gift of healing. She spoke of Salcan's sickness, his love for Laydra and her papa Kamdra. She told Wind Runner's story of the people who lived in the land and of the battle that may have killed them. She talked of the gathering of the tokens and the families, and left everyone with as many questions as answers.

Kirym asked Bryn to ensure Rargo knew the dangers of the hill. She didn't want him to investigate and put himself in danger.

With the cave gone, everyone seemed more relaxed. There was a lot more talk and laughter as a meal was prepared.

23

Kirym Speaks

Very late in the afternoon, I realised that Arbreu and Amethyst were close. I slipped away through the trees to meet them, knowing Teema and Mekrar were as aware and would explain my absence if necessary. I was beginning to feel whole again.

Amethyst had grown since I had last seen her. It felt like many moons since I held her. In reality, it was only days. The wee girl cooed and gurgled as I hugged her. I couldn't get over how perfect her features were. Her skin was delicate and creamy, but her thick black hair had grown, and now sat just above her shoulders.

Arbreu seemed taller than ever. Always thin, he had filled out since we left the valley in early spring.

Mekroe was as delighted to see me, and didn't clown around as much as he normally did. He seemed to have a maturity not there when I saw him last.

Starshine handed me the pouch of large tokens. "Mekrar

was right. It's hard to be the custodian of them. They are distracting. I don't know how you do it all the time."

I thrust them into my waistband and with Arbreu on one side carrying Amethyst, Mekroe on the other and everyone else crowding around, we walked back to the camp.

Bryn's family had withdrawn a little, aware this would be an emotional reunion. I was conscious of them grouped on the far side of the clearing looking a little lost and somewhat envious of the large family group.

Eager to include them, I grabbed Mekroe and Arbreu's hands and pulled them towards the new family.

Bryn stiffened and his arm went protectively around Jeresaya. She was pale, so pale I thought she would faint.

Both Teema and I felt Arbreu's emotions surge, shock — disbelief. Teema pushed his way through the crowd to stand beside us, wanting to protect, but not sure from what.

"Ma!" It was a whisper, but everyone heard it.

Jeresaya took a tentative step forward.

"Arbreu?"

Arbreu grabbed my hand and clung tightly.

Jeresaya took another step towards him. Then she had her arms open and he ran to her. He was quickly surrounded, everyone talking, crying and laughing.

For a while, no one made much sense. Then Jeresaya stepped back and held him at arm's length.

"I don't believe it, you've grown so much and you have a child." She reached for Amethyst.

Arbreu pulled away. "No, Ma. Amethyst is Kirym's."

Jeresaya stared at me, her mouth open. "You're a … I didn't realise," she faltered. "You're so … so young."

Smiling, I took Amethyst and handed her to Jeresaya. "I found her just before the last full moon of summer. In eighteen days she'll have seen three moons. She belongs to all of us and everyone helps care for her."

Arbreu re-met his siblings, finding it initially hard to see the children he had left behind in the faces in front of him. Larqeba had only just started walking when Arbreu saw him last and the others had seen fewer than ten summers.

The celebration lasted into the evening. As the moon rose, everyone became more comfortable with the changes in family dynamics.

24

Arbreu

"What happened to you? Arbreu demanded as everyone relaxed before the meal. "I went back and everything was buried. I thought you were dead."

"We waited for ten days. When you didn't turn up, Pa decided to leave," said Dashlan.

Jeresaya wiped tears from her cheek. "Oh my dear, we thought you were dead. We'd never have left otherwise."

"Hold on," said Storm. "Now what happened? What was buried? Why leave at all — where were you and why were you there?"

"Our home, our settlement was there," explained Bryn, taking a deep breath. "It was built at the bottom of an escarpment. It was a good area for hunting and we were protected from the prevailing wind. The cliffs were a natural home to many animals and birds. The land around was rich and the crops we planted gave a generous return. It was a good place to live; home to more than three hundred people.

Our families had lived there for hundreds of generations. Another settlement as big was almost half a day south of us under the same slope. Both were well established and happy. It was safe." He smiled sadly as he remembered. "We relied on that, and when suddenly it wasn't what it had always been, most people couldn't and wouldn't accept it."

"We had the wildest spring I had ever known," said Jeresaya, "Part of the settlement flooded when the river burst its banks. Huge trees uprooted, some had been ancient when the settlement was first established. It rained constantly. Hunting was impossible, and we were unable to forage as we did most springs. The children couldn't even go out and play."

Bryn took her hand. "I took a chance to go hunting when there was a small break in the weather. We really needed some fresh meat. I was south of the settlement when part of the escarpment fell away. It was some distance from the dwellings, but I realised the whole cliff face was saturated and very unstable. I raced home and told the elders what had happened. I pressed them to evacuate everyone.

They refused. They said I was deluded. They were sure nothing could endanger the settlement that was so established.

I argued, pointing to the tree's falling and the flooding, but they had answers for that. My opinion was ignored. Anyway, the weather was getting worse. They refused to discuss it further until it stopped raining.

I wasn't prepared to wait.

When I got home Arbreu had gone. He and Larqeba have the same wanderlust. I had given up worrying about Arbreu when he rambled. This time though, it was inconvenient. I didn't dare wait for him so I packed Jeresaya and the rest up and moved them to safety. We couldn't go too far, I needed to warn the southern settlement and search for Arbreu."

"The weather was really bad when Pa made us leave," interrupted Enliah. "It just bucketed down. I was instantly wet and there was nowhere to shelter. Larqeba cried all the time, and Ma couldn't get a fire going so we couldn't even have hot food. It was horrid. It rained for days. My hair looked hideous. I didn't have my favourite things and Ma wouldn't let me go and get them. Arbreu wasn't there to help and I had to work all the time. Qwinita kept walking outside and sitting in mud puddles in the rain. I had to go and get her. It was vile."

"Initially we sheltered under a tree, but that was as wet as being out in the rain," said Jeresaya. "While Bryn went south to talk to the community there, I erected a drier shelter, but the wind blustered in every direction. They were difficult days."

Bryn grimaced. "It was evening when I reached the southern settlement. They were as sceptical as my own," said Bryn. "It was disappointing, but after giving the message, I returned to my family. The next day, I again urged everyone to at least move away for a while. I made some of them go with me to look at the damage already done. More of the cliff had slipped away overnight.

They ignored it, said that if any more came down, they'd consider scouting for a new settlement site when the weather cleared. They got quite irate when they realised I'd been talking to my immediate neighbours as well.

Nothing I said could convince them of the danger. They wouldn't change their minds. I left them and searched for Arbreu. I left messages for him in places I thought he may check.

The next day, there was no settlement.

Dashlan and I tried to dig out the closest dwelling, but the soil was wet, and it kept moving. I realised we had to stop, or we chanced being buried as well.

Again, I travelled south, but the collapse of the cliff was extensive and although parts were still intact, the neighbouring settlement had also been buried." He shook his head sadly. "I wish I'd done more, talked to everyone individually. Such a waste. Hundreds of lives lost because those pig-headed leaders thought they knew better." Bryn flinched when Jeresaya touched his arm reassuringly. "Even those I called friend ignored me and laughed." He sounded very bitter.

Around the fire, there were sounds of sorrow and sympathy. Everyone there understood the loss.

"So you waited ten days?" Kirym asked.

Jeresaya nodded. "The weather continued to be ghastly. Bryn searched everywhere we could think of. The rivers were high and although we didn't think Arbreu would have crossed them, we knew that if he had, he could have been swept away. Despite his youth, he was sensible, but even grown men make that mistake. Eventually, we wondered if he had returned home during the night and been buried along with everyone else. We had no desire to stay there with so many memories, so we left."

Bryn sighed deeply. "It was difficult to find a safe haven. The communities we met were wary of strangers, and a few threatened us with violence to get rid of us. We heard rumours of a gang attacking people and settlements. From then on, we avoided everyone."

"How did Rargo escape the landslides?" asked Mekrar.

Bryn shook his head. "He wasn't there. We found him during our travels. That was oh, four winters later," he frowned, "or maybe late spring. He was in the burned remains of a small farm. He was the only survivor of ten. He'd been badly beaten and I didn't think he'd make it. We buried the dead and nursed him back to health. He never told us what happened — I thought he possibly couldn't remember.

There was no one to leave him with, so we kept him. I've often regretted taking him in, now more than ever.

When he was able to walk, we continued along the coast. Our path was dictated by what we met; settlements which we avoided, rivers, forests and deserts. Mainly we went north and west.

"How did you get to be here?" Arbreu asked. "We travelled across the ocean for about ten days."

"We walked," said Larqeba. "All the way."

"Not you, midget," laughed Dashlan, ruffling his hair. "You got carried. Only found your legs when we got here."

"I did not," Larqeba argued. "You were the one …"

"Boys!" said Bryn sharply. "Let's try to keep up a well-mannered charade in front of our hosts."

"Ah, just like the twins," Storm said softly, "and a few others …" He was drowned out by a loud protestation from Mekroe and laughter from everyone else.

Amethyst, disturbed by the sudden noise, began to whimper. Kirym picked her up, quickly changed her wraps and settled the wee girl on her lap to watch the proceedings.

Bryn laughed along with the rest. "The land must meet up. We went north originally and then turned west to skirt a desert. We crossed a mountain. I vowed we'd never do that again, although in the end we traversed a second. It wasn't as hard though, it was a better season, and we managed to cross a low saddle. Then it was north again and another desert. That was difficult, we couldn't travel around it. We eventually found the shore again, but it was still desert. One day I realised we'd turned south. That was good, there was often a shortage of water, even near the sea. Distilling enough to drink was time consuming, and we always seemed to be thirsty.

"I remember the desert," said Qwinita. "Even though it was winter, the days were so unbearably hot, but the nights were freezing. We stayed under shelter during the day and travelled at night. It was incredibly dark. Ma worried we'd get separated and she made us hold onto a rope. As we got tired, it was easy to let go and eventually Pa tied us together in a line. That worked."

"Except Larqeba fell asleep anyway and we had to carry him," interrupted Dashlan.

"Eventually the days got cooler. We continued west along the coast and then south when it turned. We turned west again when the shore became too rough. The hills became cliffs right to the shore, so we came inland," said Bryn. "This was land similar to that we left, and I started to think about settling. Summer before last we found a clearing east o' here. We hadn't seen people for many seasons so we stopped and built a permanent lodge.

Larqeba took after Arbreu in that he's a wanderer. A few days back he brought home news of a large animal that attacked a girl." He turned to Kirym. "I am still wary of people. The only reason I'm here is because the lad said you called for help, and you asked in my name."

"What?" Teema looked mystified. "How?

"Larqeba must have misheard me. I saw the top of his head, his hair, and thought it was Arbreu. That's who I called out to," Kirym said.

Arbreu laughed. "Pa's full name is Arbryn. Larqeba misheard you, thank goodness."

Mekroe laughed. "It's a strangely small world, isn't it?"

"No it isn't," said Larqeba indignantly. "It's huge. It's taken my whole life to get this far, and there's a lot more to see." He paused. "It'd be nice to stay here though, well for a while anyway."

"We can't lad," said Bryn, ruffling his hair. "This land belongs to Kirym's people, so we'll move on in the morning. Now we're all together again, it'll be easier."

"I can't leave," said Arbreu, "and I won't. This is my family too, Pa. I can't walk away from Kirym, Teema and Amethyst. There's something new and exciting happening here and I need to see it through."

Bryn reddened. "Staying isn't an option."

"Yes it is," Kirym said. "You are as much a part of our family as Arbreu is. There's plenty of land. Stay in your clearing or move closer to The Green Valley. You'd be welcome there, or choose somewhere else. But do build a permanent home."

"You can't give land away, Kirym."

Storm laughed. "She offered my family land, Bryn, and there are over four hundred of us. From what I hear of Veld, he's very welcoming of new people. They're good folks to be aligned to. Good neighbours. If you don't wish to be part of their family, be part of mine."

"Why don't you stay for a few seasons?" Kirym asked. "If you're not happy, then move on. I think you need to be here. The tribes are all gathering. There'll be a huge celebration and a lot of questions will be answered. You must stay and be a part of it."

"So what now, Kirym?" asked Mekroe. "North to meet Papa?"

Kirym shook her head. "There's something else I need to do first. Salcan asked me to return the small skull to the people who owned it."

25

Kirym Speaks

"Why don't you do it later, Kirym? It's a lot of energy to put into two stuffed kellich skins and an old skull. I mean," said Arbreu, "Salcan was a bit nuts wasn't he? All of those bones he had in there. It's probably just one of them and he saw it as special because it's small. It'll be a wild goose chase."

"I made him a promise and I'm going to keep it," I said. "There are things about the skull that meant he couldn't have picked it out of the ground, and nor could anyone else have."

"You mean he killed it?" Mekroe's eyes were wide with shock.

"No, no! Nothing like that," I gasped. "The skull is different, very old, but not what it seems. I need some information before I'm sure I have it right." I saw the mystified looks, but decided to ignore them for now. "Salcan was quite specific on where to take it. This place, I think he called it Churnyg, isn't too far away. He went there a few times from what he said." I stopped and looked up at Arbreu. "You don't have to come with me. No one does. Stay here and get to know your family again. I'll give it ten days, and if I haven't found the talking water by then, I'll return."

"I know where the talking water is."

Arbreu spun around. "Don't play games, Larqeba," he said sharply. "Kirym takes this very seriously."

"I'm not," he protested. "It's just over two days past where we live. All of the other streams are quiet. This one, I don't know, it babbles. I never thought of it as talking, but Salcan's right. It does."

"Well," I said, "it's the first step in finding Churnyg."

Elm snorted. "It won't be that simple. I mean, upstream? Down? Even then, what are you looking for? Bryn travelled through that area. He didn't see anything."

"Well, maybe it won't be obvious, but something is there. I'll find out and then I'll come back and tell you."

Teema came up behind me and slipped his arm around my shoulder. "You're not going off alone again. I've only just found you, Kirym. I'm not letting you out of my sight."

"I'll be happy to have you join me, Teema."

"I'm coming too, I'll have to show you where to go," said Larqeba importantly.

In the end no one wanted to be left out.

I was worried about Churnyg, although I didn't tell anyone. I had no notion what lived there, and I wondered if the tokens would be as much protection as Salcan thought. Then again, I didn't know how much of the perceived threat had been in Salcan's mind.

I thought deeply about it over the three days it took us to get to the stream, and was no closer to a decision when I reached there than when I started. We crossed a number of water courses, one quite wide the others narrow, that were obviously not what we were looking for. They were swift and quiet, muddy underfoot with grassy banks.

This one was different. It ran over stones and they created small dams and waterfalls. The water here was a happy noisy affair.

I knew our hunters had explored the coastal region to the south, and I thought that had there been anything near the coast, they would have found it. So now our search took us upstream.

It was pleasant strolling beside the stream, but as the days passed, I seriously wondered if I had misunderstood Salcan's instructions.

While I would have happily gone further, almost everyone else obviously thought Churnyg was a figment of Salcan's imagination. I put the extent of our travel upstream at the end of the fifth day, but at midday when I saw a grove of trees spanning the stream, I suggested we stop there. It was oppressively hot and everyone was ready for some time off.

The trees surrounded a large clearing with a pool in the centre that fed the stream. It was cool here, the shade welcome. At the far end of the glade was a cliff. This was one end of the massive rock I had first seen when we were travelling towards the fountainhead. Now I realised there was more to the rock than was obvious. This, I was sure, had something to do with Churnyg.

Some of the trees in the grove were giants of the forest, being dwarfed only by the massive cliff face. Some were so big, I doubted we could have stood around it and joined hands. With the biggest, we couldn't try this, because it had grown up against the huge cliff face.

We unpacked and began to set up a shelter. While I was filling the large flask with water, the men disappeared. Starshine came to help me carry the large flask and hook it into its harness for use around camp.

"You shouldn't be doing this, Kirym. It's too heavy for you.

I'm surprised the men would all go hunting without setting up first. They didn't even tell us. I didn't think Teema would go off like that again."

"We can manage, and anything we can't do will wait until they come back."

We joined Jeresaya, Mekrar, Enliah and Qwinita by the fire.

"There's really nothing here other than the trees and pool," Starshine said. "Do you think Salcan heard the water and thought it was people? He had been by himself for a long time. Larqeba mentioned — well he said Salcan heard voices, and maybe he saw shadows."

"I don't know what Salcan saw or thinks he saw," I said. "He had contact with something and he didn't call them people. But this is where we should be."

I started sorting through our packs and shaking out the clothes we'd brought from the settlement.

The clothes we'd worn on the trip back from Faltryn's Fortress had been travel stained and threadbare when we arrived in The Green Valley so everything we now wore was new. However they were travelling clothes, hardwearing and practical, and quite mediocre, not something I'd choose to wear for a festival.

Not that I had a festival in mind, but Salcan had said a number of times that I needed to look impressive and enter Churnyg as a leader and head of a visiting tribe.

Through necessity, I had needed to wear my festival dress for a large part of our trip to Faltryn. It was a difficult journey. The material hadn't been designed for such hard use and the ragged remains had become swaddling clothes for Amethyst on the trip back to The Green Valley.

When we left the valley to travel north, I had packed material with the thought of replacing the dress before we met Papa and Wind Runner. However, when I did get the opportunity to sew just before I met Salcan, I had been trying to make something special for Amethyst and hadn't had a chance to start anything for myself. Now necessity took over.

I needed to look good, but be able to move in a hurry if necessary, and I wanted to carry my herb pouch and the token pocket without them looking ungainly nor obvious. I was unsure what I would come across over the next few days when I approached Churnyg, whatever Churnyg was.

Mekrar came to help, and when I told her what I wanted, she had some great suggestions.

"We could adapt the tabard pattern we had made in Faltryn, but instead of having trousers under it, make it fuller, more flowing and remove the side splits. The tie-on pockets you usually use won't work, but we could make one so it could be carried in your hand or worn over one shoulder while you are travelling. If the material matches, it'll blend in."

As she talked, she quickly sketched her design out. Her ideas were good. The dress I normally wore took quite a lot of sewing, easy if we had time and people, but I was in a hurry.

"If we all help, it'll be finished before tomorrow," Jeresaya said

"You brought the neck piece Arbreu gave you," said Mekrar, "so we'll work the neckline to enhance that." She chose a length of green material shot with blue and gold for the dress and plain blue for insets, two in the front and one in the back, to give the skirt some movement and make it flow. She also planned a belt and the pocket out of the blue. The materials highlighted my tokens and the neck jewel.

Jeresaya, Enliah and Qwinita were intrigued by the fashioning. Starshine was dressed in clothes from our stores. Most of her clothes from Faltryn had been worn out during the trip to The Green Valley. Jeresaya hadn't realised Faltryners dressed differently. Her own clothes were very simple, and were all natural earthy colours. She had previously remarked on the lovely colours we wore, and we had talked excitedly about new clothes for her, Enliah and Qwinita, although Qwinita was more interested in the trousers Mekrar wore most of the time. While they had travelled extensively, their experience of different clothes was limited because they had avoided people and settlements.

With six of us sewing, a lot of it was done by early evening when the men returned.

Teema dropped his bow and a brace of rock kellich, and sank down beside the fire. "Nothing here, Kirym. The rock is huge and there's no way onto it, the sides are almost sheer. We'll look around the other side tomorrow, but it'll take more than a moon to search around the whole thing. I think Salcan was dreaming."

I frowned. "We knew it was huge from the view we had of it from the ridge. Why do you want to get onto it?"

Teema shrugged. "Well, there's nothing else here. I thought Salcan might have climbed up and seen something from the top."

I laughed. "You should have asked. I know where to go and how to get there."

I refused to tell them what I knew. "You'll find out in the morning," I said when the uproar had died.

It didn't distract them at all. Amid the questions and comments, I accepted that I shouldn't enter alone, but deciding who to take was difficult, especially when they all wanted to join me.

They acknowledged though, that fifteen people plus a baby was too many, and would possibly seem like an invasion. The evening was full of argument, but eventually I decided to take Teema and Arbreu.

26

Kirym Speaks

We were ready to leave at dawn. It was misty among the trees and distant thunder promised a storm later in the day. I was pleased for my cloak, but now wished I had the one Oak had given me in Faltryn. It would have set my clothes off beautifully.

Often when I travelled, I plaited my hair and looped or twisted it up to keep it out of the way, but that wasn't the impression I wanted to give when I entered Churnyg. This time, when I washed it, I combed it out and arranged it to flow down my back. I attached some small jewels to cascade through my hair and rearranged my tokens to sit in a vertical line on my forehead, the blue, the largest at the top with the green and white below.

Qwinita offered me her ear jewels. They were blue and lighter than my token and I accepted gratefully. I really wanted to impress, and my size, I'm petite in a family of tall beautiful people, meant I was easy to overlook.

Salcan had told me a lot, but there were so many questions I wished I'd had a chance to ask.

I allowed Teema and Arbreu to take a knife each. Arbreu carried his at his hip, and Teema slipped his into his boot. I insisted though that the weapons remain away, not hidden, but I didn't want any overt action made that could be interpreted the wrong way. My own knife was also hidden but accessible.

I slipped the large tokens into the pocket with my herbs. Both Mekrar and Starshine raised an eyebrow at this, but neither asked questions, and no one else noticed. On impulse, I added the toys Salcan had made.

Arbreu carried a pack with food and other supplies we needed. He also carried the skull and skins.

Teema carried an unstrung bow with a quiver of arrows on his shoulder. I warned him not to even appear to use it, but we were entering unknown territory and we had to be practical. Accepting the possibility that something may go wrong, I knew it would be foolish to enter with no protection. Teema's ability to string his bow at speed was the reason I allowed him to bring it with him.

I knew Salcan had felt threatened, although that may have been because he took the skull. I wished I knew why he had felt the need to take it.

Everyone joined us in the cool misty greyness of dawn. They all wanted to know where we were going. Finally I was ready. I walked to the base of the tree that sat against the cliff and pointed up.

The trunk was wide and branchless for a distance far above my head — all of our heads for that matter.

High above amid the leaves and branches, the trunk had split and later re-joined creating a large hole.

Mekroe snorted. "Well it may be the door, but that first step's a bit of a killer, sis. How will you get up there?"

27

Kirym Speaks

In the end, it wasn't that difficult. Nearby trees were not as tall and many had low branches and were climbable. I was used to climbing in all sorts of clothes, and although I had to take reasonable care of the more fragile nature of my new dress, it wasn't difficult. Once I was onto the first branch, it was a case of walking from one to the other until we reached a limb that led to the big tree and then, up through the branches until I reached the massive hole.

With a wave to those on the ground, I climbed onto the base of the hole, and stepped through.

It was a stretch for me to get from the tree to the hole in the rock above it and once through the tunnel it created, I stepped onto a path on the inner side of the cliff. The path was narrow, but not unreasonably so. I wouldn't have wanted to rush it though.

Below us was a jungle of trees, but with the sun still below the horizon, the land was misty, grey and damp.

The path wandered gently down the rock, widening on occasion. Just before we stepped into the trees, the sun peeped out turning the grey to green.

From the bottom of the cliff, a path meandered into the distance. The mist still wreathed through the trees, distorting the sights and sounds. More than once, the whistling of the breeze or the chattering of the birds sounded like something far more sinister. There was a feeling here I couldn't place. This was a land of mysteries. When we spoke, it was in lowered voices, almost as if we were part of a secret.

It continued to be cool, especially in the shade. The land was alive with birds and insects. We could hear small animals rustling through the undergrowth. The path wasn't much more than an animal track and if it hadn't been for Salcan's comment on it, I would have suspected that only animals used it.

We rested and ate at midmorning, just a short stop.

Something changed as I was packing to continue. The birds and insects around us stopped calling. Something else was here.

Teema and Arbreu both reached for their knives.

"Don't," I said quietly. "Nothing has threatened us."

"Yet," said Teema under his breath. He slipped into the trees on the far side of the path.

Arbreu was further away and out of sight. A few moments later, he appeared on the path holding Larqeba by the scruff of the neck.

Teema appeared beside me. "This I could do without," he murmured.

"Does anyone know you're here?" Arbreu asked.

"I told Dashlan. He'll tell Pa tonight. They won't follow at night."

"Why, Larqeba?" I asked. "Bryn and Jeresaya said you weren't to come with us. They'll be worried."

"They won't 'cause they're used to me wandering off. Anyway I told Dashlan to tell Pa I'd be with you and Arbreu. If we're not back before dinner, he'll tell them then." He looked up at Teema. "Anyway, Salcan said I had to come."

Teema looked at me questioningly. "Really?"

"He said I had to be loyal to Kirym, and I can't be loyal to her if I'm not with her."

Arbreu laughed. "Shall I take him back?" He grabbed Larqeba's tunic.

"Kirym!" Larqeba squirmed away from Arbreu. "Please let me stay. I promise I'll be good."

"If he's to go back, we'll all have to go," I said. "We'd lose a whole day and maybe the day is important. Let's try to send a message to Mekrar."

I beckoned Arbreu to me and clicked his token. *Larqeba is safe.*

We felt her acknowledgement.

Arbreu's eyes widened. "How can I have a connection with her?"

I shrugged. "These things happen. You've been part of the family for a long time."

Behind him, Teema's eyes shone with amusement. Then he grabbed Larqeba by the ear.

"Listen lad. You have no more chances. You will behave. You do exactly as you're told, or I will hogtie you!"

Larqeba went pale, but to give him his due, he straightened his shoulders and looked straight at Teema. "Would you like me to carry the pack?"

The air was suddenly chill and thunder growled in the distance. Clouds covered the sun. I drew my cloak around me, glad I'd decided to bring it.

This part of the land gave the vague impression of being cultivated. The nut trees showed signs of a bountiful harvest coming, although the land beneath them was thick with secondary growth. Ahead though, we could see the towering cliffs. This open area was minute compared to the size of the rock.

Soon the trees closed around the path again, creating a tunnel. Ahead was a wall with an arch in the centre.

If Salcan hadn't told me of the path, I would have missed it. It was very overgrown, and obviously hadn't been used for quite a long time. Once away from the main path, it was easier to follow. The path angled southeast for a distance, turned north and eventually reached the wall that had been at the end of the tunnel of trees. We followed it west to a place where it had collapsed. I stepped over the debris and into the reality of the picture I had seen in the cave above the canyon, a wide shallow cave.

It was as Salcan had described. A relief carving of six trees intertwined around the wall with a tunnel in the middle. To one side of the tunnel was a stone statue of a figure holding a platter containing what looked like large tokens. It was dim after the brightness outside and I stepped nearer to study the carvings. Larqeba, Teema and Arbreu were close behind me.

28

Kirym Speaks

"Why are you trespassing on my land?" His voice sounded ancient, cracked with lack of use.

"Visiting, not trespassing," I said. I slipped off the hood of my cloak and stared at the tunnel. It was the only place he could be, but I could see nothing.

"Pah!" he spat. "Visitors are invited. You weren't."

"In my experience neighbours don't need an invitation," I responded.

"I have no neighbours."

"I bring greetings from The Green Valley."

This time his voice was strained. "The Green Valley is deserted."

"No longer. Its people finished wandering and returned to their home. The leader has called for a great gathering. It's time for the tribes to assemble again. I bring the invitation."

"They'll never meet peacefully. Some have long memories. There'll be no forgiveness, no peace and no gathering."

There was a clap of thunder.

"It's already happening," I said. "The large tokens are together again. The other tribes are approaching. It's the beginning of peace."

"If it's the beginning of peace, why have you entered with weapons?" He sounded triumphant. "You seek to trick Churnyg, take him unaware and kill him when his back is turned."

That was interesting. It seemed that this was Churnyg. A person, not the community.

"Had we looked to kill you," said Teema, "you'd already be lying in a pool of blood. Every great leader has guards, if only to protect her from idiots. Our weapons are sheathed; my bow is scarcely usable unstrung. Kirym of The Green Valley has come in peace, bearing gifts. Are you so bereft of manners you won't even greet her?"

I turned to go. "Come Teema. If he is so distrustful of us, we'll take our gifts elsewhere."

I stepped towards the entrance. As I did, my tokens flashed.

There was a sharp intake of breath. "You wear a token?"

Teema straightened and took my arm, presenting me to the shadow in the tunnel. "Kirym of The Green Valley and The Land Between the Gorges and Guardian of the Tokens, greets you and the dwellers of this rock."

He peered out of the shadow before shuffling back into the darkness. He looked like the human equivalent of a wizened tree stump.

"Ah," he sighed. "It had to come." He waved his arm and a row of lights lit up the tunnel. Already he was at the far end of it.

Larqeba darted ahead of us, brought up short when Teema grabbed his tunic and hauled him back. He thrust him into Arbreu's arms.

"So help me! Control him," he growled. He turned and strode ahead through the tunnel. Larqeba and Arbreu followed me.

Lamps reflected the warm burnished golden brown of aged wood that lined a large room. I looked for our host, but he had retreated into a dark corner.

"Why are you here, Kirym of The Green Valley?"

"The desert people wander the desert. The cave dwellers have rebuilt their caves. Why have the tree dwellers deserted the trees?"

His hand flicked and the lamps flared showing a carved seat against the far wall. He bowed theatrically.

As we walked towards it, something crashed behind us, and when I turned, the tunnel had disappeared, now indistinguishable from the walls on either side.

I grasped Teema's arm as he reached for his knife. "We're in no danger," I murmured as I sat.

Larqeba knelt on the floor at my feet, Teema and Arbreu stood either side of me. I nodded at Churnyg to continue.

"We were the keepers of the dreams. It was our job to protect the wonders of the world. We had no special land of our own, but yes, we built our hollows in the six great trees. The dragons were our mounts, and we explored and mapped the world. Our doom came when we disobeyed the natural laws given us at the beginning of time.

We travelled west exploring the barren regions that run towards the setting sun. Deep in the centre of the sands, we spied a great city, the likes of which we had never seen before.

Our rules forbade contact with the peoples of the land for fear we would change them, and rightly our dragons would not land there. But such was the beauty of the city; we yearned to touch the jewelled walls and walk the golden streets more than anything else in the world. So we tricked the dragons, convincing them that one of the riders was sick and needed care we could not administer mid-flight. We landed at an oasis hidden from the city by a large sand dune, and while the dragons slept, we slipped away to explore.

We claimed to be dwellers of the caves for fear the inhabitants of the city would refuse us entry, for the rules were widely known. We planned to stay only one short day.

The inhabitants, cloaked and mysterious, welcomed us, entertained us with amusements, music and feasts. Our cups were studded with jewels and our plates were made of gold. They dressed us in garments that hung heavy with jewels. We slept in golden beds with blankets of woven down and gossamer thread. We had the freedom of the city, told we could enter any open door.

One day became two, then four, eight, and soon I had lost count of the time we had spent there.

In our hearts, we heard our dragons call, but we ignored them seeking to find more about these mysterious people.

One sunny day — although the sun always shone — I discovered a different building. It was plain whereas other walls were inlaid with jewels. I walked around the building, finding it had but one door — closed and guarded. Entry was impossible.

I spent the day walking around the building, searching for another entrance. My search was in vain and I had a heavy heart, wondering what was being hidden from me.

The next day I returned and the day after that and every day until I'd lost count of how many I'd spent searching the plain barren walls. It seemed all in vain until one day, I stepped into the coolness of a small shadowy corner I'd never noticed before. As I stared into the shadow, a door appeared. It was shut, but there was no guard. I pushed. The door swung open. I stepped inside and it closed behind me.

The walls inside were as plain as they were out, and it

seemed simply to be a maze of empty passages. I wondered why it had been built this way until, deep in the centre, I found a large chamber. The sun shone through the transparent ceiling and streams of water criss-crossed the floor. The walls were festooned with vines and great pots held massive trees. They reminded me of the trees I lived in and I felt a moment of homesickness, but then all other thoughts went from my head, for in the centre of the chamber was a large shell. It was lined with the gossamer thread of silk worms and the jewelled wings of butterflies and in the centre sat a huge opal. It glowed as if the sun slept within it and I WANTED IT.

There was no one there to see me. I picked it up. It was cool, inviting, and I had to keep it. I hid it in my robe.

I left the building quickly and called my friends together. We've stayed too long, I told them. Our dragons are calling and we must leave now.

Our hosts urged us to wait until the morning, partake in a farewell feast to cement our continued friendship, but I declined.

My companions were reluctant to leave, but I drove them, muttering and complaining from the city. As we reached the bottom of the dune, darkness covered the land and a great clamour came from the city. Keep climbing, I urged my companions.

I secretly exulted over the jewel.

As I reached the top of the dune, I drew it from my robes and caressed it lustfully and held it high in exaltation.

Suddenly the clamour in the city turned to a wail of grief that followed us from the city. The darkness lifted and I was exposed holding the great gem aloft.

There was a deafening crack, and it split, revealing at its centre a child so exquisite my heart melted. She reached out to me, but the stone closed over her, becoming whole and heavy, so heavy and hot I could not hold it.

It fell from my hands and ploughed down the dune towards the city, but the sand changed and I watched with horror as the opal bounced and crashed against rock after rock. At the bottom of the dune it lay broken, the small body in pieces amidst the remains.

At that instant thunder roared and the winds blew. My robes whipped around me and I thought I'd be blown to the edge of the world.

Then I felt the protective grip of my dragon, and we watched appalled as the city became dust and blew away until nothing was left.

In the deafening silence the robes of the people dissolved and for the first time we saw them.

The tall beautifully clad people appeared to be mere children.

In tears they knelt beside the broken remains of their jewel. I started down towards them, hoping to help, apologise or something, but my companions pulled me back. 'There is nought we can do,' they cried. 'We must leave and hope that time will undo the damage you've done.'

With a heavy heart I mounted my dragon and we returned home to learn that summer had passed a thousand times while we were away. Although we are a long-living people, our children had grown old and were strangers to us.

Our dragons, disgusted with our behaviour, left to convene a great summit to decide on their future. While they were away, The Cave People came to us and, in friendship, asked for our help in a battle. They had been attacked by their neighbours, the dwellers of the desert.

The dilemma was great. We could not fight against them, and we were not so treacherous as to fight for them. While we delayed, the battle came to us. We hid in the hills, but the leader of The Green Valley came down and pushed them aside stopping the battle.

We gathered the bodies of the dead and buried them in a great mound. While we watched, the mound became a mountain, sitting in an open plain to remind us always of our betrayal.

The leader of The Green Valley created large tokens for unity and peace, but my dragon declared that bright stones would be a temptation for us, and he came to confiscate them.

The great leader disagreed and fought the dragon. Many of the stones were lost and the peace token shattered. Not to be thwarted, the great leader created a rainbow from the remains of the peace token.

Each of the tribes made camp and the great leader listened to their stories. He could not make a decision, for no one told him the whole truth. However the great leader had a secret weapon. He had a child and the child, as children do, played with the other children and slept at the fires of the various tribes.

Adults talk as children sleep, and the child heard all and reported back to the great leader.

Our punishment was huge. We, who loved freedom and air, were destined to live in hollows below the ground, forever burrowing like animals in the rock. Our land was to be as arid as the desert and even that was confined within towering cliffs of The Rock.

We lost everything.

But the child of the great leader claimed the punishment was too great. 'They cannot live without hope,' she said. And so into our arid land, she guided a river. 'Let nature do what nature does', she told us. She planted a tree to mark the entrance to our land, and urged us to make peace with The Desert People, offer what apologies we could. Our last trip into the light of the day was to meet with them.

Such was their distrust of our word; they would not allow anyone to approach them. Even The Leader of The Green Valley was turned away.

Faltryn brought us a package though. Inside was the skull of the child and the message thundered through our land. 'You wanted it! Care for it better than you did when you stole it!

Our sadness was great, but again the child of the valley helped us.

When the peace token shattered, a shard had fallen from it. The child gave this into our care. 'The tokens will be found and the peace token repaired,' she prophesied. 'This shard will restore the land. Only you can make this happen.'

And so the tribes drifted away and over the seasons we heard whispers in the wind. That a new leader was born. The people were gathering. The tokens had been found. But we saw nothing and no one approached us. Eventually the wind whispered that all had left the land and forgotten us. We became the Nythesians — the only people."

"What of the shard?" I asked.

Churnyg sighed heavily. "We are a people who should not be given hope. When the trees had grown and the streams laughed and gurgled as they crossed our land, I began to take the shard into the moonlight to watch it sparkle — to remind me of the beauty of the world beyond my sight. I would roll it down the banks of the stream and watch it as it glistened and shimmered. Early one morning as it rolled into the water, a huge fish swallowed it. I chased him as he swam away, but as he neared the cliffs that surround our land, a great eagle swooped down, grabbed the fish and flew away. I could follow no longer, we are forbidden to leave the land. The bird disappeared towards the place where the sun sets.

I told my people that The Leader of The Green Valley had

come to me in a dream, bade me to give it to the birds to restore it to the peace token. They didn't believe me and gave me the lowliest job, keeper of the back door.

Even in that I have failed, for while I climbed the trees at dawn, the giant stole the skull despite our caring for it for more than a hundred-thousand seasons.

So you see, Kirym of The Green Valley. There will never be peace, because nothing can be restored. Again and again I let my people down and until I die there will be no peace among them and no peace in the world. But I continue to live and your journey here has been in vain." He took a deep shuddering breath. "Now I live in the lonely half-light of the nearest semblance of a tree I have. Go away, Kirym of The Green Valley. Leave me to my demons. Leave me to face the wrath of my people. Leave me to the death they are now debating."

He collapsed on the floor, his body heaving and shuddering with sobs.

Teema leaned towards me frowning. "If the story is true, then he has to have seen over twenty five thousand summers."

I shrugged. "There are many explanations," I said quietly. "He feels the guilt however he comes by it. But the stories don't match up. However Salcan took the skull and we can help there."

"Can we do enough?" asked Arbreu.

"More than you think," I replied. I raised my voice. "We promised help, Churnyg. There will be peace. It begins with this."

I brought out the skull.

I assumed it had been attached to the skins when Salcan stole it. The slots to attach them were worn. I had cleaned the skins and stuffed them with dried fragrant herbs. Now they looked plump and smelled sweet.

Churnyg's head came off the floor — he gazed at what I held out.

"Salcan asked me to return your property. He should never have taken it. He acknowledges he made a mistake."

29

Arbreu

Churnyg stood and peered distrustfully at Kirym. He stepped into the light and was clearly visible for the first time — a small solid dwarf, looking as if he was hewn out of an ancient tree trunk. The smile on his face was beatific.

He reached for the skull.

There was another crack of thunder. As it faded there was a distant buzz that got louder and louder, as if someone had stirred a bee hive.

Chrurnyg's eyes widened with fear and he seemed to shrink into himself a little, although he straightened his shoulders and back.

"Kirym of The Green Valley," he said softly. "The wrath of my people is great. It has been a long time coming, but now they have made their decision. Gynbere, our great leader will now tell me if I will die or be banished. Go now, back to your people while you have the time. Go quickly before they close the path, which they will do to prevent my escape."

"You have the skull now," Kirym said. "They cannot take retribution for something that no longer is. Now they will accept that things are changing, you'll be able to leave here and once again live in the trees."

"I told you that some have long memories and are not forgiving. It's my people, the Nythesians I was talking about. I let them down and they will exact punishment. I will give you time to escape. Remember me, please. Tell stories about the bravery of Churnyg."

"If everyone else is willing to forgive, they should too," said Kirym crossly. "You have the backing and support of The Green Valley and the People of the Caves."

The noise increased and appeared to be coming closer.

"There is no reasoning with Gynbere. He has made his decision and called the people together. He will not back down in front of them. He will tell me now and give me time to think about it. But I will be dead by morning." He looked beaten.

Teema now had his bow strung and his knife in his hand. "Not if we can help it," he said. "Larqeba, you stay beside Kirym. Protect her," he said. He turned to the dwarf. "If there's a threat to your life we'll fight to defend you. For now, let's listen to what this Gynbere says, and then we'll decide what to do."

Churnyg sighed. "It is a mistake for you to stay. I may not be able to get you out later."

"We will decide on the escape after we hear Gynbere," said Teema. "Perhaps we can take you with us, and thwart this bringer of death."

"Oh, very well," said Churnyg, with little grace. "Stay in the dark while I face him. He won't kill me in front of the people. There's a way they do this so that few know. There may be time after."

Kirym put the skull in his arms. "You have this. Show them it's back. They can't blame you for its disappearance if it's here."

Churnyg looked fondly at the little figure and sighed deeply. "They'd take it as proof that again I've had contact with those from the outside. It'll put you and the skull at risk, and my death may come sooner. Keep it, Kirym of The Green Valley. You care for it more than they do anyway. For Gynbere, the treasures were always an excuse to persecute my family."

Before they could argue, he flicked his hand and the lights went out.

Arbreu could hear him moving in the dark. A hole appeared in a wall showing a small dimly lit balcony.

Churnyg stepped out onto it. He was surrounded by stone flowers, these carved into the arch he stepped through, and the banister that edged his balcony.

Beyond him was a massive hall, the vaulted stone ceiling arched above, while the floor was in darkness below. The arches were heavily carved. People and animals writhed around them, entwined with lengths of stone garlands, flowers and fruit. There were more carved figures on the walls, surrounding and supporting lines of balconies around the hall.

The balconies were crowded with dwarves of all shapes and sizes. They stood in groups, talking and laughing together. The general impression was that of a celebration.

"How did all of these live in six trees?" Teema asked quietly.

"I think they were types of trees," Kirym responded. "Our Churnyg is an oak."

A spotlight illuminated the curtain-draped balcony opposite them. It was cleverly done. Stone faces peeped through the drapes in places, stone hands held the massive swags up and various other limbs, human and animal were visible.

A closer look showed chains that fettered these figures to the balcony and the wall around.

The curtains slowly opened to reveal a group of armour clad guards. They parted and a portly, ornately dressed dwarf stepped forward and waved to the cheering crowded balconies.

As the noise reduced, he stepped to the balcony rail, waved the crowd to silence and cleared his throat.

"Hrumpfff. People of The Rock," he droned. "Again and again," he paused, looking around to see the effects of his words. "Again and again … we have been let down … hrumpff … by this … this traitor." He pointed at Churnyg.

A sigh rose from the floor far below.

Gynbere frowned and cleared his throat again. "Hrumpfff! Now!" he barked. "Now we have none … none of the precious gifts … gifts we were favoured with. This," he waved his hand towards Churnyg, "this traitor has conspired … conspired, I say … to let the enemy … to let the enemy into our midst to rob us. He helped them … to steal … yes steal our precious jewels … the jewels we have saved … saved," he screamed, "from our enemies!"

There was a roar from the crowded balconies.

"Now," he thundered when they had silenced. "Now we will have … an end to it … an end, I say. Without the traitor … we will know peace."

"What a pompous idiot," said Arbreu quietly. "I'll enjoy stopping this."

"Don't pre-empt things," cautioned Kirym. "We are rather outnumbered at the moment and this is their home."

"For a long time … for a long time … the traitorous Oak family … have not been part of we people of The Rock. They have worked against us … against the good of you people. We will have this no longer ... We will not, I say. We will take his name." He paused, staring as the crowd around him roared. "We will take his spirit!"

Another roar of delight thundered around the hall. "And now," he screamed. "Now, we will banish him."

He waited again until the crowd had silenced. "He has allowed ... allowed the giant ... the giant ... from the far land ... to take the treasure ... yes our precious treasure. The treasure we have cared for ... cared for since the beginning of our time. Sadly, we know ... we know we will never ... never, I say ... we will never get them back.

We will take him ... yes, we will take this traitor ... and we will cast him out ... We will ask the birds to take him ... take him to their nest. Then he can no-longer betray us. The birds will teach him to fly. They will take him away ... he will leave and he will never return. He will fly to a land ... a land beyond our safe borders. We will see ... how he gets on ... living amongst the giants," he paused for effect, "the giants he invited in to rob us ... of our treasures!"

The roar of the crowd lessened as the leader leaned over the balcony. He pointed across at Churnyg. "Now," he roared. "Now, he can think ... he can contemplate ... his fate. We will come for him at midnight. The birds will have decided ... by dawn." He pointed at Churnyg. "Go," he thundered. "Go and ponder your destiny."

The crowd roared and the lights around Churnyg vanished. He stumbled back into his hollow and the wall closed. The lights flared.

"We're the giants?" asked Kirym quietly.

Churnyg nodded.

"So they'll send you out to us?"

"Only my bones," said Churnyg. "It's a sop to the crowds, who might object if they knew he planned to kill me. This is the way my sire and grandsire died."

"We have until midnight," said Kirym.

He shook his head. "They'll come long before then despite Gynbere's statement. He seems to be in a hurry, this is the quickest sentencing he's had. I wonder why it's suddenly so important. Maybe he's heard another whisper, although most of them are in his head." He shrugged. "We need to move fast to get you to safety. Take the skull, it'll not be cared for here. None of the precious items we had have been valued by any other than my ancestors. Returning them will only give Gynbere an excuse for more killing."

"We could talk to Gynbere, make him see how wrong this is. The world out there has changed," said Arbreu.

"Enough," Churnyg said. "He will not allow an approach by me, or anyone who may have spoken to me. If we don't move now, I'll not get you out. I want no deaths on my conscience."

The lights went out and he carefully opened the door to the tunnel and peered out.

Kirym moved up behind him. They stayed still, silent, straining to hear through the background noise. The rain had started and was getting heavier, a muted roar in the distance. There were other noises, a skittering of tiny feet along the passage, the rustle of leaves blown in by the wind, and then an explosive choked off sneeze. Churnyg quietly closed the door and pushed across four large bolts.

"They're waiting for you," Kirym said.

The lights shone dimly. "Well, they'll have trouble getting in," said Churnyg, "but they've moved faster than I thought. There must be a lot of opposition to my death, or perhaps Gynbere is getting more paranoid. I imagine he'll have arranged for them to block the path to the tree also. Thank goodness you were so stupidly obstinate and didn't leave before they sentenced me."

Kirym stared at him in horror. She crossed the hollow to

Arbreu and clicked his token. *Get away from the rock! An arrow flight at least!*

When? asked Mekrar.

NOW! Kirym responded. *Wait for nothing!*

Arbreu looked pale. "What if they've left it too late?"

Churnyg looked shaken. "There are more of you?"

"People of many tribes travel with me," said Kirym, "and more are on their way to join us. Now if this path is blocked, what can we do?"

"There's an old bolthole. It's a dangerous route ..." Churnyg frowned, deep in thought. Then he sighed. "It's our only chance. They'll breach my hollow eventually and we'd best not be here when they do."

He opened a cupboard and emptied the contents onto the floor. Pushing picks, shovels and ropes aside, he pulled out a cloak and handed it to Larqeba. "Put this on and keep quiet. If you make a sound, we'll all die." He took Larqeba's face in his hands and stared into his eyes. "They'll kill The Lady of The Valley first, so you mind me."

Larqeba gulped and nodded.

Churnyg looked at Kirym. "You'll do. Not perfect, but unless your face is seen, you'll pass." He handed cloaks to Teema and Arbreu. "Carry your knives, but keep them hidden under your cloaks. Remember, blades reflect and odd lights are investigated. You're too tall to be one of us, but it'll be dim, so we may get away with it." He grunted. "Stoop, keep your hoods low and if we meet anyone, leave the talking to me."

30

Kirym Speaks

Teema and Arbreu had no choice but stoop. The tunnel Churnyg opened and took us down was made for short dwarves and even he couldn't stand tall.

We each carried a small lamp, but only Churnyg's was lit and that was hooded almost to invisibility. I was directly behind Churnyg, followed by Larqeba, Arbreu and Teema.

The first part of the journey was quick, but the further we went, the more often Churnyg paused and listened for sounds ahead.

The tunnel ended with a wooden wall. He put his ear against it.

"Clear," he grunted.

He pushed at one side of the wall and it slowly edged out. While it was still a narrow crack, he again listened and was at last satisfied. He opened it enough for us to slip through and then eased it shut.

The wall we had come through backed a large ornate

cabinet, one of many spaced along the wall. We were at the edge of a long gallery that ran around a hall similar to the one outside Churnyg's hollow, although a lot smaller. The vaulted ceiling looked the same, but there were no carvings or ornate curlicues here. Instead the arches were deeply ribbed. This hall had galleries instead of balconies. The ceiling was high above, but as with Churnyg's hall, the floor far below was in darkness.

We followed Churnyg as he darted across a bridge connecting two galleries and then down a series of lengthy passages. We ran for a long time in near darkness, and were all quite out of breath when we stopped.

Churnyg leaned forward, fighting to control his breathing. "We'll not make it to our first safe hole," he said. "There's a patrol coming. This is the best place to wait them out."

He pushed us into a narrow alcove in the wall. "Face the wall and stay still. Eyes an' faces reflect light so keep your hoods low. If you must carry your knife, keep it hidden in your cloak. Don't move or talk until I tell you to."

Churnyg put Larqeba in the darkest corner with me next to him. Then Arbreu and Teema, Churnyg was at the end in the most exposed position. However, if he was discovered, the game was over for all of us.

"Don't talk! Don't move!" were his final instructions.

We waited in the darkness. It seemed like such a long time. My hood was pulled close to my face, but I managed to peer down the long passage. Not a lot of use. It was pitch black and I could see nothing.

The noise was subtle, just a vague vibration. Soon I realised it was the rhythmic thump of many feet.

The footsteps got closer until they seemed to be right on top of us. There was a sudden brilliant light, a discordant crash and bang that made me jump.

A column of dwarves streamed past. They carried bows and

spears. All wore black armour, and it was this that clanked and crashed as they marched. Then the light went out and with it, the noises except the sound of their feet slapping on the stone path. Again the light came on and this time we saw the noisy end of the line.

The light and clamour gradually receded into the distance and in the darkness that followed, I could feel Larqeba squirming.

Churnyg must have been aware of it too, for he hissed through his teeth.

I grabbed Larqeba's shoulder and squeezed.

He froze.

A light appeared in the distance, getting steadily closer and closer. A lone dwarf jogged towards us. The light went out and all we could hear was the slap slap slap of his feet. Then even that stopped.

I held my breath, sure the others were doing the same.

Suddenly the light came on again. The dwarf was standing almost opposite Churnyg. He raised his dim lamp, turning in a full circle, his eyes darting in all directions. His appearance was strange. His head and body were round. He had large feet and he was hairless. His eyes bulged. After what seemed like an age, he lowered the lamp and continued on his way.

We stayed hidden, the silence and darkness overpowering.

"They've gone." Churnyg's voice seemed loud.

I felt both Larqeba and Arbreu jump at the sound.

Churnyg turned his lamp up a little. It spat, fizzed and died. He exchanged his with Larqeba's and, motioning us to follow him, continued along the passage.

Again we ran fast for a long time. When next he stopped, it was to tell us that we needed to travel more cautiously for a while.

"You must obey me instantly," he said. "Your lives will

depend on it. If I say jump, you had better be off the ground before I've finished speaking. Make no sound, no matter what you see or hear." He put his face in front of Larqeba's. "Sound could be the death of us."

"He'll be quiet, Churnyg," I said.

"Hrmpfff," was his only reply.

Churnyg's lamp was now so heavily shuttered I could see only a faint glow around it if I looked at it directly. Now we travelled holding the shoulder of the person in front. Our footsteps echoed against tunnel walls for a long time, and then the echoes changed and I felt we were again on one of the galleries that criss-crossed the halls.

"Down!"

Arbreu dropped to the floor. Already I was following his example, pulling Larqeba down with me.

A light came on, shining up from the level below us. Something long and sinuous whipped across the gallery just above my head.

This gallery was different from the others — there was no rail along the edge. Had the tail hit us, it would have wiped us off the path — with a long fall into the darkness below.

A huge body spun around just below the ceiling of the hall and I was suddenly looking into the eye of a massive dragon.

It paused, and turned back, its face close to us. I reached out and stroked its nose, intrigued by the size and colour. It was huge, and a luxurious creamy white. It twisted away again. I stroked down the length of its body. Its scales rippled under my hand, thicker and looser than I thought they'd be. The dragon spun back to look at us again.

The light started to dim and Churnyg rose, beckoning us to follow him.

"Kirym!" whispered Larqeba. "Salcan had ..." and then I had my hand over his mouth.

Churnyg glared at him, his face like thunder.

I waved him on and looked back. The dragon stared after us, and as we disappeared into the darkness of the tunnel, it twisted away and its tail again swooped across the gallery. But I held one of its scales tightly in my hand.

The tunnels were as dark as ever and again we ran. Larqeba was getting tired, frequently stumbling. Arbreu reached behind me and pulled him forward, supporting him.

After a long time, Churnyg slowed and turned his lamp up slightly, aiming the light at the rock wall. He ran now stooped almost to the floor, staring intently at the crease where the wall and floor met.

Then I heard it. The slap of feet on the stone floor. Another patrol was approaching.

Churnyg stopped and appeared to be prodding various stones in the wall. A narrow gap appeared and he forced his way through. He turned up the lamp and dumped it on the floor, beckoning Larqeba through to him and then Arbreu. I thrust my pocket at Teema and pushed him through.

He struggled. I wondered why it took him so long, Churnyg was shorter, but wider in all directions and Arbreu's shoulders were slightly broader.

The noise of the slapping feet was so loud, I was sure they were almost on top of me. When, moments later, lights shone, they were so close I could see the stitching on their leather armour and the strange blank masks they wore. Three filled the tunnel. Their noise was almost deafening and they were bearing down on me at a frightening speed. These guards were huge. Their heads almost touched the roof of the tunnel, their shoulders met, and skimmed the walls as they walked.

Then Teema was through the gap and I slipped in behind him. It was a really tight fit. The rocks dug painfully into my skin, I knew I'd have scratches on my shoulders and knees. I was confused. All except Larqeba were bigger than me, yet still I struggled. As my foot left the passage, the front line of the patrol swooped past me and there was a sudden suction. I grasped the rocks as tightly as I could, but I was being inexorably pulled back into the passage.

Teema and Churnyg grabbed hold of my arms, pulling with all their strength. Churnyg actually had his feet on the wall and was almost horizontal.

I suddenly popped free of the suction and we fell in a heap on the floor. The noise diminished slightly and when I looked up the hole in the wall had closed.

Churnyg had his finger to his lips, but there was no way I could have spoken. I was still trying to find my breath.

The noise of feet and the clash and crash of the armour and weapons was so close, it felt almost as if the patrol was in the hollow with us. Then the clank and bang of armour stopped and all we could hear was the rhythmic slap of their feet as they disappeared into the distance. For a while the only sound was of heavy breathing.

Churnyg was on his feet, again prodding the wall and twisting various pieces accompanied by the grinding of rock on rock. Eventually he turned away and sat down again. "The wall is as thick as I can make it," he said.

"Why didn't they stop when they saw me?" I asked.

Churnyg shrugged. "The labyrinth patrol is blind. They'll walk over you and not stop. They can hear a mouse fart, but they won't see a thing."

"They were different from the guards we saw earlier. I felt as if I was being pulled into them."

He nodded. "That's their big weapon. There are times each day when anything not safe behind closed doors is sucked under their feet and crushed. Be thankful this hollow had a pressure door, else everything in here, including us, would be out there."

"So that's why the door was tight!" I said.

"Where are you taking us?" demanded Teema. "We must be way below ground level now. If this is a trick …"

I put my hand on his arm. "Churnyg is in more danger than any of us, Teema. Trust him."

"It's not like we have a choice," he grumbled.

Churnyg stepped up to Teema. "I go nowhere not needed, young warrior. The path we take is fraught with danger, and this is the safest route. The only route! Well the only one we can take. We are below ground level in the hope no one will think to look for us here. Others may know of the bolthole, and they can move faster than we can. The paths they use are shorter. I only hope they assume I have already left The Rock by some other means."

"So what now?" said Teema.

"We rest," said Churnyg. "The child won't last if we don't. When the moon shines, the patrols are more active."

"Moon? You're saying we've been here for the whole day?" Arbreu sounded sceptical.

"I think he's right," said Teema. "Larqeba is ready to drop, and I feel the day has past. Time spent in darkness is deceptive."

Having finally got my breath back, I sat up and opened the pack and pulled out a water flask handing it to Churnyg. He drank and passed it to Teema and then Arbreu and Larqeba. By then, I had a parcel of food laid out.

Larqeba gasped as he gulped the water. "What was that white thing, Kirym? It was like Salcan's."

Churnyg sat up, instantly alert. "Salcan had a dragon? Why didn't he …?"

I sifted through the items at the bottom of my pocket, and piled the ornaments Salcan had given me on the floor in front of Churnyg. "This," I said, handing it to him. "Is it one of your treasures?"

Churnyg slumped back and shook his head. "That? No, it's not ours. I thought you meant a real one."

"A real dragon? Why would you suppose ..." I tried to think quickly. Salcan must have been in the hall, although the dragon he made had a different stance, its face was longer, and it had two horns. The dragon in the hall had no horns.

"What's important about dragons?" I asked.

"When they return we'll be free." He shook his head and sighed. "It was probably just a dwarfling's story."

"Salcan saw your dragon?"

He nodded.

"How long was he in here?" I asked.

"He came at the beginning of autumn and left halfway through spring. He kept coming back though. Not in here, but near, watching — well that's what was said anyway."

Churnyg looked more intently at the pile of ornaments. He picked one up, the nearest thing to a smile on his face I'd seen since I handed him the skull.

"He remembered me," he whispered.

The ornament he held was his own image.

"Could Salcan have found these in here?" I asked.

Churnyg shook his head. "No one here would make these. Salcan must have."

I handed him the dragon scale. "It's made of the same material. There's a strange link here. I wish I knew what it was."

Churnyg shrugged and pushed the figures around, looking at one after another. He picked up one of the bird figures and went quite pale.

"What are they?" I asked.

"Liberty. Slavery." he shrugged and pushed the pile of ornaments aside. "Lies!"

He placed the bird with the other figures, lay on the floor

and pulled his cloak over his head. Within a short time, he was gently snoring. Teema, Arbreu and Larqeba had also fallen asleep.

I placed the dragon scale with the ornaments, and ground some harkii for myself. The slap of feet beyond the wall told me another patrol was passing. Even when the clank and clash of their weapons sounded, none of the sleepers stirred.

The hollow was narrow and long, the end stretched away into darkness. There were large black shadows against the walls. I lit a new lamp and went to explore. The shadows were twelve massive wooden cabinets. Beyond the cabinets the walls were painted. Much of it was very old, but more recently parts of the pictures had been over-painted, altering the original work. The new pictures were dark and foreboding.

I returned to the sleepers.

Five patrols went past before I woke Churnyg.

"The patrols are getting more frequent," I said.

He nodded. "They know I've escaped. The bolts couldn't hold them out forever, but they'll not find the tunnel unless they take the walls apart. Even then they'll have no idea where to look once they reach the end of it. They'll search a while and then return to normal," he said. "We just have to wait them out. You should have slept, we're safe here."

I handed him the carving of the strange bird.

He fingered it with distaste. "I've personally never seen them. According to lore, if you do, you face a grim end. Whether it's death or slavery, I don't know."

"Salcan appears to have seen them, but what are they? I saw the paintings back there." I indicated the darkened end of the hollow. "The birds are not part of the original art work. What do they cover?"

"The pictures told of the dragons' return. They gave us

hope — helped our children to dream. Then one day there were guards on the door and entry was forbidden.

Many seasons later the guards disappeared, but the door remained closed to us. From then on we had to rely on our memories. Time passed and we were told our memories were wrong. We knew the answers were in here and we demanded access.

We should have been wary when Gynbere agreed.

They'd been desecrated. A story was here, a new one, but it didn't inspire us. It told us we were prisoners of The Rock and now there was no escape.

The old stories were banned as heresy. Those who continued to tell them disappeared. We were told they had grown feathers, flown away, but had been captured and enslaved by the great eagles, to spend eternity cleaning their nests and feeding the bottomless pits that were the stomachs of their nestlings.

Our dreams were dead so this time we closed the hollow. We needed to ensure it didn't contaminate our children. It was very difficult and took a lot of planning.

There was great anger when it happened and we cowered in fear. The recriminations were massive, and much of my family was decimated. Gynbere called it a revolt and he guessed we were at the forefront of it, although it would have made little difference even if we hadn't been.

But anger cannot be sustained forever, although many winters passed before we again had the courage to enter the hollow. This time, we created a new door, one they didn't know about. We couldn't return the pictures to their original state, and so we entered less and less. Few know of it now, I may be the only one. I'm certainly the only one who can open the door. Now though, I wonder if freedom and peace are figments of my imagination, wishful stories from dreamers and fantasists."

"Have you only seen the pictures with that light?" I asked pointing to the dim lanterns we'd carried from his hollow.

He nodded. "It's all we have."

I pulled my lamp out of the pack Arbreu had carried. "Let's have a proper look," I said.

31

Kirym Speaks

The bad light had allowed a lot of the subtle detail in the paintings to be hidden.

Again and again, Churnyg exclaimed over things he'd never seen before or had long forgotten. There was a lot that had meaning to him, images that were part of his folklore.

Soon, Teema, Arbreu and Larqeba, disturbed by our noise, joined us as we explored. We found streams, trees, hills and valleys. Except for the depressing birds, it was a cheerful interesting picture.

Then I realised what it was. "It's a map of the land."

Much of it was indistinct, shown from a great height. It started on the right wall with the huge northern mountain and the three circles where we discovered the route to Faltryn.

The hills and caves around The Fortress of Faltryn was misted with smoke or fog. The back wall showed the desert. It was various shades of gold with a glowing orb on the horizon. The settlement of The Green Valley was hazy green with shadows that may have been the dwellings. High above it flew one lone dragon. The dim lights used in the past had hidden it, and the vandals had missed it.

Now Churnyg stared at proof that a dragon, part of his dream, had stayed. Two hooded figures sat astride the dragon. They were flying straight towards The Rock.

The Rock area was more distinct — closer — but a large cabinet covered most of it.

Churnyg, Teema and Arbreu heaved it away from the wall.

Although the dark birds littered the painting, most of them were pictured flying around the rock or perched in the tree in front of the sheer cliff. The cabinet had been placed to hide them. The tree was pictured as smaller than it was now, and the hole was clearly visible through the top branches. Two of the birds had dwarves' heads, the rest were more like vultures than eagles. One feathered figure lay at the base of the tree.

I took the lamp closer. The feathers were odd. They stuck out at strange angles, not sleek and birdlike. A talon stuck out of the feathers, curled around a smooth stone that appeared lemon coloured in the lamp light. The claw and talon sat proud of the wall.

Churnyg collapsed.

I wet a cloth and placed it on his forehead.

Revived, he sat hunched over, tears coursing down his face. "Gynbere was right. The birds are our death. We can't leave. We're slaves here forever."

"It doesn't mean that," said Larqeba. "The other dwarf-heads were flying, so they got away. Anything's better than slavery in here."

Arbreu clipped him around the ear, although it was half-hearted. Larqeba saw it coming and ducked.

"The stone belonged to my great-grandsire," said Churnyg. "He was carrying it when he disappeared. This verifies his death. It's proof Gynbere told us the truth this time. We can't live outside these gloomy walls."

"Perhaps that's not what it means, Churnyg," I said, grasping straws from the air. "Someone planned for you to find the stone. Only the bad light stopped that happening before this. Had it been Gynbere, it would have been far more obvious. Perhaps you have more friends than you realise. The stone returned. It belongs to you now."

"What? A sign that like it, I should remain imprisoned in this hollow forever?" he said sourly.

"Perhaps it's a sign you can leave." I pulled my knife from its sheath under my dress and went to where the stone sat in the wall. Everyone followed me.

I was surprised that Churnyg was at my elbow, but as I knelt beside the stone, I realised it was the knife that held his attention.

He took it from me and held it up, his eyes wide. "You really are from The Green Valley," he said in wonder.

"You had doubts?" asked Teema incredulously. "After all she's told you!"

"Hush, Teema. Why should he trust anything said to him when he has been told so many lies? He's right to question it. He has put his life on the line for us. We're lucky he was prepared to do that."

"Wait on," interrupted Arbreu. "How does the knife tell you where we come from?"

Churnyg shrugged and looked more belligerent than usual. "Dunno!"

I took my knife from Churnyg and used it to pry the talons open and pop the stone out.

Churnyg picked it up — he positively glowed, as did the stone. Not as the tokens glowed, but it seemed to come alive in his hand.

"It doesn't tell me I can leave," he grumbled.

I pulled my pocket towards me and opened the pack that held the wrapped tokens.

"Choose one."

He looked at them suspiciously, took a deep breath and after pulling his hand back a few times, shut his eyes and picked one up. He immediately placed it on my lap, looking somewhat apprehensive.

"Open it," I told him.

He carefully unwrapped the token, staring in amazement at the golden glow. He moved it and we all saw the sun rise and set and the moon follow it.

"This means you can live under the sun as well as the moon," I said.

He looked hopeful and doubtful at the same time. "What if you're wrong?"

"I'm not," I said with more conviction than I really felt.

"You said you used to live out in the trees," said Arbreu. "Why would that change? I think Kirym's right. It'd just take courage to get out there and do it again."

32

Kirym Speaks

Despite Churnyg's assurances we were safe and could all sleep, he was happy to help Teema guard us. When I woke, it was to the sound of the guards again streaming past us.

"It's almost continuous now," said Teema. "It's been building up for quite a while."

Churnyg nodded. "Gynbere must really be pushing for them to have gone on for so long. They'll have to stop soon. Exhaustion sets in and there is nothing Gynbere can do to make them carry on. That's when we move."

"Do they suspect we're here?" Teema asked. "It's been really intense out there."

Churnyg shook his head. "It'll be like that everywhere. It's happened before when there's been a panic of some sort. If they even thought I was in here they'd be trying to break through the wall. It'd be hard, but they are miners."

When I thought back to the patrol in the labyrinth, I had the feeling I was seen. One of the masks was different, I was sure it wasn't blind. It didn't have the blank surface of the two beside it. Maybe it was an illusion, but it worried me.

Larqeba went off to explore. He spent time looking for hidden things in the map, and then began to open each of the large cabinets and climb inside. Eventually he came back, hungry, as growing boys are.

"Two of the cabinets are locked," he said with a mouth full of food.

Churnyg had been lying on the floor with his eyes closed. He sat up, frowning.

"Nothing should be locked," he said. "Maybe the doors are just jammed." He stood and took Larqeba's hand and they wandered into the darkness.

Teema, Arbreu and I took the lamp and joined them.

Churnyg pushed and pulled at the doors, but they refused to budge. "They should open for me, they're made of oak." He was quiet for a while. "Last time I was in here, every cabinet opened. Someone else has been here."

"Friend or enemy?" I asked.

"The secret of the door is now known only to my family. The last time the door opened there were three of us here. The other two are now dead. One of them must have told someone else. I doubt they'd tell an enemy, but I have doubted many things over the seasons." His voice dropped. "I've not always been right."

He turned to face us. "It's a gamble. There's a sure way to open the cabinets, but if it's a trap, it may bring the patrol in here. What do you want me to do?"

"Open them."

I was surprised at how confident I sounded.

"Are you sure, Kirym?" asked Teema.

"The yellow token is serene, and if only Churnyg's family have the knowledge, we must trust them."

Churnyg unfastened his jacket. He pulled a small button

off his waistcoat and removed one of his earrings, joining them together. He pulled a lace from his boot and tied the end to the earring, knotting it to keep it secure. He carefully spun it and flicked it at a spot high on the door. It fell to the floor and I picked it up to hand it back to him.

He had made a small silver acorn, only obvious when the components were put together. The cap of the acorn had been his button, the earring made up the seed and the earring shaft held it all together.

Churnyg spun it again. It fell to the floor. Then again and again, until suddenly it sailed in a perfect arc and settled on a small knot near the top of the door. There was a loud click as it swung open.

We stared inside. The back of the cabinet was made of polished oak. It shone like silk except where the broken stub of a branch protruded from the middle.

Churnyg jumped up, grabbed the stub and swung from it. It collapsed down with a loud clunk — and nothing happened.

The small acorn had fallen through a hole in the knot. Churnyg picked it up and went to the second cabinet. This was taller than the first, although that one was much deeper.

Again Churnyg swung the acorn, eventually flicking it into a small hole high on the door. It swung open and again we stared at a wooden back. This one had a series of horizontal slits in it.

Churnyg began to climb, using them as steps of a ladder. He reached the top and half turned. "Teema, climb up behind me, as high as you can. Arbreu, you follow him. Then you, Larqeba. We stay holding on until I tell you not to."

When Larqeba had climbed as high as he could, there was a loud bang from the first cabinet.

I raced over to see what caused it.

The floor inside the cabinet had fallen away, and deep down I could see the edge of a wrapped package.

I lay on my stomach to grab it and managed to do that easily enough, but I struggled to haul it out. It was bulky and very heavy, and the edges of the pit were unstable. Falling debris kept knocking the package from my grasp. Using all of my strength, I finally got the end of it onto the edge of the floor. The weight appeared to be in the other end and I had great trouble hauling it out. As I finally got enough of the package onto the floor to ensure it didn't slip back in, the sides of the hole collapsed. I grabbed the package and backed away as the door of the cabinet slammed shut.

"Get out, Larqeba!" shouted Churnyg. "Fast!"

Larqeba jumped out of the cabinet, followed in quick succession by Arbreu and Teema. There was a roar of pain from Churnyg as he dropped out and rolled across the floor.

As I ran to help him, the door slammed shut. Churnyg had his hands under his arms and was using words I wished Larqeba couldn't hear.

"I hope that was worth it," he grumbled, rubbing his hands. "The slits closed up. Jammed my fingers."

All four were massaging hands and fingers, the white marks turning red and blue. No skin was broken; the bruises would fade over time.

Then they spied the package I'd pulled from the hole.

Teema, Arbreu and Larqeba rushed over and were about to open it when Churnyg threw himself on it, covering most of it with his body. And he snarled! He sounded like a pack of wolves.

Teema stepped back, hauling Arbreu with him and literally lifting Larqeba away from the pack by his tunic.

"Sorry, Churnyg," he said. "We're out of line. What would

you like to do? Can we help?"

Churnyg rolled off the pack and sat on the floor. He glowered at us.

"If it's a trap, it could kill us," he said. "I don't mind if you die, but I'd prefer not to."

"But the only way to find out is to open it," I said.

He grunted with annoyance. "So? Do it safely. We need a barrier to protect us."

After a bit of discussion, Teema and Arbreu helped him lower the smallest cabinet onto its side. It was pushed and shoved until it was closer to the package.

Churnyg untied his bootlace and hooked the acorn earring into his ear. He removed the other bootlace and his belt and tied them together.

"Need your belts," he said to Teema and Arbreu. He hooked the three together and added a piece of rope Larqeba offered.

The package was wrapped in a stiff oiled material. It reminded me of the covering on a package Papa had found in the boat cave as we were preparing to leave The Land Between the Gorges.

The material was stiff with age and Churnyg had problems making a hole near the corner, but eventually he managed to force the boot lace through and knot it. He laid the line of belts and laces over the side of the cabinet. Once we were all safely behind it, Churnyg yanked the line. There was a crash, a clatter and silence.

Larqeba's head immediately rose to peer over the top of the cabinet and he cursed as Churnyg yanked him down. Already he was repeating the words he had heard Churnyg using.

"If Jeresaya catches you saying those words, Larqeba, you'll not sit for a long time. If you repeat them in my hearing, you'll never travel with me again. Ever!" I poked Arbreu as he attempted to cover a laugh.

Finally Churnyg raised his head. "Seems safe."

A sword in an engraved scabbard, a shield and what looked like a twist of willow were scattered across the floor.

I grabbed hold of Larqeba.

"These are for Churnyg," I explained.

But Churnyg stayed beside us, staring blankly at the weapons, the slap of feet on the far side of the wall the only perceptible sound. After a long time, he stood.

"Kirym, noble lady of The Green Valley. Would you honour me by lending me your knife?"

He stared at the knife, and then took it over to the sword and shield. He looked from one to the other, and called me over.

"These weapons belonged to the Great Leader of The Green Valley. Last I heard they were in Gynbere's hollow, under guard whenever he suspected some sort of threat. I don't know how he came by them, but he never carried them. It's believed that only those who are entitled to may carry them. You already carry the knife and it goes with the sword. They belong to you."

He dropped the knife — it fell straight, and then spun towards the sword and clamped onto the scabbard.

"Not me surely," I said. "They'd belong to Papa. He's headman."

"Veld is headman of the family, Kirym," Teema interrupted. "Headman and Great Leader could be two different things. Your knife — it sat in Veld's family chest for a long time and no one claimed it. You wanted it from the moment you saw it and you've carried it with you ever since. Anyway, you hauled these things from the hole, so Churnyg must be right."

"Someone brought the weapons here from Gynbere's hollow, and someone took them there in the first place.

What about them?" I asked.

"They were taken to his hollow in a box." Churnyg snorted. "Even that was pulled by slaves. Gynbere has never dared to touch them, although there was whisper that one of his lieutenants did and died immediately. Whether he was ordered to pick it up or did it off his own volition, no one knows."

That gave me something to think about. I felt no danger from the weapons so I picked up the scabbard. It was intricately engraved with dragons, stars and trees. It was surprisingly light. The sword hissed out of the scabbard and glowed in the lamp-light. It could be used with the knife attached or they could be separated for two-handed fighting. I returned the sword to its scabbard and hefted the shield. It fitted my arm well, not as unwieldy as I thought it would be. It was etched — a willow circlet set at the top above two dragons, a shooting star and six trees. In the centre was a circle of gems, each a different colour.

The last thing lying on the material was the willow twist, reminiscent of the circlet on the shield, but smaller. Although it seemed unrelated to the sword, I had no doubt it was part of the set. As soon as I picked it up, it changed, expanding and shrinking as I moved it. It was the strangest thing. It wasn't willow at all, but some kind of metal. It fitted over my wrist snuggly, an easy way to carry it until I figured out what it was. Altogether they were surprisingly light.

"I wonder why I had so much trouble getting them out of the pit. It was a real struggle," I said.

"Maybe they were testing you. They had to know you really wanted them. When we leave here they may make the difference between us all living or dying," said Churnyg. "But you alone must carry them. We'll help with the other things, but this burden is yours. Now sleep," said Churnyg, stretching. "Soon we will need to move, and when we do, speed will be vital. Anyone lagging behind could die."

The constant slap of feet got faster and louder as we rested. Now it was continuous.

33

Kirym Speaks

Now our footsteps echoed through the tunnels. As quiet as we tried to be, the smallest sound ricocheted from wall to wall. I only hoped there was no one here to hear it. We had to balance speed against noise, and speed, according to Churnyg, was now paramount. The tunnels were eerily empty, although I wondered how long before people began to venture out again.

I wore my knife on my hip. I carried the scabbard, sword, willow twist and tokens.

The willow twist sat on my wrist. The shield was hooked over my shoulder. Larqeba held the skull and kellich skins. Arbreu carried our pack of provisions.

Churnyg led us. He, Arbreu and Teema carried bows, arrows notched ready if necessary.

We ran for a long time before Churnyg allowed us to stop for a breather. The rest was short, just time for us to drink. I handed harkii nuts to everyone. "Eat these, they'll give you energy."

Churnyg and Larqeba eyed the unknown nuts with distrust.

"Eat them," ordered Arbreu. "She's right, we need them."

We took advantage of the empty tunnels, although it was a little more fraught now. We came across other tunnels more frequently, and glimpsed caves beyond them. Teema ran at the rear as an added protection.

There were sharp corners. We had no idea what was in the darkness beyond. Now Arbreu helped Larqeba. I ran at Churnyg's shoulder.

We were cautious and expected danger at every step. Even so I was shocked when the tunnel ahead lit up.

Churnyg slid to a stop. A silver projectile flashed across the open area straight at him.

My sword hissed from the scabbard, intercepting the missile which wrapped around the sword tip, and swung just in front of Churnyg's face.

Ahead of us, leaning against the tunnel was a labyrinth guard.

Churnyg stared at the projectile. He pushed the sword away and stomped down the tunnel. "Murdering traitor," he muttered as he pushed past the massive guard.

Now I got a good look at the guard. His stature came from the helmet. It sat on his shoulders and extended well above his head, making him appear massive, at least twice his usual height, taller and broader than anyone I'd seen before.

I stared at the guard, certain he could see every move I made. I pushed Arbreu and Larqeba on. "Catch up to Churnyg," I whispered. Teema joined me and I urged him on also. "I won't be long."

I unwrapped the projectile from my sword tip and studied it in the dim light. A chain held a weighted acorn.

I stepped forward and I held it out to the guard.

He took it.

"You can see," I stated.

He didn't answer.

"Why does a labyrinth guard hold an acorn?" I asked.

"It's mine by right of birth," he said. He waved the thought aside. "That's irrelevant. There's no time for talk. Just listen."

He pointed at the sword and scabbard.

"These are weapons of power, not of death, although they will kill if need be. With each death, the power diminishes. Think carefully before you use them for that purpose. That," he pointed to the willow twist on my wrist, "is a crown. Wear it when you face your enemies or when you want to understand something important. It is said to have greater power than the sword. The shield will protect more than one. You can ask someone to carry it for you, but choose carefully. If they accept, it will bind them to you for life. They'll owe their loyalty to you before all others. That can be a heavy load to carry. It also holds a different protection for the holder. That hasn't yet been written about, but I believe it could make the difference between life and death. Protect Churnyg. He has knowledge he isn't even aware of. Remember though, as holder of these items, you are everyone's protection."

He picked up a black sack from the floor by his feet. "Something in here for you and something for Churnyg. Make him wear it hidden beneath his cloak. It may save his life. Insist on this if you value him."

He paused. He looked as if he was carrying a heavy load. "The time will come for him to return to the Rock. Tell him this —

When the dragon returns,
he will fight for your liberty.
The sound of his roar

will destroy your prison.
Heroic feats will be sung about,
your brave deeds remembered.
At the call of the dragon
your enemies will be destroyed
and your sons and daughters
will celebrate."

He pushed the sack into my hand.

"When you leave The Rock, get to the shelter of the trees. Go north. Keep The Rock in sight. There's an ancient oak grove. Rest there and gather your friends. Don't stay too long. A stronghold can easily become a prison."

"Come with us," I said.

He shook his head. "There are things I need to do before I can turn my back on The Rock. Go quickly. There's not much time. Gynbere knows where you are headed. I only hope the plans laid to hold him up have worked. Otherwise we may be doomed before we begin."

I turned away, adding the sack to the load I carried. The guard's light disappeared and a small glow appeared ahead. As I re-joined the others, a low rumble echoed up the tunnel, and dust billowed towards us.

I wondered if the guard had caused the rock fall, and if he was safely on the far side of it.

Churnyg turned away, mumbling angrily under his breath as he led the way once more. Again we ran, and ran for longer than any of us wanted. Finally Churnyg stopped and lowered the lamp, lighting up a small tunnel leading down into the rock.

"I need to go first — there are doors to be opened. Follow at intervals. Count to twenty between each of you, but little one," he took Larqeba's face in his hands, "you come with your brother."

34

Kirym Speaks

Churnyg disappeared feet first and there was an agonising wait with Arbreu mumbling numbers under his breath. Then as he hit twenty, Teema pushed him into the hole, and Larqeba followed.

I handed Teema the sack. "Something in here will be a protection for Churnyg. Make him wear it under his cloak," I said. "You go next," I urged when he stepped back to let me through.

He looked about to argue, but sighed. "If you're sure?"

"I am. I need you all safe."

He ducked down and disappeared.

I started to count, trying not to rush the numbers, but eager to leave my lonely vigil. I reached twelve when I heard a noise. The tunnel behind me lit up. In the dark it was hard to tell how close the light was, but someone or something was approaching.

I crawled backwards into the tunnel. It went down at

a sharp angle before levelling out. Ahead was the lamp Churnyg had left. I grabbed it. There was enough head room here for me to stand.

There was scuffling in the tunnel above me. They'd been closer than I had thought. As I ran to catch up with Teema, I slipped the shield off my shoulder and removed my cloak.

I turned a corner in the tunnel and found myself in a large cave. The lamp wasn't needed, light came from a tunnel to my right, showing Teema was about to disappear into it.

The tunnel opened up into a cave and I held the lamp high searching for a direction. Teema's legs were just disappearing into a low tunnel. I ran over, knelt and looked into it. Teema was on his belly, sliding towards the far opening.

I placed the pocket of tokens on the shield with the scabbard, sword and knife, and wrapped them in my cloak. The tunnel was now clear as Teema stood. I pushed the cloak-wrapped package towards him. The floor was smooth and the cloak carrying the shield scooted ahead and shot out the mouth of the tunnel. I tucked my skirts up and started crawling. I realised how very slippery the floor was, although the walls were coarse. I understood why Teema had been on his belly when my knees skidded sideways and I fell, hitting my temple against the rough surface. I paused, seeing stars, and then grabbed hold of the rocks protruded from both sides and propelled myself forward.

As I reached for the next handhold, something grabbed my boot and pulled me back.

"Teema, help me," I yelled as my hands slipped from the rock.

Teema pushed the cloak package aside and grabbed my arm. However, the smooth nature of the tunnel pulled him in instead of pulling me out.

Arbreu grabbed his legs and yanked him back, but Teema lost hold of me.

Someone grabbed my leg and I kicked out. I heard a muffled curse as my boot connected with flesh. I grabbed the rocks to pull myself on, but again my movement was arrested. For a few vital moments I remained still, unable to move forward, but not slipping back.

"The sack, Teema," I screamed.

He swung around and upended it. Two items hit the ground, one thick and black the other a long, bright, sinuous flash of gold. It flicked into the tunnel and I felt a slight sting as it grazed my cheek below my eye and then I grabbed it.

"Pull!" I shrieked.

He dropped the sack and grasped the other end, pulling with all his might. I began to move up the tunnel. I felt something pierce my instep. I kicked out again and connected firmly with whoever it was. The hands lost their grip on my ankles.

Suddenly free, I shot out of the tunnel and into Teema's arms.

As we untangled ourselves, there was the rasp of grinding rock. I turned to see a huge slab of stone roll in front of the tunnel with a loud thunk. Arbreu gave Churnyg a boost to get on top.

Larqeba was on a higher ledge. He handed Churnyg a mallet and a rock cylinder. Churnyg hammered it into a hole near the top of the slab, and then did the same to another on the other side of the stone, effectively ensuring that the block couldn't be rolled out again.

"That won't be moved in a hurry," he said as he jumped down. "Not much point in having a bolt-hole if it doesn't have a bolt. Now let's get beyond the arrows and we'll be safe and free."

We were in a shallow cave, the entrance open to daylight, but dim as it was surrounded by a thicket of trees.

I looked down to see what I held, what Teema had used to pull me out of the tunnel. I'd expected him to use the sack itself. I held a leather belt, engraved, gilded and bejewelled. The engravings mirrored those on the scabbard.

Churnyg saw what I held.

"Wondered where that was. Where did you get it?"

"What is it?" asked Teema.

Arbreu laughed. "It's a baldric."

"What's a baldric?" asked Larqeba, pre-empting Teema.

"An ornamental belt, but it's worn diagonally across one shoulder," explained Arbreu. "It'll allow Kirym to carry the weapons on her shoulder. They'll be easy to get, but not obvious."

"You've got the whole set now. You can carry them, or you can wear them. If you wear them, you accept the responsibility that goes with them." Churnyg scowled. "You have a choice, Kirym of The Green Valley. Once made, there is no going back."

"I've always worn the knife, and I've never turned aside from responsibility." I threaded the scabbard and shield onto the belt, and slipped it over my shoulder. It felt good, like it belonged there.

"You can keep the sword there, or slip it down onto your hip," said Arbreu. "Because of your height, it'll be better on your shoulder. Your knife can hook onto the sword, or sit on your hip by itself and your hands are still free."

Teema picked up the black thing that had fallen from the bag. "What's this?" It was thick and pulpy and sprung back when pressed.

It was strange, I'd seen nothing like it before. "It's for you, Churnyg. You must wear it," I said, finally getting a chance to see the guard's gift to Churnyg.

"Pah," he spat. "Gifts from a traitor," and he turned his back on me. He stepped towards the entrance of the cave, brought up short when I grabbed his hood and hauled him back.

"Be pig-headed in your own time. You will wear it because it's the sensible thing to do. Whatever the guard's agenda, would you die just to thumb your nose at him?"

Churnyg rounded on me. "You're right, we don't know his agenda. Who's to say it's not a trap?"

"Because he could have betrayed us already, but he didn't," I said. "He gave us these things, he didn't have to. What more do you want from him?"

Churnyg scowled, but took the black thing and strapped it pack-like to his back and flung his cloak over it.

"Now we can leave," I said. "There's an oak grove to the north of us. We'll aim for there. Do you know the way, Churnyg?"

"It's oak," he snarled as he turned to the entrance. "I'll find it."

Teema shrugged and pushed Arbreu and Larqeba ahead.

"Do you really trust that guard?" he asked quietly.

"Why shouldn't we? He's been honourable so far."

We followed Churnyg from the cave.

35

Kirym Speaks

Trees fringed the cave entrance, hiding it from curious eyes. After the dingy grey and black of The Rock, the restful greens of grass and trees were delightful.

There was a wide open area to cross before we were out of danger.

"Are there guards on the rock?" I asked. "And if there are, would they would shoot on sight?"

Churnyg shrugged.

I wanted to leave nothing to chance, so arranged the group carefully in the hope that the shield would cover us all. I put Larqeba and Churnyg in front with Teema and Arbreu behind them. I followed, with the shield between us and The Rock. I was pleased it was held on my back, but wondered if it would be the protection the guard promised.

We ran towards the trees in the distance. I wanted to be more than an arrow flight away, that was just common sense, although I wondered if we would be as safe as Churnyg thought.

We were almost to the trees when I heard a shrill angry bird-like scream. The whistling of an arrow overhead confirmed Gynbere's arrival on the battlements.

"Faster," puffed Churnyg. "Almost there."

"I can't," I gasped.

As much as I wanted to, I couldn't keep up. I was having problems running. My right leg felt too heavy and hot, my foot ached.

I would have fallen had Teema not grabbed me and taken my weight.

"What's wrong?" he asked, but I was too busy trying to stay conscious to answer him.

Arbreu grabbed my other arm, and with the two of them, I moved faster. A volley of arrows hit the ground around Churnyg's feet, and a harsh screech echoed from the top of the rock. The thunk of arrows came closer and I struggled to remain conscious, scared of what would happen if I didn't.

Then we were in the trees and out of sight of those on the wall. We continued in, changing direction occasionally until we were sure no one from The Rock would know where we were. Teema and Arbreu sat me on the ground in a small clearing and Teema helped me to drink.

"It's my foot," I explained, struggling to untie my boot.

36

Teema Speaks

Churnyg pushed me aside and ripped Kirym's boot off.

We were all shocked. The boot was wet with blood, her foot badly swollen and black with bruise and clotted gore.

Churnyg cursed. "One of you carry her, the other carry the … no we can't. Only she can carry the treasures."

"Harkii nut and borkan seeds," Kirym said faintly. "Grind them together, quickly."

Larqeba already had Kirym's herb pouch open and was pulling out the packets she wanted.

Arbreu and I left him to it; he seemed to know what to do.

"What happened?" demanded Churnyg.

He went pale when Kirym explained what had occurred in the tunnel.

"Those things won't help," he said. "The Yew family are skilled poisoners."

"Gynbere's family hold the yew tree as its symbol," Kirym

explained to my mystified query.

"Pah! Irrelevant facts," said Churnyg. "We need an antidote and for that I need a tanthin bush." He grabbed Larqeba's arm. "Do you know what they look like, lad?"

Larqeba hadn't finished nodding before Churnyg had him on his feet and was running through the trees.

"Guard her," Churnyg called over his shoulder.

It was an agonising wait. I alternatively paced and hovered with nothing to do but worry. I envied Arbreu who took over grinding the nuts and feeding them to Kirym.

"Do you think the poison is moving through her body?" he asked. "Should we use a tourniquet to stop it?"

"My foot is affected, not my head," Kirym giggled. "No, it's fine at the moment. The remedies help despite Churnyg's views."

I just didn't know. I thought Kirym was being brave for mine and Arbreu's sake, and if it helped Arb, I was glad.

I gathered some cool herbs, mashed them and covered a nasty bruised graze on Kirym's temple and an angry thin red mark under her eye, wondering how she got them.

It took a long measure of time for Churnyg and Larqeba to return and I started at small noises, worried it was Gynbere or his guards.

Eventually Larqeba burst out of the trees with Churnyg close behind him.

"I hope they found the right thing," I muttered as they approached.

Larqeba upended his pouch. A collection of grey lumps caked with mud rolled onto the ground.

"We need water, a platter and some sedbilt seeds," Churnyg bellowed.

Arbreu emptied his pack and handed over a platter and a flask of water while Kirym sorted through the packets in her pouch.

Churnyg cleaned one of the lumps and dumped it on the platter. He counted out twelve seeds and ground them, mashing the powder into the lump. He packed it around the wound and bandaged it with his scarf and tied it tightly.

"These grow on the roots of the tanthin bush. They can be difficult to find, but we got a good number so we can change the poultice when the sun sets and then every half day. Now we have to get to the oak grove," he said. "You can rest better there."

37

Kirym Speaks

My foot throbbed, but my head was clearer.

"Arbreu, where is Mekrar?" I asked.

He automatically shrugged, but then closed his eyes and concentrated.

"Hidden in trees, but ..."

I beckoned him to me and clicked his token.

Where are you?

We travelled north from where you left us until the sun set. Shall we come in and get you?

No, we're out and now north of you. Come to us, but be careful. They may be searching for us and might shoot on sight.

"I don't know how we do that," said Arbreu, looking pleased.

"It's your connection to Mekrar," said Teema.

"But I don't have a connection with her."

"You do now," I said as I turned to Churnyg. "With the

bolthole blocked, where is the next nearest exit from The Rock?"

"There's the tree at the southern end. I heard they were trying to build a door in the wall of the north-eastern section, but they were having trouble getting through the rock. There was another bolthole on the eastern side, but the guards found out about it, so we blocked it."

"Could Gynbere have reopened it or created something without you knowing?"

"Possible. Digging in rock isn't something you can do quietly. Tailings have to be disposed of, workers talk, people find out. Gynbere has closed areas off, mainly in north and east. It means that even if Gynbere decides to follow, it'll take him at least two days to get here. But he won't leave The Rock. He has no need to. I've gone. That's what he wanted."

"If that was all he wanted, he'd have just kicked you out," I said. "It's not as simple as that. Those he has still imprisoned in The Rock come into it. If there is no proof you died because you tried to leave, they may just decide to follow you. What does he do then? Allow everyone who wishes to, leave? He needs to show that leaving is a death sentence. What did he say about your grandsire leaving?"

"He said the birds didn't want him. They attacked him mid-flight and ripped his wings off. You saw the drawing."

"He was at the base of the tree. More likely he was pushed out."

"Possible, but he had become a bird."

"Why would the birds attack him?"

Churnyg stared at me, frowning. Eventually he shrugged. "Dunno, but a number of people saw his body, and some of them said it was the birds."

"Did you ever talk to anyone who actually saw it happen?"

He shook his head.

My foot and leg still throbbed, but less than before and I was beginning to feel better, although tired. I thought the heavy bleeding may have helped flush away some of the poisons — I was probably very lucky. The poultice would handle the wound. I would need to keep taking harkii nut, borkan seeds and a few other things until I was sure the poisons were eliminated. Fortunately the information I'd gleaned while trying to heal Salcan would now help me. That knowledge may help save my life.

Churnyg wouldn't allow me to wear the boot again until the hole caused by whatever entered my foot could be cut out and replaced, so I walked barefoot. Arbreu promised to work on the boot when we stopped for the night.

We travelled north, slower than before, and we stayed in the trees.

The trees changed as we walked. In the south, they were mainly poplar, linden and sycamore. As we got further north, pockets of chestnut, magnolia and ash appeared. No oak trees though.

We caught occasional glimpses of the rock, but saw no signs of life. The sun was getting low in the sky when Churnyg suddenly stopped and sniffed the air.

"Oak!" he said. "Lots of them. They're near."

We pushed our way through a thicket.

"Be careful. Gynbere may have anticipated our arrival."

Churnyg shook his head. "He couldn't know about the grove. The trees would mean nothing to him. We'll be safe." He stepped forward, but was brought up short when I grabbed his hood and hauled him back.

"Assume nothing!" I hissed. "There's a saying — know

your enemy. Gynbere knows what you value. Don't ever underestimate him. He knew about the paintings and he took them away. He knew you'd aim for the bolthole. Assume he knows, because he has so far."

Churnyg scowled at me, but turned away without a word.

The noises about were those of birds and insects. We ghosted through the trees without disturbing them.

This area was thick with vegetation that had flourished, long undisturbed. Our path meandered around massive clumps of tall rhododendron and thick clumps of willow.

Little by little, Churnyg slipped ahead, and I was just about to haul him back again when a scream shattered the silence.

Instantly my sword was poised ready.

Teema and Arbreu had their bows nocked and drawn. But there was nothing to attack, seemingly nothing to defend against.

Churnyg had sunk to his knees and I realised the noise came from him. At first I thought he had been wounded, but I could see no injury and there was no movement around us, and although the tall thick undergrowth to one side was too dense to see through, it would also be hard to shoot through.

I raced towards him, and glancing up, saw the oak grove. Seven ancient trees many thousands of seasons old — every one of them felled.

Everything was silent except for Churnyg's sobs. "Why?" he moaned. "Who would do this?"

"Only Gynbere has reason to."

"But he's already killed us off."

"He hasn't! That may be his intention, but," I said, "if I have anything to do with it, he won't get the chance."

We searched for a protected place to camp and amongst the massive trunks I found something special. I called Churnyg over, pointing to the many sturdy seedlings pushing through the soil.

"The trees are growing again. They'll be here long after the memory of Gynbere has died. They live as you do. They're as hard to kill off as a whole race of people."

Once the camp was set up, I wandered through the fallen debris. The trees were truly gigantic — they towered above me even though they lay on their sides. Three trees had been chopped down, their stumps ragged and torn as they fell. The other four were pulled from the ground, the roots still partially buried.

I leaned against one, watching a small herd of deer grazing in the open meadow that spanned the area between the trees and the rock. The grass was higher here than to the south, and the dear were only just visible above it. I was about to turn away when there was a flash of light from the top of the rock. Something had caught the rays of the setting sun.

Someone up there was watching the deer, and probably watching for us.

I slipped away, keeping to the shadows and told the others what I had seen, instilling in Larqeba the importance of staying out of sight.

"It's a good thing you saw it," said Teema. "I was about to go hunting. Those deer were top of my list."

The fallen trees were great as protection. We set up a shelter in a corner created when two of them fell against each other. The trunks gave us excellent protection, and we had an easy avenue away from them should the need arise. We dug a ground oven in a corner, almost under the branches to cook meals. I wanted no smoke showing to alert those in the rock to our presence, although from something the guard had said, left me with the feeling that Gynbere would arrive sooner or later.

Teema and Arbreu hunted to the west, Larqeba, Churnyg and I had collected herbs, fruit and roots to add to the meal.

It would be a long night. I organised guards before the light faded although we ate after the sun had set. After the meal Churnyg changed the poultice on my foot. My instep was still black and bruised, and the puncture was painful to the touch. It still bled a little, but was improving. I added a tisane of healing herbs to the harkii and borkan seeds.

As everyone settled down, I sat and concentrated on Mekrar's token. It was harder than using Arbreu's connection with her, but he was asleep, and would be awake for guard duty at midnight. I didn't want to disturb him.

Will you stop overnight?

We plan not to.

There's a watcher on top of the rock. He may not be the only one. Take care you are not seen.

She nodded. *There's a lot of cloud cover, and it's dim at the edge of the trees. We'll keep hidden.*

We shared guard duty, Larqeba and Churnyg took the early shift. I joined them when the moon was two hand-widths from the horizon, helped to check the surrounding area and sent Larqeba off to bed.

With a hot drink in hand, I settled down to get some answers from Churnyg. "You said that Salcan spent the winter in The Rock."

Churnyg nodded.

"How could he do that with no one else knowing?"

He looked surprised. "Oh everyone knew. He was quite popular. Gynbere looked on him as his personal pet giant. But something happened and Gynbere ordered his death. I heard about it and warned Salcan. Then Gynbere blamed me for letting him in. Not that it made much difference. Any excuse."

"He took the skull. Why was it so important to him?"

Churnyg shook his head. "You need to ask him. All he said to me was 'It's not true. The whole story is a great lie, and I'll be back to prove it.' I wish I knew what he meant."

"Salcan said that some of those who lived in The Rock weren't human. What did he mean?"

"According to lore, some of the guards change. Evidently the perimeter guards become black birds although possibly they call the black birds to them. We're told that if you see the birds, you die, although more recently it's said that those who have disappeared became birds and flew off to be slaves in the high eyries."

Teema joined me at midnight and I told him what I'd learned.

"It doesn't make sense?" he said.

"There's too much missing," I agreed. "It's obvious Gynbere and his guards know they can leave The Rock whenever they want."

Teema nodded. "So why didn't they follow Salcan and get the skull back?"

"Possibly Gynbere didn't want it. Maybe it suited his purpose to have it gone. Once Salcan had left, he didn't want him to return. He didn't know if Salcan had friends who'd search for him. So it was better to keep him away."

"But why?" Teema was quiet for a while. "Kirym, why did Salcan stay in The Rock when he said he couldn't live with us?"

"His sickness was a danger to others and he knew it. That's why he avoided us. There were times when he was fine and maybe he felt less threatened by those in The Rock for a while."

"Why haven't you told Churnyg he's dead?"

"Salcan told me about the black birds, and he made the carving of them. Churnyg knows that. I don't want anything to confirm Gynbere's silly myths, and death after viewing the birds is a deeply entrenched belief. I'll tell Churnyg after he knows he can live out here. After I prove Gynbere to be a liar."

"Can you do that?"

"I must. If I don't, then all of those poor people will remain in there treated as slaves. If we can't get them out, we could have all sorts of trouble."

"Why didn't Salcan go back in? It sounds like he planned to."

"Perhaps the injury hit too quickly. It may be that he wanted to give Gynbere time to think he was safe, then come and get us to help sort it out."

"Would he do that? Ask Veld for help, I mean."

"Oh I think so. Salcan hated inequality, especially against those who were small or weak, but he had a special love of children. He'd be incensed at any injustice against them. That's the one thing that would encourage him to come and talk to us."

Just before dawn Mekrar's party arrived, having travelled through the night. They were met by a snarling, knife-wielding Churnyg.

The rest of us raced to intervene and introduce them to him. He begrudgingly accepted them as friends, but was totally smitten when he met Amethyst. She stared at him and gurgled, grabbed his finger, pulling it towards her mouth.

An annoyed Bryn grabbed Larqeba by his tunic and lifted him off the ground. "After I specifically said you were not to go. Do I have to thrash you before you listen to me? Do you realise how worried your Ma was?"

"Arbreu was allowed …"

"That's totally different," Bryn thundered. "We knew he was going, and he's of an age to make his own decisions. I think I'll just thrash you and get it over with." He sat on a log and laid Larqeba over his knee.

"The lad helped us," interrupted Churnyg as Bryn raised his hand. "We may not have made it without him."

"That's no excuse," barked Bryn. "He was disobedient first." He raised his hand again.

"Pa, I wandered the same way at an earlier age than he is," interrupted Arbreu.

"And look what trouble that caused. Seasons of sorrow, and you were near killed before Kirym saved you." He looked down at Larqeba, reached up to the tree and grabbed a branch. It broke off with a resounding snap.

Larqeba flinched.

Bryn threw the branch to the ground. His frustration showing on his face. "What do I do?" He looked around, shook his head and stood Larqeba up. "I'm hungry. I hope you have a good meal prepared."

Over the meal we exchanged news, learned of their journey and told them about our escape from The Rock.

"So who'll you ask to hold the shield?" asked Mekroe.

"I haven't thought about it."

Mekrar raised her eyebrow in disbelief.

"We'd all be delighted to hold it for you," said Storm.

"Yes," I said, "and it will tie you for life. That's a hard ask."

"We'd accept with our eyes open," said Jeresaya. "Ask. We'd consider it an honour. I would."

"It's a lovely offer, Jeresaya, but everyone here has commitments. You have the obligations of a husband and family. I can't ask you to take this on."

"Come on everyone, this isn't helping Kirym decide," said Mekrar. "She knows we'll help as we can. Let's extend the camp and sort out the guard list."

"I'll do it," she said when we were alone.

"You have new obligations."

She sighed. "I don't have to have them. You and I would make an awesome team."

"You and Arbreu would make a better one. I won't ask that. It wouldn't be fair on either of you."

Mekrar shook her head. "He hasn't said anything. Does he even know? Anyway I think Starshine is interested in him, so maybe it'd be easier if I did hold the shield."

"Starshine likes Arbreu only as a friend. Maybe she's using it as a smoke-screen for Storm."

"He likes you," she said.

I laughed. "I'm his little sister. He wants to protect me. No more." I paused. "Arbreu has the connection to you, and he is becoming aware of it. Just tell him. That'd save time. Or I could talk to him."

"So why not ask Storm to carry the shield?"

"It would divide his loyalties. His first duty is to Wind Runner, and Starshine will need him when she becomes matriarch. The same for Granite and Elm. Churnyg will be needed by his people, Larqeba's too young and his siblings are unknown."

"And Mekroe is our idiot brother,"

"Have you noticed? He's less of an idiot now."

Mekrar looked up enquiringly.

I laughed. "He's trying to impress Starshine. Has Storm objected?"

"I don't think he knows. I'm surprised I didn't notice."

"I'd say that's more because of Starshine than Mekroe, but it says a lot that he has respected her wishes. I doubt

Storm will have much say in it if she's made up her mind. Wind Runner may be harder to convince. She's seen him act the idiot. Anyway, if Starshine has no interest in Arbreu, it makes it easier for you. Not that her interest should stop you. It's said all is fair in affairs of the heart." I paused. "So where does that leave me with the shield?"

"There's Oak,"

"A lot may have changed since we saw him last. In many ways he's an unknown quantity. Anyway, again Starshine will need him when she becomes matriarch."

"She won't need him if she has Mek and Storm."

"That's not definite, and anyway, Oak isn't here," I said.

"You've talked yourself into a corner. You're left with Teema, and I don't know why he wasn't your first thought."

"He was, but every time I thought of asking him, something said don't and I can't figure out why." I shook the unformed thoughts away. "I really think Papa should carry the sword."

Mekrar shook her head. "You have no idea how well it suits you. Anyway you are holding it, so it's meant to be. You've got to accept that. About the shield — why don't you give Teema the choice? He needs to make some decisions about his life, and it would do him good. If he isn't instantly enthusiastic, withdraw the offer."

"I need time to think. It's more than just choosing someone. I wish I'd been able ask more questions."

Just then a warning call echoed across the clearing. Mekrar and I rushed, with everyone else, to join Arbreu and Mekroe, who had been watching the area between The Rock and the camp.

38

Kirym Speaks

About fifty black-leather-clad soldiers, surrounding a large curtained litter, approached the grove.

"It's called an ibith," said Churnyg. "Gynbere's latest mode of transport.

I grabbed my knife and the shield. "Teema, would you stand by me, please?"

Mekrar gave me a strange look as Teema moved to my right shoulder.

"Do we need weapons ready for use?" Teema asked.

I nodded. "Ready, but not obvious."

Arbreu slipped in beside Teema at my left. Mekrar and the other men ranged around us.

I slipped the willow twist off my wrist. It seemed to grow and fit my head snuggly.

We made our stand in front of a large oak stump. Jeresaya carried Amethyst, and had a firm grasp of Larqeba's tunic in the vain hope of reining him in should the need arise.

"If they used the south exit," I said, "they've made a really fast trip. I wonder if there is a door you don't know about, Churnyg."

I stepped to the front of the stump. "Why do armed soldiers from The Rock invade The Green Valley?" I called.

The porters stopped and put the ibith down. There was a flurry of movement as the soldiers grouped around and pulled the curtains aside.

Gynbere found himself at a disadvantage, the grass was higher here than his seat. "Slaslow," he barked.

A portly soldier with an officer's helm ran forward and helped Gynbere out of the ibith. With only his head visible above the grass, he stamped forward to where the grass was lower.

Once there he strode pompously up and down, his hands gripping his whip behind his back.

Eventually he cleared his throat. "I have come," he paused, "for the traitor."

"We have no traitor," I responded.

Churnyg had been standing to one side of the massive stump, but now he started to pace around it mumbling as he went.

To their credit, all of those standing with me took this in their stride. The same couldn't be said of the guards. They hooted and jeered, edging closer so as not to miss anything.

"What's he doing?" called one.

"E's trying to become a tree," laughed a second.

"Trying to make 'em grow again," yelled another.

Churnyg continued to pace and chant.

Larqeba squirmed free from Jeresaya and joined him, skipping and adding his own chant and occasional hoot to the chorus.

The guards continued to laugh and jeer, cavorting in front

of Gynbere, obscuring his view. They scattered as he slashed at them with his whip. Sobering quickly, they shuffled into a group around him.

"Churnyg is a traitor! I demand you return him!" Gynbere called. "He must answer ... for his crime!"

"What crime do you accuse him of?"

"Murder!" he screamed. "I accuse him of murder!"

"If Churnyg is guilty of murder, then he will be judged, but by a Judicial Summit of The Green Valley. You can bring your evidence to that. Who did he kill?"

Gynbere growled menacingly. "One of your own!" He paused, waiting for a reaction, disgruntled when he didn't get one. "Have you no interest ... harrumph, in whom he slaughtered?"

When it was obvious he would get no encouragement from us, he scowled. "We befriended one of your people, harrumph," he droned. "Befriended him, bestowed gifts on him and bade him rest with us over the wintertime. As spring approached, Churnyg ... of the murderous Oak family ... this evil, harrumph, this evil criminal gained the poor man's trust." He paused looking around the grove. "And he killed him!" he roared. "Killed him for the gifts we gave him ... Churnyg ... harrumph, Churnyg took his life."

He looked over, trying to ascertain my reaction.

"Is this guy for real?" asked Bryn.

"He's an idiot," said Storm softly.

"He may sound like one," I cautioned, "but he's very dangerous. Just hear him out, we need to keep this from coming to a head for as long as possible."

"Having killed him," Gynbere paused, "having killed him he dropped my friend's poor mutilated body ... he dropped him deep into a hole ... one of the chasms that lead to the centre of the land. Sadly, harrumph," he tried to look crestfallen, "sadly we could not retrieve the body, although harrumph … although we tried. Churnyg must answer … he must answer for this heinous crime. Would you harrumph, would you shield … a murderer?"

"We of The Green Valley do not condone murder, Gynbere, and we would not protect a killer. This crime against one of our people must be tried by our Judicial Committee. However, I'm trying to think who you could be talking about? I'm sure all of our people are accounted for," I said.

"The crime was committed on my land. I will try him. I demand you hand Churnyg over!" He paused dramatically. "Do you not even wonder whom he murdered?"

Gynbere waited through a long silent pause with only a discordant screech from Larqeba as Churnyg took a breath in his chant.

"You haven't even missed your man Salcan!" he screamed triumphantly.

"Gynbere, you'll be delighted to know that Salcan didn't die at Churnyg's hand. We all saw him just a few days ago. I truly appreciate your concern for my people, but as no crime was committed, we'll take Churnyg with us."

There was a sharp crack. Gynbere's whip handle had snapped in two. He angrily threw it on the ground.

In the following silence Gynbere was pale with fury. He realised he had no way of countering our claim, and because he knew Salcan had left The Rock alive. He must have feared we would produce him to thwart his claim.

"I should have killed them both when I had the chance," he screamed. But I will have Churnyg! I will destroy him as — as I destroyed those trees!" He smiled nastily. "You've had the chance to accept my offer. Now you will willingly … willingly hand him to me." There was a long pause. "Now it's a trade!" he screeched.

The guards hauled a tall cloaked hooded figure out of the

ibith. Gynbere turned the figure to face us and whipped off the cloak.

A collective intake of breath and Enliah's gasp of, "Rargo," confirmed his identity.

"Oh, Bryn, what do we do?" Jeresaya murmured.

I nudged Arbreu in the shin as he took a breath ready to make a suggestion.

Churnyg stopped his pacing and stared across the open area. "I'll go back," he said.

"No!" I grabbed his arm. "There must be another way. Let me negotiate. If I can hold him off long enough, Papa will be here and they'll be outnumbered."

"No one should die for me. Gynbere would kill the boy in front of you just to spite me. Then he'll haul someone else up and kill them, and another and another. I can't chance that. Anyway, it was going to come down to something like this. Gynbere always played dirty, even when he was a dwarfling."

I wiped away my tears and hugged him. "You are the bravest person I've ever met," I said. "Is there anything I can do?"

He shook his head. "Give me time to say goodbye."

I nodded. Teema and I watched Gynbere to ensure he didn't take the chance of our being distracted to pull some trick while Churnyg said his goodbyes.

He went first to whisper to Mekrar and then to Arbreu.

Arbreu went red. "I. Well, um." He lowered his voice. "She won't ..."

"Yes I will. Of course I'll marry you," said Mekrar. She smiled through her tears, took Arbreu's hand and kissed Churnyg on the forehead.

Churnyg handed Larqeba the lemon stone. "Hold this and you become an Oakling. My people are brave. You must be too. Obey your Ma, be loyal to Kirym and look after Amethyst."

He leaned in and whispered in Larqeba's ear.

Larqeba smiled and nodded. Churnyg seemed to be ruffling his hair, but suddenly Larqeba's head jerked up and he squealed loudly. He pushed his hair back and proudly showed off a small silver acorn in his very red earlobe.

"He's too young," gasped Jeresaya.

"Hush, Love. It's already done." Bryn put a restraining arm around her shoulder.

Churnyg went from one person to another, shaking hands with the men and being hugged and kissed by everyone else. Finally he came to stand in front of Teema and me.

"I have a message for you," I said as I took his hands in mine.

"When the dragon returns,
he will fight for your liberty.
The sound of his roar
will destroy your prison.
Heroic feats will be sung about,
your brave deeds remembered.
At the call of the dragon
your enemies will be destroyed
and your sons and daughters
will celebrate."

Churnyg wiped tears from his eyes. "How did you learn that?" He shook his head. "I haven't heard it since I sat on my grandsire's knee. I'm glad you know it. You will be the best leader this land has ever known. You have the wisdom of the great leader and the justice of his child."

An icy wind sliced through the grove. I shivered and pulled Churnyg's hood up, tying it tight. "I'll never forget you," I whispered.

"Be brave," he said. "Rescue my people. Give them the justice they deserve."

I nodded.

He turned and shook Teema's hand. "You think too much, lad. Don't!"

A cold sun rose through the thin clouds as he turned away. The field in front of us was festooned in spider webs that now glistened in the pale sunshine as the wind ruffled the grasses. Churnyg trudged through them towards the now triumphant Gynbere.

At Gynbere's nod, Rargo started his walk towards us. His head was down — I couldn't see his face — and his hands were tight behind his back.

I hoped he hadn't been mistreated. I felt guilty, I should have asked Mekrar to search for him and warn him about Gynbere's guards, but to be honest I hadn't thought of him since we arrived at The Rock. I was aware he had followed us from Salcan's cave, but every time Bryn approached him, he ran away. Jeresaya and Qwinita had tried to talk to him, but he eluded them also. I wondered how he had been eating, and had suspected that Enliah had been leaving food for him.

Churnyg and Rargo were approaching the crossover point.

Larqeba sniffed loudly. "It's not fair," he said. "They get Churnyg and we get that moron."

Jeresaya hushed him, but I knew he wasn't the only one to think that way.

The wind washed across the field making the spider webs billow and surge. The webs in front of Rargo rose to knee height and he appeared to trip over them. His arm shot out to break his fall as he overbalanced.

"Churnyg!" I screamed. "Churnyg!"

He spun around and, pierced with many arrows, fell to the ground.

A group of archers, previously hidden behind the ibith, body guards and soldiers, had risen and fired their arrows at Churnyg.

I was already racing towards him, my knife in my hand. Teema ran at my shoulder. I could hear Arbreu, Mekrar and Mekroe behind us, only just ahead of Bryn, Storm, Elm, Granite and Larqeba.

Rargo picked himself up, turned and limped back towards Gynbere.

"Rargo! Rargo! Come back!" called Enliah.

He turned to her and sneered. "I don't need your charity. Gynbere appreciates my talents."

Then seeing me charging towards him, my knife drawn, he spun around and ran.

I raced past Churnyg's motionless body, realising why the feathers in the picture of his grandsire were so wrong. They too had been arrows.

"Gynbere!" I called.

He turned, sneering. "I rule without interference from you. I will deal with my people as I wish. Do not enter my land again."

"You live in The Green Valley," I called, "and we will not have our people treated in this way."

He turned his back on me and strolled casually towards his ibith.

"The dragons will roar!" I shouted. "They will take their revenge on you! Those you persecute and kill for the love of it will rise up. You will be judged by them, and they will have their freedom!"

He stopped and turned back.

"The Rock is impenetrable. Stand outside the walls and do your worst," he sneered. "My walls will be standing when the trees have died of old age and pathetic dwellings of The Green Valley have turned to dust."

I was closer now. I reached behind me and pulled the sword from the baldric and brandished it along with the knife.

He gasped and went white. "It's a t-t-trick." He took a

deep breath. "A lie!" he screamed. "The weapons were ..." His eyes bulged. "I destroyed them! All of them!"

"You can't destroy what you cannot hold, Gynbere. They are mine, and the knife has always been mine." For the first time, I really felt the weapons truly belonged to me. "Never forget," I shouted. "The dragons will return and you'll pay the price for what you've done! We will rescue our people."

I began to walk towards him.

He lifted his robes above his knees and ran, his guards streaming after him.

His ibith was left behind, upended in the rush to leave. Attached to the back were large bundles of extra arrows. I made a mental note to come back and inspect it after we had buried Churnyg.

Teema and I returned to the crowd around Churnyg's body and knelt beside him.

The arrows were strange, made for close shooting. The black fletching was long, taking up at least half of the shaft. Shot deep into Churnyg's body, he looked like a dead bird.

"Carry him back to camp," I said. "We will bury him beside the great oak."

"Oh, I wouldn't like that," said a small voice. "Well, not yet anyway." Churnyg opened one eye.

"Yahoo-hoo," crowed Mekroe. "How ..."

"Stop!" called Churnyg. "Celebrate later. They think I'm dead. Let them keep that thought. We don't want them to return and try again. Perhaps you should carry me back. Keep up the act. They're probably watching from the walls."

He was draped across Storm's shoulder. Larqeba led the procession back to the camp. Teema and I brought up the rear.

I turned back as we reached the trees. "Hold on, Teema. I need to check on something."

The cobwebs lay thickly on the ground in the places no one had walked. They billowed in the wind, ragged around the spot Rargo had fallen. I groped down through them exploring the ground. Eventually I found and held up a thin chain with a heavy silver acorn on the end.

"I wondered why Rargo fell." I twisted the chain around my fingers, swung it in a circle and slapped it onto my palm. "Ouch!" There was a red mark where it hit.

"Where did that come from?" asked Teema.

"Let's find out." We walked towards the trees in the south.

Flattened grass in the shadow of a large tree showed where someone had stood. With no track leading away, I scanned the adjacent trees. There was nothing in three of the nearest, but solid branches of a number of trees entwined and some distance away a dark shadow clung to the trunk of an ancient ash tree.

"You can come down," I called.

The figure lowered itself gingerly, losing its hold halfway down and thumping heavily onto the ground.

We finally got a look at him — a labyrinth guard.

"How did you know where he'd be?" Teema asked.

"These are tree people. Where else would he be? Anyway, generally it's a good place to hide. Most people don't look above their eyebrows."

His guard uniform looked incongruous in the daylight. He eyed Teema warily.

I held out the chain and acorn. "It's heavier than the last one. Why?"

"That one's a weapon. It temporarily numbs what it hits. I had no other way of warning you it was a double cross. You were betrayed."

"What do you mean, betrayed?" I asked.

"The boy! He followed you into The Rock. He searched out the guards and made a deal with Gynbere. That's why Gynbere acted so quickly. He wanted Churnyg to attempt an escape. If Churnyg managed to get to the entrance hole, he was to be shot or pushed from the tree. If they managed to shoot him, they'd say the birds rejected him. If he had to be pushed, Gynbere would tell everyone he had ordered the guards to let him go, but he slipped and fell. But the guards had been told to kill you all one way or another. Somehow Churnyg figured it out and when the door remained locked, Gynbere knew his plan had failed. He knew about the bolthole, and with the tree death failing, Gynbere assumed he'd go there next. The obvious choice."

"How did Gynbere get here so fast? I'd have thought he'd take at least one day longer and possibly more," I said.

"When he lost you at the bolthole, he disappeared into one of the walled gardens. I'd forgotten about it. We all had. It had been sealed off a long time ago, something about a fault in one of the walls. I wonder now if Gynbere planned it as an escape route if there was a rebellion." He sighed. "I was too far behind him to hear what was being said, but I thought he would rest and plan his next move in the morning, so I went south to the tree."

"What about the guards there?" Teema asked.

"They were on high alert, but I managed to get past. It wasn't easy, but neither Gynbere nor Slaslow were there to give orders. I assumed Gynbere would be behind me. In fact, he was a step ahead all the way. I was still a long way away when I saw his him being lowered over the wall in his ibith. I knew then I was too late to help Churnyg. I should have told you about the boy when I saw you in the tunnel."

"If you had taken the time to do that, they'd have captured me," I said. "They nearly did. What would you have had

Churnyg do?"

"Run! I thought if he wasn't with you, Gynbere would give up. He didn't have any real argument with anyone else. Now Churnyg is dead and all of the plans are ruined." He looked terribly unhappy.

"You know Churnyg wouldn't have run away, even to save himself."

"I hoped."

"However," I said. "Not all is lost. You can take over, do what he would have done."

"The people won't follow me as they would Churnyg. He was respected. He's always opposed Gynbere and he has saved a lot of lives. They look on me with as much suspicion as Churnyg did. Maybe because he did."

"You may be surprised. However together you can do a better job than either of you could do alone."

"They won't follow me, even if I use his name."

"He's alive."

"But he can't be. He fell. I saw him."

I smiled. "You did give him that protective thing."

"He wore it?" he asked incredulously. "I didn't think he would. He's a stubborn old grouch and he doesn't trust me. He thought my becoming a guard was a betrayal of everything he fought for."

"We need to get back," Teema interrupted. "They'll be wondering where we are, Kirym. You'll join us now, won't you?"

He shook his head. "Churnyg won't welcome me and I don't want to cause more problems."

I wondered if all of the inhabitants of The Rock were as exasperating as those I'd met. "You don't have anywhere else to go. You certainly can't go back to The Rock. Now's the ideal time to make your peace with Churnyg. How can he change his mind about you if he doesn't know what your reasoning was? Right now he knows you saved his life, so that's a good place to start. We need you if we're to challenge Gynbere and free your people."

39

Kirym Speaks

Churnyg had been divested of his cloak of arrows — it lay under a tree looking like a large dead bird. The fire had been built up and when we approached, Churnyg stood and offered his hand to the guard.

"Get rid of the clown clothes before I do that again," he grumbled.

"What's your name?" asked Larqeba.

"I'm just a Labyrinth guard. We don't have any other title."

"But before you were a guard," Larqeba insisted, "you had a name then."

"It was taken away." He looked embarrassed.

"Harrumph! You didn't deserve it," growled Churnyg. "That name was given to a noble Oak, and you weren't." He scowled. "Still, maybe you've changed. So yeah, you can have one. Not the old one though and not if you look like them."

"A new beginning then. Let's start with fresh clothes," I said.

Mekrar and Jeresaya sorted through the goods we had brought with us and finally settled on Mekroe's spare sleeping robe and Dashlan's old cloak. It was the best we could do; the dwarf was shorter than all of the men except Larqeba and he had rather large feet. He was taller and slimmer than Churnyg, but obviously related.

Churnyg looked him over critically. "I can still see a shadow," he grumbled. "But all right, I'll acknowledge your nosiness helped us a little and you showed some spirit, although in that uniform you were probably just at the right place at the right time. Still we can give a nod to your maman's people. You can answer to Ashistar. When you've shown proper respect to your heritage I may give you a second name. Until then you are an Ash."

Ashistar wasn't the only one who looked bewildered.

I patted him on the shoulder. "He said you were brave and intelligent, and he has named you for those qualities."

"What gave them away, Kirym?" asked Churnyg, as we settled to a very late breakfast. "Had you not yelled, I'd never have turned. They'd have shot me, I had no chest protection."

"Rargo swung his arms to try to keep his balance."

"I don't get it," said Teema. He wasn't the only one who looked blank.

"He gave the impression when he began his walk," I explained, "that his hands were tied behind his back. For some reason that was the impression he and Gynbere wanted to give us."

Ashistar explained how Rargo had approached Gynbere

with his plan to betray us.

"If we'd realised that, we could have called Gynbere's bluff," said Mekroe.

"No," I said. "Make no mistake; Gynbere would have killed him anyway. Rargo may have gone there of his own free will, but once there, he would simply be another pawn for Gynbere to use. I doubt he'll be allowed to leave unless he is of no further use. Even then, I suspect Gynbere will find it easier to dispose of him than allow him his freedom. He'll have learned the lesson. Letting Salcan live came back to bite him." I turned to Ashistar. "When I saw you in the tunnel, you said you had other things to do before you could leave The Rock. What needed to be done?"

He looked devastated. "There were others who supported Churnyg. Their lives were getting harder, and we planned an escape. I thought this was the ideal time, but when I went to get them, they'd all disappeared."

"How were you going to get them out?" asked Churnyg.

"The bolthole initially. But Gynbere was screaming about it being blocked after you escaped, so I then planned to take them to the tree. I thought I could spin a good enough story to get them past the guards."

We hauled Gynbere's ibith into the trees to be examined. It was very heavy, much heavier than we thought it should be for what it was.

Once those on The Rock could no longer see us, we took it to pieces.

The seat was sumptuously padded and the wood used on the back and sides were intricately carved. The arms contained compartments which, when opened, revealed containers of powders, seeds and vials of potions. There was a different puzzle to each of them and fortunately the puzzles were all quite simple.

"Pah! Cheap imitations. Those with real talent refused to work for him."

"The carvings are good though," said Bryn.

Churnyg nodded. "Yes, and all of them were taken from something else. Gynbere destroyed old works of art and had the materials used to make this."

I knew a few of the seeds, but most were foreign to me. Those I knew were highly poisonous. The seat held a blade, its edge dark with poison. I wrapped it carefully, knowing I could burn the poison off, but not wanting to contaminate the fire we were using. I'd do that sometime in the future when I could light a separate fire up-wind of everyone.

The ibith as such was demolished, although we tried as much as possible to keep the intricate art intact, in the hope we could return it. Teema and I destroyed what poisons I knew and hid the items I couldn't identify. I would handle them at a later date if they continued to prove unidentifiable. I wondered if this was Gynbere's entire store or if he had more stockpiled elsewhere. I hoped he had been paranoid enough to not trust anyone, and this was all he had. However knowing he might have another supply of them meant I could not ignore Gynbere for long.

Churnyg and Ashistar added the arrows to the store we carried. Mostly the shafts were of oak.

"These were stolen about ten season cycles back," said Ashistar. "Wondered why?"

"Gynbere would have had a perverse pleasure in killing me with my own wood," said Churnyg. "If it adds to our strength and reduces his, it must be good. The odds are levelling out."

40

Kirym Speaks

We talked of future plans over our evening meal.

Ashistar was sure we were safe for the time being. "Gynbere won't antagonise The Green Valley. He has always said The Rock was the most defendable fortress in the world, so he'll feel quite safe inside. He'll lock himself in, but he'll discourage anyone who approaches. He thought Churnyg was the last of the Oak family. Thinking him dead means he'll relax."

"Until he discovers you've gone also," I said.

"He won't find out."

"Someone will know, one of the other guards perhaps. Won't they tell him?" I asked.

"Nah. Gynbere doesn't accept bad news well. He's inclined to take it out on the bearer, so no one'll put themselves or their families in danger. Anyway they know I helped Churnyg occasionally. They'll think I'm lying low because of that. It'll be ignored for a while, and then when they realise

I'm gone, they'll have left it too long to tell anyone."

It made sense.

"I don't understand why Gynbere turned on Salcan," I said, "Churnyg said he liked having him there."

Ashistar settled himself comfortably against a tree, a platter of meat and vegetables on his lap. "Oh, this food is so good. Best I've ever eaten. Um, yes Gynbere was very taken with Salcan or at least he seemed to be," he said licking his greasy fingers. "It was strange and there was a lot of whispering about it later. It was at a feast. Now nothing Gynbere does is without reason. The feasts, often at a time when food has been scarce, are put on to make Gynbere appear generous. However he and his guards control the food distribution, and not everyone is invited. Anyway Salcan was invited along with the rest of us. Not to the top table you understand, Gynbere wouldn't be that friendly in public. The size difference between them made Gynbere look ridiculous, and he wouldn't allow that again. This feast was well-attended, there was always good entertainment at Gynbere's feasts, juggling, dancing and singing, and it was one time where everyone there was sure of a good meal. Salcan sat with the dwarflings. He was there when the tumblers and jugglers performed. Everyone screamed and cheered at their latest tricks. There was a lot of jumping up and down. When they settled Salcan had gone. For such a big man he could move with amazing stealth. He was there, and then he just disappeared.

He'd been gone for a while when Gynbere suddenly jumped up and started screaming about disloyalty. Said there was a plot. He ordered the guards get everyone out of the hall and lock them in their hollows. No one really knew what was going on, not even the guards. Generally they're given an idea of who and what he suspects, normally nonsense, but they have an idea of some sort. Suddenly he was screaming about multiple plots, but before everyone was even out of the hall, he demanded the guards all search for Salcan. Ordered them to kill him. He's known for his massive rages, but this was worse than anything I'd ever seen. The guards weren't sure what they were supposed to do first, search for Salcan or empty the halls. There was a rush to leave, but in reality the return to the hollows took ages."

"Aye," said Churnyg. "I wasn't there, but a Beechling told me to find Salcan and get him out. He was popular with the dwarflings. There were a lot of patrols, but they were hindered because not everyone knew what was happening and where they were supposed to go. Those who did were rushing around looking for their families and getting them to safety.

I found Salcan in one of the carving areas. He wanted to talk to me, but someone saw him and shouted for the guard. He made a run for it. It was touch and go, but there were people who liked him or disliked Gynbere, so there was a bit of interference and he got away. Afterwards I realised he had taken the skull."

Ashistar nodded. "Initially the guards assumed he'd already left The Rock, so they didn't set sentries at the tree. That was fortunate for Salcan. Gynbere was furious. The following day he said he'd uncovered Salcan's plans to murder everyone in The Rock including him. It was a foolish statement; we all knew Salcan would never hurt the dwarflings. We might have believed it if he'd only named himself."

"Salcan spent a lot of time with the children?" Kirym asked.

Ashistar nodded. "There was always a group with him. He told them stories and showed them things from other places." He paused. "He left some of his figures in the great hall." He put his platter on the ground and pulled the uniform to him. After sorting through compartments in the massive helmet, he pulled out a large linen sack.

"I took a shortcut through the hall after everyone had been driven out. These were sitting on the table where Salcan left them. I hoped to return them to him, but he'd gone of course. Later Gynbere asked for them. He described the sack, and said it and the contents had been stolen from him. Not true though. I watched Salcan making some of them, and anyway some of them were of things no one inside had seen."

"Why didn't you hand them over," I asked.

"If Gynbere wanted them, I figured it wouldn't be good for the rest of us. Anyway it was never wise to put yourself in front of him. He's far too easy to irritate. So I wasn't about to tell him I had them. Eventually he said Salcan had been seen taking them with him."

"Why did he lie?" asked Bryn.

Churnyg shrugged. "He wouldn't like anyone to think he'd been thwarted in anything. Gynbere always had to win. I wonder why he thought these were so important."

"Kirym, Salcan gave his stuff to you, so that means these are yours too," said Larqeba. "So you can show them to us."

Laughing, I opened the sack and tipped the contents onto my lap. Some were wood, but most were made of the same material as the platters and were similar to the ornaments Salcan had let Larqeba play with.

Salcan made what he saw, dwarves — one looked like Gynbere — children, dwarflings, guards and a single bird, similar to those in the picture. He sculpted us — the people of The Green Valley, Papa and Mama, Armos sitting in a small boat, Teema holding his bow, me with large tokens. He made copies of Dragon Quest and Seeker, the boats we travelled to The Green Valley in. Everything looked very realistic.

The most significant were the trees, a number of oaks, clearly those around us. Salcan had portrayed their fallen state well, but there was also a whole standing tree and another stump, both complete with roots.

The stump was smoothed across the top, the age-rings in fine detail. I wondered where it was. When trees were chopped down, the stumps tended to be as rough as those around us. I knew about tree rings because Findlow told me, but I didn't think he ever had that conversation with Salcan.

Along with the ancient oaks, Salcan had made a number of younger trees, most similar to the nut trees growing within The Rock and they put the size of the oaks into perspective.

Ashistar picked up one of the people Salcan had made. "It's very similar to one that was in The Rock."

"We saw it by Churnyg's front door when we went there," interrupted Larqeba.

"Ah, so that's where it got to. Gynbere wanted it destroyed, but it disappeared. I guess no one who visited you told him."

"It looks like you, Kirym. Is it?" asked Ashistar.

"If he made it before he saw the statue in The Rock, then probably."

Churnyg grunted. "He had that one with him when he arrived. It's made of oak. He showed me for obvious reasons, and asked if people would object to him carving in their wood. If they were, he'd not have used wood while he was in The Rock. He was very proud of this one though."

Ashistar wiped his greasy fingers on the grass. "Best meal I've ever had," he said, belching with satisfaction.

Larqeba giggled and burped in imitation.

Bryn picked him up by his tunic and sat him between him and Jeresaya. "Stop it!" he said quietly.

Larqeba went red, but grinned with satisfaction.

"When I saw Salcan's carving," Ashistar continued, "I thought of the statue and wondered if there was a connection. No one has an explanation for ours. Occasionally someone would talk about the objects on the platter and all sorts of suggestions were made about what they were. Then Gynbere banned the talk, but that just turned it to whispers. What are those things you're holding?"

"They're tokens, similar to those we wear, but bigger. They have different meanings, too."

He nodded. "My great-grandsire carried a yellow stone. He said it was a salute to something held by an old friend."

"Churnyg's grandsire carried a yellow stone too," said Larqeba. "We found it. Did his grandsire know your great-grandsire?"

Ashistar looked embarrassed and started rearranging the carvings.

"Salcan told stories to the children," I interrupted. "Maybe Gynbere heard something he didn't like."

"They were too far apart for any conversation to have been overheard," said Ashistar. "Salcan had been gone quite a while before Gynbere exploded, and leaving the hall wasn't a problem because people came and went for all sorts of reasons. It had to be something else."

The next item I picked up was a strange little brush. It was made of animal hair, half the width of my thumb. The fibres had been tied together and glued between two pieces of wood. The wood was smoothed and inlayed with coloured triangles. The ends of the hair were dark, not the natural colour though. Near the handle they were pale, almost white.

I picked up two more items that had fallen from the bag. First glance had me thinking that Salcan had made more platters. But I quickly realised these were quite different.

Both sides were flat, but one was extensively scored. The lines were black, filled with charcoal dust, and while they were quite visible in the firelight, it all looked like so much scribble. The last item was a bag of crushed charcoal.

"Salcan told me how he had made these things," I said, "and it was a lot of work. He mixed clay to a special recipe, formed the pieces and let them dry. Then he cooked them in an oven, but it had to be for the right time — a long time — and at the right temperature."

"So you think if he had made and kept them, they had to be important," interrupted Mekrar.

I nodded as I started to sweep the charcoal out of the lines, realising why Salcan had included the brush. It wasn't easy. Some were scored a lot deeper than others. When I had cleaned charcoal from the shallowest lines, I realised what Salcan had done.

Both plaques held a number of pictures, each engraved at a different level. Isolating each layer showed what he had drawn.

The first picture — the shallowest lines — was a simple sketch of the canyon wall with the three caves. With the addition of extra lines, it evolved into Dragon Quest, our large boat, tied up at the rock path. That then became The Green Valley soon after we had finished the first three dwellings. Finally it showed the oak grove, but with younger trees as well as the ancients. With people and dwarves beside them, it showed the impressive size of the oak trees which disappeared when they were drawn by themselves.

The second plaque was simpler and was possibly Salcan's initial attempt of this craft. Its first picture was a dwarf. He became part of some standing stones, then more standing stones, but these were set among trees, and the final picture was a dragon.

Teema picked up the first plaque and stared at it. "It

doesn't make sense, Kirym. Could a picture turn Gynbere against Salcan?"

"A number of things could have influenced him, and maybe not the pictures. But Churnyg, if Gynbere thought Salcan was telling the children about the oak grove, would that explain his reaction?"

Churnyg stared at the slab and nodded slowly. "It might. He said the old stories of living in trees were lies, made up by those trying to destroy us. He said trees could never grow that big, but the men on the wall told everyone what they could see. Gynbere said it was an illusion caused by light or mist or our enemies, those who would destroy us if they learned where we lived. Eventually the stories were banned, so of course they were passed on in whispers. We organised guardians of the past to learn and remember. No one knew everything. We felt it was too much to be learned by one only and we couldn't chance the whole history disappearing with one simple death or murder. It was a mistake though. I'm sure some of them died without passing the stories on. We tried to protect those who did volunteer to learn, but knowledge is a heavy responsibility and fewer people came forward. It just took a whisper in the wrong place to sit a death sentence on someone. My people stopped trusting each other. My grandsire and great-grandsire each knew part. But they're both dead."

"I'm sure they passed it on," interjected Ashistar. "They valued our history. That devotion was fed to their children and grandchildren."

Churnyg sighed deeply. "Even if they did, it only takes one person to forget something vital, and the rest is irrelevant. Even a small piece would make a difference. I've lost my part. I was so sure I got it right, but it didn't work." He sounded so sad. "Always I let my people down."

"Oh!" Finally Ashistar looked beaten. "We need the history

to bring life back to what it was." He brightened up. "But even without it, we can still be a whole people. Perhaps your part wasn't so important."

"Could the two of you work together to remember?" I asked.

Churnyg shook his head. "My part was special. What I learned in secret could only be used in times of exceptional need and at a distinctive place. We have the place, but without the song, there is little use us being here. Even then it ..." His voice faded.

"Wait, wait, wait," said Teema. "A special place — I guess that's here in the oak grove. Why don't you start reciting? Maybe it'll come back to you."

"I did," said Churnyg sadly. "I marched around the stump and sang, but nothing happened. I must have got it wrong or maybe the trees need to be standing. My song called for help, but none came."

"But help did come," I said. "Ashistar came. Without him, you'd be dead."

Ashistar brightened, but Churnyg continued to look miserable. "It was supposed to call the dragons back. Each spring, we would call the dragons for the spring celebration. Everyone knew how to sing that, but this song was different. It told of a great need that only the dragons would be able to help with."

"Could Larqeba's involvement have altered your song?" asked Bryn.

"No," said Churnyg, smiling fondly at the little boy. "The lad's an Oak at heart, and any who desire can sing their song as we call. My great-grandsire told stories of spring nights when every person in the land gathered and joined in. There were hundreds of hundreds singing and dancing."

"Maybe you didn't sing long enough," said Larqeba. "We could do it again. It was fun."

Churnyg looked sceptical, but everyone else was enthusiastic.

"Hey, Sis," called Mekroe, a wide smile on his face. "No time like the present. Can we do it now?"

Teema was on his feet as I nodded. "We'll need light, so let's get the fire over there. There's a stone outcrop in front of the big stump. Put the fire on that."

"If the guards on the wall see a fire," I said, "will they investigate?"

Ashistar shook his head. "They do nothing without Gynbere or Slaslow's express order and Gynbere's anger at almost everything is widely known. Gynbere will be so angry, no one'll approach him about anything short of the walls falling down. And Slaslow's as bad, because if something goes wrong, he gets it from Gynbere and he'll take it out on the nearest person."

"Gynbere may have given the order to be told of anything that happens over here," said Teema.

"True," said Ashistar, "but when he left The Rock, he was in his ibith. I think he needed it to get in the same way. So he may still be on his way back to the tree entrance. Even if he was told of a fire here, he'd probably think it's a trap."

I packed Salcan's statues back into the pouch and stood, adjusting my hold on Amethyst.

"You dropped something." Ashistar leaned forward and picked it up.

He held the bird pictured on the wall of the locked hollow.

There was something in the way he looked at it.

"Ashistar, did you show Salcan the pictures of the birds?"

He nodded slowly.

"What?" Churnyg had overheard us. "So Salcan saw them in the hollow? There and not at the tree?"

Ashistar nodded again.

Churnyg frowned. "He still could have seen them as he was leaving. Others have."

"I've not found anyone who has seen them in the tree or flying around it," said Ashistar. "I've seen feathered bodies at the base. I was told they had turned into birds, but the eagles rejected them and tore their wings off. But I've never found anyone who could look me in the eye and tell me they actually saw it themselves. I have seen the guards in feather cloaks, but they always returned to The Rock. In view of what happened to you, Churnyg, I think the feathers in those bodies were actually arrows."

"So," I said, "If Gynbere saw this on the table at the feast, he may have realised where Salcan had been ..."

"Which means," interrupted Teema, "he knew the hollow was open again. He'd also realise that Salcan was in close contact with those he looked on as enemies, because no one else would have shown him what the birds looked like."

I nodded. "And may have worried that his schemes were beginning to fall apart."

"So you had free access to the hollow," accused Churnyg.

Ashistar nodded.

"Who told you how to enter?" asked Churnyg.

"My grandsire took me there." Churnyg went pale. "And he and his sire taught me the key."

"Who put the stone in the wall?" I asked.

Ashistar shook his head. "I don't know."

"Who locked the two oak cabinets? I asked.

"I did."

"Why?" demanded Churnyg.

"Because I knew you'd discover them, and find a way of getting the weapons out to safety."

"You put the weapons there?"

Ashistar shook his head. "No. I got a message telling me where they were. All I did was lock the doors."

"Why didn't you just tell me?" demanded Churnyg.

"I didn't think you'd listen."

"And I wouldn't talk to you anyway." Churnyg lowered his head. He obviously had a lot to think about.

41

Kirym Speaks

Mekroe, Larqeba, Granite, Bryn and Dashlan helped Teema haul deadfall from the surrounding area, and soon there was a large pile of wood waiting to be fired. While Arbreu carefully covered the coals of the camp fire, the rest of us moved to the large stump. Mekroe brought out his pipe and started playing softly, warming up for what was ahead.

Larqeba took the dragon statue and sat it in front of the large stump. "The dragons should know it's them we want," he declared.

I carried Amethyst over as the fire was lit. She was awake and alert, watching the sudden flurry of movement. There was an air of celebration as the fire caught and Churnyg started his march around the stump. Almost immediately he was joined by Larqeba. Mekroe picked up the tune on his pipe and slipped in behind them. The younger members of the party rushed to join them and one by one we all linked into the procession.

Churnyg's chant became a song, and we soon picked up the chorus which seemed to be a series of noises ending with a loud wolf howl. That left Churnyg, Larqeba and Ashistar to carry the rest of the melody.

The song eventually ended and we sat by the stump to rest.

Larqeba screwed up his face. "You said you didn't know the words to Churnyg's song, Ashistar. But you did. You sang it with him."

Ashistar shook his head. "I sang a song from my childhood. I'm not sure where I heard it."

"Hrumpfff!" snorted Churnyg. "He was sitting on my grandsire's knee when I was learning it. He was supposed to be asleep, but he was obviously a sneaky little troll then too."

"So you knew Ashistar when he was little," said Mekrar.

Churnyg scowled. "I took him with me occasionally when I went places," he said grumpily. "He had no friends. Dislikeable little beast."

Larqeba looked from Churnyg to Ashistar. I saw the realisation dawn.

"Churnyg's your Pa," he exclaimed smiling broadly. "That explains the yellow stone."

Jeresaya hushed him. "People are entitled to their privacy."

Churnyg went red, coughed and harrumphed for a few moments. "No Jeresaya. The lad's right. It should never have been a secret. I should have had courage enough then to stand up to people and claim him as mine. I have bravery enough to support the downtrodden masses, but it's never extended to those I was close to." He sighed deeply. "Many disapproved because his mama had different roots. She was an Ash," he said by way of explanation.

Amid a rush of comments, Ashistar glowed with pleasure.

A sudden downdraught of wind flattened the fire and rattled the branches around us. Moments later there was a huge thump, and the earth shook.

"Earthquake?" gasped Mekroe, staring wide eyed at me.

I shrugged, unsure and dropped to my knee, leaning protectively over Amethyst. This was different. The ground vibrated, not at all like the earthquake and aftershocks I remembered from The Land Between the Gorges. It was strange rather than frightening. I was reminded more of a large herd of stampeding deer. The noise seemed to come from further south.

Moments later another crash sounded, north of us, over near The Rock. There was a strange howl and I heard the distinctive sound of rock hitting rock. It petered out, just an occasional kathunk as a rock dislodged and rattled across others.

"I don't know," I said diffidently. "It sounded more like an avalanche, but what could fall? I don't think it was an earthquake."

After the initial silence, everyone started to talk.

"Quiet," I snapped. Then in a low voice, "Storm, Elm, douse the fire. Arbreu, we need a heavy guard circling the camp two hundred paces out. You and Bryn take the north to east quadrant. Starshine and Granite take north to west, Storm, Ashistar, east to south. Mekroe, Dashlan, south to west. Mekrar, Jeresaya, get everyone to safety in the camp area. Make sure that fire is well covered. I want nothing to indicate its presence. Churnyg, take care of those in camp, keep Larqeba beside you. Those not on guard, get some sleep." While I was talking, I gathered the items scattered around the stump and handed them to Jeresaya.

I clicked Amethyst's token and handed her to Mekrar. "Feed her, change her wraps. She'll sleep."

"What are you planning to do?" asked Teema.

I picked up my knife, sword and shield from where I'd left them leaning against the stump. "We are going to see what made that noise."

He grabbed his bow and quiver and followed as I ran across the open grass area towards The Rock.

I was sure the sound had come from there, but heavy cloud made visibility poor. I watched the ground carefully mainly to ensure I didn't trip on something, but also because that was all I could see.

Nearer The Rock the grass reduced a little in height. Recently fallen rocks on the ground some distance from the wall explained the noise, and as the clouds parted momentarily, we saw a gaping hole in the wall of The Rock.

"Did it happen naturally or was something done from inside?" I wondered aloud. "Teema, check to the south, see if the same thing happened there. Then get back to the others and warn them. Gynbere could be attempting something, and we need to be prepared. Get everything not actually being used ready to take should we need to leave in a hurry. I'll meet you back there."

Teema disappeared and I stood still, listening. There was no sound of anyone climbing over the rocks. So far as I could tell, nothing was coming through the wall, but that didn't mean they weren't planning to.

Time passed and no new noises came to me. I turned away, but as I got clear of the debris, something large streaked past me.

After a moment's hesitation, I followed.

It moved fast, but slowed when it reached the edge of the open area. That allowed me to get closer. In the dark of the trees, I lost it. There was an animal track of sorts, I followed that.

"Nnngg! Nnngg!"

I headed towards the sound.

The noises stopped, but something was breathing heavily, gasping for breath. Whatever it was, it was hiding in the bushes ahead.

"Why are you chasing me?" it asked crossly.

"Because you were running away."

"Oh!" He, it was male, paused. "Well I'm not now so you can go away."

Again the clouds parted and something on the grass shone. I touched it and rubbed it between my finger and thumb, catching the tinny smell of blood.

"You're hurt. Can I help?"

"I'm not hurt! Go away!"

"If you're not hurt, why are you bleeding all over the grass?

He sighed deeply. "If you must know I've got a splinter in my foot. I can't pull it out."

"Perhaps I can." I stared into the trees, trying to see who I was talking to.

"Phit! Puny human. If I can't, you won't be able to."

"I'd like to try."

"Nnnnngg." A large scaly foot edged out of the shadow, but it was difficult to see much more in the dark.

"It'll be easier to see with a fire, I'll collect some wood," I said.

"Be patient. The clouds are about to disperse and enough of the moon will shine for you to see."

"I'm Kirym. What do I call you?"

"You don't!" he snapped. He paused. "So what's a Kirym?"

"It's my name. I come from The Green Valley. We're trying

to ..."

"People from The Green Valley are travelling the land again?"

"You sound surprised."

"You went away. Everyone did and I didn't know where you were, or how to get you all back. I thought I heard the call, but everyone said I was dreaming."

"You heard the song? Churnyg and Ashistar will be delighted."

He brought his head down out of the shadows, the clouds parted and I got a good look at him.

A dragon!

42

Kirym Speaks

He looked similar to the hanging in The Rock although he had four horns, while that swinging in the gallery had none. This dragon didn't seem to be the creamy colour of that one. His scales were pale with a tracery of dark around each of them. However the moonlight distorted the colour.

I reached up and rubbed his nose. He shook his head a little and then settled down again. Blood dripped from his lip.

"Oh, you've cut your lip too."

"I tried to bite the splinter out," he pouted. "It's very sharp."

The splinter was a shard of rock, long and thin, the edges were like razors. It had stabbed deep into the top of his foot.

I picked some long wide leaves and wrapped them around the shard, and then draped part of my cloak around that and pulled. For a brief moment it didn't move, and then it came so quickly I almost fell over. Blood gushed from the wound.

I quickly cut the hood off my cloak and pressed it onto the wound. Holding it firmly with my knee, I opened my herb pouch and chose some herbs to inhibit the bleeding.

"Why didn't you come sooner?" I asked as I sprinkled them on.

"Sooner?" he huffed. "I came when I heard the call. Soon enough!" He paused. "Oh all right, I got lost," he said crossly. "It was more a whisper than a call. I couldn't get a bearing on it. I'm not old enough to follow the sound. Hunng!" He winced as I pressed the wound. "But no one else would come, so I had to. The call started again, but it stopped as I zeroed in. I was tired. I flew a long long way all by myself. I landed on a big rock to rest, but it fell over. I flew towards another rock and it attacked me. That's when I got the splinter." He sounded terribly young and rather petulant.

I ripped my petticoat into strips and wrapped the pad of my hood onto his foot finishing it with a bow. He held it up, looked at it and nodded approval.

While I told him how Churnyg and Ashistar called him, I rubbed his nose again. He seemed to like that. I shivered, the wind cut through me. I explained why the song finished prematurely when Churnyg first started it.

He closed his eyes and appeared to be thinking. "I don't understand what's happening here. Things are different. Nothing makes sense. My memories seem wrong. I heard the call. I shouldn't have, I'm too young. Egrym thought it was just an echo in time. He may not believe me even when I tell him. I have to let Iryndal know though. Even that may not be enough to move any of them into action. However I will urge them to consider a return to the land. They'll make a decision to come and see — or not. I don't understand what lives in The Rock. It was never there before, however, it seems I might have let it out. Because I created that path, I will warn you of things you need to be aware of." He paused, frowning. "To the northwest are fires. A great army is heading this way. They are getting close."

"What are their intentions?" I asked.

"I can't read their hearts. Make a judgement call. If you are wrong, people could die, so get it right." He took a deep breath. "Don't assume evil in everything that approaches, but be prepared. I know something happened in the desert." He frowned and then shook his head. "I don't understand. It's all so different now. Protect yourself and tread carefully. The closest danger is The Rock, but not everything there is malevolent. You decide what is good and what is bad."

"You're not responsible for Gynbere, Dragon. He was able to leave The Rock before you came here, and he has many times over the seasons."

His eye's narrowed. "Harrumph! You could have told me before. I didn't have to tell you anything. Faltryn was right. Everyone is devious."

I stiffened at the mention of Faltryn, but the dragon didn't notice.

"You warned me of danger because you have a noble spirit, Dragon. If lives can be saved because of this, many will sing your praises over their home fires."

He looked pleased.

"Now what other dangers are there?"

"Faltryn! He's angry. He said we were deceived and betrayed. He said he'll never forget and he'll never forgive. He's not of a mind to be cooperative. He's not inclined to be overly familiar with you people."

"What made him so angry?"

The dragon was quiet for a short time, obviously thinking. "I really don't know, Kirym. He won't talk about it. But it isn't wise to cross him, and I think that might be what we are doing here. He'll be angry when he finds out, but then he's always angry."

"There are stories, Dragon, and none of them add up. It seems to me that people need to know what happened. Then they should be allowed to make their own decisions. There are many problems needing to be sorted out, and Faltryn avoiding them isn't helping."

"Ah, you've heard a story," he said sarcastically. "Is it true or not? That seems to be irrelevant to you."

"We still need to understand what happened. Would he return to make things right?"

"Faltryn? Harrumph!" he snorted. "Probably not! But who said his decisions were wrong, anyway? Dragons are deep thinkers. It's easy to hear a story and be wise, Kirym. And things look different in hindsight."

"I agree, Dragon, but why was Faltryn the one to make all of the decisions? If everyone knew the truth then, there may not be the problems there are today."

The dragon growled in the back of his throat. "Stop calling me Dragon. My name is Borasyn. The people of The Green Valley are still opinionated, I see. Arguing this with me is a waste of time. We can't change the past."

"No, but the mistakes of the past shouldn't be repeated. Everyone needs to be responsible for their actions, even Faltryn."

"Hinck, hinck, hinck." It was a while before I realised he was laughing. "Faltryn may meet his match in you, if he decides to come here. Now, I must depart." He brought his damaged foot to his heart. "I will return. I want to see if you are as wise in action as you think Faltryn should be."

He struggled to his feet and stretched his wings.

"One more thing, Borasyn. The large tokens are now together. The prophesies are coming true. Faltryn needs to know that things will happen whether he's here or not. With the wall down, the people of The Rock will flood into the land to enjoy their freedom."

He frowned. "I don't understand about the rock or tokens, but I think things have changed. It seems I have to trust you to do what's right. I hope my trust is not in vain."

"The tribes are gathering. Those needing homes will be welcomed to The Green Valley."

"This Gynbere tried to kill you. Will you offer him a home too?"

"What he has done to his people is worse than anything he did to me, and he'll answer to them. But as I said before, the stories don't add up. People act on what they know, but if what they know is untrue, then everything'll go wrong. I have the skull Faltryn gave to the people of The Rock. The story he gave with it is a lie."

He stared at me, and I realised he had no idea what I was talking about.

"Just tell Faltryn," I said.

Dawn revealed the gaping holes in the wall. The rocks were jumbled in untidy piles and scattered across the grass. In the strengthening light the southern gap became clearer. Now we could see a low wall with a line of men looking over it. Many more crowded in behind them. They stood silently staring at the trees around our camp, where we hid in the shadows.

"Shall we invite them to join us?" asked Mekroe.

"Not just yet," I said, "and do stay out of sight for now."

"Why? I mean, we can tell them that Churnyg is here, and they can come and —" said Dashlan.

"Kirym's right," interrupted Ashistar. "We don't know why they're there. We don't know who they are, nor who is leading them. Anyway chances are they wouldn't climb over the wall."

"But ... but," stuttered Dashlan, "if they think they can be free, they may want to join us. Gynbere's a monster, isn't he? Why would they want to stay with him?"

"He hasn't attacked every family. Those not in fear have no reason to want change. To many he provides food and clothing, their great protector. In their eyes he's kept them safe for a long time," said Churnyg.

"He's kept them locked up," said Mekroe. "Not quite the same."

"It depends on your point of view. Most of them think living out here is a death sentence. Remember, we know more than they do," I said.

Churnyg pulled Larqeba back into the trees as the sky lightened further. "Until recently, even I thought we couldn't survive out here. I was amazed to waken this morning and find myself alive."

"There's something wrong, Kirym," said Teema quietly. "When I checked the gap last night, the centre of it was clear. I walked right into The Rock."

I frowned. "And yet now it seems the wall is intact to about head height. Can they build that quickly, Churnyg?"

"No they can't. But if there's a discrepancy of any sort, then Gynbere will be behind it."

"So we must take care."

"To my mind there's too many o' them to be Oak supporters," said Ashistar.

The sun rose further and bathed the trees in light. We retreated back into the dappled shadows and I checked that nothing we wore would show up. The soft wind ruffled the tree line and helped camouflage our movement.

Starshine and Jeresaya took Amethyst back to camp to feed and change her. When they returned, they handed out the last of the fruit and I passed around my flask.

"Yesterday's fruit and cold water for breakfast," moaned

Enliah. "We have a perfectly good loaf under the embers. Why can't we pull it out and eat it?"

"Because we could smell it," explained Qwinita.

"So? We've smelled it before."

"With the wind blowing towards them, they would too," I said. "That would give our presence away."

"It might encourage them to join us. Don't we want them out here?" said Enliah.

I took her hand. "You're generous in wanting to share your meal with them, but we must remain invisible until we know who they are and what their intentions are. So we leave the fire covered as it is, and make our decisions when we know more."

"Aye, Kirym is right," said Bryn. "This is an unknown situation. But if they're friendly when they do come out, you can help feed them all."

Dashlan laughed quietly. "Oh she will love doing that."

I nudged his shin, and he grinned down at me.

"Could they be building the wall up again, Churnyg?" I asked.

"No," said Churnyg. "To move rocks that big would take an army. They'd need pulleys, ropes, overseers. Well actually, they wouldn't need overseers, but they'd get them, more than required. It's noisy demanding work. They're not workers. They're not even moving around." He shook his head. "I have a strange feeling about this."

For half the morning those in The Rock remained still and quiet, staring at the trees. It was quite unnerving. Then the centre rocks suddenly disappeared and a large box holding a seat was carried out and placed on the ground. Presently a black-clad figure climbed onto it and the box was lifted to shoulder height. A thin cry echoed across open area.

"Gynbere," snarled Churnyg.

"And soldiers," I gasped. "Move!"

With a roar, the mob raised their fists. Suddenly the grey rock changed to a sea of black-clad men carrying spears, swords and pikes. The line of men surged forward. They poured out into the open area, surrounding the seated figure.

"Teema, Storm, take the frames," I called. "Elm, Bryn, help them. Go west. Don't get caught. The rest of you, get up the big chestnut by the magnolia. If we all run, we could be captured."

"You're right," said Teema. He grabbed his cloak and Ashistar's guard uniform and threw them on the frame. The four men picked up the frames and disappeared quickly.

Dashlan and Granite pulled half dead branches across the gouges in the grass, camouflaging the flattened ground where the frames had sat.

At the nearest chestnut tree, Jeresaya was pushing a complaining Larqeba up the trunk after his sisters. Ashistar virtually ran up the tree trunk, grabbed Larqeba's arm as he went past and took him with him. Starshine followed them, carrying Amethyst.

I glanced around the area we had used. The rest of Gynbere's deconstructed ibith was stacked on the far side of the clearing. The poisons had been destroyed or buried, but I could do nothing about the rest.

Churnyg's arrow-pierced cloak and protector lay under a nearby tree. I grabbed them. With no blood on them, it was something I didn't want Gynbere to see.

I saw nothing else that might give away our presence here, other than some flattened grass and the blackened residue of two fires.

The charred branches of the large fire near the big stump still smoked. The smaller camp fire nestled in the sharp angle where two felled trees met. There was a pile of wood in front of it, but the fire itself had not been stoked since before midnight. If uncovered it would still glow beneath the ash and soil I had covered it with during the night. I was relieved we hadn't added fuel as we usually did each morning. It might remain undiscovered if they didn't search the area too closely.

Skirting a fallen tree I threw Churnyg's cloak and protector up to Qwinita.

"Hang it over a branch," I said as I leapt up to grab a branch. Churnyg had waited for me. He pushed me higher to be out of sight before the first of Gynbere's men arrived.

I could hear the soldier's approaching, still screaming their attack cry, the sound muffled by the surrounding undergrowth. It was impossible to tell how close they were.

Churnyg followed me up the tree. He had the ability to almost walk up the trunks. He swung from branch to branch with ease. Ashistar was also in his element now he was no longer hampered by his guard uniform.

I grabbed a higher branch to get into the leaf cover. It broke as it took my weight, and I lunged for another, grasping it with my finger-tips. A twig caught my dress and it ripped from the waist down.

"I've got you," grunted Churnyg, grabbing my arm.

I tried to get a better grip on the branch, but my fingers were slipping. Churnyg grunted as his grip, too, began to fail. He swung down and pushed his shoulder under me to take my weight, but the branch he held on to was too big for him to hold properly.

Another hand grabbed my arm. I hooked my foot onto a solid branch and pulled myself up. "Higher," Ashistar grunted, dragging me into the thick leaf cover. I stepped onto a branch, but my foot rolled off it. Someone grabbed my foot, and then I was safe. Something thumped to the ground below the tree.

"Where's Churnyg?" I gasped.

"Where'd you expect me to be?" he muttered from the branch below me. "It was just a dead branch." He climbed to a comfortable perch above me.

Qwinita tossed me a new green cloak. "Thank you," I mouthed, relieved at her forethought. The cloak I'd worn since leaving the settlement, while still usable would not have hid me nearly as well as this did. I wrapped it around my shoulders and pulled on the hood. Everyone else had done the same. Starshine had reversed hers, the dark lining hiding the bright yellow material. Everyone had taken care to cover colourful clothes.

The first soldiers entered the clearing at a run, still screaming their attack cry.

As I fingered the damage to my dress, deciding it could perhaps be stitched again, but only by someone with more skill than I, my pocket slipped from its place around my waist. I grabbed it. The ties were broken, probably when the branch ripped my dress. Something on the ground caught my eye. I glanced down. Two large tokens, the green and yellow, lay under the tree.

Churnyg gasped. He'd spotted them too. "I'll get those."

I grabbed his arm. "Leave them. You'll be seen."

"But ..."

"Tokens look after themselves. Shhhh!" I clutched the token-pocket tight and willed my body to be still, my breathing soft and controlled as more soldiers and guards charged into the clearing, their swords drawn.

43

Kirym Speaks

As one, the guards and soldiers stormed across the open area. The line broke up as they ran into obstacles of fallen trees, stumps and bushes. They were quite unruly, there was a lot of unnecessary shouting.

As the obstacles stopped the front-runners, more men piled in behind and the early arrivals were pushed hard against the barriers. It quickly turned into a skirmish. Waves of soldiers rushed in. By the time new arrivals could be convinced to move away, quite a few sported wounds, some quite serious.

As we weren't in any immediate danger of being discovered, I risked a quick check of the rest of the tokens. They were safe. The pocket would need to be replaced. I tied the frayed ends together as best I could.

The last of the soldiers and guards were now in the clearing. The men following them were not in uniform. Most of these were without weapons, but pulled or carried large baskets. Trailing behind were women and children, most carrying packs of one sort or another. The Rock was being evacuated.

Small groups of soldiers hacked their way through the overgrown areas around the fallen trees. Some pulled the smoking remains of the big fire apart, throwing the wood aside and kicking the ash away from the rock base. Others were doing the same with the stacked remains of the ibith. One soldier raised an axe to split one of the panels.

"Stop that!" An old man advanced towards them. "Just stop it. It's obvious there's no one hiding inside the wood. You're desecrating works of art."

"Gynbere said to destroy everything they left …" interrupted a soldier, who wore a plume on his helmet.

"You know they didn't own them, Gawryn. They belong to Imolay Beech and …"

"Shut him up," yelled Gynbere from his new ibith, as he was carried into the clearing, still surrounded by his bodyguards.

The crowd around the old man thinned noticeably, as a guard approached, his sword raised. A younger man stepped in front of the guard. "Forlgen is right. There is no reason to destroy the artefacts. Why should he be arrested?"

Some of the crowd moved closer, their comments rising in volume.

"Get out of my sight! Both of you!"

Forlgen and his saviour melted into the crowd.

"Slaslow! Where are they?" asked Gynbere.

"Ahhh, they're not here, Sire. They must have left in the night when they realised your power had surpassed theirs."

"And the body?"

"It seems they took it with them."

"I want it," Gynbere raged. "Where'd they go?"

"They left no signs, Sire. They've just disappeared."

"Find them!" Gynbere screamed.

The soldiers milled around not having been given any direct orders, but the people of The Rock spread out and stared up at the fallen trunks of the great oaks. There were many conversations, a few getting louder until "Who destroyed the trees? When ..."

"Our enemies," bellowed Gynbere, swinging around to face the questioner. "I have kept you safe for hundreds of seasons." He paused and drew a deep breath. "But in trying to break the confines of the prison they built around us —" he intoned, returning to his usual mode of speech, "— and contain them as they grew in strength and tried to kill you all, I was unable," he shook his head with dramatic remorse, "... to continue to extend my protection ... to this group of trees as I have for many many seasons. Sadly ... and I am in tears at this destruction ... they were able to devise their evil plans over the last few days ... while I concentrated on destroying the walls to facilitate your freedom. This is a warning from our enemies, and they will do the same thing to us if we let them. We must destroy them ... before they destroy us. So let's find them ... and kill them!" His final words were drowned in a roar of approval from the guards. Most of the people were silent.

"It would have taken many men to destroy the trees, and yet the guards who saw them over the past few days say there were fewer than ten people here. They could not have done this," said the man who had argued for Forlgen. "I looked over the wall during winter, and the trees were down then."

A wave of murmured comments erupted as the crowd debated this.

"They used magic to blind the eyes of you who looked from the walls," screamed Gynbere, "and they will use it against you next. They were destroying the trees while the giant Salcan was trying to kill you all in our own home. Without my power, you would now be corpses in that cold mausoleum." He waved expansively towards The Rock. "I thwarted him, and I will do the same to them." He turned his back on them and gestured angrily to his advisors.

There was a lot of muttering.

Gynbere chose to ignore it.

Most of the packs and containers being carried were placed at the edge of the meadow, and the men, women and children wandered around the felled trees, staring at the destruction. One small boy skirted the nearest fallen tree and stared up at the huge exposed root system.

A cascade of flowers tumbled down the drying roots. He jumped to grab some, pulling the trailing vine towards him. With a handful of blooms, he scrambled over the debris towards the trees we were in.

Churnyg drew a sharp breath as the boy pounced on the tokens. He slipped them into his pocket, turned away and climbed back towards the clearing.

"I know him," murmured Churnyg, breathing again. "Shormel Willow. He'll return them when I ask."

Suddenly Slaslow slipped out from behind a thick branch and stamped down beside Shormel. "Whatcha got there, boy?" he demanded.

"N-nothing, s-s-sir."

Slaslow grabbed him by his tunic and slapped him around his ear. "Then ya won't miss it, will ya?" He stared into his face. "Willow spawn! I might ha' known it. Unless you want to be an orphan by midnight, you'll hand it over." He snatched Shormel's pocket from his waist, dropping the boy as he did so. The contents scattered across the ground as he tore the flimsy material apart. He pounced on the yellow token, rubbed it on his trousers, and pushed it into his padded jerkin. "Lousy little thief," he snarled. "Ya find my stuff, ya return it. Anything like this, it's mine." He lifted Shormel off the ground by the front of his tunic. "If ya breathe one word o' this to anyone, you'll find yourself minus a family." He dropped him on the ground again, and stamped away.

"That makes it a bit harder," mumbled Churnyg. "Still, we know where both tokens are."

"Where's Larqeba?" Jeresaya gasped.

My eyes searched through the branches of the tree, then Ashistar nudged me and pointed.

Shormel was being helped to his feet by another lad.

Larqeba was wearing the cloak Churnyg had given him just before we made our dash for the bolthole. He had pulled the hood up, hiding his blond hair. His sun-browned face was streaked with mud, which also dulled the few stray curls that escaped the confines of the hood. With a glance at the retreating Slaslow, he helped Shormel to gather his dropped property, including the green token, and pushed it all into his own kerchief. He tied the four corners together and handed it to Shormel.

"Keep it hidden," Larqeba said, nodding approval as Shormel stuffed it into his tunic. He put his arm around Shormel's shoulder and together they walked towards the milling crowd.

Just before he disappeared, Larqeba glanced back at us with a big smile and raised his thumb.

Jeresaya had moved from where she had been sitting down to a branch beside me. "I have to go and bring him back."

Ashistar swung down from his branch, grabbed her shoulder and pushed her firmly against the trunk. "If you get captured, and you will," he said in a low voice, "they'll kill you both. Then they'll look for the rest of us, and they'll find us. If the lad's found, they'll let him be. Even Gynbere wouldn't get away with hurting a child, no matter who he is. He's a bright lad, clever enough to have a good story if discovered."

"Aye, he'll be protected," said Churnyg as the soldiers below rounded everyone up.

We watched Gynbere climb aboard his make-shift ibith and his guards closed in around him. They lifted him to shoulder height and moved off.

The soldiers herded everyone else over to pick up the packs and they followed along behind them.

A few men picked up the carved wood panels.

"He didn't even let them eat," Churnyg said in disgust. He stood and swung down to a lower branch.

"Wait!" I hissed. "They could have left a guard."

Ashistar grunted softly and nodded. "I would have. How long should we wait?"

"Until it feels right," I murmured. I settled back against the trunk, grabbed Jeresaya's hand and held tight.

"I know you're right," she said softly, her eyes drifting in the direction of the departing crowd.

Amethyst was restless and her wrappings were damp. She had slept for most of our wait, but now she was hungry and she realised my finger was not the meal she wanted. Even jiggling her and tickling her tummy no longer worked.

"I have some harkii," whispered Starshine, "But my water flask is with Teema."

Churnyg mumbled something, and groped in his robe, handing me a small bladder. "Not much," he murmured, "but it may suffice for now. Will she drink it cold?"

"I think so. Well some at least, and until we get down from here, it's all we have," I said.

Already Starshine had begun to grind the nut to a paste,

and Jeresaya helped dribble the water in. The cloth I used to sieve Amethyst's mixture had also gone with Teema, and I hoped she would manage without choking. She was still so young, and not ready for anything even remotely solid.

She took a breath to remind us of her needs, and I quickly grabbed the hem of my dress and ripped off a square. It's never going to be repaired now, I thought with some regret, remembering the work that had gone in to making it. I hoped the sound of the material ripping hadn't been too loud. I swiftly dragged it through the mixture and placed the end in her mouth. She sucked at it greedily.

It worked, although being hungry she made more noise than I liked.

A nearby bird began to sing, drowning the sounds a little. I glanced up thankfully, and realised the song came from Churnyg.

Red in the face, he rolled his eyes, but carried on. Soon real birds fluttered around the trees and joined him.

The sun moved towards the west and still we waited.

"I'm hungry," Enliah whispered loudly.

Churnyg glared at her, Jeresaya looked panicked.

The birds flew away, and Churnyg again began his birdsong, enticing them back and settling them down once more.

Just as I was about to accept that there was no one below, there was a movement in the clearing.

"Gunyon! You there?" A fallen branch was pushed aside and a guard stepped into view. "Gunyon! Where are ya, man? Come on, let's get going. This place is creepy. There's all sorts o' weird sounds around."

Another guard crawled out from under a branch of a fallen oak. "It's too soon. Slaslow said we were to wait until dark.

What if the sounds are …" He paused. "I dunno, what are we watching for?"

The first guard rolled his eyes. "There's been birds singing. I once heard Churnyg say birds only sing when there's no danger."

"You listen to him? He's a rebel."

"He may be a rebel, but he knows things. Even Slaslow quoted him a few times. Anyway, what's wrong with that if he's right? Listen, the birds stopped when we came out. I think it's 'cause they're scared of us. Anyway if anyone was here, they'da showed their-selves by now and besides, the birds wouldn' have been singing. There ain't nowhere here to hide. You think we didn' look when we first come 'ere? We been all over here, first thing we done. Slaslow's a bully. Probably laughing fit ta bust at us sittin' here for nothin'. If we wait any longer, we'll never catch up with them, an' it'll be night time. We'll lose 'em in the dark and we'll get eaten by a monster or something."

"There are no monsters. That's just a stupid story."

"Ya think so? I 'ad to take a message up to one of the top guards an' I heard something roaring an' screaming down here. Even the guard was scared. Said ya wouldn' catch him on the ground by his-self for all o' Gynbere's jewels. Only thing keeping him on the wall was Slaslow. Threatened to throw him an' 'is family off the top if 'e caught him slacking. Mind you, Slaslow didn' hang around up there. Anyway I'm going. You can come or not. Up ta you." He turned away.

"I dunno. What if he catches us? He'll kill us," said Gunyon.

"How's he gonna find out? If something attacks us he won't be back ta save us. He won't even remember we're here unless we remind him. Then 'e'll be angry cause we din' find nuffin. Anyway, I'm goin'. When I catch up, I'm gonna lie low for a few days. Then Slaslow will've forgotten about me. They have a special destination. Only Gynbere knows where. If we're left behind," he shrugged. "Well, I ain't gonna be." He started to walk away.

"Wait up!" called Gunyon, glancing around fearfully. "If we turn up too soon and Slaslow finds out …"

"He won't. We'll follow 'em, and stay out o' sight 'till just after dark."

"Yeah all right. We'll go together. Wait!" he called. "Wait for me."

"You reckon that's it?" Dashlan asked quietly.

I paused a while longer, and then stood, stretched and nodded. "We go carefully, weapons ready. We climb down on the far side of the tree.

"Wait!" said Churnyg. "Ashistar and I'll go first. Keep your bows handy. Dashlan, you and Granite come next, but wait until we're in the middle of the clearing before you make a move."

Our staged descent took time, but before long, we were all grouped in the middle of the clearing.

"What now?" asked Granite.

"A meal and I'll find out when Teema can return."

Jeresaya wandered over to where our buried camp fire had remained undiscovered. With Granite's help, she raked away the top soil and ash, and pulled out the loaf we had put in to cook overnight.

I sat back and thought of Teema. *Were you followed?*

No, and we didn't go too far. Are you safe?

All's well. When will you get back?

We'll come now. Be there before dark.

"They all right?" asked Mekroe, handing me a piece of loaf.

I nodded and took a bite, relishing the tender meat and berries and the crisp crust. I continued as I chewed. "They weren't followed. Be back soon. Thing is, do we stay here, or move elsewhere for the night?"

"Will Gynbere return?" asked Jeresaya, handing me a hot drink. "Do you think we should leave in case he does?"

I shrugged. "He has no need to. He was savouring the myth of destroying the walls, and leading his people to freedom. His story has changed. Previously he said he built the walls to protect them. Now he's torn down walls built up by an enemy."

"None of that's in our history. Gynbere thinks the people are stupid, that they won't realise he has changed his story. But they do and they will distrust him more and more," said Churnyg.

I paused, thinking. "Churnyg, Ashistar, what was the special place the guard was talking about?

"There was a whisper of somewhere up north I think. Something to do with secrets and power," said Ashistar. "A throne too I think. I only heard it on the last day. Slaslow was talking to someone in another room, it got a bit loud and excited. At the time I thought they were trying to trap someone. If it was said back to them by the right person, Slaslow would accuse them of spreading treason. I don't know if Gynbere knew what was being said though, because it seemed to come from Slaslow."

Granite leaned forward. "What do you mean? You said Gynbere's in charge. He must have known."

Churnyg shook his head. "Slaslow is the fist behind the power. When Gynbere says do it, Slaslow finds a way and his way is generally a lot more violent than necessary. Of course he blames others if something backfires, but Slaslow is a toadying little snot. Now, you saw him earlier, openly taking goodies for himself. He's changed. I guarantee Gynbere won't even see the token he just stole, and yet before this, Slaslow would've taken it straight to him, and strutted around basking in glory. There was a whisper that he'd slyly picked up a few things left lying around Gynbere's hollow. Now he's collecting openly."

"Before when there were whispers, they were shut down fairly quickly," said Ashistar. "Lately, it's been different."

"How?" asked Granite.

"Guards never walked away when they heard those sorts of whispers. Lately they seem to have been actively encouraging them."

"And the guards belong to Slaslow," said Ashistar.

"So is he trying to take everything? The power and wealth. How far would he go to get it?" asked Starshine.

"And who would be the more dangerous opponent?" I said quietly. "Still, Gynbere was taking the credit for getting them out of The Rock, so at the moment, he's in charge, and he's going north. So we'll stay here for now."

"Kirym." Ashistar looked troubled. "Before when tokens were mentioned, Slaslow pooh-poohed the stories. Gynbere took them more seriously. I don't think Slaslow has any idea what tokens really are, well I haven't either. But the point is, watching Slaslow when he found the token, well he didn't recognise it for what it was. When Gynbere caught a glimpse of a drawing of the girl holding them, well he went nuts. Ripped the picture up. Demanded to know what the dwarfling had seen. Her uncle said it was a bad drawing of her sister holding a platter of bread. Gynbere let it go, but had them watched for a long time." He frowned. "Well it may mean something or not. But," he shrugged.

44

Kirym Speaks

The fire was revived. I resolved to keep it small, for cooking and heating water for drinking and washing only. Granite and Ashistar followed the trail left by Gynbere and his men, and reported back that they had gone slowly north, but kept going and seemed unlikely to return.

"No subtlety about their trail," reported Granite. "It looks like a migration of sqilute has gone through."

"Messier though, evidently," said Ashistar.

"What are sqilute?" asked Dashlan.

"Um, large animals," said Mekroe. "Mainly brown, long necks, bad tempered, smelly breath."

"Sweet, fluffy, gentle animals, who object to being harassed by nasty little boys. Mekroe had an argument with one," Starshine explained. "He didn't win."

"There's been a change too, Kirym," interrupted Granite. "The soldiers are up just behind the guards, the people are behind them. No rear guard, nothing."

"What's happened to Gunyon and his mate?" asked Mekroe.

Granite laughed. "They're very close behind. If anyone looked back they'd see them."

"When they do?"

"The guards and soldiers can't because the people are in the way. I doubt Slaslow will remember the task he gave them, even if he sees them," said Ashistar.

"To him, all soldiers are faceless," said Churnyg.

Teema, Storm and Bryn returned just as the sun touched the horizon.

"How's Elm?" asked Teema as he dropped beside the fire, and accepted a hot drink.

I tensed. "What do you mean? He was with you."

"Was," said Bryn. "Fell and hurt his leg. Couldn't put any weight on it, so we helped him hide and said we'd return for him. He said he'd try to walk back slowly, if he could. He was gone when we went back, so I assumed he'd started. He's had more than enough time to get here."

"Did you trail him as you returned?" asked Mekroe.

"Of course. He was on-track, limping, but moving well," said Teema.

"Explain the trip from the beginning please, Teema" I said.

"From here we went to the far side of the trees and then south to get around a low hill. Then we followed a dry watercourse east. That was good, left no trail. It fed into a south flowing stream and we took to the water. We went north until we came to a scrubby thicket and west again until we were sure no one was following. Coming back, we went to where we left Elm and tracked him to the thicket.

I assumed he'd reverse the outward journey and when we didn't see his tracks, figured he'd taken to the water again. We didn't expect to see any sign of him on the stones."

"We came down the far bank of the stream, didn't see the point of getting our feet wet again," said Bryn. "We crossed where it was shallow." He frowned. "I didn't really look for Elm's trail, but I'm sure I would've seen if he'd left the stream earlier than I expected."

"Could he have accidently turned upstream instead of down?" Qwinita asked.

"He wouldn't make that mistake," said Granite. "He's a river-man."

"What if he missed the place you entered the stream at this end?" asked Dashlan.

"The dry watercourse was lined with big flat stones," said Storm. "They were distinctive, like an arrow pointing out the direction to take. Elm actually commented on it as we stepped into the stream. Said it was a good way of remembering where to start east again when we returned. It was one of the most obvious points on the bank and it was quite visible."

"We crossed over when we were opposite it. It was one area where we didn't leave any tracks, and we followed it until we saw the hill, and then came around the west side of it. No sign of him leaving the track at any stage," said Bryn.

"But also no sign he actually followed it?" I asked.

Storm shook his head. "Elm's a bit of a stickler for rules. So I expected him to follow the track back. He wouldn't even take a shortcut, which we'd have done if he'd been with us."

"What can we do to find him?" asked Starshine.

"Nothing for now," said Mekoe, grabbing her hand. "It's too dark to see any trail, and if we try, we'll cover any sign he may have left. We'll go at first light."

Dashlan sat forward. "Four of us could do it. Pa, Mekroe, Qwinita and I could go, couldn't we, Pa?"

"What do you think, Teema?"

He shrugged. "This doesn't make sense, Kirym. Elm's not the best tracker, but he can read the sort of trail we followed. He commented on the distinct lines we left in the long grass, said it was more obvious when we dragged the frames rather than carrying them. He asked what we'd do if Gynbere's guards followed us."

"And you told him?"

"Saw no reason not to," said Teema nodding. "He asked extra questions too."

"If you were followed and he was captured, where would it most likely have happened?" I asked.

"At the thicket where we left the water," said Storm. "Anyone waiting in there wouldn't be seen by Elm as he approached."

"But why would they capture him?" asked Dashlan. "Wouldn't it make more sense to follow him and get us all, or follow Elm's trail back to you, Teema and Pa?"

Teema nodded his approval. "We'd have seen if he tried to evade anyone."

"Unless he took to the water from the thicket," I noted.

"He might have, and if they did too, they'd have left no trail, except where they entered the water, because that's the only place they could have been," said Bryn. "Then again, we would have seen their prints, unless they were waiting in the stream, and you'd have to wonder why they'd do that."

"What if he chose to leave us?" said Mekroe.

In the following silence, Starshine's eyes widened. "He wouldn't. He's one of us. Where would he go? We need to start searching as soon as possible."

"We will, Starshine," I said.

"What about Larqeba?" asked Qwinita.

"What about him?" Bryn looked around. "Where is he?" Jeresaya sighed and explained what happened.

"He's turning me grey, that boy." Bryn turned to Ashistar. "You're sure he'll be all right?"

"He'll join Shormel's family. His sire is trustworthy. Slaslow will have forgotten about Shormel by now anyway," said Ashistar.

"Until Larqeba manages to retrieve the token Slaslow stole," said Qwinita.

Churnyg snorted. "Nah! If the boys do that, they'll make themselves very scarce. Slaslow can't make a fuss without admitting he withheld something from Gynbere. He may be greedy, but he's no fool."

"Unless he doesn't care any longer," said Mekroe.

"Did anyone see Rargo?" I asked.

"I didn't think to look for him," said Jeresaya. "I was too worried about Larqeba. I'm sure I didn't see him. If I had I would have remembered, I think."

I nodded. "Three cloaked guards came late to the party. They stayed near Gynbere," I said.

"I noticed them," said Ashistar. "Gynbere's spies and bully boys are always masked and hooded when they're working. The anonymity is a safeguard, and it means if they're heavy-handed, they can't be identified. Two of them guarding Rargo? They would keep him nearby and under guard. Gynbere would be wary of Rargo double-crossing him."

"Why would Rargo be so heavily cloaked?" asked Dashlan.

Ashistar laughed dryly. "After the fiasco with Salcan, Gynbere was very vocal on not trusting anyone from the outside. If he was now seen to hobnob with one, it would lead to questions. He wouldn't want that. One of the cloaked people was taller than the others. So probably Rargo, but could he be a threat to Larqeba?"

"After Rargo's treatment of him when he was trying to rescue Kirym from Salcan, Larqeba will avoid anyone in uniform and he'll know to watch out for Rargo," Bryn said.

"He knows how to avoid trouble when he has to, but there's something else to consider for tomorrow," interrupted Ashistar. "There are still people in The Rock."

Dashlan shrugged. "Maybe Gynbere left a few guards so he could return if he wanted to."

"No!" interrupted Ashistar. "If that was the case, he'd have left a whole company. Every commander and security chief went with Gynbere. I'm sure of it."

Churnyg nodded. "Guards wouldn't bother me, except to be wary when we leave here."

"Anyway I only missed a few people and they were all rebels or related to them. They were those I was going to help escape yesterday."

"They could all be dead," said Storm.

"Did you notice that no one left through the north hole?" I asked. Everyone looked blank.

"Maybe the fall blocked the tunnels there," said Bryn. "If they'd investigated them during the night, no one would need to check it again."

"Blocked from one direction doesn't mean no access from another. Surely Gynbere would be inquisitive. No one looked at it," I reiterated.

Jeresaya sighed. "That implies they knew there was no need to search."

"It could be simpler than that," interrupted Ashistar. "There's a section there that's very dangerous. The internal rock is rotten. Collapses without reason. No one in their right mind would go there, and it's long been blocked off. So I wouldn't read anything into it, Kirym."

Churnyg cleared his throat. "The stories about that area

are frightening. However, consider this. Gynbere took his time arriving at the hole this morning. He does that. Gets everyone there before dawn, but he takes his time. He'd sleep in, have a good leisurely meal and wander along when he's ready. But he could equally have been waiting to hear that the people he saw as a threat had been dealt to. There's a few stories out of there, and it's possible you wouldn't have heard them Ashistar. Just whispers, but I put a lot of weight on whispers."

"We have three jobs to do in the morning," I said. "Bryn, can you and Dashlan look for Elm?"

He nodded. "We'll follow the stones to where we joined the stream, and work up from there. What if there is no sign of him after the thicket?"

"You're sure Elm couldn't have missed the stones?"

"Only by choice," interrupted Storm.

"Then continue past the thicket for as far as is reasonable."

"What do you mean, reasonable?" asked Dashlan.

"You can only travel against a deep flow of water for a short time. After that, you get cold and tired, and you go faster on land," said Bryn.

"When you're following," I said, "I want you to look at the land from Elm's point of view, but think about how he would see it if he was being pursued. If there's no sign of him, return here and we'll re-evaluate. Teema, I want you, Mekroe and Ashistar to help me find out how Gynbere made it appear that the wall was partially rebuilt. Just a quick look. We'll leave before dawn."

"I could help there," interrupted Dashlan. "Pa can take Qwinita. For a girl, she's not bad at tracking."

"I'd like you to do it, Dashlan. You're nearer Elm's height and that could make a difference," I said. "You'd see things Qwinita may miss because she's shorter."

Dashlan still looked miffed.

"I'd be happy to change jobs," said Qwinita. "I'll be cooking and changing Amethyst's …"

"A good guard does what his leader demands, Dashlan," interrupted Mekroe. "Even lesser jobs are important. It's essential to learn obedience."

I giggled, Teema and Mekrar roared with laughter.

"Mekroe had a problem with that when he was younger," Teema explained. "It's nice to know Armos managed to drum some sense into that thick head."

Mekroe's face was bright red. "Most of it came through the seat of my trousers," he said with a laugh.

"What about the northern hole?" interrupted Churnyg.

I nodded. "We'll need to look there, so later on after we return from the wall."

45

Kirym Speaks

The sky was just beginning to grey when Teema, Mekroe, Ashistar and I arrived at the southern hole. The stones from the wall had tumbled to the sides, and now there was a large open hole.

Inside The Rock, it was as Teema had described, an open space, part of a wide tunnel running north and south just inside the wall.

Teema opened the lamp he held, and aimed it in both directions. The tunnels disappeared into the distance, empty for as far as the eye could see.

"This is a guard-only tunnel," said Ashistar. "It allowed them to travel quickly with no one knowing. Slaslow used them to launch lightning fast attacks when Gynbere dreamed of shadows. No one seems to be here, but do you mind if I check the nearest guard post, Kirym?"

"Take Teema. Be quick and careful." I was interested in the ground. As Teema had swung around to follow Ashistar, his lantern highlighted a number of dark mounds on the ground. The tunnels we had travelled, were cut through rock, all of it smooth.

I hunkered down to look. Mounds of fabric. I lifted a piece up and shook it out.

"Cloaks, no robes! Hundreds of them."

"What?"

"On the ground, Mek. Start collecting them. I want to take as many as possible with us when we leave."

"Why?"

"Because they're an anomaly, and I want to look at them in daylight. Anyway why would we leave them to Churnyg's enemies?"

Dawn was breaking when we arrived back at the camp, each laden with the robes. I held one up. The mottled greys and greens were intricately woven together.

"That's Papa's hunting robe," said Mekroe.

"What?" Teema frowned. "That's weird, why would they have ...?"

"Papa's was very old when he got it. Mama gave it to him when they joined. Nothing was known about its history except it had been in the family for a long time. These appear identical. They could be as old as ..." I paused, not sure where my thoughts were taking me.

"Could Mama's ancestors have battled Gynbere's?"

"A number of explanations come to mind, Mek, but at this stage there are other things we need to do. If possible, I'd like to collect the rest of the robes and store them safely until we can find out about them."

After handing one to Churnyg, Ashistar put one on. It fitted him across the shoulders. "They're all too long, which would be why they were left when they launched their attack yesterday, but I'd have liked one of these when doing guard duty at night. Very warm. I wonder where they were kept, and why they weren't used."

"Why burden ourselves with more than one each and a few spares?" asked Churnyg.

"Because against The Rock," I said, "the wearer was virtually invisible. When Papa used his, he was very hard to see in most circumstances. Against rock, trees, and even on an open plain you could easily miss him even when moving. Had the guards and soldiers worn the hoods up, we wouldn't have seen them. I don't know the connection to Papa's robe, but I want to find out."

Ashistar folded the robe carefully, delved into his sleeve and pulled out a small scroll. "Almost forgot. Found this at the guard post. I couldn't read it there, it was too dark, but there may be something relevant." He rolled it out and placed it in front of me.

It was in code, unintelligible to my eyes, but I was intrigued by the makeup of the scroll. Sections had been added as needed, and the papyrus was very fine. The outwardly small scroll had a surprising amount of information in it. There were a few empty leaves at one end. Messages were short.

I pointed to the symbol that appeared to indicate the end of each message. "Do these mean anything?"

Ashistar frowned and rolled the scroll open for quite a distance. He pointed to one symbol near the end. "See here, well this is a new emblem." He then pointed to a different symbol nearer the beginning. "This one signifies the message is from Gynbere. At the beginning of the scroll, the messages are all Gynbere's." He paused and skipped back a few sections before speaking again. "I know all of the early messages, they went to most of the guards. The latter ones with this new symbol seem to be specific to some guards, not all. I suspect this new symbol represents Slaslow."

"Gynbere's symbol is a yew leaf, and that makes sense. What's the other?" asked Teema.

"Lately Slaslow's personal guards were spouting a story of his ancient lineage back to a different tree. They called it a fire tree, and implied it was a nobler tree, and took ascendance over all others."

"How did Gynbere take that?" asked Storm.

"I doubt anyone had the courage to tell him. And I only heard a whisper."

"That doesn't look like any leaf I've seen," said Bryn. "It looks a bit like a faceted stone to me."

"I think that's it," said Churnyg. "I suspect it implies a bit of Slaslow's long buried history. What do you know of it, Ashistar?"

"Yew of course."

Churnyg snorted. "He wanted us to think so and possibly he is, but I doubt it. He was born in the red-stone tunnels, and nothing is known of him. Donima took him in, everyone thought her daughter was his maman although there was no proof of that. He sidled up to Gynbere early on and did his dirty work. Been doing it ever since. Now, anything in that scroll, or do you just want a history lesson?"

Ashistar glanced at the section in front of him. "They started to assemble the people before midday yesterday. They planned to take them all out through the tree exit. Soon after midnight, Gynbere changed his mind. Possibly he learned about the breach in the wall and saw the potential of an easier exit."

"Is the other hole mentioned at all?" I asked.

Ashistar shook his head. "That's it really."

"So what happened at midday that made Gynbere change his long term plans?" asked Teema.

I thought back. "His plan to get Churnyg was thwarted,

but he still had Rargo. Maybe different information became relevant."

"Rargo secretly listens to people, and he uses what he hears, especially if he can make trouble," said Enliah spitefully. "Who knows what he passed on?"

"That's very helpful, Enliah. I'll have to think about it." I glanced at the dawn sky. "We need to move, check the other hole in the wall."

Churnyg picked up a pack. "Yes let's not waste time."

"Where are you going?"

"To save my people."

I grabbed his tunic and pulled him back into the shadow of the trees. "Oh, no you don't. If you return to The Rock what will convince people they can survive out here? Anyway did you personally know all the guards?"

He shook his head.

"So some may still be in there. One archer in hiding may be delighted to shoot you for a reward from Gynbere or Slaslow. I need you here, but stay out of sight until you see the red lining of Mekroe's cloak displayed on that debris." I turned to the others. "Keep him safe. Sit on him if need be. Teema, Mekroe, Ashistar, let's go."

"An archer could shoot Ashistar," grumbled Churnyg.

"And they could shoot me, but there's more chance of it being you. The clothes you wear are rather distinctive. I assume you still object to using Mekrar's other sleeping robe as a disguise?"

"Damn dress," he grumbled. "Why would I?"

Mekroe, Teema and Ashistar had packs, knives, bows and a full quiver of arrows each. I took my knife, sword, and shield.

"Do you both feel as vulnerable as I do?" asked Mekroe.

"Yes!" Both Teema and I answered at the same time.

"But that's silly really," I said. "There's probably no one on the wall anyway and we have the protection of the shield."

Mekroe laughed. "For all your reassurance, I don't know if I'd be with you if you didn't have that shield." He looked back, measuring our progress from the trees. "Why is Arbreu not doing this? Actually, I haven't seen him today."

"I sent him and Mekrar to check on some fires in the northwest. I need to know what caused them."

"I wondered where they were. I assumed they were off umm — well gazing deeply into each other's eyes."

"Just like you and Starshine?"

He went red. "Umm, you know? Oh, well umm, ahhh, how come you're worried about a little fire at a time like this?"

"I'm not, Mek. I'm hoping they're Papa's sentry fires. But if it's a wildfire, then we need to know the extent of the burn off. I'd hate to be driven into the flames by Gynbere or his guards. Anyway, I want to at least be forewarned."

"How did you know about the fires? I haven't smelled smoke."

I laughed. "Neither have I. A dragon told me."

Teema's eyebrows arched.

Mekroe snorted. "Well don't tell me then." He pointed to my hip. "What's that?"

"It's a rock shard. I found it last night. I'm going to ask Findlow to fashion a handle for it when I see him next."

"Wow, I never find things like that," he said. "Why change the handle? What you've got on it looks good."

"I plaited fush fibres, but the stone edges of the handle are sharp and I think they'll cut through fairly quickly. Wood will be a better option, unless Findlow or Armos can round the edges of the handle area to make the fibres safe."

The first boulders were easy to walk around, but soon we were climbing up and over them to gain entry into The Rock.

The open area just inside the wall narrowed quickly to a passage heading east. For the most part, this tunnel was roofless. Although the outside walls still towered above us, some of the internal walls here were lower. Twenty steps in, a partially open door indicated another tunnel going south. Fallen debris blocked the door, and prevented it from opening or closing.

"Through there," said Ashistar, pointing, "is the other end of the tunnel we were in this morning. I wonder why the door's been opened. Never been before. Generally it's guarded by Slaslow's men."

"Why?" asked Mekroe.

"He said it was to keep people safe."

"But that's a guard only area," Mekroe said.

"Guards have been known to disobey orders. Maybe he was just being careful. The interior rock in this area is rotten. You can break it with your bare hands. Walls collapse for no reason. It'll be particularly dangerous now."

Teema put his shoulder to the door, but was unable to budge it. "Well, I doubt anyone could get through. The guard's uniform would definitely make it too bulky for them, but a smaller guard without his uniform might make it. Is that likely?"

"No. The uniform is a badge of office even for the lowest. It's very prestigious, worn with pride. They'd never take it off. While on duty, it's against the rules."

He turned away and we followed the passage east into The Rock. It was clear to a corner a few hundred steps on, and most of it was roofless, although thick debris on the ground showed it hadn't always been so.

"Is this collapse recent, Ashistar?"

He nodded.

We moved cautiously towards the corner, and peered around. It was clear to the next corner where a dark narrow tunnel went to the right.

"Wait here," grunted Ashistar. "This goes to a storage area, I'll check it." He and Teema disappeared, returning a short time later. "No way through. We found two other tunnels, both blocked. It may be that an area right across this section of The Rock has collapsed. If that was known, it could be why no one came over to check on it. There are no people in here and Slaslow would know ..."

"We can't take that for granted, and anyway, you and Churnyg said faces were missing." I said.

We continued on. Dust and debris showered on top of us.

"Someone's up there," gasped Mekroe, flattening himself against the wall.

I pointed back along the tunnel. "They've had ample chance to check us out. There's a lot of dust falling all along here, Mek. That implies there are lots of people up there. They haven't challenged or attacked us, so it's more likely to be the wind moving the dust across the top of the wall."

Mek nodded and stepped to the other side of the tunnel, squinting up to the ledge high above us, his arrow nocked, but not drawn.

Fifty steps further, another tunnel branched off, and again Teema and Ashistar disappeared to search it. Mekroe and I continued cautiously onward, stopping when we could see two more tunnels branching off, one to the right, and one to the left. The ground here was covered with dried reeds. I leaned forwards and flicked some away with the point of my knife as Ashistar and Teema caught up with us.

"The rushes make it safer," said Ashistar. "It gets muddy when it rains. The water seeps through cracks in the rock layers. In some places the ground is always damp. Let's move on. Teema, you go left, I'll go right. You two wait here."

Mek laughed quietly under his breath as they disappeared. "He has no idea. Lead on, Sis."

He followed me to the next corner, and when that showed a clear passage, I moved quickly up to the next junction. The tunnel that led off had collapsed almost to the entrance, so we moved on again. This passage had a lot of rock debris from the corner to about half way along, but there seemed no danger, so I clambered over the rocks to another corner which I peered cautiously around.

"What's there?" asked Mek, when he realised I had paused longer than usual.

"A body," I murmured. "Looks dead, but ..."

"I'll go get Teema."

"Stay put," I snapped.

The body was face down. A fly buzzed over it, landing on solid thick fingers.

Male, I thought.

He wore a grey robe, familiar although I couldn't remember where I had seen one before. The fly settled on his face, and with three others took off again. They circled and returned, landing out of my sight. He made no movement.

The passage ahead turned to the right and darkened. The roof was intact there, but there was a sliver of daylight beyond, where it had collapsed. Roofless again, the tunnel curved back to the east.

Keeping low and against the southern wall, I moved to the body, knife in hand.

I reached forward and touched his hand. It was cold and firm. I scanned the area ahead — no movement and no sound. On the ground just beyond the body was a lantern.

The flame had scorched the dry rushes that covered the ground. The ground and the body were covered with a dusting of small rock flakes, debris from above. I hefted one of the largest of them. It was not big enough to have knocked him out.

I placed my knife on the ground, lifted the body by the shoulder and heaved him onto his side. Almost instantly something hit the northern wall above my head and clattered to the ground. I leaned forward and picked up a feathered bolt.

Mekroe sucked in a breath. "Leave it, Kirym. I'll go get Teema."

"No need." I took a deep breath. "There's no danger, Mek."

The body had three similar feathered ends protruding from his chest. The front of his robe and the ground under him was covered with drying blood. By the amount I figured he had died quite quickly, and its dark colour suggested some time ago, probably about midnight. I allowed the body to roll onto its back and again bolts hit the wall and fell to the ground. I checked the pulse in his neck. He was dead. The front of his robe was covered with sticky blood. The right shoulder had a series of thick black chevrons pointing down, three close together followed by two further apart. A metal badge showing an arrow piercing a bleeding scroll, was pinned above the chevrons.

I remembered five men dressed similarly, standing near Gynbere on the day Churnyg was sentenced to death. They nodded to each other as the sentence was given.

Unable to see the flight line, I crawled forward, keeping low to the ground. This time two bolts hit the wall. They came out of the darkened recess ahead. All hit the wall at about chest height for someone Churnyg's size. None came anywhere near me. Whoever was there, was shooting blind.

How though did they know I was approaching?

Mekroe was at my shoulder. "Kirym, we should go back."

"Why? Carrying on would make far more sense."

"If you want to die, it might. You're being shot at. And they're accurate."

"No they're not. They haven't hit me, and they won't."

"Kirym!"

I leaned forward and looked behind to where Teema, his face tense, stood with Ashistar just behind him.

"Get down, Teema." I urged crawling forward. More bolts hit the wall, singly for the most part. The ground ahead was clear of everything but dried reeds.

"Why is there a thick layer of reeds covering the ground here, Mek?"

"Ashistar told you. The rain makes it muddy."

"It rained heavily a few days back, and yet the ground here shows no sign of it." I leaned forward and flicked the reeds away from the path. Four vines lay about a finger height above the ground, running along the passage. I pushed one down. Nothing, but when I released it, a bolt hit the wall. I did it again. The same result.

I moved forward again, keeping close to the southern wall. At the corner I peered carefully around and quickly pulled back, evaluating what I'd seen.

Incredible! No danger. I looked again, taking as long as I needed.

Around the walls at various heights were ten small bows. They were fed from above by a silo of bolts. I pressed one of the vines. Through a series of cogs and levers, one bow-string pulled back and fired when I released the vine. Another bolt rolled from the silo onto a notched board, and slotted into the bow.

"Kirym! What's happening?" Mekroe hissed.

"Wait! All of you keep down. I'm going to try something."

I cut the line of vines. Every bow fired.

"Ahhhhh!"

I glanced behind me.

Mekroe lay flat on the ground, looking embarrassed. "Sorry, you should have warned me." He grinned sheepishly. "Yeah, I know. You did."

More bolts slotted into place, but now they were harmless. I made sure I had disarmed all of them and stood up. "It's safe now. Come and look."

Ashistar and Teema gingerly stepped over the body and joined me in the shooting gallery.

"Very clever." Ashistar was hoarse with awe. "Oh, my goodness! I thought I knew about all of Gynbere's devices. But this is new." He was silent as he looked around. "Never been mentioned. I wonder how it was done without word getting out."

"The dead guy out there could have done it," said Mekroe.

"Him? No he wouldn't have the expertise, although he could well have thought it up. I wonder when this was set up. The area has been off limits for a long time."

"So why didn't you and Churnyg try to escape this way? Before the bolts were set up, I mean," Mekroe asked.

"It was tried in the past, but this rock makes it intrinsically dangerous. Some of those who chanced their luck in here, didn't return. Those who did weren't prepared to try again. There was no way over the outer walls, and the rock in here shatters with no warning."

"Two different types of rock, Mek," I said. "In this area, they've shattered into flakes, while the outer wall fell in big boulders."

"Ashistar picked up a flake. "Small here, but big enough to kill elsewhere. Even these are dangerous though. If enough of them fall on you, you get buried alive, and digging out is nearly impossible."

"The question we need answered is, what is Gynbere hiding?" I asked

"Why do you think he'd be hiding anything?" asked Mekroe.

Teema snorted. "Silly question. This is Gynbere we're talking about."

"No, Teema. Questions are good, and Mek should ask them," I interrupted. "Mek, these bolts are here for a reason. A lot of work has gone into setting them up."

Mekroe nodded. "Could it be a safeguard to protect people? Stop them entering."

"You don't protect people by killing them. Why not tell them honestly. They're hiding something here," I said. "Ashistar, tell me about the dead man. I saw similar robes near Gynbere when he sentenced Churnyg."

He nodded. "He's one of the Urfit triplets. A nasty piece of work, they all are. Their job was to spread disinformation, altering our history and creating a pro-Gynbere version." He pointed to the badge. "They were constantly harassing Sirasha Beech. He keeps the written archives. The Urfits wanted to destroy the lot, and Sirasha was constantly under threat. Sirasha played the game well though, and so far, he hasn't lost. I wonder why this one," he nudged the body with his foot, "walked into the trap."

"He was running from something," interrupted Teema, "and if he knew about the bolts ..."

"Oh he would have. He probably organised them," said Ashistar.

I nodded thoughtfully. "Then something terrified him so much he forgot. Possibly it was the wall falling in the passage back there. I wonder, though, how anyone got past here earlier."

"Perhaps there was some way of removing the tension on

the vines — something in one of the closer tunnels. What alerted you to the danger, Kirym? He could've been hit by a rock."

"The roof shattered, but the pieces here were small, too small to have killed him. The floor was covered with rushes, but there was no mud as there was back there, so the rushes had to cover something else. The blood was sticky, the flies were just beginning to find him." I pointed to the charred rushes. "His lantern had been glowing. It happened at night."

Mekroe picked up a bow and bolt. "These are lethal, but the bows are so small. You could use them, Kirym, they're just your size."

"What were they protecting? We still have no idea. What's in this area, Ashistar?"

"So far as I know, nothing! The rock here shatters and can't be worked. There's a few caves, but some have collapsed, so they're of no use for anything."

"But something important is still here," I said.

Mekroe shook his head. "They might have removed it already."

"Then why would they reset the bolts?" I asked.

"Oh!" Ashistar nodded. "All right. We'd best check then."

"Collect the bows and bolts first," I said. "We may not return this way, so best we take them with us."

Teema grabbed those ready to be fired and handed them to Mekroe. More slotted down to where they had been. "This'll take too long." He climbed carefully onto a ledge and hoisted himself up towards the top of the silo. As he did so, he dislodged a stone balancing on a couple of rocky nobs. Behind it were some containers. He dropped them down to Ashistar. "What are these?"

"Aha, quivers. Good, makes it easier to carry the bolts."

Teema handed down handfuls of bolts to Mekroe, who

managed to place most of them in the quivers. Ashistar and I detached the bows, and I picked up the arrows Teema dropped. I put most of them in Teema's pack, but kept one. In a lull when I wasn't needed I stepped into the open, nocked a bolt to the bow, and began testing them.

The bow was smaller than that I normally used, and it felt springier. The ends were curved back, different from any bow I had ever seen. I fired. The bolt flew to the end of the passage, and hit the wall with surprising force. It fell to the ground taking a section of rock with it. It was heavier at the nose than the arrows I was used to. I fired five bolts. Then I was sure I would be reasonably accurate at this short distance. I really wanted to test them in the open to see the full range and power. I felt they would be a formidable weapon. I wandered down and picked the bolts up. Despite hitting the rock, the stone points weren't damaged, although the wall had flaked considerably where each bolt had hit. I took them with me, picking up those that had been fired earlier, noting the same damage to the wall there.

"Woo-hoo, you're lethal with those," said Mekroe, coming up behind me. "Great weapons. Teema sent me to get you, we're ready to move on." He slipped the bolts into his quiver.

I followed him. "If they're as good over a distance as they are close, I'll enjoy using them. I hope we can make more, somehow."

As we walked through the now stripped armoury, Mekroe picked up the sacks and other quivers. "There's a few that were really dirty. I've left them there." He pointed to the ground.

I picked them up. "Let's take them. There are a limited number, and if they can't be replaced, these may be needed in the future."

"But they're filthy, and it's caked on."

"A little water does wonders, and if it doesn't, well, I'll figure something. I'll carry them, if you don't want to."

"No, no. I'll do it. Anything for the lady of The Green Valley."

I laughed and we ran to catch up to Teema and Ashistar.

46

Kirym Speaks

Beyond the trap, the tunnel turned again, and now we went north. Further on we found similar set-ups. Some set to fire in the direction we were traveling, designed to stop people returning. Again, we cut the vines and took the bows and bolts with us.

Three caves were empty, and showed no signs of being recently used.

There were four more traps, aiming in both directions and now we knew about them, they were quickly dismantled. Now we all carried full quivers, and Mekroe hauled three sacks of bows and extra bolts.

The paths here were mostly open to the sky, and there was no evidence they had ever been roofed. In some areas the walls had fallen, and we travelled with more care.

Finally we turned a corner and found our way blocked. Ahead the passage seemed impassable with the fallen debris from the walls. These were bigger boulders, but there was a lot of dust and smaller rocks, some of these were still falling.

"A dead end, and getting more dangerous too," said Ashistar. "Let's start back, there should be a good meal waiting for us."

"I want to check the face of the fall," I said.

I walked on towards the rock pile, pausing and stepping aside when a large rock fell from the top and rolled along the passage towards me.

Ashistar darted forwards and grabbed my shoulder.

"If you get hurt, Churnyg will kill me," he growled.

A smaller rock clattered to the ground, and something flashed across the space beyond it.

"Wait here." I pulled free of his grasp and darted forwards, climbed onto a rock and then a ledge, and leaned forward to glance through the hole.

An old woman, her face pale, stared defiantly out at me. She took a deep breath. "Are you attacking us?"

I laughed. "Four of us? That'd be a bit foolhardy wouldn't it?"

She smiled weakly. "Against an old woman and a handful of children? I imagine it would be rather easy. Mind you, we'll fight."

More faces joined hers. Dwarflings.

"Are you going to kill us? asked a boy.

"No! My goodness no. We're here to help you escape."

The old woman shook her head. "Thipin said there was a plan to kill us. He wanted us to wait here until it's quashed."

"We don't want to kill you, and other than the falling rocks, all other danger is gone. Let's clear some of this debris and get you out."

This rock fall was small, and soon the hole was big enough for me to climb through. Teema followed, while Ashistar and Mekroe made the hole larger and safer.

Shurlyn, the old woman was accompanied by fifteen dwarflings, two of which were babies. An old man sat against the rock wall in the shade. His eyes were closed, and he was very pale.

Why did you come here?" I asked.

"Thipun Urfit brought us here yesterday. He said he'd discovered a conspiracy against Gynbere. We'd been accused by those who were behind the plot. He wanted us safe here until he could prove who was responsible."

"You two and children?"

"There were forty six of us, but as soon as it was light, we tried to find a way out. The others were clearing a path further along there," she pointed down the passage, "but the rocks came down. I've heard nothing of them since. Old Mrilan," she shook her head, "well he had a strange turn. He's not really spoken since then. The children and I can't move the stones, they're too big, but I don't think there's any point."

Mrilan, ancient and pale, was coherent. He accepted water, but refused food. "Give it to the dwarflings," he insisted. I tried to convince him we had enough for everyone, but he was adamant.

"Leave him, dearie," said Shurlyn. "He may eat later."

"Not likely," he muttered. "Women! They think you'll change your mind just 'cause they nag."

"And grumpy old men lie down and try to die because they can't get their own way," growled Shurlyn.

"Tell me about the rock fall," said Teema.

"It just collapsed onto them," said the biggest boy.

"No it didn't," said a girl. "The other end started to fall, and some of them ran this way, and then a big rock got lodged above them and the rocks fell there." She pointed to the left of the rock-face.

"What do girls know?" interrupted the boy. "They were flattened."

"I watched and I saw," she said, her hands on her hips.

Ashistar and Mekroe had set out the food, and Shurlyn ushered them over to it.

"Who's right?" asked Teema.

"Wait until Shurlyn returns and ask," I said quietly. "In the meantime, there could be survivors, so we need to start moving rocks."

Teema, Mekroe and Ashistar began work, helped by a few of the older dwarflings. More waited to take over when they tired, although they were each eager to continue until they fell. The younger ones stayed close to Shurlyn, staring in awe at the food we put in front of them. Despite their obvious hunger, they were reluctant to eat it until Mekroe bounded over.

"Not eating? Well all the more for me — and this is my favourite." He took a large bite of cold venison wrapped in a piece of flat bread. "Mmmm!" he rubbed his tummy and rolled his eyes.

The little ones giggled. A tiny girl reached out and touched his tunic, pulled back and tried to hide when she realised he'd felt it. Mekroe sat on a rock and pulled her onto his knee, breaking off a portion of bread and meat for her.

She took the food and put her hands behind her back, trying to slip off his knee.

"Eat it, Varitza. There's plenty for the rest of them," said Shurlyn.

Mekroe held another morsel in front of her mouth, and she tentatively ate it. "You'd best join in," he said to the others. "Otherwise Varitza and I will have to eat the lot, and then we'll blow up and go pop." He handed the food out, and still no one else ate.

"Eat up. These are nice people. They won't take it away,"

said Shurlyn. "It's a real feast for you."

Finally they started to eat, although they still eyed us suspiciously.

"Don't rush, it's all yours." She turned away, her eyes bright with tears. "They've never seen such a feast. Well not one that wasn't snatched away as soon as it was obvious they wanted it."

"Why would someone do that to children?" I was aghast.

"Gynbere believes we're dissidents. Generally someone in our families is or was." She shook her head bleakly. "It's hard to be a rebel when one has children. It's good of you to share your food."

"Who would be more believable, the boy or the girl?" I asked, handing her a roll of bread around some meat.

"Both, I'm not sure." She shrugged. "Aziavar, the girl was closer, and she tends not to speak unless she's sure. Yarlyth, the boy, well, he is a boy, and boys like to be considered, especially around the men." She took a bite of the meat roll. "Ah, this is divine. I've not eaten venison for — oh, eight, ten seasons, more probably. Even then it was just a tiny morsel, smuggled out of a feast by a friend." She handed some of the roll to Mrilan, who broke a fragment off the edge and nibbled it.

"Here." He grabbed one of the bigger boys. "Take it up to the workers. I don't need it."

"Mrilan. There's plenty for all of us, and we've more close by if we run out. If you are too weak to walk, the children and Shurlyn will have to carry you out. They are too young or ..."

"Don't say Shurlyn's too old," interrupted Mrilan. "She'll not take it well, and she'll make me wish I was already dead." He scowled. "There's never enough. When you leave, I'll remain here. I'd just hold you up and there are few enough stores to warrant wasting them on an old man too close to death to bear worrying about."

"If we run out here, I'll get more. If you don't eat, I'll have to return later with more food to prove it. It'll make my life very difficult if I have to constantly return here with food for you, especially when I wish to take the children to safety."

He took a small piece of bread and sliver of meat. "You sure?" At my reassurance, he began to eat.

Shurlyn brought over a flask of water for him.

"Why did you trust Thipin Urfit?" I asked.

"We didn't," said Shurlyn. "But we could hear yelling, the clash of weapons. He said he would be happy to see us dead, but this plot was serious, and he'd prefer to get the real offenders."

Teema and Ashistar were making progress with the rock clearage. They passed the rocks down to the bigger children who stacked them against the walls. There were a lot of rocks.

I took a flask of water over to the workers.

"STOP!"

I froze. Ashistar paused, just as he began to prise a big rock free.

Mrilan pushed past me. "You," he pointed to one of the older girls who'd been helping Ashistar and Teema. "Get all of the dwarflings back to Shurlyn." He climbed up to Ashistar, who was still holding the rock. "Wedge it back in." He pointed to the wall on the left. "See there? If you take that rock, the next one will roll out and the rest'll collapse. Then we'll have to dig you out too. Can you wedge it back in?"

"I can." Teema balanced a smaller rock under it, and hammered it in with a fist-size rock.

Ashistar pounded another rock in with the heel of his hand. "If we can't take this one out, how do we go further?"

"Get down from there, and let's look at the whole picture."

Once everyone was on the ground, Mrilan stood and stared at the rocks. "All right, let's do some support work here. I want big rocks, about that size," he held his hands apart, "about as big as you can lift. The older dwarflings will help, even if it's just rolling them to you. I want to build a support wall here," he pointed to the right of the big rock, "and then we'll open a hole there." He pointed to the left about halfway down the rock-fall.

"Won't that bring down the ones above it?" asked Teema.

"Probably not, but if it does, it should fall away from you and we'll be able to try something else."

"Should?" Teema gasped. "I hope you're right."

After initially trying to do as much as Teema, Mekroe and Ashistar, Mrilan conceded defeat. "I no longer have the strength," he grumbled, having tried to lift a large rock onto two others. "In my youth, I'd have had this finished by now, and with one hand tied behind my back." However he proved to be a good foreman, intuitive about the best way to lift and fit rocks into the wall.

The children and I could do little more than roll more along to them as required. It was midday before they again began to remove rocks, but this time they moved faster. True to Mrilan's prediction, the top stones held, and a narrow tunnel began to form. It lengthened as the sun moved a hand-width across the sky.

Ashistar was almost fully in the tunnel, Teema was in head and shoulders, and Mekroe was hauling a rock away, with Yarlyth's help. The rest of us remained with Shurlyn, out of the way and providing drinks as required.

Suddenly, two large rocks fell from the top of the rockfall, followed by a cascade of smaller rocks and shale.

The girls screamed, but Mrilan moved faster than I thought

possible. He pushed Teema to one side, and hauled Ashistar out of the tunnel by his belt.

As Ashistar gained his feet, we heard a muffled shout. Mrilan immediately climbed the rocks until he was near the top of the fall. "Don't move," he bellowed. "Can you go back a way, and come in lower and to your right?" He listened to the muffled reply. "No, won't work, you must go lower, or you'll be buried." He climbed down to rocks and walked over to Teema and Ashistar. "Are you all right?"

They nodded.

"Can we help them?" asked Teema.

"No."

It seemed such a long wait. Occasionally more debris fell from the top of the fall. My heart was in my mouth as one heavier rock fell, and then another and another, but Mrilan wouldn't allow us to go closer to help or advise.

Then, with a shower of dirt and small stones, a large boulder rolled out of the tunnel, and fell to the ground. As the dust settled, there was movement in the tunnel, an arm waved to clear the air. Then a face appeared.

"Sire!" Yarlyth ran forward and threw his arms around the man's legs before he had gained the ground. Both had tears in their eyes as they walked clear of the dust. The next man out paused and helped others out through the debris.

"Vimble." Yarlyth's sire extended a hand to Teema, and then glanced behind.

I felt little arms around my legs, and glanced down. Varitza had her head buried in the folds of my dress. I bent down and picked her up.

"I want my maman," she sobbed and buried her head in the nape of my neck.

Then more people climbed out of the dusty tunnel, many needing help as they clambered over the broken ground. Almost all showed obvious bruising and abrasions.

Shurlyn nudged me as a dust covered young woman was helped out. Her nose was broken and her eyes black. Someone had wrapped a dusty cloth around her head, but it had proven inadequate for the job. Her wounds still leaked, the blood slowly tracking through the grime on her bruised face and dripping off her chin.

She came straight over to us. "Varitza?"

"Hey, honey," I whispered to Varitza. "Who's this?" Her head moved a little, she opened one eye and then covered it again.

"She was standing next to me when the rocks fell. It looked like you were eaten up by the fall," Aziavar told the woman.

"It's all a bit overwhelming. She'll come right," I said. "Get some food and a drink. Then we can get everyone to safety. I'll look after her for now."

"Oh, I must be unrecognisable," she said numbly. She tentatively touched her swollen cheek and winced. "I'm Rosisha. Thank you for looking after her." She rubbed Varitza's back, but the wee girl clung tightly to me trying, it seemed, to push her head through my shoulder.

Puffs of dust spurted out of cracks in the long walls of the tunnel as they creaked and groaned, and more rocks tumbled from the fall.

"We have to move now," said Mrilan. "This wall will collapse soon. Anywhere is safer than here."

I raised my voice. "Is there any wound that can't wait until we are safe to be dealt with?"

In all, forty-one people joined us for the trip out. Five had died, and were left buried in the rock fall. It was a devastating loss. All of those who had been on the far side of the fall were sporting cuts and bruising of one sort or another. There were two broken arms, a dislocated shoulder and other minor injuries.

I dealt with the dislocated shoulder as soon as I could, while Shurlyn and Teema coped with the broken arms. Those injuries would have held us up more had we left them.

The return trip to the outer wall was fraught. The rock around us creaked and groaned. There had been more minor falls since we had come in. We clambered over and around them, but our journey took longer. Luckily they held, although the noises they emitted were frightening.

Varitza finally returned to Rosisha, although whenever we stopped to rest, she skipped between the two of us.

We were just a few steps away from the only shored up section where we saw the third set of bolts when it crashed down in front of us.

Everyone had been eager to look over land that was free, albeit a little unsure of stepping away from The Rock, but they were now reluctant to move on through the tunnel.

"You can't go back, the tunnels behind us are more likely to fall than those in front," I said. "If you stay here you'll be buried."

There was a lot of muttering, but Mrilan backed me and pushed everyone through. Then a long rumbling crash behind us heralded the truth of my prediction, and the last few in the line rushed through.

Passing the body of Thipun Urfit slowed them down. Although there was a palpable fear of him and the rock behind us, they were intrigued to discover he too had been as vulnerable to other forces as they were. Teema had explained the traps we had destroyed as we passed the first of them, and now they saw the results.

"So he planned to leave us here and allow us to be killed as we tried to find our way out," said Shurlyn. "I'd wager he staged that fight to get us in here."

"Well he got what he deserved," snorted Mrilan. "Couldn't think of anyone who deserved death more, although there are a few lining up pretty close behind him."

Aziavar stared at the body. "It serves him right. Wish I'd seen him die. He's watched enough of us suffer."

"Don't copy his bad behaviour," I said. "You're so much better than him."

She stared at me, frowning. "But ..." she paused. "All I remember of him is him hurting people. He loved it. He was rich because of it."

"And he's dead because of it," I said softly. "He fell into his own trap. That's a good lesson."

47

Kirym Speaks

Leaving everyone in the safest place we could find, Teema and I approached the outer wall alone. Initially we wanted to see that nothing had changed since we entered, but also we didn't want anything to frighten the people we had just saved. Their deep-set beliefs in the dangers of leaving The Rock would be pushed to the limit soon, and I wanted there to be as few problems as possible.

We paused in sight of the hole in the wall, looking at the field beyond. A stag and two does grazed there. As we watched, their heads snapped up, and they wheeled around and disappeared.

"Did they see us?" asked Teema.

"No. We're still hidden from them, and we made no noise. They were looking up, so I suspect whatever spooked them may be on the wall."

"Could Gynbere have returned?"

"Unlikely. It's more probable a rock fell from the wall, or

possibly a bird distracted them. The guards might have used them for target practice in the past. I'm going to check it out. Go back and keep everyone safe. I'll be as quick as I can." I handed him my pack, retaining my weapons, a bow, a quiver of bolts and my knife.

Teema disappeared, and I climbed the rubble to the partially blocked door and peered through. Ahead was a wide tunnel.

Debris on the other side of the door had lodged it tight, but there was plenty of room for me to climb through, although I had to remove the shield first. There was nothing in sight, and no noises to indicate anything here. I glanced up. The wall towered above me. A narrow staircase zigzagged up — I was in for a stiff climb.

I felt vulnerable climbing the steps. I was visible to anyone walking along the tunnel below, and I suspected that someone on the top of the wall may have a direct view of me. From the steps, I could see nothing of the top, but I assumed there must be a space of some sort. The guards could not have just stood on the top step to watch the area below. The guard I had noticed from the trees below had been further along the wall, and this was the only route to the top.

A quarter of the way up, I found a cave-like area cut into the wall. Fortunately it was empty. It couldn't be seen until I had reached it.

It showed how very thick the wall was. I took twelve steps across it, the area was three times longer. A number of openings looked over the tunnel below.

They were too big to simply be places for guards to pass each other. There was enough space for some to stay here for extended periods of time. I found three more similar spaces further up the wall.

The higher I went, the more vulnerable I felt.

When I safely reached the last cave before the top, I took a moment to breathe deeply. A vat of water gave me a needed drink. Beside it was a pile of rope, and nearby there was a cache of weapons, mainly arrows, but nineteen bows also. An interesting number.

At the top of the steps a path went in each direction, narrow, although two people could pass with ease while on it. It sat below the crest of the wall allowing anyone on it to see everything in the meadow below while remaining hidden and protected. A similar but lower wall sat on the inner side, allowing a view over the path below. To the north, the wall ended abruptly with the rock fall. To the south the path rose to a crest.

With a bolt nocked into my bow, and ready at my side, I followed the path. Near the crest, I hesitated and peeped over. Ahead I could see as far as the southern hole, where Gynbere and his people had emerged.

Just past me the path widened to an area surrounded on all sides with a small battlement. In the centre sat a guard.

I placed the quiver on the ground by my feet and readied the bow although I kept it low; my knife was loose in its sheath. "Hello."

He spun around and raised his bow, his mouth open. He looked shocked and uncertain.

"Who are you?"

"Kirym."

"You're not one of us. Where'd ya come from?"

"Out there."

"I didn't see you."

"It was early this morning. I'm going back now. Would you like to come with me?"

He shook his head. "Can't. Working. Anyway, no one can. Once you're here, ya have to stay. If ya leave, ya die. Everyone does. Always been like that. If you try to leave, I have to shoot ya."

"Oh, I don't think I'd like that."

"You'll be all right if you stay."

I smiled at him. He really wasn't sure of me, his bow never wavered, but it didn't actually point at me.

"Why do you think people die if they leave?"

"Slaslow said. Anyway, everyone has. Always been like that."

"What did you do yesterday?"

The change in subject confused him. "Um, I cleaned out the soldier's food hall."

"You had help?"

"Nooo." It was a tentative answer.

"That was usual?"

"Sometimes, but I'm a guard and a guard always obeys." He paused. "I do anyway," he said proudly. "Why're you asking?"

"And today you came up here alone to guard the wall?" He nodded. "Have you seen any of the other guards today?"

"What's it to you? Why are you ...?"

"Because I doubt you've seen anyone since Slaslow told you to clean up, and took the other guards away. What's your name?"

"Baketer." He lowered his bow.

"Baketer, you know that Gynbere and Slaslow took almost all of the people out of The Rock yesterday at about midday. Have you seen anyone since then?"

He frowned.

"You say that everyone who leaves here dies."

He nodded.

"So why does Gynbere want you to shoot them? I mean if they are going to die anyway..." I let the comment hang in the air. Then I pointed across the open area. "You see over there?"

"What, in the trees?"

I nodded. "At midday yesterday, Gynbere and Slaslow were over there with almost everyone else from The Rock. Can you see any bodies?" I waited for him to digest that. "I came in to rescue the few people who'd been left here. They're ready to leave. I'd hate you to hurt them."

"Where were these people?"

"In the area beyond the door." I pointed north.

"No one lives there." He raised his bow again. It pointed somewhere over my left shoulder — I didn't think he had ever shot anyone before.

"Who said?"

Slaslow and the ...." He paused. "I can't tell you that. But no one goes through the door. It's my job to stop them, 'cause it's dangerous."

"You're right it is dangerous, but there are people there. And if Slaslow and Thipun Urfit told you that no one was there, they lied."

He blanched and his eyes widened at mention of Thipen. It seemed I'd hit a nerve.

"Thipun Urfit took people through there, and left them to die," I continued. "He set traps on the path so they couldn't return. We rescued them this morning, and they're all waiting to leave."

"Well, I'd believe it of an Urfit,"he paused, "but it's his job to keep us all safe. Those people could have been criminals."

"I doubt children, dwarflings would be classified as lawbreakers. A few of them aren't even walking."

"Dwarflings? Through there?" And I knew I had him. He was scandalised.

"Come with me and check. If you find I'm wrong, you can always come back." I picked up the quiver, and slipped it and the bow over my shoulder as I turned away.

He gasped, and I turned back.

He stared at me, wide eyed. "You're an elf." He was pointing to the quiver.

"Is something wrong?"

"You carry them. Carriers of elf-bolts. The stories and," he paused. "All right, if everything else you say is true, I'll come with you. But if there's one lie, I'll kill you and anyone else I find." He paused. "Well, not you, cause you're an elf. Can't kill elves. But I'll be angry, and I'll keep you here until I can ask Slaslow to figure it out."

Baketer followed me down to the ground and north along the path. "I can't go there. I won't get through the door."

I pointed south. "The wall has fallen down there too. We could try for that hole."

"It's too dangerous. It's about to collapse. I checked earlier."

"Oh dear. Ummm. Is there another route we could take to get you out? Maybe back through tunnels in The Rock."

He frowned, now not sure what to do.

I paused not wanting to push him too fast.

Suddenly part of the inner wall just south of us creaked and collapsed. The dust billowed towards us. I pushed him into the corner between the door and the inner wall and managed to cover both of us with my cloak before we were showered with dust and fragments of rock.

It seemed ages before the dust began to settle. When it had a little, I stepped back from the wall.

"Are you alright?"

"Why'd ya' do that?"

"Well I didn't want you to be hurt."

He stared at me, I couldn't read his expression.

"We need to go. I don't think this wall will hold out much longer."

Around us, the rock screeched and groaned.

Baketer eyed the door, still nervous about going through,

I waited.

"I can't fit," he said.

"If you take your jacket and helmet off, you'll manage."

"But ... but," he spluttered. He looked horrified. "It's my uniform. "I'm a guard. It's ...""

"I could take your jacket and hand it straight back to you when you come through. Then you can put it on again."

"What about my helmet?"

I looked up. "Well, no it won't fit, but you could try throwing it over the wall."

We both eyed the wall towering above us.

"It's a bit high."

I nodded. Then I had a sudden thought. "I could attach it to a bolt, and try to shoot it over. You can collect it on the other side."

"How will I find it?"

I ripped a strip from my skirt. "I'll tie this to it, and it'll be easy to see."

A bolder fell from the top of the wall, and rolled towards us.

"All right I'll go first with my jacket and you can come after me, but shoot my helmet over first."

I smiled my agreement. Suddenly he grabbed a length of rope off his belt. "Just to be sure you come through." He seized my wrists and began to wind the rope around them.

"If you tie both of my hands, I'll not be able to use my bow."

"Oh!" He paused.

"What about one wrist," I suggested, "but keep the rope loose, otherwise I won't be able to shoot accurately."

The rope wasn't very long and once Baketer had climbed up the pile of debris and pushed through the door, it was almost too short for me to be able to shoot. Trying to help, he stood right against the door with his arm extended. The rope jerked as the bolt left the bow, but the shot remained true, and I watched the helmet sail over the wall.

I squeezed through the door.

Baketer had slipped down the rocks as the rope slackened and was struggling to regain his feet.

"Are you all right?" I asked as I helped him up.

"Where's my helmet?"

"It went over the wall." I untied the rope from my wrist.

"I didn't see it land."

"It went that way." I pointed towards the field.

His went pale. "Outside?"

I shrugged. "The angle was too great to shoot in this direction. It limited my aim."

Before Baketer could say anything, a rock clattered across the path behind us and he swung around to see Teema and the men of The Rock approaching, followed by the women and children. Vimble carried Mekroe's knife, the others had fist size rocks. Baketer backed against the wall, looking angry and scared as the men surrounded him. He lifted his bow, the arrow aimed at me.

"No one will hurt you, Baketer," I said, stepping closer to him. "Baketer was also trapped in here. He's agreed to join us."

"Lower your bow," snarled Vimble. "Otherwise, it'll be the last thing you do."

Baketer swung his bow closer to me.

"Lower your weapon, soldier," said Ashistar. "These people are ..."

"No!" Baketer looked belligerent and the arrow stayed where it was.

"Luntow!"

Baketer lowered his bow and stood up straight with his chest out, as soon as Ashistar spoke. "Yes, Sir, Thez!"

There was an instant change in the atmosphere, as the

men stared at Ashistar.

"You're a Thez?" What in the ..."

"What's a Thez?" asked Teema.

Vimble pointed to Ashistar. "Him! I might have known this was a trap."

"It isn't a trap," I assured him. "We're helping you to escape, and if you don't want to come with us, you can go anywhere out there you like."

"But what's ..." interrupted Teema.

"They're part of Gynbere's hierarchy," explained Shurlyn. "Slaslow is top of Gynbere's army, and below him are two groups. The shadow group with the likes of the Urfits' are on one side, they do propaganda and try to alter our memories, and the Thez are the counterbalance, the action men. Either way, I smell treachery."

Baketer edged to a position between Ashistar and Vimble, not sure who to support. His arrow, although no longer aimed at me, wasn't far off.

Behind us was an ominous rumbling, followed by an explosive rush of dusty air. This part of The Rock was beginning to crumble.

"We have to leave," I said. "It's safer out there, and we can discuss this over a drink and a meal."

"This could be a trick to kill us all off," said Vimble.

"It would have been easier to leave you all in there. You had no food, no water and no idea of how to leave. Add the traps and you wouldn't have made it, even if the walls had been sound. Let's get to safety and then decide what to do."

As I spoke we heard a crash from beyond the gate suggesting some of the walls there were collapsing. I picked up Varitza, and took Aziavar by the hand, knowing that Shurlyn and Rosisha would follow. Vimble pushed Ashistar ahead of him, his knife poised. Baketer followed him, his arrow ready, but still unsure of his loyalties.

As we reached the edge of the wall, Shurlyn stopped. "We could die. My great-grandsire told us that. He never lied."

"Perhaps it was the truth as he knew it," I said, "but Gynbere and Slaslow also knew this truth, and they left yesterday morning. It's not the only time they have been out there either."

"I think she's right. There are no other guards on the wall, and I haven't seen anyone else since yesterday," said Baketer.

Vimble snorted. "So why were you left?"

Baketer went red and hung his head.

I knew I would have to follow up on that question.

Mrilan snorted. "They might already be dead."

"Would you believe Churnyg?" I asked.

"A lovely man, but even he said it was death to leave the protection of The Rock," said Shurlyn. "Thipun took great delight in telling us about his death when he eventually did try to leave. He thought it was funny. 'The last of the real rebels,' he said."

I climbed onto the rocks beside her. "Mekroe, can you wave your cloak so the inside shows?" He swung it around his head, settled it, inside out on his shoulders and pointed across the open area.

"You see the people by the trees?" I said.

Shurlyn nodded.

"Churnyg is with them. Thipun lied to you. Churnyg is alive and proof the prediction is false." As I spoke, Churnyg climbed onto a tree stump and put his hands on his hips.

Shurlyn shaded her face and stared. "Ach, my eyes are old and not as good as they were, but I must say, it does look a bit like that young dandy." She turned and peered into my eyes. "Eee, you've an honest face. I'll trust you, but if you're wrong and I die, I'll be most annoyed."

She turned to those behind her. "I'm going. If I were you, I wouldn't stay around too long. Those walls sound ominous. When Slaslow discovers we've escaped, he'll do something nasty, and we'll be blamed for Thipun's death too I imagine."

Rosisha joined her. "I don't care if the old predictions are true. At least Varitza and I will die free, and that's better than living as a slave.

As I helped them down, others clambered over the rocks to join us. More took their places watching to see what would happen. When we had covered half the distance to the trees, they began to follow.

Baketer spied his helmet, and raced over to get it, clamping it firmly on his head.

At the clearing, we were welcomed by the smell of hot food. Starshine, Qwinita, Enliah and Jeresaya had worked through the day, anticipating our return with people. Storm and Granite had spent part of the morning collecting robes from the northern hole. They had been folded and stacked on a new hauling frame. A number of them had been shortened so they could be used if necessary.

"You!" said Churnyg, glaring at Mrilan. "I heard you were walking the halls of the underworld."

"I turned down the invitation when I was told you'd be part of the welcoming committee."

Insults gave way to backslapping, handshakes, and to Churnyg's disgust, hugs and kisses. Then Vimble pointed to Ashistar. "You know who this is, Churnyg?"

Churnyg nodded.

"You know his job?"

"I know the job he had," said Churnyg guardedly.

"He's a Thez."

Churnyg's eyebrows raised. "That high! Hmmm. So that's how he knew what he knew."

"What did he know?" snarled Vimble.

"Enough to get us safely out of The Rock." He glanced around at the sceptical faces. "Without his help, Gynbere would have killed me, killed all of us. He got Kirym. Poisoned her as we were escaping. She's put her life on the line for all of us."

"Ashistar led us to you," I interrupted. "He knew the danger of the rock area where you were, although not about the traps that were set."

"You sure about that?" asked Vimble.

"Yes I am. He planned to lead us through the tunnels, and would have been shot had I not been ahead at the time."

"And how did he manage that? So you'd be killed instead of him?"

"No!" interrupted Mekroe. "He told Kirym to wait and let him go first. She's not one to be ordered about."

Vimble stared at Ashistar. "What's to say this isn't just a huge plan to deliver us back to Gynbere?"

"Because," said Churnyg, "as much as I'm loath to admit it, he used his position and knowledge to save many lives over the seasons. There's been an occasional whisper about a guard who helped the rebels."

"Oh yes, I've heard about that," said Shurlyn.

"Well it seems it was him." Churnyg paused. "And there's one more thing." There was a long silence. "Ach! He's m' son."

In the stunned silence after Churnyg's declaration, there seemed to be nothing else left to say.

"And what about him?" asked Mrilan, pointing to the guard. "Why'd they leave him behind?"

With no answers forthcoming, Mrilan turned angrily to Baketer. "Well?"

He shrugged. "Never included in much," he mumbled. "Got the dirt jobs mainly. Only been on the wall in really bad weather. Otherwise scrubbing floors and worse."

"Why?" asked Bryn.

Baketer studied his feet and shrugged again.

"Who's your family? Where'd you live?" barked Ashistar.

"Beech. Lived in East Low until I was a guard. Sire was Vorthain."

"Ahhhh, that's it," said Churnyg. "Slaslow's beginnings. Born East Low, formerly called The Red Stone diggings. Vorthain lived a couple of hollows over from Donima. He had an accident, ohh about ten winters back. How many winters had you seen then, lad?"

"Eight."

Churnyg nodded. "Why did you join the guards?"

"Didn't have a lot of choice. Just after m' sire died, our hollow burned out. Slaslow came an' said he'd let me join."

"Slaslow at his best," said Ashistar. "There were a lot of fires down in that area. Deaths too, and then they closed it off. Few families got away intact. You got any other family?"

"None who'd claim me."

"Your maman?'

"Never knew her. She died. She was Chestnut."

"So he was controlled," said Churnyg. "Given a job, but kept ostracised. You had no friends, did you lad?"

Baketer couldn't have looked more embarrassed.

"That stops now," I said. "Baketer's treatment seems to have been every bit as bad as that dished out to the rest of you, but at least you knew why, and could support each other."

Teema nodded and held his hand out. "I'm Teema." He began to introduce the others.

I turned to Bryn and Dashlan. "What did you find?"

"Nothing," said Dashlan.

Bryn shook his head. "It's not only that there was nothing, it was the lack of anything that concerned me."

"What do you mean?" asked Teema.

"When we followed Elm's track back yesterday, we turned away when we sighted the thicket, thinking he'd simply backtracked. But today, well we lost him at the thicket."

"Could something, an animal or animals have covered his tracks?"

"He got to the edge of the thicket, but didn't appear to go through it," said Dashlan. "No prints at all. Even so, we went upstream. Checked the bank right along. About a thousand steps on there was a large rocky outcrop coming right down to the water. We checked the edges of that, no sign of him. Further on from there was another one. Smaller, but he didn't use that either."

"He couldn't have left the water without leaving a sign unless he climbed onto the rocks. But to leave the rock pans into quite thick grass implies a knowledgeable grasp of tracking, one I didn't think he had. And it was the same downstream. We went about seven hundred steps beyond where we left, but there were lots of smaller rocky areas, and no sign of him. Unless he stayed in the water ..." Bryn shrugged.

"What do you think, Kirym?" asked Starshine.

"From Bryn's description of the flow, Elm wouldn't stay long in the water going upstream. He'd know that going down-stream will bring him to the coast. If he then went west, he'll come to the stone path where we tie the boats, and from there he could get to The Green Valley if he chose too."

"That's implying he planned to leave us," said Granite.

"He's always been a bit of a loner," said Storm. "Perhaps he was overwhelmed by having people around all the time."

"What are the other possibilities, Kirym?"

"That he has gone north, and is wanting to hide from us. That opens a lot of options, and some of them are dangerous. The lack of tracks worries me, but Ashistar, do Gynbere's guards have the skills to cover their tracks and others?"

"Not that I know of, but it seems there were a few things I didn't know."

"Watching the way they stampeded into the clearing leaves me thinking they don't, but it only takes one or two people with the knowledge …"

"I think that's something that would be taught to at least some of the others," interrupted Ashistar, "and I'm sure I would have heard about it."

"Which leaves us nowhere," said Mekroe.

A loud thump brought us all to our feet. A plume of dust rose from beyond the northern hole in The Rock.

"We need to leave here," I said. "If that thing goes we have no idea of what will happen and I want to be far away."

"It's almost dark. Should we wait until morning?" asked Storm.

"We don't know when it will collapse. Waiting could be more dangerous than travelling now," I said. "There's some light left. Let's get as far as possible before full dark." While I was speaking, Jeresaya and Starshine began to pull food from the ground oven, and settle it into some baskets.

Teema and Storm gathered the hauling frames together, and I strapped Amethyst's travel sling on and tucked a blanket around her. She was sleepy still, and I knew the movement of walking would settle her for a while although she would be demanding her meal soon after dark.

"What if Elm comes looking for us?" asked Starshine.

"Hopefully if he can follow a trail, he will. Otherwise he's aware of how to get to The Green Valley."

The dwarves crowded together clearly worried. They constantly glanced towards the east, but were happy to help when asked to. I organised the usual guards for travel, and was pleased when Vimble, approached Teema and offered the use of his men and boys to share the job.

Baketer made the same offer to Ashistar. Before long, they had been organised to carry the smaller children and loads, and pull frames. Bryn hauled out a rope to be used if we decided to travel beyond dark. I asked Jeresaya and Churnyg to lead them off. The line extended, everyone found a place that suited them.

I took one last look around the clearing and picked up a flask that had been overlooked. As I turned away, I caught a glimpse of something in the tall grass under a tree. Baketer's helmet. I picked it up, and caught up with Teema and Bryn, the rear guards. "Slip that on one of the fames, please, Bryn," I asked.

His eyebrow raised. "I don't think he wants it."

"Maybe, but the decision was made too quickly and he may regret it. Anyway I'm loath to leave our castoffs just lying on the ground."

He nodded, and I sped up to say a word or two to the others as I moved to the front. With my bow ready and a bolt nocked, I increased our speed. That wasn't sustainable for an extended walk, but I wanted to get as far as possible before darkness stopped us.

Dawn found us camped in the lee of a small hill. It was more exposed than I liked, but the bulk of it was between us and The Rock. All of those who had been on guard through the night reported occasional cracks and bangs from behind us, but nothing loud enough to suggest the whole rock or even a large part of it had yet collapsed.

By early morning, we were again travelling. Dashlan and Mekroe organised the children able to walk in what Dashlan called a walking snake. The children holding onto alternate sides of a rope, Mekroe at the front and Dashlan at the back. Amid shrieks of laughter, Mekroe wound around trees and bushes, through large tufts of grass, speeding up and slowing down as the whim took him. He and Dashlan had as much fun as the children.

As they travelled, Churnyg's people underwent a transformation. As a people, they were drab and uniform, their clothes all greys and browns. Churnyg, with his purple waistcoat, green jacket, blue trousers and yellow scarf was flamboyant when compared to them. I now appreciated Shurlyn's description of him as a dandy.

There were small changes initially. The girls and women picked posies, pinning them to bodices or hair. Ribbons and scarves appeared, small snippets of colour peeped out from under wraps and jackets. For the men, bright kerchiefs appeared around necks or peeped out of sleeves and pockets.

A tree laden with ripe plums was gazed at with awe, but no attempt made to pick them, until I called a short halt and sent Ashistar and Dashlan up to hand down the sweet ripe fruit. There was plenty, but many of them simply held the fruit reverentially and smelled the fragrance of it. In different circumstances it would have been amusing.

It took a lot of encouragement to get them to bite into the deep red flesh. For all except the oldest, this was the first plum they had tasted.

"What happened to the fruit and nuts from the trees inside The Rock, Shurlyn?" Teema asked.

"It all went to Gynbere and his favourites. Chosen people harvested the crops, but few of us got to taste the fresh produce. Some of it would arrive on the tables at a feast, but we were rarely invited to them. If we did, we'd avoid them. Slaslow used the invites to trap those he wanted to arrest and imprison." Shurlyn indicated a group of young people eagerly eating their second plum. "Few of them have even seen fruit, although we always told them of the food they would find when our prison walls fell. We just never believed it would happen, and when the storyteller doubts his tale, so does his audience."

We travelled northwest away from The Rock, attempting to put distance between us and danger, and perhaps get closer to Papa, wherever he was. I tried to contact Mekrar and Arbreu, but got no response.

Churnyg's people could prepare the food they were offered, but they had no idea of how to collect from the land we passed through or find their way back to the campsite. That work had fallen on the twelve members of our party although Enliah made friends with two girls and disappeared with them whenever she could.

In the afternoon we found a sheltered clearing to spend the night and the meal was started.

I took time off to play with Amethyst. She was far more alert now and grabbed at things held in front of her. She needed to be watched, everything went into her mouth.

I'd had the opportunity through the day to practice with one of the bows I'd found in The Rock. Springier than the bow I usually used, it was strong and accurate at quite a distance. When I practiced a shot at the limit of my usual range, the bolt was buried up to the flights into the hill I shot at.

I foraged widely as usual and took a few people with me every time I wandered. Cooking the food when it was produced was set to with pleasure. Three kellich and two ducks became stews, and a deer was spit-roasted over embers. Fruit, nuts and vegetables were also cooked and served up in a variety of dishes. There was enough for everyone with plenty for the next day.

Guard duty was another new experience. The dwarves picked up the rudiments quickly. Most of them had some skills, having watched the guards inside The Rock, but there they relied on noise to panic and intimidate. Out here was very different. Here, silence to read the night sounds was more important. Even Baketer needed guidance.

They had no idea what caused the noises of the night, and tended to be jumpy. They assumed danger in every little movement and sound. Shadows scared them. They assumed every noise they heard was Gynbere.

Trees and bushes were frequently challenged through the early nights. Learning was slow and by the third night, still jumpy, more than one of them carried bruises from a misunderstood noise. Fortunately we had foreseen this, and the weapons they carried were simply sticks.

Two days of bad weather kept us in one place, but gave them the opportunity to practice.

Teema and I checked through the nights as usual, finding six to eight people inspecting the perimeter with the guards. We were challenged so frequently in the early part of the night, we organised half of our experienced guards to check an extended perimeter. This worked well, and we walked a great circle two hundred steps away from the camp edge.

I still had plenty of time to enjoy the company and the evening before we slept each night was the time for stories, songs and questions. During one evening, I had a good look at the dirt-encased bolts we'd found in the tunnels. The casing was solid, it almost looked as if it had been baked on. I carefully scored the surface of each one, and soaked them overnight. In the morning the dirt was soft, and I began to scrub it away.

Marking in the dirt gave me the initial thought that the shafts were engraved or carved, but as I scrubbed the last of the dirt away, I realised they were all encased in a tracery of sliver filigree. Once clean, they glowed, beautiful although clearly not for everyday shooting. As I dried them off, those sitting around the fire discussed them.

"Not from our history," said Churnyg. Mrilan and Ashistar agreed.

"Well of course they're not," said Baketer.

"What do you know boy?" said Vimble.

Baketer reddened. "Well, umm, they're Kirym's. It's obvious."

"Is it?" asked Teema.

"O' course it is," said Baketer. "She's the only one who's used them. Anyway those is elf bolts and she's the only elf here."

"You're probably right lad," said Storm, smiling broadly. "Anyone much bigger than her would look ridiculous. I certainly have no desire to ever try them."

Dashlan laughed. "Oh, I think I'll sketch that. It'll give us something to ..."

"Laaad," interrupted Bryn. "Show some respect."

"Ach, no, Bryn. I think I'd be laughing with the best o' them," said Storm. "You can draw it Dashlan, but I'll claim the drawing. I'll find some way to show it off."

48

Kirym Speaks

It was a busy time and I spent less time with my family than I liked. Teema in particular threw himself into teaching hunting, foraging and guarding. For a few days, I only saw him when he was asleep, or surrounded by those he was teaching.

"They're getting the idea now," I said. "Only practise will make them better. Why don't you and I range ahead tonight and get a view of the land ahead?"

"What if Gynbere attacks? Shouldn't we keep our full strength here?" he asked.

"We're well guarded and there's been no sign of him nor any of his guards. Why would they be looking for us here? Anyway Ashistar said Gynbere loves huge fires and being out of the confines of The Rock would give him an opportunity to have them. We've not seen any, nor smelled smoke."

"So that's why you have guards up the trees. Could he have lit the fires Mekrar and Arbreu are checking?" he asked.

"No," I replied. "He was still in The Rock when I found out about them so it points to something or someone else."

"Ashistar got around, didn't he? From what I've heard there's a strict hierarchy with the guards. He was a labyrinth guard wasn't he?"

"Ask him. You won't get an answer though. He's not too forthcoming about anything until he's sure about you."

"We could die saving his people. He should trust us."

"Rargo was one of us."

"Oh!" The memory of Rargo's betrayal brought him up short. He nodded. "I suppose he has good reason to be wary."

We left when the night was half gone. There was little light from the moon, but the stars lit up the sky, and we were able to get some distance ahead. We travelled slower than I would have during the day, but the still of the night meant we heard and smelled things we might otherwise have missed. The night animals were searching out their nests and dens when we turned back towards our camp.

As the sky slowly changed from black to grey, there was a rush of wind overhead.

Teema grabbed my arm. "That happened just before the wall fell. Gynbere must have done it. He's here. We've got to warn everyone."

"Not Gynbere," I said. "A friend. Come on, I'll introduce you."

As we slipped through the trees along the banks of a stream, there was a thump, a crash and a muffled curse.

"Borasyn?"

"Hello, Kirym. I said I'd be back. Did ya miss me?" He giggled.

He sounded — different.

"Borasyn?"

"You were expecting someone else?"

I laughed. "You took a long time. I thought you'd changed your mind about returning."

"Naha. I was held up. I died again and I had to wait until I was reborn."

"You died?"

"Oops! I wasn't supposed to tell you that. Some things are secret. You can't tell anyone. Promise me? Promise, promise, prooooomise?"

Now it was light enough for us to see him properly. He was different — he seemed younger and sillier. Cleaner, as if he'd been scrubbed, and he was acting weird — but this was Borasyn.

Teema clutched my arm. "Is that a …?"

"Yes."

"It's purple."

"Yes."

"But, well then … Well what did we see at the inlet?"

"I don't know, but come and meet Borasyn." I introduced them.

Borasyn stared into Teema's face, frowning slightly.

"He's a bit strange," he said in a loud whisper. "Let's leave him here."

"No," I said. "He's my special friend, just like you are."

"Naha!" He turned his back on Teema, snubbing him. Suddenly he grinned and held up his bandaged foot. "My foot feels better, but I like the pretty bow, so I hid it when I died."

"So that's what happened to your petticoat," said Teema.

"Why did you hide it?" I asked Borasyn.

"So Faltryn wouldn't know. He's such a grumpish."

"Faltryn?" Teema looked shocked. "Are the stories in Wind

Runner's books true?"

"Parts of them are, Teema. Borasyn, did you tell Faltryn what I said?" I asked.

"Tried to! He ignored me." He snorted loudly. "He has no interest in anything. He's soooo ooooold. All he does is sleeeeep. But we can make it right together, Kirym. So where do we start?"

"Information first. Someone felled a huge oak tree. The stump was smoothed off. Do you know where it is?"

"Will I get in trouble?"

"You did it?"

"Oops!" He had the distinct look of Mekroe when caught in the middle of doing something he knew was wrong.

"Did you fell the tree?" I asked, suddenly wondering if I needed to apologise to Gynbere.

"Oh, no! No, no, no. It was lying on the ground." He drew circles in the dust and looked away into the trees. "I just played with it. I thought it had fallen over. They do that you know."

"Can you take us to it?"

He nodded eagerly. "Too far to walk though. Can you fly?"

I shook my head.

He frowned. "That's right. Bird flies, butterflies and dragon flies." He nudged Teema's shoulder almost knocking him over. "Does that make me a dragonfly?" He rolled on the ground laughing, batting his wings and raising a dust storm around us.

"My stars," muttered Teema. "You've found a right one here."

Borasyn composed himself with difficulty. "If you can't fly, you'll have to ride. I can teach that." He bounced up and down excitedly.

"You'll need to be very gentle," I said. "This is new to us."

He settled down and I climbed onto his knee and then his back.

"Sit in front of my wings, but not too far forward. I need to be able to move my neck. Hold on with your knees.

I was surprisingly comfortable, although not at all sure of my ability to hold on as he suggested. However, he had ridges along his neck, and seemed happy when I gripped them.

"Do we haaave to take him?" Borasyn edged away from Teema.

"Yes we do," I said firmly, giving Teema a hand to climb up behind me.

"I have the horrid feeling we are getting into deep trouble here," Teema murmured.

"We'll be fine," I said, patting Borasyn's neck. "He'll look after us."

The dragon shivered with delight, a strange feeling for us on his back.

"I wish I had your faith. I think he's crazy." Teema grabbed me tightly around the waist.

Borasyn's wings swooped down and suddenly we were above the ground, above the trees and swooping away from the stream.

The flight went well. It was exhilarating. The wind raced past and now I knew what it was to be a bird. First we went straight up and hovered, Borasyn's huge wings beating slowly to maintain his position. The land stretched out below us, much like Papa's maps. The bird's eye view showed me details of the area I could not have learned any other way. Even in the dim grey light of dawn, the colours I could see were amazing.

The glow of fires was quite close now. Three to the north were close together, and to the south east, one huge fire had four smaller fires close by. None of them had the appearance of a forest blaze. I made a mental note to contact Arbreu as soon as I could. He and Mekrar should have reached the fires to the north by now and must know who set them. If they were Papa's we should meet him very soon.

Borasyn flew fast. He took us high in the sky and hovered there, enjoying the sight as the sun slowly rose. He dived down, and we were in shadow below the sun line, but he again took us up to give us another sunrise and yet another. Three in one day, it was something I'd remember forever.

We went east, flying over The Rock. The two holes stood out blackly against the lighter grey of the stone. From above, we could see the open areas of trees and gardens, some down at ground level, but many higher. I caught an occasional glimpse of the stream that meandered from the north. A large section of the area where we'd found Shurlyn's group had collapsed. The paths we followed were gone, and that section of The Rock looked flat and dark.

The cracks and groans we had heard from our campsite were ominously loud here. I wondered how many more walls had fallen since I was there with Baketer.

I was intrigued by a number of large piles of rocks heaped against the eastern wall, and wondered where it came from. The wall there seemed to be intact. Before I could suggest a closer look, a puff of dust shot into the air. An ominous rumble grew louder and louder as the dust thickened and mushroomed up and out, caught by the rays of the rising sun. Borasyn's wings flapped strongly as he endeavoured to climb high to get above and away from the dust cloud.

"Will anyone be within the dust area?" asked Teema as we turned to watch it billow over the land.

"We travelled well, and we've chosen a protected camp site. I think we'll be all right. I don't know about Gynbere's people. They were travelling very slowly, and I don't know if he'd think of that sort of protection. I only hope no one was left in there."

Borasyn soared away from the clouds of dust, flying now towards the west. Most of the land was still in shadow, but as the first rays of sunshine washed across, it came to life.

Flocks of birds joined us, until Borasyn, with a flick of his wings left them behind. It seemed that in little more than a few gasps of breath, we swooped over land that had taken us days to cross.

It was cold. I wore my blue cloak, but because I had cut the hood off, it gaped at the neck.

Teema wore one of the mottled robes we'd found in The Rock, and I was warmer when he wrapped it around both of us.

Borasyn took us up through thick damp cold clouds. Once above them the lighter layers glowed as the sun hit them, many-coloured for the dawn. Frequently we could see through them to the land below. I struggled to take it all in and I could see why Churnyg grieved over his loss of freedom if this was part of it.

Then Borasyn circled west. There were many details in the land I wanted to remember, and information I needed to pass on to Papa and Storm. As the light strengthened, I saw more trees, streams and grassy hills.

The flight back was different. Borasyn slowed down, and we watched the land come to life. The lighter it got, the lower he flew, eventually snaking through the trees, around and over hills and skimming across the surface of a small lake. It was as exciting as the earlier trip, but scarier. Everything went by at such speed. By the time I'd noticed a tree ahead, Borasyn had twisted around it, and the next and the next.

Suddenly we were out of the trees, across a lake, up and over a small ridge and Borasyn was slowing rapidly.

The ground shot past us fast — too fast. He hit the grass

and we tumbled head over heels, coming to rest against the northern bank.

"Hinck, hinck, hinck."

His laugh was catching and I joined in.

"Are you hurt?" Teema asked breathlessly.

Borasyn gasped. "Hurt? Oh no. You shouldn't be. It was just a little bump. I do it all the time. I'm not very good at landing you see. I need to practise more so ..." He paused.

I rolled over to see what was wrong.

Borasyn, still lying on his back with his bottom against the bank, was looking at the shield which I'd lost hold of as I fell. He righted himself, staring wide-eyed, and gingerly reached for it, pulling his claw back quickly without touching it. His eyes wide he looked at me.

"Why didn't you tell me," he said huffily. "I didn't recognise you. I should have, but it was so long ago. Faltryn stopped teaching me."

"What do you mean?" I asked, but he ignored me, closed his eyes and screwed up his face.

"Mellith, Tamweir, Zandahem, Oakenrock," he intoned slowly. "Mellith, Tamweir, Zandahem, Oakenrock, Mellith, Tamweir, Zandahem, Oakenrock."

When he opened his eyes, he seemed a bit different, almost reverential. "You should have told me who you are," he said grumpily. Then he brightened and grinned. "It's good flying eh. Landing's a bit hard though. Dragons aren't much good at that when they're young. Are you all right?"

With a glance at Teema, I reassured him we were fine, but Teema was staring open-mouthed at the massive arena we stood in.

It was surrounded by a tall embankment, a perfect amphitheatre and mirrored the canyon in size although the surrounding banks were much lower and not sheer. There were three entrances, one each to the north-east, north-west and south. There were pools with flowers around them in the north and just northwest of the southern entrance. Just north of the centre was the gigantic oak stump — the trunk lay nearby.

Part of the bank that stopped our flight had collapsed at some time in the past. Grasses growing on it implied that most of the damage had been done a few seasons prior to our arrival.

At my feet were a number of large shiny clay flakes. Many had lines scored across them, and most made no sense, but one was a perfect eye.

I sifted through the other flakes against the bank and turned a few over. Some were missing, possibly mashed into dust, but I retrieved enough to create part of the original form, a dragon. Not Borasyn, this dragon seemed more regal. Pretty too, I thought it was female.

"Who did this?" I asked.

"Ummm." Borasyn lay on the ground with his head on his front feet looking like a naughty child.

"You? Wow, they're very good. You're so clever."

He brightened up immediately. "You're not angry 'cause I broke the hill?"

Teema laughed. "They're wonderful. Why did you destroy them?"

"Naha. Not me. It happened when the tree fell over. I redid some, but they got broken too. I was going to do them somewhere else, but I had to find the right sort of hill. This stuff is good, but a lot of hills don't go gloopy."

I decided not to ask what 'gloopy' meant. I glanced along the bank. It was obvious that a lot of it had recently been destroyed. "What were the pictures of?"

Borasyn sat up. "Things I saw. Things I remembered." He lowered his voice conspiratorially. "Not all of them are broken, only the ones that could be seen."

Teema looked as mystified as I did. "Can you show us?"

Borasyn ambled along the bank to where the grasses grew down from the top. He pulled long stringy strands away. The grasses had not rooted into the hard shiny surface of the bank, but they were firmly embedded at the top and bottom. Teema and I set to and helped him clear it away.

Teema was quiet for a while, yanking angrily at the long strands. Then he sat back on his heels and stared at me.

"Kirym, why didn't you give me the shield to carry? Don't you trust me?"

"Oh, Teema, of course I trust you. I was going to ask you to, but then I realised it would be a waste."

"What? Why?" He looked mystified.

"I know you're loyal to me. You're my friend, always. If the shield does what is claimed of it, then it's a valuable asset. To confirm what I already knew would be a silly thing to do. I'd gain nothing."

Teema looked happier and more relaxed than he had for quite a long time. "So how do you decide who to give it to?"

"I can't just give it to someone. They would have to agree to carry it."

"So if you offer it to someone you're not sure of and they refuse, you'd know to distrust them."

"I wish it was that simple. It could suggest fear or perhaps a belief they don't deserve the honour. Acceptance could imply greed for power or position."

"You're talking yourself into a corner." Worry flitted across his face. "What if you give it to the wrong person? Could it turn on you?"

"Whoever accepts the shield couldn't betray me easily. However if they had an ulterior motive, I wonder if it would turn on them. For instance, if I offered it to Slaslow, what would it do to him? It comes down to what loyalty is, and how does that conflict with the person's inner desire?"

"Why don't you offer it to Gynbere? Could you control him that way?"

I shook my head. "It would be playing with fire. If it has the power it's perceived to have, he'd still try to use it for his own purposes. He'd have to be loyal to me, but it wouldn't mean he'd work for the good of others, nor to do the right thing. There are many ways to undermine a person you claim to support. Anyway, I doubt he'd take it even if I offered it. He'd think it was a trick."

"So where to from here?"

"Prophesies are strange things. They rarely mean what one imagines them to. It's claimed the load is heavy. If it is as we're told, it could drive a person to madness. I'd not wish that on anyone, not even an enemy."

I took his hand. "I'll always need you beside me. You're there because you want to be. That's of more value to me than wondering if you stand there because you hold the shield."

We were interrupted when Borasyn tumbled down the bank and lay beside us giggling. "It breaks off if the roots don't come out," he said, holding up some long strands of grass.

The grass had covered three pictures. I stepped back to study them. The first showed seven dragons and a number of people amongst some standing stones.

"Is that the stone circles?" said Teema.

"I don't know. "There's not much shown of the stones themselves. They're slightly different." I pointed to a stone that sat at an angle. Below it was a smaller obelisk. "If it's the stone we know, the small one has gone."

"Well Borasyn could have been seen it a long time ago. Maybe hundreds of seasons have passed between seeing the stones and drawing them, so things would have changed, wouldn't they?" I had no answer.

The people were interesting. Borasyn had managed to capture the different clothing and builds that identified the separate families. There were those from the Valley, the tree dwellers, Faltryners and so many children.

I moved onto the next picture. This showed three boats sailing through the sea arch. The people shown on the decks, the tallest of those he'd depicted at the stones, came from The Green Valley. One boat was through the arch and had sails unfurled and billowing in the wind. One was in the centre of the arch, the sail hanging limply in the dead air and the third was in the bay, its sail still furled. There were men up the mast, on the cabin roof and the decks. On a distant rock sat a dragon.

The next picture showed the massive trees with dwellings and dwarves in them.

Borasyn stroked the side of the picture. "It was autumn when the water birds left. The trees were full as usual, but by midwinter they were empty. I never saw the people again. I wanted to tell someone, but Faltryn had told me not to fly into the land, ever, ever, ever! I was scared. After the water birds went away, the whole land emptied. I finally mentioned it, he said I was dreaming. I wasn't! Arymda saw the water birds leave, but she doesn't know I saw her watching.

A long time passed and two birds returned. Then there were people in The Green Valley again. I thought we should talk to them. Faltryn said they'd kill us if they saw us. But then you talked to me Kirym, and you asked me to come back, and you didn't even try to kill me."

"Why did Faltryn think we'd kill you?"

"He said you were annoyed because you wanted us to go back to the stars and we didn't go. Arymda tried to ask more, but he yelled at her. She got scared, 'cause Arymda was his favourite and he was usually nice to her. He was always angry with me though, especially when I talked about before. Before when the land was full of people. Before when we flew with them." He paused. "When we were happy." He signed deeply. "He said my memories were wrong. They weren't, but I didn't tell him after that. He wouldn't approve of me making the pictures." He snorted and danced along the line of the bank. "But then he doesn't know and it was fuh-hun."

"Wait on," interrupted Teema, "where do birds come in to this?"

"The people of The Green Valley used them," said Borasyn.

"He means the boats, Teema. Three left, two returned. The land emptied between those times. Wind Runner said we went to search for the people who disappeared, but that it seems, is wrong." I frowned, trying to put it all together. "There is so much I don't know. What a shame these were destroyed. I think they'd have told us a lot."

"Do ya like them?" asked Borasyn enthusiastically. "Cause I can do them again. There's two more, but they don't show anything much. They were the first ones I ever did."

He took us along past those we'd seen to where the growth was particularly thick. This was harder to clear, the grass was well rooted at the bottom and top of the bank.

"It's just the standing stones from a different angle. There were trees there then," said Teema, and he dragged me to the next picture.

This showed an arid flat place similar to the desert where I found Amethyst, although there was more sand here than stones.

In the centre, a few large bricks were almost buried in the

sand. It looked as if a few more gusts of wind would cover them.

"That's after it disappeared," said Borasyn.

"Disappeared?" asked Teema. "What disappeared?"

"The desert cave. It was strange. Iryndal said it was there long before we came to the land. It was big and the walls were straight, not like normal caves in hills. It was there before we died. When we were reborn, it was gone. Faltryn said I must have looked in the wrong place. Later he said strange things happened. He said the night lasted for a long time, and it was much darker than usual. Then he said it looked as if the stars died, and when morning came, the desert cave had disappeared. He made it sound really spoooky."

"How do you do the pictures?" interrupted Teema, fingering the crumbly soil. "It may not work now the top layer has gone. It's very flaky."

"Naha, it'll work." Borasyn bounced over to a clear area of the bank. "It's all in the way ya do it."

49

Kirym Speaks

I turned and looked at the huge clearing we had flown across. Near the centre sat the stump, just as Salcan had seen it.

This was why we had come here.

I wanted to race over to look at it, but I remembered there were things I needed to do.

"Wait," I said to Teema and clicked his token, sending a message to Arbreu.

Are you with Papa?

We arrived last night.

A long trip.

Umm, we were held up.

I decided to let that one go.

Did you find any fires?

Veld's, he responded.

Where?

To the north.

I nodded, relieved.

Tell Papa to travel southeast until he reaches the large amphitheatre. Pass a message on to Mekroe. He must walk one hand width west of north. Warn him that Gynbere's guards are wandering away from the main group. He must keep all scouts close to camp, and allow no one to go out alone. Avoid fighting if at all possible.

Arbreu nodded.

Teema shook his head. "I was so taken with flying, I noticed the fires but didn't think who had started them. Will those from The Rock ..."

He stopped as Borasyn nudged him roughly aside and stared at my tokens.

"Hmmmmm! Pretty!" He lowered his head and nudged them with his forehead in imitation of Teema and me. The air seemed to vibrate and sigh. His forehead pulsed and a small circle darkened. He closed his eyes and shook himself like a wolf coming out of a pool of water. And then he giggled.

Teema stared open-mouthed.

"My stars!" he exclaimed. "Purple. Is he the final token?"

I shook my head, opened my pocket and pulled out the token I had found in the cave above the canyon. I touched it to my forehead and then to Borasyn's. The circle above his eyes bulged slightly and deepened to a dark purple. He tried to look at it, cross-eyed in his attempt.

The token shimmered and the air around us quivered.

"Where did you get that?" Teema didn't know whether to be shocked, surprised or angry.

"I told you about the cave above the canyon. Things happened before I could show anyone the token, and then Salcan grabbed me and the time was never right to tell anyone."

He went red and nodded, remembering his reaction when I arrived back from my trip up the hill.

"Well what do we do now?"

"What we came to do." I put the token back in my pocket. "Let's look at the stump."

It was smoother than I thought possible, even more than the top of Findlow's favourite chest after he had spent a whole season rubbing it with sand, ash and beeswax. This was much bigger than anything Findlow had ever done, and the top glowed. The life rings of the great tree seemed to be very deep.

"This must have taken you a long time to do."

Borasyn frowned. "Time is nothing if that's all you have."

"How many dragons are there?" I asked. "I mean if you're all reborn, then it must add up over time."

"Na-ha. Dragons don't easily reproduce. Anyway, the eldest makes the decision about new-borns, and all the eggs have to be there together. It didn't matter though, but even though the rest of us all wanted them, Faltryn said no. So no eggs will be laid until he's no longer the eldest, but that doesn't happen anymore."

Teema snorted. "That doesn't make sense, Borasyn. Surely he is the eldest or he isn't."

"Ahh! Well this is the way of reborns. Not all dragon families are reborn, and many are suspicious of them, so that's why we're here and that's why things have gone wrong. Anyway, it seems we might not be soon, so I don't suppose it matters."

"Now I'm really confused," I said.

He sighed deeply and settled with his head on his front feet. "We came from the stars. As I said, dragons don't breed easily, and the flight I was born to was no different. They had almost died out before any eggs were laid. Finally though, the nursery was full and they waited as the eggs matured.

One egg was different and it was treated with suspicion. It was massive, bigger than any of the others in the nursery and it was black when the others were green. Most thought the shell would be too thick for a baby dragon to break, and the other parents wouldn't allow it to be near their eggs. So it sat by itself in a corner of the nursery. Through the seasons of incubation, Mama protected it fiercely as many tried to sabotage it.

Dragons eggs hatch at midsummer, but this one didn't. When the nursery was full of hatchlings, their mama's complained about the egg remaining. They called for a meeting to demand it be destroyed.

Mama didn't go to the meeting. She used the time they were arguing to take her egg and hide it. She carefully carried it deep into an overgrown gully, crawling down through the giant thistles, convolvulus and jasmine and easing the egg down after her.

When they found she was gone, the other dragons searched for her, but their hunt was half-hearted at best. They were too tied up with their own hatchlings.

Mama cared for the egg over the summer and autumn, but as the winter approached, even she began to think it infertile. On the first day of winter, she dug a hole to bury it, but when she picked it up she heard a faint sound coming from inside the shell. Elated, she made plans to care for it over winter. As the first storms arrived, she realised the shell was cooling, and so she wrapped her wings around it to keep it warm, refusing to leave it even for a day.

As the full moon rose at midwinter, the egg began to shake. At midnight it cracked. A small white dragon emerged. She named him Faltryn, amazed that such a massive egg had produced such a tiny dragon.

Just as Faltryn was born, a great storm began and she was unable to leave the gully. So she stayed where she was and cared for her son. At dawn Iryndal broke through an inner membrane of the egg and crawled out to meet her mama and brother. Ubree hatched at midday, followed at sunset by Othyn. Egrym came at midnight, Arymda at dawn, and I, the seventh dragon was born at midday.

With my birth, the shell shattered and the storm ended abruptly. Mama ushered us up the steep overgrown gully to be introduced to the family.

The nursery had been destroyed during the storm and the hatchlings and their mama's had fled for their lives. Had our egg remained there, we would have been crushed. Now though, there was great rejoicing as we joined the flight.

As midsummer arrived, everyone was greatly distressed when I died. My sister Arymda stayed with my body through the long dark night. She sang of our lives together, and told me the things she knew that I didn't. As dawn broke, I was reborn. My family rejoiced.

However there was a lot of superstition and many looked on rebirth with distrust. It wasn't a common thing you understand. There were stories of reborn dragons in the deep archives of our history, but many of the flight leaders had labelled them as myths. Most of the dragons wanted them to remain as such, because the birth of reborns heralded an era of change. There were threats to my life.

Time passed as everyone argued about it, and again I died, but this time Arymda died also. Egrym mourned, singing for us as Arymda had done for me.

This continued through the early seasons of our lives, until the time came when six of us died. Faltryn and our mama, mourning deeply, protected us and sang Faltryn's experiences to us.

We were again reborn, but a short time later Faltryn died. We waited, hoped and sang, not knowing what would happen. Our songs were full of sorrow, but also of hope for the future.

We waited for much longer than with the previous deaths.

This time the rebirth was different. When he was reborn, Faltryn returned younger than me, and for the first time, I was aware of the responsibility of a younger sibling. The cycle continued, and each cycle got longer as we learned more. Eventually, I was the oldest, and I cared for my younger brothers and sisters.

The other dragons on our home star became more and more suspicious of us. Now open threats were made on our lives. Their fear of us was great, but what stayed their plans was the fear of what would happen if they killed us. That fear was greater. They didn't know if our murder would begin the annihilation of the whole flight.

They feared us alive, and they feared us dead, and a lot of time was spent discussing the best way to be rid of us.

Finally, they came to a resolution. We would be exiled. They reassured us that they would bring us back to the land we called home once they came to terms with the changes we brought. They chose a place for us, a planet far away from our Dragon-Star and we were sent here. They never called us back.

But here was a good place. We approached the guardians who cared for the people and the land. They generously offered us Winterisle, a land we loved, and a position within their society.

Slowly over time, we began to meet more of the people, and then a few of the different families of the land. As they became comfortable with our presence, we began to integrate our lives with theirs. Some of the families though, the guardians felt, needed more time to learn of us, because of our size in relation to theirs. We agreed to meet them at a time the guardians felt was right, and when they were prepared to invite us in to their lives. We agreed with this and for us, life was wonderful for many seasons.

We offered to assist the guardians in exploring and

mapping the outer reaches of the land. These journeys became the highlight of our existence. We began to feel at home and grew to love the people. Our memories of the distant Dragon-Star began to fade.

We learned to recognise the calls of spring, and we'd fly in to pick up our riders wherever they were and celebrate with them. I remember watching the tree dwellers build a massive fire, and salute the birth of the year, singing, dancing and feasting. Many would join them for their spring celebration.

When everyone dropped with exhaustion, we would take our riders and fly away for an adventure.

Each spring we would choose a new place to go. We explored the wild Melundym oceans, the desolate mountains of Empeat, the unexplored forests of Leniarm and many other exciting places. During the autumn and winter, we helped to draw maps and write of the adventures we shared so it could be passed on to those who followed.

But we kept our deaths a secret. We were at our most vulnerable then, and we felt it was knowledge others didn't need at that stage. As each midsummer arrived, our riders would find a community to visit. We would stay hidden until we knew we were safe, or had been reborn and were ready to fly again. The time we spent dead was short and by keeping it secret, we safeguarded ourselves."

"Didn't the riders wonder why you didn't join them on those visits?" Teema asked.

My token started to throb, Teema's mirroring it, and I was aware of a sound that wasn't part of nature.

Borasyn lifted his head, copying the sound. It vibrated across the clearing, echoed and intensified as the large tokens joined in. Wind buffeted us from above, and a second dragon appeared overhead, spiralling down to land at a run on the far side of the stump. She was bigger than Borasyn, her pink scales were edged in red and she had two horns on either side of her heart-shaped face.

"Pink," gasped Teema. "This is …" His voice trailed away as she came close and stared at us, her scales erect.

She turned menacingly towards Borasyn. Her scales lowered slightly. "You told them?" She looked very intimidating.

Borasyn slipped his front foot under him and sat down. "I would have told you first, but you were asleep,"

"You know the rules! How many times does Faltryn have to yell them at you?"

"This is my sister, Arymda," Borasyn said brightly. "Arymda, this is the holder of Oakenrock. If Oakenrock is here, then the universe is repairing."

"Not by itself it isn't. And even if it was, you should have told Faltryn."

"Naha! Faltryn never listens," he said lightly. His tone darkened. "He's a bully and he tells lies and I don't believe his stories anymore. Look where we are. And we're not dead. Anyway if Oakenrock is here, Tamweir, Zandahem and Mellith will be close and that means everything is changing."

"What are these things," I interrupted.

Arymda hissed. "See, it doesn't even know. You've been tricked, Borasyn."

"No one tricked me," he said belligerently. "The shield you hold, Kirym. It's called Oakenrock. Four powers to balance the four corners of the world. A crown, and a shield and ummm, some other things."

Arymda rolled her eyes.

Borasyn continued as if she wasn't there. "Faltryn said they'd all been destroyed. It's better if the four powers are together but even one means we can dream again."

I slipped the crown off my wrist. It grew, but this time it was different. It seemed to be more alive. I placed it on my head, picked up my cloak and pulled the baldric from the folds, and the sword from the scabbard. There was a subtle change in the attitude of both dragons.

"Borasyn, you said the riders didn't ever ask why you dragons stayed away from the settlements at midsummer," Teema interrupted. "Why not?"

Borasyn turned his back on Arymda, ignoring her thunderous glare. "That was the way we wanted it at midsummer. No one questioned it. Some of the communities were not ready to meet us anyway. For the others, well, Faltryn was able to influence their thoughts a little, that's one of our gifts. We said we slept, and that was true, but our sleep was sometimes in death."

"So what went wrong?" I asked.

"We were mapping the western desert when midsummer approached. Our deaths were due, the big death if it happened. That would affect six of us. We died as usual, but something changed. When we woke, we had no new knowledge. Faltryn said we wouldn't waken when he sang to us. He said the planets realigned and the universe changed while we slept."

"Faltryn said our death was greatly extended," said Arymda edging closer to her brother, "but I didn't think we had been dead for much longer than usual. I worried about the riders and wondered what had happened to them while we were dead. Faltryn brought them to us. The changes in them were strange. We had watched these people get older over the seasons, but this was different. They looked much older than they had when we saw them last, but suddenly I couldn't tell one from the other. I asked Faltryn about it, but he said it was an illusion because of the light. It scared me because the sky felt black. I remember looking up and being surprised to see the sun was shining in a bright blue sky."

"Why didn't you tell me?" Borasyn grumbled. "I doubted myself. When I asked questions, Faltryn just told me to be quiet. I thought I was the only one who saw the changes."

"At least you asked questions. No one else did. The riders wouldn't even talk to us. In the time it took us to return them to their homes, they never spoke a word. I asked Faltryn and he yelled at me," said Arymda. "I was scared. Egrym said it was because they were disappointed in us. We had deserted them in the desert, had worried their families. It was our fault, and I felt bad. I wanted to tell them what happened, they were always so happy to discuss things in the past. Egrym said they didn't want to hear my pathetic excuses. When I asked him why they talked to him, he said they only wanted to talk to the men. I got upset, but later he admitted they hadn't. He was just repeating what Faltryn said."

Borasyn frowned. "Just before we left the desert that day, I looked back at the massive cave our riders had visited. It was gone. There was just a huge hill of dirt blowing away in the wind."

"But I saw that too," gasped Arymda. "Faltryn said the cave was where it had always been, and that I must have looked in the wrong direction. For a while I thought my perceptions were incorrect. He said lots of time had passed, but there were none of the changes I'd have expected. Rivers hadn't altered and trees were no bigger. Coastlines were the same, and yet the riders were ancient."

"Faltryn kept saying I remembered wrong, and then he said if I mentioned it again, he would banish me to Irunish Mountain, and I'd have to stay there by myself forever," said Borasyn.

Arymda patted his head. "It was a mean threat to make. I was going to tell Irundal, but every time I went to tell her, I told her something else. I couldn't understand why I always forgot. Returning the riders had none of the joy of previous journeys. When we stopped at night, they didn't light a fire, talk, sing or play their music. No stories or laughter. Faltryn said they didn't trust us any longer, and yet I didn't understand why they wouldn't let us explain. They turned away and I felt a barrier that had never been there before. At night they all lay on the ground and none moved until dawn. Then they mounted and we flew on.

A few nights before we reached their home, we stopped as was usual, and we slept, which was unusual. Normally we watched over our riders. When we awoke they were gone. Faltryn said they'd decided to walk the rest of the way. He told us they had ordered us to return to the Winterisle. They didn't want us to have any more contact with them or any of the other people of the land." Arymda looked beaten. "I looked for the riders as we flew home, but it was as if they had vanished. I talked to Iryndal about it, suggested we at least follow them to ensure they arrived back at their settlement safely, but Faltryn overheard me. He got really angry, and told Iryndal off. Said she had no right to encourage me. He was the oldest and it was her obligation to back him up."

Borasyn sidled up to her and snuggled close. "Eventually Faltryn said the travelling and mapping was over. The riders had all the maps they wanted. He said they'd changed things so if we entered their land, we would die. Iryndal said we had an agreement and should demand they honour it. Faltryn said he'd approach them again. He was away until the end of summer. When he returned he said he'd failed. Then he refused to talk about it ever again. He said if we entered the land we would die, and so would they. The agreements made when we arrived here were now cancelled. We had to remain in our own land until we could return home or inhabit another star."

Arymda sighed. "Faltryn is the eldest and he's in charge. He knew the most. Until he died, we had to obey."

"It got worse." Borasyn frowned as he remembered. "He didn't die. We realised eventually that without his experience, we couldn't grow. He said it was our fault. He had sung to us, but we wouldn't listen. Time passed and again I died. The cycle restarted, but it never ever ended." He laid his head on Arymda's shoulder.

She folded her wing over him. "Our deaths are becoming more frequent, and it's harder to reawaken. Soon we will become the unborn and not exist at all. It may not be a bad thing. There is no meaning to our lives. We sleep most of the time anyway. We can't fight it because we don't know how."

"Why did you come back into the land, Arymda?" I asked.

"I love the autumn flowers. One day I was picking some and I realised I had strayed over the border the guardians had set. I was so scared, I thought I'd die instantly, that's what Faltryn had said would happen. But then I saw Borasyn. I realised he had been even further into the land. I started to follow him when he flew here, and he didn't die. He even flew over places Faltryn had mentioned as fatal, so I knew something was wrong.

I asked Faltryn to search for the people and talk to them again. He refused to cross the border, but said he'd go to a place where the guardians had agreed to meet him on occasion. When he returned, he said the land was closed, even to him. I knew he was lying, but I couldn't understand why. I decided I'd try to find the guardians and talk to them myself. Then I saw the water birds flying through the arch. I thought they must be leaving because I'd entered their land."

"They didn't," said Borasyn. "I saw the people at the start, but I was too scared to approach them. You came a long time after that."

"You knew! Why didn't you tell me?"

"Well you saw me and you didn't say anything," said Borasyn. "Anyway I hoped as time passed everything would be all right again. I realised that the planets hadn't changed. All of those I knew, were in the places they'd always been."

Arymda sighed. "Many seasons after that horrid trip back to Winterisle, I began to search large parts of the land. I found the trees, but they were empty. The dwellings of The Green Valley were in ruins, and there was no sign of the desert people. I thought they must have died because I came into the land. Recently I thought to check the caves of the river dwellers. Another big change! They'd disappeared. The ledges where we had landed to celebrate with them had fallen away and the cliffs were now tall and straight. The people had vanished. But the hills smoked and I was scared. As I flew the land, I realised it had changed. Not the massive changes of eons, but slower subtle fluctuations. I thought then that I had slept more than I should. Recently Borasyn told us he heard the spring call. Egrym and Ubree said he was dreaming. They warned him to stay away because of the curse. I wanted him to talk to Iryndal, but he wouldn't wait for her to waken."

Teema shook his head. "Does this make sense to you, Kirym?"

"It's beginning to, although there's still more to find out." I turned to Borasyn. "How did you manage to smooth the top of the stump? It would have been rough and ragged like the others near The Rock when it was destroyed."

"I'll show you," he said, snapping out of his sorrow. He went to the fallen tree trunk and pulled away a thick branch that had broken off when it fell, and pushed one end into the ground. Then he snorted onto the rough end, ejecting a stream of fire from one nostril.

"Wow, impressive," said Teema.

The flame instantly charred the smaller broken ends, but didn't allow the more solid pieces to catch fire. Borasyn flicked a few glowing embers with his foot, stamping them out on the ground. He did it again. "It takes a bit of time, but once the rough stuff's off, I rub it and that makes it all shiny." He brushed the burned section with his scaly foot and I could see the difference immediately.

"What's that?" asked Arymda, pointing to the bandage on Borasyn's other foot.

"Oh! It's a fixer. Kirym gave it to me." He lifted the foot from the ground and looked pained. "I hurrrt my foooot," he wailed.

Arymda rolled her eyes.

"Can you all breathe fire?" I asked.

"Of course," snapped Armyda. "We're dragons!" She took a deep breath, her eyes on Borasyn as he hobbled around the stump. "On dark spring nights, we would fly in a circle and send rivers of fire into the sky. It was great entertainment for the children." She looked sad. "I loved hearing their squeals of excitement. Their laughter. And listening to them talk about it later, they were so delighted. We haven't done it for a long time now. Faltryn said it was stupid."

"And Faltryn has been secretive since the visit to the desert." I took a deep breath. "Well, the tribes are returning, Arymda. You need to be here too. You and your brothers and sisters."

"Even Faltryn?"

"Especially Faltryn. He's vital, because part of this is down to him. Not all though. How can you get them here?"

"They'll come," said Arymda. "There's something calling us. It was faint, but it's getting stronger as time passes.

50

Kirym Speaks

Lost in thought, I was only vaguely aware of Arymda wandering away to sit in the shade of the felled tree.

Borasyn dragged Teema over to a clear area of the bank to show him how he made the pictures.

Arymda was almost hidden in the branches of the big tree. I was concerned at how sad she seemed.

As I approached her, she shook her head and sniffed. "You're right. It'll all come to a head now. Everything has changed. But I think Faltryn was right too. This will destroy us and maybe everything else."

"Why do you say that? Everything may return to the way it was."

She shook her head sadly. "It's already happening. Borasyn is fading. He's the youngest, the one with least knowledge. First he'll go, and the rest of us will follow."

"I don't understand. He seems fine to me. Healthy and very noisy."

"He's disappearing. It's as if everything's vibrating and you're all getting fainter with each pulse."

She was right about the vibrations. They seemed to come from the large tokens. Was that what was affecting her? It was the only thing I could think of.

Arymda sighed. "What's he doing?

I stood on tiptoe to see over a branch. "Teaching Teema how to spit," I giggled.

"It's nice that he's happy when our lives end. He hasn't been for a long time." An enormous tear trickled down her cheek and plopped on the ground.

Now the tokens I wore were throbbing. I reached into my pocket, chose the red token, and clicked it to mine.

Arymda didn't react at all. I was mystified. She seemed to see everything except the tokens. She had made no comment about the purple lump on Borasyn's forehead, nor the tokens Teema and I wore. I wondered if she could even see them. Perhaps she needed a connection before she could.

With the token in plain sight, I moved close to her. "Arymda ..."

She nuzzled her face into my shoulder, and began to sob. I put my arms around her neck and she hugged her. I wondered how to begin explaining when she brought her head up suddenly and we bumped heads.

She jumped as if she'd been stung by a bee. Then she swung around and raced towards Teema and Borasyn. I ran after her, wondering what had happened. Arymda swerved around Teema and grabbed Borasyn by the shoulder, hauling him around to face her.

He had been about to spit on the bank again and only just managed to avoid spitting in her face, lowering his head slightly and depositing a glob of saliva on her shoulder.

She ignored it, turning his face back to her.

"Wow he could spit for a living," laughed Teema, before

realising something else was going on.

Arymda stared at the purple lump on Borasyn's forehead, touching it gently. She had a small pink swelling just showing on hers, and I realised her forehead must have touched my token when we banged heads. I held up the red token and she leaned her brow against it, and then turned back to touch Borasyn's.

She took a deep breath and snarled. Her scales rose, she reared up and roared. The noise thundered around the clearing. It died away and she preened her scales as they settled back in place.

"Hmmm. Faltryn has a lot to answer for. He stole our memories. How dare he! It's just not acceptable. I will have answers from him. He has deceived us and I'll not tolerate it any longer. Just wait until he gets here."

With time on my hands, I wandered over to have a closer look at Borasyn's broken pictures. The surface material was similar to the platters and ornaments Salcan made, but the colour was different. The platters had been pale, almost bone-like, whereas these were the colour of the soil. The top surface was hard, shiny and impervious to rain. I started trying to piece one of the pictures together.

The damage was extensive and nothing among the flakes made sense. As I sorted through the pieces, I found a long piece of solid metal. One end of it was pointed, the other flat, but sharp. Half way along, through the thickest part of the metal, a broken handle protruded. A miner's pick. I'd seen one like it on Churnyg's floor as we were preparing to leave his hollow, another attached to Ashistar's uniform.

"How did you make the pictures, Borasyn?" I called.

He bounded over to a clear portion of the bank, spat on

the soil and mixed it around, now I understood what he meant by gloopy, adding more spit as needed. When the consistency was right, he smoothed it and started to put lines into the surface.

He breathed fire on the finished picture, drying the surface. "Not too hot to burn it, but hot enough to dry it deep," he said. "I usually take longer drying it or it won't last for much more than a season. Done properly, it'll last for many winters. This just shows how it's done, and I'll redo it later so it stays up."

I stared at the lines in the bank. It pictured the tree while it still stood. A huge dragon sat under it, a dwarf in front of him. There was a scroll, a quill and a small, half-filled bladder at his feet. Borasyn had drawn some grass and flowers under the tree, along with what looked like a couple of thick bricks lying together to one side. Almost hidden behind the tree were the head and shoulders of a man. He appeared to be sleeping, his hand resting lightly on a shield.

"When did this happen, Borasyn?"

"Oh that was the first time Faltryn went off to talk to the guardians."

Arymda was outraged. "You followed him?"

"He didn't say I couldn't," said Borasyn defensively.

"What was happening?" I interrupted.

"Dunno. Couldn't get close enough to hear, but they were both happy at the end," he said, "although the dwarf yelled a lot before then. Faltryn didn't go anywhere near the guardians though."

"And him?" I pointed to the sleeping man.

Borasyn shook his head. "I don't know. I've only just remembered him and every time I try to think about him, my mind runs away."

"And how's that unusual?" mumbled Arymda, who had wandered over to peer at the pictures.

I glanced at the sun, almost mid-afternoon, and realised I was hungry. I hadn't eaten since last sundown. Teema and Borasyn were making more pictures, and Arymda was studying those already made.

Slipping the crown onto my wrist, I wandered through the north-western entrance of the amphitheatre and walked towards some fruit trees I'd seen when we flew over earlier. It took very little time to gather enough succulent fruit for Teema and me. I spied mushrooms and roots that together would make a tasty evening meal and gathered them also. I wondered what the dragons would eat. Lost in thought, I was startled by a rough voice.

"Well, well, well. What 'ave we 'ere then? A good capture I think. We'll get a big reward for this one."

I looked up in alarm. Five dwarves, Gynbere's guards, stepped out from behind trees, their spears pointed at me.

I stood warily. "So brave. Five brawny men against one unarmed girl." I silently cursed my stupidity in not being more alert, although if they had been resting quietly in the shadows before I had arrived, I'd have no way of knowing they were there.

I looked them over carefully. Although their guard uniforms made them appear similar, there were differences. One wore a medallion on his chest, one a plumed helmet, and one had red hair hanging onto his collar. The other two were clad entirely in black, and had kept their helmets on, their faces covered.

These men must have been sent here as soon as they left the clearing outside the walls. For them to get this far, meant they came here pretty much directly, and at speed.

"Did you hear that animal roaring earlier?" I asked. "It sounded huge."

The red headed guard nodded.

"Do you know what it was? It sounded close. We could all

be in danger," I said.

They looked around suspiciously, more nervous now than before.

They've not ventured from The Rock before, I thought. I slowly stepped away from them.

The guard wearing the plumed helmet spat on the ground. "She's just trying to frighten you." He seemed to be the leader.

"Yeah, but there was an animal," said one of the black twins. "We all heard it. What was it?"

"Nothing! It was a trick," said plumed helmet. "We'll take 'er with us."

"But we're here to get the great leader, Rookam," said red hair. "It's not her. We waste time with this chit of a girl, instead of finding this leader. We'll pay with our lives if Gynbere's not happy, and he'll be irate if we turn up with the wrong person."

"Gynbere said the leader would be here, Borboncha" said Rookham.

"Gynbere also said the land was empty," said Borboncha. But there are people all over the place. We keep hearing them. He said we should wait for the leader in the big round meadow. We haven't even found it, and even if we do, how do we guard a huge area. Anyway Gynbere said the leader wouldn't be there until tomorrow, so we're too early. He said this leader would be with Churnyg, but Churnyg's dead, so how can he be?"

The medallion wearer snorted. "Cause 'e isn' dead, fool. Someone lied."

"Limuba said he and his men shot him. They don't miss. So what happened? Why don't we get answers? Who do we trust?"

"Just do as ya told, Borboncha. Do as I tell ya," snarled Rookham. "An' stop questioning every single order I give ya. Maybe we can trade 'er for this leader. If we leave 'er 'ere, she may warn someone. We need to take 'er or kill 'er."

"Ahhh, you wouldn't be threatening my little sister, would you?" said a voice from behind me.

A wave of relief washed over me. Unexpected help. The spears moved to my left, pointing now at Tarl.

"You're not threatening me as well, are you?" Tarl sounded shocked.

"Ya should 'ave approached with a better weapon than a smart mouth," said Rookam.

"Oh he didn't need to." Sundas stepped out of the trees beyond Tarl. "He brought a pile of his friends."

The guards paled as they saw his immense size. Rookam backed off, and quickly the others followed, Borboncha the last to leave having dropped his pack when he first saw Sundas. He grabbed it by the base, righted it, and picked up a few of the items that had fallen out. He turned on his heel and melted into the trees leaving the rest of his possessions on the ground.

Laughing, Tarl picked me up, clicked my token and planted a kiss on my nose. "It's been so long, little one, and you're growing up."

Giving him what I hoped was a look of disgust, I hugged him back, squirmed out of his arms and turned to hug Sundas. "We'd best get away from here before Rookam realises there's only two of you. We gained a lot of information and it'd be silly to waste it by allowing ourselves to be captured."

Sundas picked up my cloak containing the food I'd collected.

"What information?" asked Tarl as I checked the prints of the guards, and collected the things Borboncha had dropped.

"I'll tell you when we're safe," I said. "I presume you're advance scouts."

"Aye, Lass," said Sundas. "We'll get you back to safety and then let Veld know he's aiming a bit far east."

Tarl followed me away from the trees and, with his knife drawn, slipped past me to follow an animal track to the west.

"Come on, let's get away from here," he said.

"Before you follow the wrong path," I interrupted, "we'll be approaching strangers who don't know you. Perhaps I'd best take the lead."

"Yes, yes, yes," he said impatiently. "Arbreu and Mekrar told us about Churnyg."

"It's not Churnyg, nor the other Tree People who've escaped. They're still at least a day away with Storm and Mekroe. Did Wind Runner tell you about her home and history?"

"You mean her memories from the books?" asked Sundas.

"Yes, particularly those about Faltryn. Not the Fortress, but the dragon."

Tarl smiled indulgently. "So little one, you've found Faltryn, have you?"

"No," I replied. "His brother and sister."

Tarl turned back, a look of amusement on his face.

"Come lad," said Sundas as he scanned the sky. "There are things here we don't understand. Sometimes Kirym is not just your wee sister. Do ya mean it lass? You've found the dragons?"

"They found us. Only two, but the others are on their way. I'm not sure how Borasyn and Arymda will react to you, so stay behind me until you've been introduced."

"You named them?" Tarl started to laugh. "Ahh, you wind us up well, Kirym."

I turned on him and drew myself up to my full height. "These are dangerous times, Tarl. Those guards could well have killed us. Count yourself lucky they were inexperienced, and scared of open spaces. Be thankful they were intimidated by Sundas' size. If there's one group around here, there could well be more. This is not the time for jokes." I stepped closer to him. "Mind me well, Tarl. One wrong move could mean death. Yours and others."

"Come on, lad." Sundas clasped Tarl's shoulder. "Let's just do as we're told. This is unknown territory for us. Kirym seems to be in charge. Let's get to safety and find out what's going on."

51

Kirym Speaks

Teema and Borasyn were still making pictures in the clay, but Arymda was aware of Tarl and Sundas as they slipped through the entrance behind me.

She raced forward, hissing and spitting, her scales erect. Angry, she looked even bigger than before. She slowed when she recognised me, but was distinctly wary of the two men.

"This is my brother Tarl and my friend Sundas, Arymda," I said. "They're the vanguard of the tribes due to gather here."

Her scales flattened a little, but she was still suspicious of them.

Tarl was shocked into silence, his face pale, but Sundas bowed theatrically towards her. "This is the most beautiful dragon I've ever seen," he said.

Arymda blushed prettily, then suddenly spun around and raced towards Borasyn. "Iryndal! She's coming!" she called.

Borasyn ran to her side.

"If you value your lives, cover your weapons and do not move," I said to Tarl and Sundas.

Removing the crown from my wrist, I ran over to Teema, and clicked his token.

Tell Papa to come south now, I said to Arbreu. "Put your bow and knife on the ground and cover them with your cloak," I told Teema.

Placing the crown on my head, I slipped in between Borasyn and Arymda.

The air vibrated as it had when Arymda appeared, but this time the tokens remained quiet. Then a massive blue dragon snaked over the rise that surrounded the clearing. She was many times bigger than Arymda and very elegant. There was an air of experience about her I had not seen in either of the younger dragons. She flew gracefully, and stopped with ease. None of the bumbling head-over-heels tumble of Borasyn, nor even the lighter running-landing of Arymda.

"Children," Iryndal said, "there you are." Her voice was light and musical, but there was an edge of steel to it.

"You mustn't roam like this. It's so dangerous. The land is full of people. They could hurt you."

"Naha!" Borasyn snorted. "Faltryn said the people had gone and wouldn't return."

"Things change for no reason," said Iryndal. "You mustn't question it. Faltryn is the oldest. He knows best."

"No he doesn't," said Arymda. "He wants to die. Every day he brings death closer to us. He's told so many lies. The people have returned to The Green Valley, and we should talk to them."

"Let's return then to the Winterisle. Faltryn can approach them."

"Like last time?" asked Borasyn. "He never went near them. He keeps secrets, and we are dying because he won't tell us. I'm learning some of the things he's hiding from you.

It's not fair that he won't do what he is required to by old law."

"That's as may be, Borasyn," Iryndal said with a little less patience than before, "but he will have his reasons, and we must trust him."

"Why?" said Arymda. "If his reasons were valid, he'd be honest with us, but he isn't. He just gets angry. We have the right to question, and you should too. We were told we would die if we came here, but we're still alive. I've seen the shield of Oakenrock. Faltryn said he saw them destroyed. What else has he lied about?"

Iryndal frowned and shook her head, as if trying to get rid of an annoying insect.

52

Teema Speaks

With Kirym's words of caution in our ears, we stayed quiet and waited for the argument to run its course. The three dragons faced each other seemingly oblivious to the four of us. The only movement in the clearing was Borasyn and Arymda's entwined tails thumping gently on the ground.

The blue dragon had not yet acknowledged Kirym. She looked so small and fragile standing between Borasyn and Arymda, and I wondered if Iryndal even realised she was there. This was so different to meeting the younger dragons.

The tokens had not responded to the arrival of the blue. I wondered if there was a problem here. If there was, could it be sorted out before Veld and the rest of the family arrived. I wondered what an irate blue dragon would be like. Having seen Arymda annoyed, I was sure I didn't want to this this one angry.

The younger dragons were suddenly quiet. Something was affecting the blue, and I realised I was too far from Kirym to be any support if something went wrong.

Kirym's admonition to keep my weapons hidden was one I would not and could not ignore, but her caution to me was different to the one she gave Tarl and Sundas. Even if she didn't need protection, she should have my support.

I quietly walked up behind her, stepping over Borasyn's and Arymda's tails, and touched her shoulder to let her know I was there. I realised she held the large blue token at chest level, something I hadn't seen from where I had been standing.

Iryndal didn't acknowledge me even when I moved.

Kirym's tokens throbbed violently, mirrored by my blue token.

Suddenly Iryndal rose and hovered just above the ground. Her forehead began to pulse in time to the token. A silent force shot out from her. It hit us hard — Kirym staggered back with the force of it. Had I not been there she would have been knocked over.

I only stayed upright because Arymda had moved closer, and supported me as I did Kirym.

Kirym raised the large blue token to eye level. The colours in the stone swirled, the movement increased with each pulse, until I thought the stone would surely explode. Then a ray of blue light erupted from it and connected to Iryndal's forehead, arched over to Kirym's, and then to mine.

I had never seen the large tokens do this before. Previously the stone had merely glowed and pulsed before connecting with our tokens.

Iryndal's reaction was amazing. She reared up and roared.

It was a while before I realised she made no sound, but the air vibrated, and the fallen tree shuddered. The ground beneath it was suddenly adrift as a wave of dried leaves and branches were dislodged from the massive trunk. The polished stump shook and the ground we stood on trembled.

Iryndal returned to the ground, shook her head and opened

her eyes. The light from her forehead was still connected to our small tokens, but now there was a lump on her forehead as prominent as our jewels, and it pulsed in time to ours.

Belatedly I realised that our tokens had connected to Tarl, Sundas and the younger dragons.

As the lights faded, Irindal rested her head on her front feet. She looked exhausted.

"Come here," she ordered.

Kirym walked up to her.

"Has everyone been deceived?"

"Yes," said Kirym, "and some more than others."

"You wear Mellith." Iryndal nodded towards the crown on Kirym's head. "What of the other treasures?"

"I carry a shield, sword, scabbard and knife."

Iryndal nodded. "Egrym, Ubree and Othyn, my brothers and sister are approaching. They will be easier to convince than I was. However, many people are travelling towards this place and we must plan or there will be problems when they get here. It seems not all have the same desire for a return to what originally was."

Kirym nodded. "Even with the best of intentions, it can't be the same. Too many things have changed. I've sent messages to two of the groups coming. The people from The Green Valley and from the northern caves known as The Fortress of Faltryn are coming from the north."

Iryndal raised an eyebrow at the name Kirym gave for the caves.

"A few of the Tree People also approach, one desert dweller, along with people from lands beyond the sea to the south east." Kirym continued. "Gynbere of The Rock is bringing the rest of people, but his intentions may not be peaceful."

Iryndal nodded. "I wonder of those missing. We need all of the tribes here. Could the desert dweller lead us to the rest of the desert people?"

Kirym shook her head. "I found her soon after her birth this summer. It may mean her people survive in their homeland. I hope to be able to search for them once the other families are all together and settled."

Iryndal nodded. "There is still much I don't remember, and more that is merely a vague shadow after so long. I have reservations about some things I don't understand. I hope time will help that." She looked up as again the air vibrated.

A green dragon sped towards the amphitheatre chased by a bronze. Just as it seemed the green would crash into the ground, it levelled off, but so close, we were buffeted by the wind it created. It raced around the amphitheatre, still pursued by the bronze. The green dragon slowly drew ahead of the bronze until they were on opposite sides of the field.

"My brothers," said Arymda, with the slight sneer sisters have for the boys in their family.

The brothers continued to circle, getting faster and faster. Suddenly they turned in towards the centre, seemingly on a collision course.

At the last moment they twisted, met shoulder to shoulder and spun around each other, their colours beginning to blur. They drifted south until they were almost out of the amphitheatre.

Together they snorted a stream of fire into the pool of water near the south entrance. Very quickly, the water boiled and a cloud of steam rose and hung over us.

Iryndel's tail thumped the ground. She seemed to swell with annoyance, the scales on her neck and back rose.

The two brothers ignored her, and continued to spin.

From the west, a yellow dragon streaked across the sky towards us. Without reducing speed, it turned its head and barrelled its shoulder into the two males, knocking them head over tail in a tumble of wings, legs and a shower of scales.

The boys lost control, disappeared over the eastern edge of

the amphitheatre and hit the trees with a crash and a shower of leaves and small branches.

"Yay, Othyn go!" said Arymda. "Girls rule." She glanced smugly at Borasyn.

"Naha!" he sneered. "You couldn't crash like that. You snivel if you land on a pebble."

"I do not!"

"Do so!"

"Do not!"

"Children," snapped Iryndal. "I have enough with those two. Please!"

"Just like the twins." Kirym smiled.

The yellow dragon circled sedately and landed softly near the north-western entrance. She sashayed towards us, her tail snaking two and fro across the grass, obviously making the most of her entrance.

The two males crawled over the eastern edge of the amphitheatre and raced towards her.

Iryndal stepped in between them. "Ubree! Egrym! Behave yourselves! We are guests here. What will our hosts think?"

I stared at the circle of dragons. "I never thought they'd be different colours. I hope I can learn their names."

"Well you know Borasyn, Arymda and Iryndal already," said Kirym. "The bronze is Egrym, Othyn is gold and Ubree is green. You'll soon get used to them."

I put my arm around Kirym's shoulder. "Well this is it, Kirym. A brilliant end to your quest. You really have found the dragons."

She leaned against me. "The quest for the dragons maybe, but I think this adventure has only just begun."

If you have enjoyed The Trail to Churnyg, please leave a review on the website of the seller you purchased it from. Good reviews are the life blood of independently-published authors, so please take a few moments to let others know what you thought of the book.

Thank you for reading.

Do look for further adventures as
The Token Bearer series continues.

www.wordlypress.com